THE COMMON BOND

ALSO BY DONIGAN MERRITT

Possessed by Shadows

DONIGAN MERRITT

THE
COMMON BOND

— a novel —

OTHER PRESS • NEW YORK

Epigraph on page vii translated from the original Spanish, *Del sentimiento trágico de la vida*,
by J. E. Crawford Flitch (NY: Dover Publications, 1954; originally published
by Macmillan and Company, 1921). Gregory Corso poetry excerpt on page 44 from
"Marriage," published in *The Happy Birthday of Death* (NY: New Directions Publishing
Corporation, 1960). Joseph Conrad passage on page 78 from *Lord Jim* (NY: Penguin Books,
1989). "If You Wanna Be Happy" lyric on page 186 by Jimmy Soul (LeGrand-S.P.Q.R.
Records, 1963). "Goodbye, Cruel World" lyric on page 192 by Gloria Shayne (Rhino Records,
1961). Poetry excerpt on page 294 from "To His Coy Mistress" by Andrew Marvell. Ludwig
Wittgenstein aphorism on page 366 translated from the German by G. E. M. Anscombe
(Berkeley: University of California Press, 2007).

Production Editor: Yvonne E. Cárdenas
Book design: Natalya Balnova
This book was set in 11.9 pt Fournier by Alpha Design & Composition of Pittsfield, NH.

10 9 8 7 6 5 4 3 2 1

Library of Congress Cataloging-in-Publication Data

Merritt, Donigan.
The common bond : a novel / by Donigan Merritt.
p. cm.
ISBN 978-1-59051-306-4
1. Widowers—Fiction. 2. Trawlers (Persons)—Fiction. 3. Ship captains—Fiction.
4. Hilo (Hawaii)—Fiction. 5. Loss (Psychology)—Fiction. 6. Psychological fiction. I. Title.
PS3613.E7765C66 2008
813'.6—dc22
2008002476

Publisher's Note:
This is a work of fiction. Names, characters, places, and incidents either are the product of
the author's imagination or are used fictitiously, and any resemblance to actual persons,
living or dead, events, or locales is entirely coincidental.

This book is lovingly dedicated to Holly Murten.

And to the cafes where much of it was written:
Café Aedes, Berlin
Caffe San Marco, Trieste
Café Bonaparte, Georgetown, DC

We pity what is like ourselves, and the greater and clearer our sense of its likeness with ourselves, the greater our pity. And if we may say that this likeness provokes our pity, it may also be maintained that it is our reservoir of pity, eager to diffuse itself over everything, that makes us discover the likeness of things with ourselves, the common bond that unites us with them in suffering.

—Miguel de Unamuno
The Tragic Sense of Life

PART ONE

RAIN

[*Hawaii 1981*]

ONE

It rained again.

Rain streaked the window. Jalousie slats opaque with dampened dust. Palm fronds drooping, turned brown. Cinder block walls, yellow like dried mustard, clammy from the heat and the slow rain, contained him and the memory where now he lived.

He was in the most tenuous element of consciousness, neither asleep nor awake, thinking and remembering, without control. He knew what he could see so clearly wasn't actually happening, that it was a memory of this same place, but another time, more than a decade ago. Although it did seem so real that his body responded to the image: Of Victoria breathing like a racehorse and as slick as a sea lion from the sweat and moving in such a way it would be impossible to say if she's fighting or fucking.

He's thinking, Victoria loves having her clothes off, a compliant self-focused nude, undisturbed by bodily conventions, as volatile as mercury, as exciting as fireworks. In one angle of light the carefully trimmed triangle of fine hair between her legs is nearly invisible. Soft puffs of air blown across the mound of her sex makes that hair tremble like ripples across a field of calm golden wheat. Studying his dick as it rises near her face, she tells him it's a dichotomy: simultaneously hard and soft, sweet and salty, a special hardness that is somehow both limitless and fragile. She teases it with the tip of her tongue but no more, as if any further generosity could leave it empty and wasted.

A car on the wet road outside sounds like plastic sheets unraveling. She is spectral, the woman who seems so close and so real in his memory, but who is dead now and does not exist in the categories of time and space.

A fingertip pressed to her nipple makes it seem like she might simply slide away.

Turning onto her back and raising her arms she grabs the wicker headboard and the wood responds with a human squeal; she stretches, pulling her breasts into high, elongated ovals; she scissors her legs out of the sheet and offers a warm inviting place for the man she decides to tease no longer. Torch lights from the café leak through the rain-streaked jalousie slats and illuminate in stripes the beads of sweat, translucent pearls, on her breasts and belly.

"How many times are you able to do this?" Victoria wonders, using two fingers to open herself for him.

What had he said? It's entirely the company, maybe. That is how he remembered it now. He says, "It's entirely the company."

Her breasts are so white against her tan that they seem to shine, to lighten the room, to attract and compel fingers-hands-lips-tongue.

"I love being naked," she says, casually smiling and looking down across her body.

She is very inviting.

"I love fucking you," she says.

Now he was supposed to say something to her. While he worried about what he should say, she moans, or maybe it is a whimper. He is already in love with her and afraid to say anything that might seem stupid; he wants her to imagine him as her lover.

"I will die. Fucked to death," he says, finally.

She laughs.

Then she tells him, "It can be your epitaph. Here lies Morgan Cary, a Kona fisherman, fucked to death in the Sunset Lanai, on Friday, whatever the day in May this is in the fine year of nineteen hundred and seventy."

They could put a plaque on the door, he might have suggested. Why was it he remembered so much about her from that ancient night and so little about himself?

She smiles over the idea of a plaque, then exhales loudly and sighs when he enters her.

Love covered him like rain slapping the outstretched fronds of a palm.

Another car passes on the driveway outside. He was not able to say if it was now or then, in the memory or in the moment. He is caught within both times.

Victoria goes to the bathroom.

He had managed to treat that night, those few hours, as if it were the span of eternity, the full scope of their lives. Nothing came before, nothing would follow.

It was a question that had waited all night. Victoria proclaimed that men always want to know this. They seem to believe these words validate their prowess. She said men were babies, when they weren't busy being bastards.

The toilet flushes and she comes out, still naked, with a towel wrapped around her hair. She has a perfectly proportioned body. Men propositioned her, suggesting that they could make her a top model or an actress or a very rich mistress. She would say they were stupid and obvious; she was used to this kind of thing and far from being impressed. From the doorway with both hands clutching the towel on her head, she finally answers him.

"I suppose I do love you, but I wish you didn't think you needed to ask. That was love we just made, yes?"

It might have been sex and that's what he had really been asking: Was it love or sex? For her? But then he was afraid to say anything else, because she had given him the magic words; she could take them away just as quickly.

A gecko clicks high in the opposite corner. Victoria turns to look. Seen, the tiny green lizard spins in its own length and disappears so fast maybe it isn't there at all. Victoria removes the towel from her hair and drapes it over the back of the only chair in the room.

"Tioni?" If he was so afraid of what she might say, why did he keep pushing?

She sits on the edge of the bed, kissing, touching, playing.

But he knew, although she hated these questions and the feelings from which they came, she must have understood that she must say more. She must have been able to see he was sinking in guilt.

"We've just been dating."

"For almost five months. Tioni is in love with you, I'm pretty sure."

"He hasn't said it."

"He has to me."

"Yes, I suppose he is. And I'm sorry. But I didn't make him do it."

"You made me do it just by appearing in my space."

Victoria laughs.

"I still hate the way it makes me feel," Morgan says.

"I suppose you'll end up hating me."

"That will never happen."

"That's just the orgasm talking."

Victoria picks up her wristwatch from the bedside table, its green numbers flickering like a bit of phosphorescence in a boat's wake. How, he wonders, could she make such normal motions? How can she not realize that nothing will ever be the same again?

"I didn't know it got light this early," she says.

"False dawn. The sun won't be over the mountain for about half an hour."

"I better go."

How can she even think of this?

She dresses quickly. There are only her underpants, red shorts, a white T-shirt, sandals. They can't spend the rest of their lives in a motel room. Morning has come. Outside waits illumination, discovery, revelation: Tethers to both ecstasy and misery.

She leans over the bed for a final kiss, then says, "Let me do it, okay? I don't want you fighting about it."

"We won't fight. I don't fight with Tioni. I've known him almost my whole life."

"Men fight about things like this."

"Men fight over a bar bet. Tioni is my best friend."

"Which makes it worse. Still, let me tell him my way, in my own time."

"How much time?"

"Today."

"Then what?"

"Then . . . we just go on living happily ever after."

She blows a kiss from a smile and goes out the door.

Only seconds pass.

The door opens and she steps back into the room, her eyes wide and the tips of her fingers at her lips. She catches Morgan pulling up his underwear.

"He's out there!"

"Tioni?"

"Yes. He saw me. He looked right into my eyes. He was crying."

Cheapening the night beyond recovery.

The engine of Tioni's pickup truck starts, tires hissing as he drives out on the morning-damp road.

Victoria explodes. Morgan sits back on the bed, astonished and agonized. "Goddamn it all to hell!" she screams, kicking over the night table, then kicking the broken lamp against the wall.

"Shit, Victoria, stop it!" Morgan restrains her in an embrace. "I'll take care of it. Just calm down."

Then he realizes that she has bitten into his shoulder and drawn blood.

Morgan went to sleep finally and the memory remained a dream within a dream.

TWO

Earlier that day, the Aloha Airlines plane he had taken home descended beneath thick, pearl-colored volcanic haze and settled fast over a coral reef where blue water broke white before fanning out pacified and green into the lagoon. The flowered airliner passed low over the shoreline, chasing its crinkled indistinct shadow across the rumpled field of laupahoehoe lava surrounding the Kona airport; lava as dried out and hard as an old chocolate cake, kiawe trees clinging to the crust as brown and dead as tumbleweed.

Morgan searched for the high green mountain slope while the plane taxied toward the open-air terminal, but it was only visible in outline through the strange and extraordinary haze.

When the door opened for the ramp, a heady warm perfume meandered through the cabin—gardenia, plumeria, ginger, a strong overlay of kerosene. Passengers descended into a diffused but still radiant sunlight to the accompaniment of drums and steel guitars, playing tropical

Muzak. A trio of lei girls in skirts of plastic grass and bras of plastic coconut shells waited for a tour group. Two round-bellied taxi drivers in Aloha
shirts hovered near the baggage carousel drinking Cokes in cans. By the
gate, a young Japanese woman held up a clipboard sign and a rainbow-
striped umbrella.

Morgan descended the ramp behind a Japanese man in a white terry-
cloth hat and white short-sleeve business shirt. As they moved toward the
exit gate, the man's wife walked backwards step by cautious step to cap-
ture her husband's arrival on a minicam.

Morgan found a taxi and threw his bag into the back seat. Right away
the driver wanted to tell him that the haze came from the ongoing eruption of Kilauea. "We call it *Vog*. Means volcanic fog."

"How long this time?"

"The eruption? Off and on forever. This one, a couple months."

They turned out onto the road toward Kailua town.

"It's killing tourism."

Morgan wondered if that might be a mixed blessing.

"Yeah," the driver laughed. "Careful what you pray for, right, brah?"

As the taxi neared Kailua, he could discern the softly rising, thickly
vegetated slope of Hualalai mountain.

Before Victoria, he was a fisherman. His house was up there on the
lower slopes of Hualalai, the cloud-shrouded purple and green mountain
backdrop to the village of Kailua-Kona. It was a small house, really a
shack, unpainted and constructed single-wall, with piles of books and
stacks of paper holding his own ambitious stories, all of it being curled
by humidity and gnawed on by bugs. The tin roof leaked and tangled vines
threatened to sneak in through the koa wood flooring. Originally the
house was used by seasonal coffee pickers. It sat well back from the main
road, along a rain-rutted trail through a jungle of such massive tropical
profusion that the house materialized from the background like a phenomenological trick. Electricity came into the house from a single drooping

feeder line that ran up from the main road in an arc like the slope of an old horse's back. There was no water piped up from the town below. Rain captured in a cistern was diverted to the house via a gravity-fed pipe. The toilet had its own tiny shed in Nature. It was about a mile and a half to the bay where the sport fishing boat Dolphin moored; he walked down to work in the mornings at sunrise, which doesn't vary much at that low latitude. He was habitual, always eating breakfast at the Seaview Café, which had no glass in windows with panoramic views over the sea wall and harbor and out over the omnipresent Pacific. He ate heavily, fresh papaya halved in a koa bowl and doused with lime juice, fresh pineapple chunks on cottage cheese, fat round soft pancakes with strips of bacon crisscrossed on top and smothered with papaya syrup, two cups of black Kona coffee, and a sixteen-ounce mason jar filled with ice water. He would not eat again during the day as they trolled offshore ledges for Pacific blue marlin, yellowfin tuna, Hawaiian mackerel, and dolphin fish, except for an apple and some soda crackers. He would go through two quarts of water to keep hydrated against the clutching heat of the tropical sun. At night, it was usually sunset by the time Tioni and he had cleaned the boat and put away the gear, Morgan would get a grilled ahi sandwich or a fat hamburger at the Red Pants, a bamboo, tin-roofed bar directly across Alii Drive from the sea wall. He would stay to drink a few beers with other Kona fishermen. It was their bar. They told hours of lies, shot nine-ball, hustled the few brave female tourists who wandered in, and sometimes had painful but unimportant fistfights. Years ago, when Morgan was a boy in grade school, actors went slumming there; Richard Boone and Lee Marvin kept fishing boats in the harbor. Then Morgan would hike back up to his house and write page after page describing what he had seen, had heard, and could imagine. These stories he never showed to anyone, not even Tioni.

Morgan believed that those days were lived on the verge of being the perfect life.

The taxi let him off at the Sunset Lanai, a motel on the southern fringe of Kailua town, across the road from a small cove at the edge of the harbor. The single-level, rectangular motel with a veneer of black lava rocks covered with red bougainvillea and yellow hibiscus was shaded by tall, curving coconut palms, ohia and kukui trees dropping their black nuts all over the property. It was hardly visible from the road. The only sign pointed to the café behind the motel, a café with open walls and a palm thatched roof where mourning doves nested.

It was not the kind of place appealing to persons wanting a lounge with a floor show, a Polynesian revue with dancing girls, tom-toms, flaming batons, slick songs, and sweet mai tais. You never saw there banzai-marching Japanese in matching aloha clothes and porkpie hats, tagged like children traveling alone. The Sunset Lanai was not on the lists of mainland booking agents. It had ten rooms, each with yellow-painted cinder block walls, a tin stall shower, and simple, cheap wicker furniture. The rooms were seldom all taken.

But from those rooms one could hear the wind-rippled sea washing over the black rocks in the cove across the road, the trade wind breathing through the trees, the clicking of geckos prowling for supper, the soft and beautiful mourning doves on the café roof. The air smelled salt clean, pungent with exotic flora, lacking the intemperate, disgraceful noises and odors of tourism, from which the town had lately fed.

Locals went there to fuck in secret or to eat fine papaya pancakes in the café.

It was to honor a memory that he returned there, where a decade ago he first spent the night with Victoria.

Eight o'clock. He had a dreadful headache behind his eyes. He'd been trying to sleep but had only lain naked and sweating atop the sheet, nursing the inevitable treacherous passage of airline frou-frou drinks through his body.

Open jalousie slat windows filled much of the wall opposite the narrow bed and a palpable, embracing air invaded the room. Through the windows he could see the deep purple sky, the island rolling away from the sun. He dozed for a while before awakening to a mosquito's whine. He reached back and turned on the rotating fan affixed to the wall above the bed. Faintly, he heard music from the café, then slept again, until the sting of stomach acid in his throat awakened him. He was dreaming of pretty brown-bellied girls, their bellies made for bouncing.

In the shower, facing the hard, sweet spray, letting the water churn and bubble from his mouth like rising from a deep pool, he scrubbed hard, but apparently it took more than motel soap to wash away grief and guilt.

He felt swollen.

Sometimes, especially in bed while trying to fall asleep, he had the distinct feeling of expanding, swelling, becoming heavier, sinking into the mattress, being swallowed, suffocating. He knew it for a phantom, like the occasional pain behind the ugly, ragged scars on his right leg, the pain that really wasn't there any more, pain that remained only distinct as an aspect of memory. Was it real if he felt it? Was it not real because it was a phantom?

He didn't remember packing. He didn't remember going to the airport and buying the ticket that brought him back to the island. He was drunk. The contents of his duffel bag were like surprise gifts when he emptied it onto the bed: Four pairs of shorts, six T-shirts, a pair of flip-flops, a pair of jeans, a black windbreaker, a toiletries bag; no socks and no shirts, except for the things he wore on the plane, which now lay on the floor scattered between the bed and the bathroom. He brought two credit cards and three-hundred-forty dollars in cash.

He had run out of whiskey. Alcohol was pain's only refuge, the only means he had for delineating the eye of the hurricane, for becoming calm, for finding the inside of that small circle of self-protection there might be amid the whirling, precarious storm of guilt he could not penetrate.

He pulled on a pair of shorts and a T-shirt before heading out to find a drink, but the walk to the road proved he wouldn't be able to do that tonight. His knees suddenly rested and he settled toward the sidewalk like a leaf, before catching himself and lurching into a pretense of erectness. It happened now and then, knees went on a sort of coffee break, fingers let go of their own accord, vision came and went, the sidewalk rose to meet him on the way down. But, then, he really hadn't been a blind, stinking, fucking drunk long enough to get used to the surprise of its distinct attributes. He could still embarrass himself and went back to his room hoping he might sleep.

There were only the memories now, the dreams. He fell asleep remembering the first time he was here with the beautiful and mad woman who would become his wife.

THREE

In the wind-swept morning, tiny bits of trash mixed with floral debris tumbled down the sea wall promenade beside Alii Drive, curling like snakes around the ankles of determined tourists. Clouds rode over the sea and smashed into the slopes of Mauna Kea and Mauna Loa, spinning like gray cotton balls caught dancing in a draft from an open window. Five miles out to sea it was raining and would be in town before long.

A sidewalk artist stood where the sea wall ended and the grounds of the old summer palace began. He painted with a palette knife, canvas held to the easel with U-clamps. A bottle of Mount Gay rum, finger-printed with acrylic paints, anchored the palette against the wind. Moving as furiously as the weather, he rendered precisely the cotton ball storm clouds above the mountain peak.

He was skinny and dark, wearing a hat of pandanus leaves strapped below his chin with a string. The hat's fringes flapped in the wind like birds tied to lines. A chewing gum wrapper tossed by the wind grazed his cheek then spun along the seawall before falling into the bay to float like a lure. His paint-splattered white pants were ragged below the knees and the faded yellow shower thongs on his feet were thin as paper.

"Aren't you afraid it will rain?" Morgan asked, stopping behind him.

"Be done before."

The artist stopped the knife but held it in place as he turned slightly to look over his shoulder. Just a glance. Then he went back to work.

Morgan came around the easel and watched for a moment. There were four Japanese men standing politely out of the way. They whispered softly to one another, as though the sidewalk could be a temple and the artist its priest. All of them held down their hats against the wind, like a cartoon.

"Justin, do you remember me?"

The artist smiled blankly and shook his head.

"Well, it was more than ten years ago and I didn't have this beard."

"Sorry." The painter smiled. It was obvious he could remember more if the sale of the painting was up for discussion, or more likely, if he had less rum running through his blood.

A long time ago, Morgan was in his last year of high school. Justin Petaín, Bob Kennan, and Morgan Cary built a thirty-five-foot double-outrigger sailboat in the yard behind a rented corrugated tin warehouse, where Morgan had a sleeping space on a platform built in the lower branches of a massive banyan tree just outside. The walls of the tree house were formed from woven palm fronds, the roof from a sheet of thick, opaque plastic, through which a muted moon moved among the branches like a distant, glowing smudge pot. There were bugs and warehouse rats and to piss Morgan had to climb down a rickety sixteen-foot ladder. Girls were intrigued by the place and liked going up there with him, at least until they saw a rat. It was better than sleeping on the beach, where Morgan, penniless and petulantly trying to punish his father, was until Bob Kennan hired him to help build that boat.

He had this idea for a snorkel cruise: taking tourists out to a calm bay, putting them in inner tubes with face masks and offering a little underwater show. It would make Bob Kennan rich.

Justin glanced over his shoulder again just as Morgan turned to walk away.

"Why, hell yes!" Justin called out, waving the palette knife in front of him like a saber.

Morgan turned around.

"Cap-i-tan Morgan." Justin saluted with the palette knife. "Fisherman."

"In another life," Morgan answered. They had called him Captain Morgan, not Captain Cary.

"Didn't you just leave for California or some other mainland hole?"

"Ten years ago, Justin."

Justin looked puzzled, continued painting, then stopped again and asked, "Where's the beautiful Victoria?"

"Not here."

"Now there's a pity, brah."

Morgan walked a few steps closer. "You still do beautiful work."

"Uh," Justin grunted, shaking his head.

Morgan offered a brief wave and continued toward the pier. Justin had wanted to paint Victoria and probably fuck her, but they left the island before either might have occurred. He wanted to tell Justin that Victoria was dead, that he had come home to recover something he could put into his now-empty places. But he just continued to the pier, where his life had been.

Widely spaced drops of rain, thrown nearly sideways by the wind, approached the pier. A curved-tail poi dog investigated Morgan's ankles, circled him twice, then trotted off to piss on the banyan outside Tanaguchi's market. The bay was choppy, white caps inside the harbor, fishing boats hobby-horsed against their mooring lines.

Morgan watched the Mele Kai for a moment, the boat he helped Bob Kennan build, remembering a storm so bad that Bob couldn't get out to the boat in the dinghy. Almost lost her. In those days people were afraid of Bob Kennan. He was big, bull-necked, strong, and temperamental. Morgan got along with him well enough, but couldn't work for him, no one had ever worked for him long. There were arguments, then threats, then impotent apologies. After building the boat, Morgan lasted only a few months living in the tree house, helping out with the charters. Now, there was the Mele Kai on her mooring in the bay and Morgan wondered if Bob was still around.

Two fishing boats came in earlier and were now secured to the dock with stern lines. In the increasing storm, their positions at the dock became precarious. It was hopeless now for charters. Aboard one, Tommy Aki prepared to take his boat out to a safer mooring, away from the pier's concrete threat.

The rain made five decades of fish blood sticky on the pier. Morgan wore flip-flops. Oil and grease on the concrete was as slick as verglas under his feet.

He moved aside for a jeep. It stopped behind the only other boat at the dock to disgorge a pair of young men as brown and round as cookies. They were shirtless and shoeless, wearing only oversized baggy shorts slung low below their successful bellies. It was dangerous in the bay then. The boat bucked between lines lashing her between the stern and the anchor. The boys jumped onto the pitching wet swim step and climbed over the transom into the cockpit. One went up the ladder to the flying bridge to start the engines while the other released the stern lines and shoved the boat away from spastic tire fenders, then headed forward to take in the anchor. Morgan enjoyed them, he thought it was beautiful, but it all made him sad and nostalgic for the life he had given up. He sat on a fat bollard. To light a cigarette, he had to cup the match against the wet. He managed only two puffs before a fat raindrop fatally extinguished the ember.

He had come to the dock assuming Tioni would be at sea and they would not accidentally meet, but in this weather he could be anywhere, he could show up anytime. Morgan decided to go back to the motel before he ran into Tioni and had to tell him that Victoria was dead. In California, Morgan thought he wanted to see Tioni again, but not now, not when the possibility was this real. What could he have been thinking?

He was thinking what a bad idea it was to imagine that coming home was a magic fix for anything.

FOUR

He rented a car and drove across the island to Hilo and took a second-story room on a gently sloping street in town, above a grocery store where stalks of bananas hung from wire lines and bushel baskets of mangoes, papayas, and guavas were displayed along the wide sidewalk with bins of vegetables. On the corner stood a Catholic church advertising bingo on Wednesdays. He could see the marquee for the ramshackle Palace movie theater. In the alley beyond the stairs to his room stood a house that commercial buildings had surrounded and consumed like a cancer. The rear wall of the old house was completely covered with shoes—flip-flops, sandals, tennis, and athletic shoes—each secured with a rusting nail. An odor of marijuana often emerged from it.

He ate Chinese food at Sophie's Place and Vietnamese food at Me Kông. He took day-long hikes out to Rainbow Falls on the Wailuku river. Hilo was not his home, but he loved the verdant tropical fishing town, the harmonious cacophony of its tin roofs pinging in the rain that fell during some part of almost every day, where the lawns were a maze of gardenias, eucalyptus, pandanus, tamarinds, alligator pears, roses, fuchsias, clematis, begonias, water lemons, and bamboo. There wasn't a building in the main section of town higher than the tallest coconut palms.

He chose a bookstore, buying a book every week to take on hikes into the jungle. He sat and read by the falls, often drifting into a nap for half an hour or so in the deep, cool grass. Sometimes he stayed up late into the night finishing a book. Some books were abandoned when he saw that the writer used obvious tricks, the way a film lost its magic if he could visualize the set or see the actors acting. Others he read through twice, because in them the fictive dream never wavered. They were important in his life, like air and water and light; they piled up on the floor around the armchair in his room, until he began to wonder who he might give them to, although he really wanted to keep them. Their solid and sensual presence in the room comforted him, like quiet friends, like a lover watched sleeping.

He liked walking back from Sophie's in the dark, along the sidewalk that took him to his room, a sidewalk brightened in spots by small white fluorescent tubes below corrugated fiberglass canopies. It was a poor area of Hilo. Four or five languages were spoken in the neighborhood. It was certainly not a fashionable street, although rich and poor got mixed up in the islands. Simple dresses and flower-patterned blouses in shop windows there could be purchased for less than ten dollars. Cheap plastic rafts, shiny tin pails, a chain saw, tool belt, kids' fishing set, and beach umbrellas were displayed in the window of the hardware store. Shoppers came in pickup trucks that said Gecko or Hang Loose in the rear window, cheap Nissans old enough to be called Datsuns. There was a pawnshop and a liquor store. At the barber shop you could also get your shoes shined and your clothes pressed or watch the barber sleeping on the cloth sofa against the back wall, where the best breeze crossed between two big windows. There were wooden benches along the sidewalk where old people could rest and gossip. At night, most people left. The merchants lived somewhere else and the coffee shops closed early. Sometimes young Asian boys loitered by the old theater and smoked clove cigarettes. That smell joined stale beer, faint urine, old wet bricks and fruit rotting in alley trash bins where maggots blissfully bred.

He had acquired a distinct feeling of healing, so he made some rules, just some things to help keep him on track, on the planet. He would try not to drink in the daytime, although he confessed to still needing some whiskey to fall asleep. Actually it was a lot of whiskey. He started trying to stop smoking; it wasn't easy.

The rest of April passed.

FIVE

In May it rained less and only at night. There was something reflective of his childhood during that time. He had almost no responsibilities and knew that in this, at least, he was lucky. He had nothing but time, although he threw away his watch and tried to ignore other means of marking it. Local people recognized him now as someone who sort of belonged and sometimes he was acknowledged with a wave or greeting. Marilyn, the waitress at Sophie's Place, mothered him. She brought her daughter around to meet him but nothing came of it. They went to a movie and hardly spoke all evening. He didn't know why, because she was a nice girl, pretty, with silken black hair and miraculous teeth. She was a few years older, divorced, had no children. The first time they went out, she said, "I am barren; you should know that up front." Her body was sensual and inviting. Morgan found his lack of interest annoying but was welded to it. He wondered what she thought of him? Probably only that he was boring. Sometimes he passed her on the street and they exchanged warm greetings, as if they were friends.

It wasn't long before he was spending his days along the Hilo water-front, naturally attracted to the boats, to the bustle of life around the motley windward side fishing fleet, to the cacophony and salty tang of the fish market. He often stopped for a few beers at a fisherman's bar with an enormous Pacific blue marlin mounted on the wall and a display of the variety of lures common to windward fishermen.

Morgan took some pleasure talking with an old fisherman named Ben Kamakani, who had a haole sampan named Noho Kai—sea saddle—that he built in his backyard almost forty years ago. Ben was sixty-seven and had thick white hair and skin the color and texture of a bomber pilot's weathered leather jacket. His feet looked swollen and cracked with dis-ease, but were in fact strong enough to hammer nails, because Ben had never worn a pair of real shoes in his life, except the day in 1941, when he married Anna. The rented shoes rubbed blisters so badly that blood flecked his toes. That night, Anna kissed his toes. Morgan couldn't be-lieve Ben told him those things, but liked that he did.

"I got married one week before the Japs bombed Pearl," Ben said.

"I wasn't even alive then."

"How old you?"

"Thirty-six."

"Almost same like my boy Joseph. He's thirty-nine."

"He fishes with you?"

"Joseph? Hah! Joseph's a singer. He live in California."

"I used to live in California. He's a singer I might have heard of?"

"He has one band, they go 'round all the Holiday Inn places and pretend they some kine Hawaiians."

Morgan knew those bands. There was nothing to say about it, really. There was too much disgust in Ben's tone to pursue that line. Morgan occupied himself drinking from a sweaty beer mug.

Ben shifted on his bar stool and turned toward Morgan.

"But I also got me one daughter, live here in Hilo. Ana give me one grandson. Her name is Ana Mana'o'i'o—same first name like my wife, only wife is Anna with two n's and daughter Ana only with one n. The boy is called Ben Iki. After me."

"Little Ben."

"You know some Hawaiian language?"

"I lived here for a long time, Ben. Most of my life, actually."

"You born Hawaii?"

"Sort of, you could say. I was born at the Pearl Naval Hospital on Oahu. My father was in the Coast Guard, so we moved a lot. He was stationed in Hawaii three times, and I finished high school Kona side, where he went to live after his retirement."

"I thought you pretty good with da kine talk for one haole."

"I don't know Mana'o'i'o."

"Mean like faith, or having faith. She was big surprise for old folks."

Slack key guitar music played from the jukebox: Gabby Pahinui singing *I Ka Po Meke Ao*. Morgan tapped his fingers against the side of the mug. The bar was full. It always was that time of the evening, between six and eight o'clock, when well drinks were half-price. The bar girl flirted, the bar man joked. Most of those men would wander home for supper pretty soon, including Ben Kamakani. Morgan stayed sometimes until closing because there wasn't anything waiting for him but a room with a bed, a bureau, a mirror, a toilet, and a bottle of whiskey. Most of the time he walked the mile back through town around ten o'clock. He left good tips and he was always served immediately. No one except Ben asked his name.

"Your father still Kona side?"

"He's dead now."

"Sorry for that."

"Long time ago. He smoked himself to death. I wish he were here, even though sometimes we had our fights."

"Like fathers and they sons."

It rained. Water drops pinged on the asphalt roof like BB's. Wind shook the palm fronds. Nobody paid much attention because it rained like that all the time. It would stop pretty soon and the wind would die down for the rest of the night.

Morgan ordered a hamburger and fries and another beer for Ben, so maybe he would stay a little longer and talk about his life. Ben clinked Morgan's glass in thanks. Cigarette smoke curled around them. Music too loud but they could talk.

"What kind work you go do?" Ben asked.

"That's not such an easy question to answer, Ben. I've had lots of jobs. I used to be a writer. I was even a Kona fisherman once upon a time. But a bum might be more accurate."

Ben laughed hard enough to slosh beer from his mug. "Most us guys bums, but da kine doan go say it. You write books, or what?"

"Book. Not books. One."

"That's about how many books I read ever," Ben proclaimed proudly. "I like radio. I like the Hawaiian music radio shows come on Sunday. I like this kind a music," he inclined his head toward the speakers above, still Gabby Pahinui.

"How you *used to be* one writer?"

"Writers write. I wrote."

"All a same to me. You got one book what have you name on it, right?"

"Right."

"What name you give him, that book? I never met nobody actually wrote one book."

"It's called *Decompression*."

"What's it about?"

"I guess you'll have to read it and find out."

"I can tell you right now I'm no interested in reading no dirty book." Morgan couldn't tell from Ben's look if he were serious or just playing with him. "How long it take for write one book?"

"Oh, can't say really, in general. I don't know when I started it, only when I finished. Or when I stopped, more accurately. Quite a few years, I'd say."

"You can sit and write for years?"

"Not all the time. I go to the toilet sometimes, sleep a bit."

Ben laughed, ordered another round of beers. Morgan pushed aside the residue of his hamburger.

"I'm curious what make somebody think go sit down and write one book?"

"Truth is," Morgan began, "I got girlfriends doing it."

Ben hooted with laughter.

"Really. Writing things down always came easy to me, it was one of the few things I could do easily and well. When I was fourteen, I got a major crush on the most beautiful girl in eighth grade. Her name was Maile. I wrote a poem for her, left it on her desk unsigned, but she knew it was from me. I lost my virginity to her."

"Whoa! No ack!"

"Nope, I'm not exaggerating. I wasn't a jock, didn't play football, didn't surf, so I used writing to do what athletics does for most boys."

"I never wrote nothing more than my own name after go from school." Ben seemed to ponder the possibilities for a moment. "I tell you, brah, I didn't go get my wife from having wrote something." He laughed again, generously and easily. "And doan go thinking I'm gonna tell you how I got her, no how."

"How'd you get any woman to marry you, Ben?"

"Well, I tell you. I got really big feet." Ben laughed outrageously.

They talked about fishing again until twenty minutes later Ben got up, said "bum bye" and went home. Morgan stayed on for another beer, waiting for the rain to stop. When it did, he walked back to town, back to the room, to sleep, to the place where oblivion could appear.

Three days later Morgan noticed Ben at the dock preparing to go out for the day. "You doing nothing," Ben called out when Morgan greeted him, "may be we go hele mai and chase some fish?"

It started that simply. Morgan went out that day and the next and the next. After that Ben turned their fishing trips together into a job, paying him five percent of the money he got for the catch at the fish auction. "You doan go for take it, we have plenty pilikia," Ben said. Morgan took the money because he didn't know how to refuse it without hurting Ben's feelings.

Morgan would have been happy to pay Ben for those days, for the sanctuary from the hard, dark shadows of imagination, for those brief escapes from the brutal images controlling his empty hours.

In what seemed only an instant, they were together two months.

They fished with rods and reels, four set out at a time—two from outriggers, two flat lines. They used lures Ben made from fiberglass molds or they drifted over the ledges with live bait. Some of the fish they caught were too big to fit inside the cockpit so they were towed in alongside the Noho Kai.

Ben teased Morgan about daydreaming when they were out on the water. There wasn't always much to do. Morgan often took the helm, but because they made long, straight runs that did not require much attention, his eyes sometimes glazed over and Ben might stare at him for a minute or two before Morgan noticed.

Ben asked Morgan what he dreamed about so much.

"I'm not always dreaming," Morgan answered.

"You go for sleep with you eyes open?"

"I was thinking about the nature of possibilities just then."

"Say huh?"

"About possibilities, how they can be disheartening."

"Disheartening? You full of poop, Morgan."

"No doubt."

"Possibil-itis," Ben said more or less to himself.

"Possibil-itis? Is that what you said?"

"Possibil-itis. That's what you got, brah. You swole up with too much possibility. Your possibles got itis. You done swole up with it."

Ben laughed out loud and went back to check the lures.

Morgan knew that Ben was exactly, perfectly right.

"You know what, Morgan?" Ben said over his shoulder as he pulled down the outrigger pole and adjusted the clip. "I been fishing all my life, since I were still in the elementary school. I never no man work for me. You see what I'm saying?" Morgan nodded. "Now I got me this one crazy haole dreams about stupid things all day and writes da poetry so he can get sex from some huhu wahine. Eh?"

Morgan didn't ask, why me? He had long ago learned not to ask questions you don't really want to have answered. Instead, he gave Ben the finger.

A frigate bird swooped low over the swells and Morgan eased the helm to port, following its path.

"Watch the birds," Ben warned, although he knew Morgan had already reacted to the sign. An Ahi would be good. It usually brought a dollar-fifty a pound, maybe even one-sixty, but the long-liners were playing havoc with auction prices, Ben complained.

Morgan was anesthetized by those hours spent on the glaring, silver-blue water, following sea birds and chasing fish and having his attention focused only on the simple details of the present, where time was not a part of what had been and what might be.

The frigate climbed a thermal path and circled again, two hundred feet high. The black, forked-tail bird worked alone. There were a few gulls waiting to scavenge and a pair of pelicans bobbing atop swells like carnival ducks.

Ben noticed the piece of jetsam when it appeared on a swell, just before it slid back into the trough between the waves. It looked like a hatch cover, although it didn't so much matter what it was, only that it was there and they had found it.

"You see 'em?" Ben cried out when the jetsam popped up again.

"I see," Morgan said, turning the wheel hard starboard.

Morgan lashed the helm on course and went back to the cockpit to help Ben bring in the outrigger lines. They needed to hurry and were not particularly neat about it.

Ben prepared two small feather lures with barb-less hooks, and when Morgan passed back one of the flat line rods, Ben removed the fiberglass lure and secured a feather lure in its place. Morgan stowed the outrigger rods and rigged the other flat line rod and reel with a lure. The feathers happened to be red and yellow, but that didn't matter by then. Those fish would strike a single exposed hook, the pull tab from a beer can, a piece of line, anything at all.

Mahimahi, dolphin fish, would find these improbable objects, in this case a house door complete with rusting hardware, adrift on the sea, areas of shade in a vast wet desert, then ride tightly packed beneath them to feed on tiny shad attracted to barnacles attached beneath.

Morgan slowed the boat to idle speed but left it in gear, then lashed the helm to guide the boat close to the door before returning to the cockpit to take up one of the rods. Ben had already spooled out a length of line to pass a lure to within five feet of the door. Mahimahi could be seen flashing their blue-silver-gold colors just beneath the surface, like electrical sparks arcing within a high tension field.

They hooked up within seconds of one another. Ben first. They pulled in four fish on the initial run and Ben hooked up again as Morgan rushed forward to turn the boat around. On the next pass they boated six fish that flopped around in the cockpit like water drops on a hot pan.

When there were more than a dozen mahimahi in the cockpit, Ben left his rod and began killing fish with a billy club, the fat end of which held a spike to penetrate the brain.

After two more passes around the door there were maybe thirty fish in the cockpit.

Seeing the action, crews of two other boats bore down on the Noho Kai at full speed. Ben waved to the men on the sport fishing cruiser Hilo Lady and the crew of the commercial boat Malia Nani. He didn't care if they joined his turkey shoot. He had so many fish aboard that they would need to stand balanced on the gunwales if they boated any more.

Ben ordered Morgan to turn out. He walked along the edge to the wheel house and cocked the helm over to head the boat for open water. Ben bludgeoned mahimahi right and left until his chest was wet and sweat dripped from the kinked white hairs.

After they died, their vivid color faded and they became a cold lumpy slab of gray. The smallest fish probably weighed around ten pounds, the largest might go forty. There was probably three hundred pounds of fish in the cockpit.

Morgan smiled, knowing how happy Ben would be after the auction. He would want to stop at the Paniolo Kai bar and buy beer for his friends. Good fishing made for a good time talking-story, for late nights, for good-spirited drunkenness. Morgan was still smiling as he turned to make for the breakwater channel. Ben, Morgan thought, was probably wondering if his deckhand had gotten another case of possibil-itis.

When Morgan looked over his shoulder to say something to Ben, expecting to see him stowing the gear, he saw Ben sitting on the engine box, bent over like he might puke, his arms braced against his legs as if to keep from tipping over, his back rising and falling like the swells rolling away from their wake.

"Ben?" Morgan called out loudly over the engine noise. Dropping the rope loop over the top spoke on the wheel, he made his way aft through the muck of dead fish.

"Ben, are you all right?" Morgan placed his hand on Ben's hard shoulder and found it surprisingly cool and damp. Ben's breaths came hard, heavy. "Is it your heart, Ben?"

"Maybe bettah we go mo' quick," Ben whispered, not looking up.

"Okay, Ben, we're going in, we're on our way right now."

Morgan kept an eye on Ben and headed the boat at full throttle toward the channel. Black carbon smoke from the stack made the haole sampan seem like a burdened locomotive. Keeping his voice low—he didn't want Ben to hear, to worry—Morgan used the CB radio to call the harbor master, to ask for an ambulance to meet them at the dock.

SIX

Ben Kamakani died first in the ambulance, then again and finally on the table in the Hilo Hospital emergency room.

Morgan didn't know until later. He took the fish to auction at Suisan Market on Lihiwai Street. Because Ben had asked him to. The three hundred pounds of mahimahi did well at auction. Gabby Tanaka made the check out to Ben and gave it to Morgan.

"Ben will be him all fix up, don't you worry," Gabby told Morgan. "He strong like one whale."

Morgan hung around for a little while to watch, absorbing the smells and noises. The auctioneer cried out lots of ahi, aku, ono, mahimahi, and opakapaka in three languages, all flavored with pidgin. Roger Chin, the Hilo Kai's deckhand, who had helped Morgan unload the fish onto pallets and get them into the back of Ben's pickup truck, offered a can of beer and said he knew Ben would be all right because he's so strong. "He strong like one whale," Roger also claimed.

But even whales die, Morgan feared.

By the time tourists were served those mahimahi on their plates at the Naniloa Hotel that night, the fish, which had traveled a few miles down Banyan Drive, would be up to thirty dollars a pound. Morgan thought of Ben at the hospital, the bills, the time off work, and considered the spread from a dollar or so for the man who caught it, to thirty dollars charged to the man who ate it.

Ben's old white Toyota pickup truck was like Ben. It smelled like Ben, which meant to smell like fresh-caught fish and hard-earned sweat. It lumbered over the earth, unlike the beautiful way Ben's sampan seduced ocean swells. But the rattling truck was also strong like Ben, taking the ragged pot holes that spotted Manono Street without losing any parts. Strong like a whale, Morgan repeated. A mantra.

He put Ben's check in the ash tray, which was already stuffed with receipts, loose change, pencil stubs, and old grocery lists, and headed mauka, up the slope out of town to Ben's house.

Ben's square house was constructed of wood planking painted white with green asphalt shingles on the roof and green shutters framing the windows. The front yard comprised entirely a tangled flower garden. Two kids were raised there and the debris of their childhoods remained to be used by Ben Iki, Ben's only grandchild: a simple red swing set, a tire hanging by a rope from the limb of a banyan tree, bicycles hanging on hooks from the garage rafters, a vine-entangled surfboard leaning against the tilted wicker fence across the backyard, a new skateboard by the backdoor, a windsurfer sail and mast against the garage wall. The garage itself was crammed with tools, toys, and some partially remodeled furniture, with space along one side for the workshop table where Ben kept the molds for making fiberglass lures.

The truck's tires crunched through the white crushed shell driveway as he pulled all the way forward. Anna Kamakani's white Dodge was gone. Maho barked in the backyard. Seemed no one was home. Of course, they'd be at the hospital. Morgan wondered if he should go there, see how Ben's getting along? But no, tomorrow would be all right. It would be better if just the family saw him tonight. Ben would be okay. Morgan decided to visit tomorrow. They'd have some laughs and maybe a couple of smuggled Olys.

He got the fish check and slid it beneath the front door with a note written on the back of an old grocery list pulled from the ash tray: "Tell Ben I'll stop by tomorrow. Truck keys are in the ash tray." He signed it Morgan Cary, as if Mrs. Kamakani might not know him.

It was a long walk back to town from Ben's house, which was on a side street a few blocks off Manono, not very far from the Ke Kilohana O Ka Malamalama Church. Ben told Morgan that his family worshiped there as members of the small Hawaiian-speaking sect, Hoomana Naauao O Hawaii.

Morgan's room was in the center of town, some miles away. He didn't know how many. It was twilight as he walked back and people hadn't yet closed their curtains to the night, so they might take in the last of the day's breezes through open windows. He had to walk around the Wailoa River Recreation Area and stay on the main road to avoid getting lost. Traffic was heavy and it still surprised him that in a place like this people commuted to jobs as if they were in California, as if they didn't know where they lived and what they had here. Sometimes he wanted to stop them, shake their shoulders, scream into their faces.

Finally he was able to cut off into the neighborhoods that fanned out along the ridges and soft slopes that rose like a curtain from the mauka side of downtown Hilo.

The people he saw through those open windows were presumed to be living lives of great depth, while Morgan saw himself as skipping over the surface of life like a flat stone hurled across a pond. He envied them painfully. He wanted that life. With such a life he might be able to shed the horrible weight of hopelessness that hovered around him like an impatient executioner.

It was fifteen minutes before Sophie's 9 P.M. closing by the time Morgan got there. Marilyn served him a bowl of Peking-style noodles and brought him an Oly. He sat at the counter because Marilyn had already cleaned up the tables. He was the only customer and hurried to be out of their way by closing time.

It was becoming more difficult to reach the eye of his hurricane. Some nights harder than others. He finished half a bottle of whiskey and still couldn't sleep. He turned the easy chair to the window and sat naked facing the slight breeze roaming up from the street. Maybe if he had not eaten he'd be drunk now. But then he'd just be sick later. He hated that part, being sick. He hated it because it placed him at the mercy of the body, which he knew was the same thing as hating life. He wanted life to be distinct from the body, he wanted there to be something of Morgan Cary that lived independently of the body's demands.

There was no one on the street. Fluorescent lights below the canopies made even stripes on the sidewalk, receding toward the Palace Theater like a shadowy railroad track.

He was not able to focus his attention on any one thing when drunk, the salvation of drunkenness. Thoughts simply staggered across the field of his mind, sometimes joyfully, but too often morbidly and always without relevance. He allowed none of his thoughts to remain in place long enough for the swordsman of grief to catch him by the neck. He got drunk in order to pretend that he wasn't going mad. Alcohol sickness, the toll taken by the pretense of sanity.

He knew this all too well. He also knew that if he were compelled to think soberly, he might think himself to death: dying to avoid dying. That was Morgan Cary's way.

He buried his face in his hands and dropped his head to the window sill. He could not cry in the same way that often he could not puke when necessary. The flood would rise in his throat, but stop there as if dammed. He could only shake his head from side to side and dig his fingernails into his damp skin.

He slept restlessly all night, worrying about Ben.

It was too far to walk again, so he took a taxi out to Ben's house. The Dodge was in the driveway, behind Ben's pickup truck, still parked where Morgan had left it. Morgan asked the taxi driver to wait.

The woman answering the door had to be Ben's daughter—tall like Ben, with his flat nose, deep brown eyes, and a lot of his big-boned bulk. Except for the rich brown eyes and thick, long hair, she was a plain-featured woman; Morgan was attracted to her because she seemed so much like Ben and Ben was such a fine man, and maybe because he empathized with her sadness.

"I'm Morgan Cary. I brought Ben's truck back."

She wore a long black dress with a sheer black lace edge around the high collar. He could not determine how old she was.

"Thank you."

"I hope Ben's better."

Morgan realized then that Ben was dead.

"My father died in the emergency room." Words widely spaced, distinct, considered, hard-spoken, tottering on the brink of impossibility or absurdity.

"Oh no," Morgan blurted out, but unsure if he had actually made a sound, added, "I'm sorry."

"Mama's resting right now, but I know she wants me to tell you how much we appreciate . . ."

Morgan shook his head.

"She knows that Papa . . . that we owe you some money from the catch yesterday."

"No. Please. No. You owe me nothing. I only wanted . . . The services?"

"Will be at the church," she indicated down the street with her gaze.

"I know it."

"Tomorrow at one o'clock. We hope you will come, Mr. Cary. Papa thought much of you. He told stories about the things you say." She smiled, maybe recalling one.

Morgan nodded and tried to smile but couldn't. It twisted his mouth into a grimace, as if he had just felt a sudden, sharp pain.

"He would want you to be paid."

"I understand. But please, no."

She nodded her understanding.

"Please give my condolences to your family. I'm very sorry."

They nodded to one another and she closed the door, releasing Morgan from any need to remain.

He paid off the taxi driver. He needed to walk. The sky was bluer than the ocean, mountain ridges held the only clouds. There was a soft sea-borne breeze. It would have been a fine day for fishing.

SEVEN

It did not rain for six days. The sun bathed the entire island with inexhaustible light and heat, sky densely blue, shadows thin and brittle. Sea and sky ran together indistinguishably, motionless. A single boat on the horizon seemed painted on a backdrop. Tin rat rings around palm trees pinged and popped from the diurnal cycle of heating and cooling. There were no more puddles, mud turned to dust, a fine white powder tickling the nose and chalking everything.

Most mornings Morgan walked down to the fish market and ate hamachi and toro sashimi for breakfast, then continued to the dock to help Ben Kamakani's son Joseph prepare the Noho Kai for sale. They had scrubbed her clean, varnished the teak and were in the process of painting everything above the water line.

Joseph had no nostalgia for the Noho Kai, the vessel that put food on his table, clothes on his back, and paid for the music lessons that gave him a kind of career. Joseph only wondered what it was worth, since it was an old boat built by one man in his backyard and towed to the sea behind a rented truck before Joseph was born.

Joseph often frustrated Morgan, although he tried not to let it show. It was not his business, after all. But to not respect Ben's boat was the same as not respecting Ben. There were times when Morgan worked alone in the bilges, in the bowels of the vessel, when he thought he could hear her mourning, whining like a dog waiting at the shore for the master who would never return. He chose not to believe it was only the creaking of seasoned wood under fresh paint.

A "for sale" sign hung from the slanted silver exhaust stack that rose ahead of the wheel house. There were inquiries; none serious yet. Joseph claimed that his mother asked too much. Joseph had tried to convince her that the old sampan couldn't be worth that amount and it would never sell. Morgan sort of hoped Joseph was right, although he supposed Mrs. Kamakani could use the money; she was waiting for the Noho Kai to sell before paying Morgan for his time and labor helping to fix up the boat. He didn't ask for pay. It was just as impossible to argue with her about money as it was with Ben.

Joseph would go back to Los Angeles Tuesday. There was very little else they could do to the boat. She sparkled in the sun like a new silver saddle, her namesake. One had to look closely now to see the scars of forty years of fishing.

Paint did not cover the hole in the transom where a still-green marlin rammed her bill through the wood. Morgan was surprised to find out that Joseph had never heard the story. It was one of Ben's favorites. Morgan had heard it three times.

"Ben said it went four-hundred-twenty pounds," Morgan told Joseph, who was filling the hole with wood spackle. "It took the short inside flat line, eighty-pound test, a blue straight runner with a red eye. Ben says it shredded line off the reel so fast he had to start backing down on the damn thing before the reel melted."

"Yeah, uh huh. Say, Morgan, when that spackle go dry, you like go slap on one dab of paint. Try to blend it in like all ah same. Okay, man?"

"Sure. So, Ben says suddenly the line goes slack and he almost falls back into the wheel house. Naturally he thinks the line broke. But unh unh. The fish had turned on him, charging the boat. Wham!" Morgan unconsciously imitated Ben telling the story, spinning in a half circle, plunging his fist through the air to show how the fish struck. "Ben says it felt like a truck hit the boat. Then he sees the bill. It's a good five or six inches through the transom."

Joseph wasn't listening anymore, if he ever was. He was already off looking for something else to spackle.

"So anyway," Morgan determined to tell the story whether Joseph wanted to hear it or not, "Ben sawed off the bill, rock-salted it, and left it there for about a year."

"Yeah, I think maybe I did hear that one," Joseph said, closing the spackle can and putting it away. "Listen man, I'm outta here. You'll lock it up?"

"Sure." *It*, my ass, Morgan thought. A boat is a *she*, not a fucking *it*.

After Joseph left, Morgan sat on a fat black bollard and finished the last couple of beers remaining from the twelve-pack in the cooler. It was two o'clock in the afternoon. Hot. The sun seemed to singe the hair on the back of his neck, like a campfire on a winter's day. The breeze off the water cooled his face as the sun broiled his back.

Tommy Hu's haole sampan moved down the river and out into the harbor, heading for the fuel dock. Morgan recognized by then the men working on those boats without knowing most of their names. Nor did they know his. Although they always greeted one another by waving a hand with the thumb and little finger extended and when someone spoke to him they called him "buddy," or lately, "brah," because he was a fisherman and among those men that mattered more than the haole whiteness of his skin.

From the fuel dock, a deckhand called out to Morgan, "How's it, brah?"

"Good."

"You go have one offer yet?"

"Not a good one," Morgan replied, holding up the beer in his hand, offering.

"Nah, anyway. I got to bring this bugger over to Suisan."

Morgan nodded and turned his attention back to Ben's boat, which in the ripples of a passing skiff tugged a little at her mooring lines.

There were very few of the big, gleaming, fiberglass sport fishing cruisers on Hilo side, not like across the island in Kona, where fishing was a business to hook tourists rather than supper, where the boats were carpeted and had VCRs for the slack times and were owned by corporations in Tokyo, Los Angeles, and Sydney. In Hilo, those mostly wood sampans were entirely utilitarian, form following function. When Morgan looked back on his time as a fishing boat captain in Kona, he supposed that he was only a glorified tour bus driver at sea. Wasn't that what Tioni always said? "I drive da bus, brah, and you go li'dat captain stuff. Da fish doan care no how."

He finished the beer and took the empty to the trash barrel. He dumped the ice into the river channel and stowed the cooler back aboard the boat. All the paint, all the varnishing and sanding had not obliterated Ben Kamakani. Morgan half expected to hear Ben's voice: "We hele mai, make huhu with them fishes." They had been fishing together only ten weeks when Ben died.

Finally there was nothing left to do, nothing to keep him at the dock. He wondered what kept him in the world?

EIGHT

"I wonder what would happen if ever I tell you there's no Peking noodle?" Marilyn teased Morgan when he placed the order, always the same one. She had brought with her an Oly, the beer he always ordered.

"I guess I'd get something else."

Marilyn laughed. A not unpleasant kind of uproar.

"I think I'll have a hamburger tonight."

"You no go have da kine," Marilyn told him. "I mean you can have whatevah, but Mrs. De La Cruz already fix up you noodle."

His bowl of mixed seafood and noodles sat steaming on the pass-through from the kitchen.

"I'm too old to eat burgers, anyway. It just turns to fat."

Marilyn squealed again. "You old? Hah! You still like one keiki, hair on you face or no." Then Marilyn, who was maybe seventy, waddled off to get the big bowl of noodles.

Morgan nodded to the old man sitting at the table beside the wide front window where a neon sign blinked Oly and Primo logos. They had only a nodding acquaintance. The old man, a Filipino, was there every time Morgan was, usually at the same table. Habitual like Morgan. The old man's white Panama hat with its tapa cloth band hung on the back of the chair. He wore a wild print shirt and black polyester slacks, worn rubber sandals, his hair as white as talcum, his skin as dark and ridged as tree bark. Morgan knew nothing about the man and here was the only place he ever saw him. Hilo wasn't so big. He probably lived nearby, maybe one of those cinder block studio apartments on the street behind Sophie's. Morgan supposed that the man might have worked in the cane fields along the Hamakua Coast, north of Hilo. There was some logic at work behind the assumption: the ridged skin, his parchment-cracked hands, his bent back, the fact that he was a Filipino man over seventy, maybe eighty. He might live alone. Morgan had wondered about him before. What did he do in his room at night? Did he read, drink whiskey, go to the Tuesday night Tagalog movies at the Palace, look out the window to see how closely approaches death? That was how Morgan lived with his own loneliness. Marilyn deferred to the old man. Was he related to her? Was she maybe his daughter? Wife? He always drank two cups of coffee. Marilyn didn't bring the pot around after that, the way she did when anyone else's cup was empty, as if imposing his limits. But maybe he wasn't alone. Maybe he only liked to have his supper that way. Some time by himself. Maybe he went home to a big house with a big family and watched TV with his grandchildren. Maybe he was happy and satisfied.

What if . . . ? Morgan wondered, reminded of Gregory Corso's poem on marriage: *What if I'm sixty years old and not married, all alone in a furnished room with pee stains on my underwear?*

What day was this? Sunday? Morgan scanned the walls looking for a calendar and found one hanging on the counter below the cash register.

Sunday. He could call the bank tomorrow. There must be enough there for some kind of decent down payment. At least that much.

Later, he stopped at the phone booth beside the Palace Theater and called Mrs. Kamakani. She said she would be happy for him to stop by. He should come for lunch.

They were seated around a picnic table in the backyard; Mrs. Kamakani and Joseph on one side, Morgan opposite. The residue of lunch spread out from one end of the table to the other. Mrs. Kamakani, dressed in an unadorned black holoku and a cloth apron in a tapa pattern, poured lilikoi punch into all three glasses. Ben built this picnic table, Mrs. Kamakani told Morgan. Ben could build anything, she said. He had been dead for less than a month. Morgan could see how difficult it was for Mrs. Kamakani to survive with half her body missing. Joseph seemed only interested in knowing what Morgan was after.

"Mrs. Kamakani," he came to the point, "I would like to buy Ben's boat."

"You?" Joseph exclaimed. "Wat's dat?"

To Mrs. Kamakani, Morgan continued, "I am able to offer a good-faith down payment today, if we can come to some agreement. I will pay the balance within a hundred and twenty days."

"How much good faith you gonna offah, eh?" Joseph asked.

"Joseph. Please." His mother made it an order, not a request.

Mrs. Kamakani glanced into Morgan's eyes, then away.

"I'm sorry . . . " She paused. Morgan realized that she could not recall his name. He wanted to give it to her but hesitated, not wanting to cause her embarrassment.

"Mr. Cary," she continued finally, as if she had just spotted the answer written on a cloud. "I am took by surprise. I thought you came here because of the money Ben owed to you for the working."

"No. I just want to buy his boat. Ben owes me nothing."

"You have dat kind money?" Joseph asked.

"For what you be rude?" Mrs. Kamakani told her son.

"This is business, Mama."

"It's your papa's life!"

Joseph turned away from his mother's hard look and feigned interest in a scrap of potato salad.

"I have the money, Mrs. Kamakani. I will pay the asking price."

Joseph shook his head. Dismayed. Cautious.

"The Noho Kai is price more higher than market value," Mrs. Kamakani acknowledged. "You do know that?"

"I don't believe that market value applies to Ben's boat."

For a moment the light returned to Mrs. Kamakani's eyes, the light that must have made her a beautiful young woman when Ben fell in love with her. For that moment, Morgan also loved her. He watched the light refracted through the sudden dampness around her eyes. He could see color on her cheeks. Mrs. Kamakani excused herself and walked directly to the kitchen. Morgan understood that until that moment, she really hadn't come to terms with the possibility of seeing Ben's boat go.

"She's one sentimental woman," Joseph said. "So, you want buy the old man's boat? No wonder you do such good work fix her up, let us pay for varnish, paint, engine parts, all da kine."

"I think the price will thoroughly encompass those expenses, Joseph."

Morgan could see that Joseph was wondering now if his mother had priced the boat too low, wondering what Morgan might know that he wasn't revealing.

Joseph laughed, then exclaimed, "Truly awesome, man! One haole owning the great Ben Kamakani's boat."

Morgan watched as a single fly patrolled the potato-salad debris. Joseph fired up a cigarette and stuck the match into the mushy shell of a papaya. It surprised Morgan that he didn't want a cigarette, happy to have something else he didn't share with Joseph.

"What a big surprise," Joseph said, smoking stylistically.

Mrs. Kamakani returned with a large plastic tub and put it at the end of the table. "Joseph, will you please tidy up?" Then she turned to Morgan. "Mr. Cary, would you like go see Ben's workshop?"

"I would love to." Morgan put his plate and silverware into the tub.

They went through a side door into the garage. Mrs. Kamakani turned on the light, although it was already bright enough from two large windows.

A worktable jutting out from the rear wall was cluttered with fiberglass molds, tools, and thin sheets of red and white rubber used to make skirts to disguise the hooks on marlin lures. There were tubs of resin, glue, and rubbing compound. In the near corner rested a dozen ocean rods in various states of repair. A box sitting on the floor next to the worktable held parts from Penn Senator reels. There were spools of braided Dacron line and spools of monofilament. A kitchen matchbox held pieces of mirrors, sections of spoons, and small vials of gold, silver, red, and green glitter.

Morgan picked up a Konahead lure, pale blue with a mirror inside, the eyes from a doll, painted red. The skirt hadn't been attached. In his hand the lure felt as substantial and beautiful as a custom knife. He put it down next to a straight runner carrying the marks from the blows of countless marlin's bills.

"Are you a fisherman long time, Mr. Cary?"

"I lived on Kona side when I was a boy, grew up and went to high school there. After that, I deckhanded part-time while in college, and then I got my license and skippered a thirty-one-foot Bertram called the Dolphin."

Mrs. Kamakani nodded. Her eyes turned toward Ben's work chair.

"Hilo fishing not same like Kona fishing."

"Yes, ma'am."

"Ben didn't think too much of fishing like one sport."

"That's for sure."

"Would you be fishing here, or maybe Kona side?"

"The Noho Kai would stay in Hilo, Mrs. Kamakani."

"I think you know that I am not wanting to sell Ben's boat."

"Yes, I know."

"And . . . I do not mean to offend you, Mr. Cary, but it is a fact of our lives, of Ben's life: You are a haole."

"That's true."

"It's not your fault," Mrs. Kamakani waved her hand to dismiss the accident of his having a Caucasian birth, even though it had occurred sort of in Hawaii. "I get a big surprise when Ben tell me he go have one haole helping him on the boat. Haoles did many bad things to Hawaiian peoples."

"I understand, but that was a couple of hundred years before my birth."

"It hasn't already stopped, Mr. Cary. But never mind. This is not about that. Ben tells you are one strange, unhappy man, but have also good instincts for fish, good skills on the water. Your unhappiness troubled Ben. Ben was a Christian man. Man of charity."

"Mrs. Kamakani, I can only promise you that Ben's boat will remain in Hilo and that I will take good care of her. I liked Ben very much and if the choice were mine to make, I would rather Ben were still alive so I could just go on working for him."

"I will sell you the boat," Mrs. Kamakani stated directly. "The price go a little high, but not so high, I think. You should also take any of this for you can use. There is one outboard motor in the shed behind the garage. It is one-year-old Evinrude. You may also go take that, please. Do you know where he keep the dinghy?"

"Yes, ma'am. In the storage shed at Suisan."

"Number ten. I will get the key for you."

She offered her hand and they shook on it. It was a hard hand, but not as hard as Ben's.

"Ben's truck goes with the boat," she added. "It's an old truck."

Morgan nodded and followed her out of the garage. Then she stopped, turned back toward him and said, "Ben Iki . . ."

"Your grandson."

"Yes. He loves the boat."

"I know. He went out with us a couple of Sundays. He's welcome aboard anytime. He's a good boy. I like him. I mean that."

Mrs. Kamakani nodded and went quickly back into the yard.

"I have sold your father's boat," Mrs. Kamakani informed Joseph.

"That's fine, Mama, but let's make sure his check go through before we go get carry ourselves away."

NINE

Morgan took to wearing Ben's hat. He found it on the floorboard of the pickup truck. It was a billed cap, khaki, stained from grease and fish blood, although some of the blood was probably Ben's, who lost the tip of his right index finger in a twisted line, slashed his foot on the razor sharp teeth of an Ono, jammed a size 10/0 hook into his left thigh and had to push it on through to cut off the barb, and so on.

Morgan started smoking again. The boredom and all the time alone, he told himself. It's because everybody else at the dock smokes, smoking is an act of ritual bonding. He always lied easily to himself, an imagination easily confused in confrontation with reality. He watched smoke rising before his tired eyes while waiting for the light to change at Waianuenue and Bayfront. His mouth was hangover dry. He sipped from the bottle of beer in a paper bag between his legs. The radio was tuned to the Hawaiian music station from Honolulu, but the static was bad.

When he turned right onto Bayfront heading toward the Sampan Harbor boat dock off Lihiwai Street, it started drizzling.

It had been only a matter of days, three or four, since he cut the last bonds to the mainland and his life there. The house he had bought only a few years before Victoria's death was in escrow. He was a fisherman again. He must go out in the rain. There was a lot of rain in Hilo.

The windshield wipers streaked. He turned them off and the radio static diminished. Tires squished on the wet pavement. Not sunrise yet, but the misty rain was so thick it would be impossible to see much difference. Light from the street lamps smudged across the wet asphalt. The Toyota truck's headlights were the only signs of life along Bayfront until he turned toward the dock. A few boats already headed into the bay, disappearing into the mist like phantoms passing across the glow of a lantern. Crews loaded supplies onto waiting boats: ice in blocks or bags, some groceries, lures. Men worked at their usual pace, the weather making no difference.

Morgan parked in the space designated for the Noho Kai, the boat's faded name printed on the creosote guard rail in peeling white letters. It rained harder, but it was also warm and he would dry fast when the sun came out. It would come out. It always did after some time, especially that time of year, autumn. Only wet or dry marked the seasons.

Tourists hated this weather, he remembered from his few years as a tourist hustler in Kona. Most of them despised it to the point of canceling their charter when it was stormy. Losing a charter cost the Dolphin's crew money, because the boat's owner only paid the crew salaries when they went out. Morgan didn't always mind those cancellations. He was hardly more than a boy, living on junk food, beer, sex, and dirt-cheap marijuana. Often when a charter canceled he would go out fishing in the rain with Tioni Brown, the Dolphin's deckhand, who had taught Morgan how to fish Kona waters.

Tioni was the third generation of his family to fish Kona. His father was a captain, but Tioni had never been interested in taking on any more responsibilities than were necessary. He lived at home with his parents and brothers and sisters, proudly claiming to have no particular ambitions. He made enough money as a deckhand and simply did not have the kind of personality it took to hustle tourist fishermen (or their bored wives) the way a captain needed to. Tioni understood instinctively that an accident of birth had given him a special life, a life that for many men constituted the supreme fantasy. Tioni and Morgan were the same age and had attended school together twice, as Morgan came in and out of Hawaii with his father's Coast Guard transfers.

They were unusual friends in those days. Hawaii was a typically coagulated melting pot: haoles stayed with each other and locals stayed with each other. It is unlikely Morgan and Tioni would ever have passed more than a few casual words in a classroom or hallway if, when they were fourteen, Morgan had not plunged headfirst, fists swinging, into a melee of haole football players attacking a solitary Hawaiian boy after their team had lost a game and Tioni taunted them. Morgan got a broken nose and Tioni lost both his upper front teeth before stadium guards put a stop to it. Tioni's sense of humor produced the claim that he lost those teeth playing ice hockey for the Hawaiian Olympic team.

Tioni's house was the first local Hawaiian home he was ever invited to. Tioni's father as a silent thank you began taking Morgan out fishing with them when he didn't have a charter, what they called holo holo fishing. Sammy Brown was unarguably Kona's best sports fishing boat captain, teacher of movie stars and hopeful rich sportsmen. Morgan learned eagerly.

"Why did you fight for my boy?" Mr. Brown asked Morgan when he first visited the Brown's home, fresh bandages on his busted nose. The implication in the question was why did a haole fight for a local, against other haoles?

"Just seemed like the right thing to do," Morgan answered shyly, not used to having to explain anything he did.

When Morgan was ten years old, attempting to protect his lunch money from the grade school Mafia, he earned a pair of black eyes. When he went home, hoping his father was going to go out and kick some ass, what he got instead was a lecture.

Mitchell Cary said: "Morgan, some men frighten easily, always worried about getting hurt or losing something; these men live long and badly. Other men never frighten; these men live short, probably, but well. A man always has the choice which it'll be for him. You don't have anything to be afraid of, son, because you don't really have nothing to lose, not like it might seem to you now, anyhow. You just can't hold in such high regard things you're afraid to give up if need be. Money is one of those things. Honor, fair play, are not among those things."

Morgan didn't pay much attention to the speech, since what he wanted was for his father to defend him. He was only ten. But years later he would think of it; then he understood that his father wanted his son to know that "things," that objects, were not worth defending if the price got too high. These were the kind of things his father commonly referred to as "the stuff that going after ain't any smarter than chasing a dime up an elephant's ass."

What had subconsciously soaked into his freshly forming mind was something altogether different from his father's point. Morgan took him to mean that he should avoid forming attachments to things he might end up desiring so desperately that he might risk pain, even death, to protect them. This left Morgan with the awkward notion that if he didn't possess "things to lose," he could live well and free from painful encounters.

None of this became clear to Morgan until many years later, after he had plunged into the fight with Tioni. He realized his father was not saying that nothing was worth fighting for, only that *things* were seldom worth it. Morgan had lunged into the fight because he saw something worth defending, the principle of the fair fight.

Some years later, when Morgan got his captain's license, he asked Tioni to come work for him on the Dolphin. They had been together two years when Tioni met Victoria Novak.

Morgan could see that day clearly, even when he tried very hard to block the images.

Silver rain. The other boats sitting on their moorings because their charters had canceled. The Dolphin stern to the pier with Tioni sitting on an engine box cover, sheltered by the cabin overhead extension.

"They canceled," Morgan told Tioni, who had already figured as much. "How about we go holo holo?"

"All a same, not today."

"There's big fish out there, brother."

"Big fish out there all a time."

Obviously, Tioni meant to take off. He had already put away the rods and reels in the overhead rack.

"Since when does Tioni Brown turn down a holo holo?"

"Since he eyeball da new waitress at Huggo's."

"Ah. Now the picture becomes clear. So, what's the story? What's she look like? Nice tits? She a haole?"

"Haole part can't be helped. But brah, let me say you: she make a blind man see, a cripple run, a dead man go suck him up air like he coming back to life."

"How poetic."

"You want see some kind poetry, brah? Turn you ass 'round."

Morgan did.

She stood behind him. Almost close enough to touch. He was struck first by her long and luxurious hair, not exactly blond and not auburn. Ash, he decided. Her eyes were almost too big, like a child in a Keene drawing. She wore no makeup, the sheen on her face came from the baby oil she rubbed in to keep her skin moist in the sun. He smelled the oil. She had a deep tan and a little of her bathing suit line showed in the cleavage inside a bandanna halter top. She wore ragged blue jean shorts and flip-flops and carried a string bag over her shoulder.

Morgan thought she was beautiful, but the islands were filled to overflowing with pretty girls. There was something else, something more powerful than pretty, but he couldn't name it. She looked . . . she was confident, strong, compelling. She projected sexuality.

"Victoria Novak," Tioni made the introduction into their awkward silence, "this is Captain Morgan Cary."

"Hi, Cap'n Morgan."

Morgan demanded his voice, but it wouldn't come. He realized she had probably heard the stupid "nice tits" remark. He stared, mute, and nodded politely.

"So, you're the captain of this here vessel?"

"What that means is he don't got to do some real work," Tioni joked.

"That is pretty much what the title means, all right," Morgan finally spoke.

"A brains–brawn thing?" Victoria said.

"Except he don't got neither one," Tioni said with a quick and wide smile.

"That is also pretty much true," Morgan continued, beginning to feel in command of his voice again.

"So we're going to split," Tioni announced, a tone of seeking unnecessary permission.

"Have fun, children," Morgan said.

Tioni mock-saluted and said, "Tomorrow, skipper."

"Nice meeting you, Cap'n Morgan."

Her smile locked his tongue again. He nodded, then turned to make himself attentive to nonexistent chores as they walked away.

It was only after they were off the pier, both Tioni and Victoria glanced back over their shoulders and smiled, that Morgan realized how flagrantly stupid he seemed to be. He supposed they were laughing at him. He already knew his life was changed.

A horn honking returned him to the moment and Morgan, standing in the Noho Kai's cockpit, waved at Gabby Tanaka driving by the parking lot. He wished he had brought more pictures of Victoria and he wished he had taken at least one picture of her from when they met. He wished he had not talked her out of posing for Justin. To possess such a painting would be more valuable to him now than owning the *Mona Lisa*. The pictures he had saved were in a box stored under a bunk in the forward compartment, although he did not open it often. His favorite was from their delayed honeymoon trip to San Diego. Still poor, making a cheap holiday in a motel at Mission Bay. Victoria, in a red one-piece swim suit and Morgan shirtless and in jeans standing by the rock jetty in front of the Hotel del Coronado. A Mexican man had taken the picture. It was his favorite because Victoria still glowed with what turned out to be erratic periods of happiness. She did not know how to be happy and Morgan had been too selfish to find out how he could show her.

TEN

Morgan turned off the pickup's engine, stuffed the cigarette pack into the pocket of his T-shirt, grabbed the lure bag off the floorboard, and stepped out into the Hilo rain.

The Noho Kai waited starboard side to the dock so her bow headed upstream as spring lines held her off. The locked wheelhouse dripped water like a woman's hair as she steps from a shower. Expectancy came from the vessel. Morgan picked up a dock line and pulled her close enough to step aboard. After opening the combination lock, he went into the wheelhouse and dropped the gear bag onto a seat cushion. There remained a lot of Ben's smell, most noticeable when the boat had been closed up overnight. Although by then there was also some of Morgan's smell.

He considered using aku nets. Big fish catches from lures had been negligible for three days. He looked through the salt-pocked glass of the wheelhouse to see how crews of the other boats were preparing. The Moku

Maru's boys were clearing nets, and Kenny on the Lani Kai set out rods. It was a mixed bag all the way down the dock.

Up the street, the crew on a city truck removed from light poles rain-soaked poster boards advertising the circus that spent a week in the park, two months ago.

Morgan blew the bilges and engine compartment, checked the pumps, then started the GMC-671 diesel engine, which announced itself with a belch of black smoke from the stack. The engine warmed up while he got the rods, having decided to start with lures. He liked fighting the fish, not just netting them in like some trapped weight.

The sun came up, a feeling as much as an event. It was warmer and the drizzle slacked off. Soon he would need dark glasses over his dilated eyes. He hauled the rods and reels out one at a time, fixing each in its holder, putting the two big Penn Senator reels along the sides to run from outriggers and the two smaller ones at the stern to lay flat out in the white water. The deck vibrated comfortably below bare feet.

He couldn't say how long Ben's twelve-year-old grandson, Ben Iki, had been sitting there on the parking rail. The boy wore surfer baggy shorts and a faded gray T-shirt with Waiakea Intermediate School Athletic Department printed on it. Morgan waved and called out a hello. Ben Iki waved back and approached the boat.

"How are you, Ben Iki?"

"Okay, Mr. Cary. You getting ready for go out?"

"Pretty soon now, yeah."

"No more rain for a little while, eh?"

"Guess I'll go either way. Shouldn't you be heading for school?"

"It's already Saturday, Mr. Cary."

"So it is."

"No school Saturday."

"Yeah, I suppose not."

"Can I help you with something?"

"Sure. There's plenty to do. Hop aboard."

Morgan took up one of the spring lines and pulled the boat close enough to the dock for Ben Iki to step across. Ben Iki jumped agilely down to the cockpit sole.

"You can bring out the lures while I get the leaders tied on. They're in . . ."

"I know. The big drawer, left side sink. What kind you like for start?"

"Well . . . what do you think?"

"What kind fish we go after?"

"Ahi, with luck. Ono, more likely. Maybe a marlin for fun." Morgan considered the *we*.

"Then I say we use da kine blue Konahead and one silver guy from the outriggers. Starboard side flat line we put on da kine straight runner with the gold spoon. What you think about maybe using one rubber squid, port side?"

"Sure. Sounds good."

Ben Iki went into the wheelhouse.

"Do your folks know where you are? I mean, you're welcome to go out with me, but you'll have to have their permission."

"My father, he's not really around here. It's okay with Mama. She know I come down here already."

Ben Iki shuffled around in the deep drawer to find the lures he wanted.

"Are you sure, Ben Iki?"

He nodded and pretended to be attentive to the lure search.

"You could get me into a lot of trouble if she doesn't know, if you don't have her permission. You know that, don't you? I'm happy to have you along, brah, but you really do have to get your mother's okay first. Do you really have it?"

"I could maybe call her right now," the boy decided, looking up from the drawer, the blue Konahead in his hand.

"Okay, let's do that. What do you say?"

Ben Iki wanted to get the lures out first. After finishing that and placing each one by the rod he wanted it attached to, they walked up the dock to the phone booth outside the supply store.

Morgan handed Ben Iki a quarter for the phone.

"Mama," Ben Iki said when she answered. "You know Mr. Cary. He buyed Papa's boat? That man? Uh-huh. Him. Well, I was already down here, you know? And Mr. Cary he was wondering if maybe it would be all right for me to go out fishing with him on Papa's boat today? Because, you see? Mr. Cary is by his self and everything like that, so he can use my help a lot!" There was a pause, to which Ben Iki listened. Morgan felt like laughing. "Uh-huh," Ben Iki answered. "It's the truth! Really! Mr. Cary say I got to have your permission already." After another pause, Ben Iki turned to Morgan and said, "She want talk now with you." His eyes were wide with hope and expectation and plea.

"What's your last name?" Morgan cupped his hand over the phone to ask Ben Iki.

"Napela," Ben Iki answered.

"Mrs. Napela, this is Morgan Cary. I think Ben Iki would make a fine deckhand for me today, if it's all right with you."

She had a soft, musical voice, a rustling, airborne voice that seemed on the verge of song. It was familiar to him and he presumed she was the woman he met at the door the day he found out Ben died, so that was the face he put to the voice. She told Morgan that Ben Iki had been very sad since his grandfather died and she thought it would do him good to be on the boat again. She asked Morgan to make him wear a life jacket all the time and he assured her. By that time, Ben Iki couldn't keep still. He skipped around the phone booth like a boy needing a toilet.

Ben Iki came to his side when Morgan hung up the phone.

"Well, Ben Iki, let's us hele mai and chase some fish."

"Okay, okay," Ben Iki cried, prancing five paces ahead back to the Noho Kai.

By mid-morning the clouds went away like a dream on waking, tumbling above the sea and bouncing against the slope of Mauna Kea to end up clustered around the peak in a lenticular cap. The trades picked up speed in the warm high sunlight. Swells lost their shape and white foam appeared atop crumbling wave ridges; a little rougher than usual for even the exposed side of the island.

Soon after turning north to troll along the fifty fathom ledge, they picked up an ono that went forty pounds. It hit the port side outrigger and snapped the rubber band striker with a pop like a firecracker, ripping off a hundred yards of Dacron line before Morgan could get the rod out of the holder. Ben Iki brought the fish in and they put it on ice in the reefer, along with the three small aku picked up casting a feather lure into a school they found working some bait just out of the harbor. Morgan took the filet knife and sliced a slab of flesh from the side of an aku he had just killed with a stab into its brain. He cut the slab into halves and handed a raw, red, warm piece to Ben Iki. "Sea candy," Morgan said. "I like caramel corn better," Ben Iki replied as he swallowed his piece of tuna.

They chased birds for fifteen minutes, then turned back to the ledge when the birds scattered. They were only scouts.

The Noho Kai was three miles beyond the breakwater on a northerly heading, toward the Hamakua Coast. The fields of cut cane along the shore stretched mauka like scars, although not as distinct as the black scabs of lava marking leeward coastal slopes. Smoke from a sugar mill stack stretched out flat toward the mountain. Brown water stained the shore where mountain streams met the sea. If they went far enough north they would see waterfalls tumbling white through the multi-hued green curtain of the Hamakua pali. Morgan thought of trying to make it that far if they weren't delayed with fish, although being delayed with fish would be preferable.

It was hot in the sun. Morgan agreed to let Ben Iki remove the life jacket, as Ben Kamakani had allowed his grandson to do previously. The

Noho Kai was stable, the seas weren't that bad and Ben Iki was confined to the wheelhouse and cockpit when he had the jacket off.

Ben Iki stayed in the wheelhouse most of the time anyway. He liked to steer. Morgan sat in the fighting chair in the cockpit with his feet propped on the stern railing; every once in a while he glanced back to check on the boy. Ben Iki, a baseball cap reversed on his head and Wayfarer sunglasses making him look like some little brown James Dean, concentrated on holding the course.

Anybody else would be using nets. Anybody else wouldn't be just as content to cruise like some tourist cattle boat along the Hamakua Coast as to catch fish. What kind of fisherman am I? Morgan thought. Trolling with lures simply because he liked catching fish that way. If he didn't catch fish, he wouldn't starve or be unable to pay the bills. After escrow closed on the house, he would have something over fifty thousand dollars left from the mortgage. It was enough to live that way for a year or maybe two.

Nothing more than holo holo fishing, he thought.

But the lures worked beautifully and were mesmerizing to watch. Each lure had a discernibly distinct action. The pair of Konaheads working from the outriggers, although they were, except for the color of their shiny inserts, identical lures from the same mold, were set to create separate illusions: the starboard side let farthest back so it ran, veritably leapt, from crest to crest, shooting up a rooster tail of white water in its wake, imitating fleeing mackerel, while the port side outrigger was set to run in the troughs between the swells and hardly ever break the surface, leaving a long, solid trail of smoke-like bubbles in its wake. It was that lure the Ono took earlier. The rubber squid on the port side flat line, which was not let out too far behind the boat, ran silent and deep, leaving very little trail, while the straight runner on the other flat line made a wake like a torpedo.

There's something here for all of you, Morgan told the fish. What do you see, you fish? What attracts you? What compels you to strike?

But somehow fish were tempted to the boat. He supposed that it was something in the sound of the boat itself that urged fish toward it, maybe the engine rumble vibrating through the water in some compelling pattern of sonic waves. That's why some boats were called "lucky." They had a sound that pulled fish to them.

The Noho Kai was always a lucky boat.

They were off the Pepeekeo School House when he had Ben Iki turn outbound and head for deeper water. For ahi. Morgan started pulling in both outriggers to change lures.

At noon they ate. Ben Iki lashed the helm and sat with Morgan in the cockpit. There wasn't much. Morgan hadn't expected company. They shared a can of sardines, eating the fish atop Saltines. There were four apples and a wedge of yellow cheese. Morgan drank beer. There was only water for Ben Iki. Morgan seldom ate much at sea, a full stomach made him drowsy.

The beers forced him to piss every hour or so. He stood on the leeward rail with his arm wrapped around the outrigger pole to do it. Should he fall in, would Ben Iki know how to bring the boat around? He looked down at the water rushing past the hull. Deep, dark water still frightened him. Although there was something compelling about it, something that seemed to urge him, call to him, accept him. The memory of what lurked below made him involuntarily shiver.

He was still pissing when the starboard outrigger let go.

"Hit 'im!" Morgan cried out, spinning around the outrigger pole and jumping into the cockpit.

Ben Iki shoved the throttle forward to the stop and the Noho Kai brought up her bow, surging into the coming swell with her slanted stack spewing black smoke. White water sprayed through the wheelhouse ports. Morgan scrambled along the cockpit railing to the rod, now bent in a deep arc as the line, taut enough to whistle, peeled away beyond the wake.

"Neutral!" Morgan commanded, pulling the rod butt from the holder and pointing the tip toward the place where the line disappeared into the water. "Bring her back, bring her back!"

The fat, black reel quickly lost over a quarter of its spool of 130-pound-test Dacron line. He tightened the star drag a quarter turn and tried to pull back the rod.

"Big fucking fish!"

Ben Iki set the throttle to idle and placed the gear lever into neutral. He dropped the rope loop over the top wheel spoke and ran out to the cockpit.

"What is it? Marlin?"

"I think it's an ahi."

"Big guy!" Ben Iki watched line shred from the spool so fast that puffs of smoke rose from the wet line.

Morgan tried to move backwards toward the chair without giving up pressure on the rod. He managed two steps by pointing the rod tip at the fish like the barrel of a rifle.

"Can you get the harness?" he asked Ben Iki. "Do you know where the harness is?"

"I'll get it," Ben Iki cried, dashing toward the wheelhouse.

The explosion was as loud as a pistol shot next to his ear. By the time Ben Iki turned toward the noise, the rod had already slapped Morgan between the eyes, the reactive momentum knocking him off his feet and back into the wheelhouse bulkhead.

Morgan would not remember it.

ELEVEN

He was certain it was a dream, the kind of dream it took a long time to wake from, the kind where it was difficult to recognize any distinction between conditions, between what one thought was consciousness and what one thought was sleeping. Maybe he was only dreaming about a hospital, while really he was napping on the sofa in his California house. In fact, he began to realize that the dream was of his house in another life, of having an afternoon nap on a long, desert-brown sofa, the scattered wads of paper lying on the floor. But it took some minutes to understand the difference, and a voice kept interfering with his concentration.

"Mr. Cary!"

It was a very loud voice, a screaming voice, too loud, destroying all his hopes of concentrating on where he was and what was going on.

"Mr. Cary! Can you hear me?"

Then he could both see her and hear her, so he didn't understand why she kept shouting.

"You've been in an accident, Mr. Cary. You had an accident. Do you understand?"

Morgan believed he was trying to acknowledge her.

"Can you hear me, Mr. Cary?"

Why, for Chrissakes, was the woman yelling! Just behind her stood another woman. Nurses. The one with the loud voice wore a stethoscope around her neck. A tube ran down from an inverted bottle of clear fluid. He had the motherfucker of headaches.

"Yes," he heard himself saying clearly for what he thought was the third or fourth time, although it was only the first.

She smiled at him and he believed that he smiled back. The nurse lowered her voice, leaned closer, and touched his cheek with the back of her hand.

"How do you feel, Mr. Cary?"

"I have a headache."

"I imagine you do."

She listened to his chest with the stethoscope and held his left wrist in her hand. She was a Filipina and caused him to think of Marilyn at the café and that helped him remember that he lived in Hilo, so maybe this was the Hilo Hospital.

"Do you remember what happened, Mr. Cary?" She removed the stethoscope from her ears, turned to the woman behind her, and said, "One twenty over seventy. Pulse, sixty." Then, to Morgan, she added, "You have a pretty healthy heart, Mr. Cary."

The other nurse was a haole, very young. Maybe a candy striper or student nurse.

"I don't remember what happened."

"You fell on your boat, hit your head. You have some stitches back there."

He reached back to feel for the stitches, but the pull of the tube in his arm stopped him short.

"Careful with the IV," the nurse warned. "You've got a concussion, which probably accounts for why you don't remember what happened. Don't worry, your memory will probably come back."

"When did I . . . ?"

"Yesterday."

"Yesterday?"

The nurse gave him two pills in a paper cup for the headache and asked if he might feel hungry. Displeased he was not. In a second bed across the room, an old man slept. A heart monitor beeped from the machine above the bed. There were many vases of flowers and potted plants, greeting cards lined up along the window ledge. Through the large window he could see the top of two palm trees in a misting rain. The young haole woman left without Morgan noticing. He saw a vase of flowers, bird of paradise, on the table next to his bed. He noticed, but couldn't reach the attached card.

Ben Iki. He remembered Ben Iki.

"There was a boy . . ."

"He brought you in, brought the boat in, I mean. Quite the young hero."

"He's okay?"

"Oh, just fine. He was smart enough not to move you. He put a towel behind your head and stopped the flow of blood. He called the Coast Guard and brought the boat in all by himself.

"The doctor's on the floor," she continued. "He should be around in a few minutes to look you over. After that, I imagine he'll let your visitors come in, if you feel up to it."

Morgan wondered what time it was. There was no clock. Visitors?

The nurse had started out when the doctor came in. She turned around and followed him back into the room.

"Well, Mr. Cary, did you have pleasant dreams?"

"I thought this was the dream."

The doctor smiled then looked at the chart handed him by the nurse. "I'm sure you wish it was. You must have some headache. How does it feel, the head?"

The doctor touched the bandages wrapped around his head, then looked into his eyes with a pen light.

"This is the worst hangover I've ever had."

The doctor had a name tag and it required concentrated focus to read it.

Dr. Takiyama laughed. Then he had Morgan look this way and that way, following the light. He had Morgan grip his hand and squeeze. He checked the bottom of Morgan's feet with the tip of a pen.

"It took a dozen stitches to close the cut in the back of your head, Mr. Cary. You have a concussion, of course. But I believe you may count on a complete recovery, with no recurring symptoms. Scalp wounds are terrible bleeders. You got four units of blood. That was the initial problem. You'd have bled to death if you hadn't been brought straight in to us."

"Ben Iki."

"I'm sorry?"

"The boy who was on the boat with Mr. Cary," the nurse answered for Morgan. "The young hero."

"Ah, yes. Ben Iki. Little Ben. Some hero, your little Ben. He saved your life, Mr. Cary."

Dr. Takiyama had a cursory look at the IV, made a note on the pad handed him by the nurse, told Morgan he would check back in the evening.

The nurse drew the curtain between the two beds and also left.

Morgan was alone for only a minute before Ben Iki and his mother appeared in the open doorway.

They seemed afraid to come all the way in and violate the space guarded by humming machines, dangling cords, and antiseptic sprays. Ben

Iki stood in front of his mother, her hands on his shoulders as if for support rather than restraint, in dependence rather than in domination. Or was it pride? Morgan wasn't sure. She looked like Ben, that is, like her father, a female variant of Ben Kamakani. She was tall, probably six feet, as tall as Morgan or maybe taller, and her brown skin stretched over large bones. She wore a formless shift, which didn't hide the fact that her breasts were large, as were her hips. Her hair was up, tied in a bun behind her head, although he remembered from the first time he saw her standing in the door of Ben Kamakani's house that, unleashed, it fell nearly to her waist. There were white streaks in her black hair. Ben's hair had been almost entirely white. She had thick eyebrows and large eyes, eyes now staring at the top of Ben Iki's head.

Ben Iki pulled away from his mother and walked over to the bed. Morgan smiled, offering a free hand to him.

"Thanks, Ben Iki," Morgan said as they shook hands awkwardly.

The boy shrugged and looked at the ceiling.

"You make good crew. If you ever want a job . . ."

"It weren't no big thing. I'm glad you okay."

Ana Mana'o'i'o Napela stood next to her son and put a magazine on the bedside table.

"I brought you one magazine to read," she explained, picking it up again so he could see the cover: A boating magazine.

"Thank you. That's very thoughtful. I haven't read this one yet."

"You look like a 'saw me,'" proclaimed Ben Iki, his eyes on the bandages around Morgan's head.

"Swami," Ana corrected, smiling in spite of herself. To Morgan, whose eyes she had only just now let herself look at, she explained. "He saw a film at school, about India. You know? Snake charmers and like that. He thinks the bandages . . ." She stopped, realizing she was just twittering. "Remember what the nurse said," she told her son. "We can only stay for a minute."

His headache was blinding. He wouldn't mind if they left, but he wondered if he would ever see them again? Morgan extended his hand to Ben Iki once more.

"I owe you."

"Nah," Ben Iki sloughed it off.

Ana put her hands on Ben Iki's shoulders again, began pulling him back.

"I'm very proud of my son, Mr. Cary."

"With every right," he answered. His vision was blurring. He wanted them to stay, he wanted to talk longer with them, but the pain was too distracting.

"His grandfather would be proud."

"He isn't called little Ben for nothing."

At the door Ben Iki stopped, said, "And don't you worry already about the Noho Kai. I keep my eye on her for you. I'm watching all a time."

"Then I won't worry."

His lips involuntarily formed a grimace. Ana Napela hurried her son out. He reached for the buzzer to call the nurse to bring drugs.

TWELVE

Morgan was aware of the presence as he awoke, sensing someone watching him. The noises and smells of the hospital were confusing and at first his eyes opened without focusing, he saw only a blur of light and shadows.

"Captain Morgan?"

He turned his head to the voice.

"How's it, brah? You finally gonna wake up now?"

"Tioni? How . . ."

"You're looking pretty good for a man damn-near supposed to be dead. Growed a beard, huh?"

"How did you know?"

"Somebody picked it up on the radio when it happened. Lot of CB chatter about it. I knew you'd passed through Kona side a few months ago already. I knew you were fishing over here with Ben. I knew you bought his boat. It's Hawaii, already. That's some bandage."

"I'm supposed to look like a swami."

Tioni laughed. "Sure. I can see that. Swami Morgan Cary. Better than Captain Morgan the Pirate. Hey, you're smiling. You must feel pretty all right?"

"Dope. They won't stop giving me the stuff. That's not a complaint."

"You have like a concussion."

"Right now I'm in a pharmacological fog."

"Ooh wee, some kind a famous writer talk, big fucking word."

Although it was clear Tioni was offering friendly sarcasm, Morgan knew in that moment how many years of great friendship were lost. That knowledge landed in his stomach like a hot rock.

"How long have you been here?"

"Couple a minutes before you stirred. They told me you was awake so I just come on in."

Morgan had no concept of time. It wasn't dark. Sun still out. Clouds drifted like figures before a screen, casting shadows along the ceiling. Was it Sunday? Wouldn't Ben Iki have been in school if it were Monday?

"You with me, man?"

"Sorry. Guess I'm a little spaced out. I remember being on the boat yesterday. I remember waking up in here this morning. That's about it."

"Well, the story is, you had a fish on. It must have been a big guy—ahi kind. The line broke, the rod he pops back and hits you right there." Tioni pointed to the discolored area on Morgan's forehead. "Then you fell back and bang you head on some kind a thing. They tell you how much blood you done give up?"

"A bunch, I guess."

"Yeah, a goddamn bunch of blood. Shit."

It felt like watching a fog lift. Like the world around him brightened. Every few seconds he seemed to see things more clearly. Only now he fully began to realize that Tioni Brown was really there, he wasn't dreaming again.

"I think I'm just going to sit down." Tioni slid over a chair and plopped across it with one fishhook scarred, bronzed leg dangling over the side. "I think I'd of recognized you anyway, even with that hippie beard."

Morgan would have recognized Tioni on any street in any city anywhere in the world, although he was at least twenty pounds heavier than he was the last time he saw him, and his skin had weathered more noticeably.

"You want something?"

"Nothing, thanks. I'm surprised anybody remembered me."

"Everybody remember, brah. You got famous."

"Famous? What for?"

"The kanes still talk about when you go and leave the rubber off that marlin's mouth." Tioni laughed. "Remember that?"

Morgan smiled, remembering.

"Just about the funniest damn thing I ever did see," Tioni continued.

"If I'm associated with something, I'm glad that's it."

"What about being one famous book writer?"

"I got fired."

"How you get fired from book writing?"

"When you aren't writing one and when nobody buys your book much anymore."

"I bought it. Were just one, right?"

"Yeah, just one. But didn't you tell me after high school you'd never open another book again?"

"Didn't say I read it, did I?"

Morgan managed a laugh.

"I was wondering, you know, if anybody yet told your wife what happen to you?"

So, finally the time had come.

"Victoria's dead, Tioni."

Tioni stood and walked to the window, his back to the bed. Morgan couldn't see what expression had come to his face.

"She killed herself. It was my fault."

Tioni turned around and walked back to the chair. He sat, waiting.

"Pills and alcohol. I found her on the floor . . ." He could see Tioni didn't want to know that. "I thought she was sleeping until I saw . . ."

"Why'd she go for do something like that?"

"Because she thought I didn't love her anymore. I suppose she thought I was leaving her."

"This is true?"

"I loved her. I was stupid, but I loved her, Tioni."

"I am sorry about this, brah. I am very sorry about this. But you know, I got over it already, a long time ago. I doan speak bad about the dead, but she would have chewed me up and spit me out. I think maybe it's not so much da kine surprise, she was heading that way all along?"

"I suppose so, but maybe I could have done more to stop it."

"Well, Cap'n Morgan. I got someplace to be now. You know how it goes."

"Okay."

"Maybe some other time, okay?"

"I hope so."

But maybe Tioni didn't hear that, because he was already out the door. Morgan had not believed a word of what Tioni said. Tioni still loved her. Morgan believed that he would never see him again.

The young haole nurse came in as Tioni went out, asked if he needed anything, she was going off shift. Morgan asked if she would do him a favor and she quickly agreed. He asked where his things were—keys, wallet, and such. She opened the bedside table drawer and showed him. He took out the key chain.

"I would like some clean clothes," he told her. "Just shorts and a clean shirt."

"You want me to go to your house?"

"It's just a room downtown. It's easy to find." He put the keys into her hand. "It's next to the house with the shoes."

"Everybody knows that place. You're giving me the keys to your room?"

"It's okay. I have nothing worth stealing."

Morgan closed his eyes and slumped into a shallow sleep, still vaguely conscious, memories coming into awareness.

A vision of the Kailua pier as clear as if he were actually approaching from the bay, tour buses parked along the King Kamehameha Hotel side of it, herds of tourists milling about in studied confusion, in new gaudy clothes, more women than men, all of them quite old from Morgan's youthful perspective, waiting for the fish to arrive on incoming boats, a spectacle described and promoted in their guidebooks. The charter vessel Dolphin arrived first and had a marlin aboard. Not a big one; it would weigh two hundred fifty pounds. Morgan and Tioni took care of the busy work in preparation to dock, Tioni dropping the bow anchor, then coming astern to leap to the dock and secure the aft lines. He helped the fishermen disembark. After showing them where to stand while the fish rose on the hoist, he jumped back down into the cockpit to help Morgan prepare the marlin for weighing and photographing. As Tioni started to wrap one of the thick outrigger rubber bands around the marlin's bill to hold its mouth closed, Morgan stopped him.

"Leave it off, Tioni."

"What for? Stomach fall out then," Tioni looked at Morgan as if he had gone silly.

"I know. Look up there." Morgan pointed toward the group of tourists now gathered around the hoist, cameras ready, waiting for the fish to be hauled up.

It took Tioni only seconds to understand Morgan's intention. Snickering quietly, he put the rubber band around his wrist instead of around the marlin's bill and mouth. Morgan secured the tail rope and slipped it around the hoist hook.

"Stop laughing," Morgan ordered. "They'll figure something's up."

Barely able to contain himself, Tioni jumped back to the dock to operate the hoist. As the marlin rose from the swim step, Morgan watched the tourists moving closer to the scales, jostling one another for a picture angle as the fish was raised with its head down, the bill trailing across the blood-stained concrete.

Keo Usher, who ran the fish auction, told Morgan he had forgotten to secure the mouth.

"I didn't forget," Morgan answered.

The man who'd caught the fish stood beside it, his hand resting on the dorsal fin, while his partner framed a picture. Tourists pressed closer, ooing and ahhing, forming a tightening circle around the dead fish. One woman bravely leaned forward and reached out tentatively to touch the gray, cold skin of the marlin's belly; her friends applauded the heroism and took her picture.

It began that moment, first a faint gurgle, followed by a loud slurping noise. All eyes moved down the marlin's length, following the path of the noise, just as the fish regurgitated its free-floating stomach and its contents, slithering out in one inverted mass of partially digested squid, tuna, and unrecognizable strings of acidy, rancid who-knows-what onto the bloody dock beneath its sword, the tainted odor assaulting the crowd.

It looked choreographed. The women nearest the fish added the contents of their stomachs to that of the marlin's. The woman whose hand was on the fish's stomach crumpled into a faint, landing across the marlin's regurgitation.

Morgan and Tioni fell into one another's arms, laughing and slapping each other on the back. Laughter rolled up and down the pier from crews on other docked boats; even sour, mean Charlie Manu, deckhand for Puna Kehoe, started to laugh. Morgan pointed to Charlie for Tioni, they had never seen Charlie laughing before.

After picking up his charge from the marlin's stomach and trying to wipe the slime from her aloha dress, the Hawaiian tour guide stormed over to Morgan crying: "Wassamatta you fool? You done it on purpose!" The fainted woman, now revived, was helped toward the bus by her companions. "Wassamatta you?!" Morgan laughed too hard to answer. There was no answer.

It took the tour guide ten minutes to round up his group and get them back to the bus. The dock again belonged to the fishermen, the drinkers, and the keiki urchins. Morgan went to the Red Pants as Tioni took the Dolphin out to her mooring. The marlin, having the last laugh, headed for the auction shed.

Morgan smiled as his drugged sleep deepened, he turned his head on the hospital pillow, and the memory faded.

THIRTEEN

And there are things—they look small enough sometimes too—by which some of us are totally and completely undone.

From a Conrad novel, but he couldn't remember which one. Things by which we are completely undone. Small things. Lots of small things, one after another after another. Morgan wanted to turn off his brain, and to do that he needed an awful lot of whiskey.

They had taken the old man away a few minutes ago. Slid him onto a gurney and rolled him out. Now, two Filipina orderlies speaking Tagalog to one another made up the bed. When they left, one took Morgan's dinner tray and praised his slight but returning appetite. The curtained window revealed twilight. It was almost seven. Where would they take the old man so late?

He could hear sound from a television across the hall, see people passing the open door. Many looked in curiously. Children were open about it. They would stare unabashedly until an adult pulled them away.

Children wanted to know, to understand, to have everything fully explained. They were not afraid to know something, they did not yet fear information; it beckoned them like the moon pulled at the sea. In understanding, they might find answers. It would be much later before they had to confront the pitiful reality that there could be answers they did not want to know, that you lost hope when you lost your innocence.

Visiting hours started again; Tioni might return. But no, he didn't think Tioni would ever want to see him again. Tioni's visit forced Morgan to think of Victoria and now he could not stop remembering the small things by which he would become completely undone, following the path she had apparently always been on.

Victoria had not been able to find Tioni anywhere after she had seen him sitting in his truck watching her come out of the motel. Morgan took the charter alone when Tioni didn't show up. He had no feeling that Tioni would do something stupid or something dramatic. It wasn't in his character. But who could say? Victoria had turned Morgan into mush. What had she done to Tioni?

He got a small marlin and an ono that day. While the marlin was being strung up on the pier's scale for the weighing and photographs, Morgan looked for Tioni. The other fishermen already knew. Morgan did not exist, they looked through him or past him. No one spoke to him. No one offered the usual congratulations for the fish. Morgan silently helped Keo load the fish onto the auction truck after the tourists had their photos, then he put the Dolphin back on her mooring. It was sunset by then.

He had to get it over with. He couldn't live with that kind of nonexistence. He walked across the street to the Red Pants bar, already filled with fishermen. He pushed open the saloon doors and presented himself to an instantaneous silence. Tioni sat alone at a table all the way back, with a bottle of Primo and a full ashtray. Morgan walked directly toward him and stopped across the table.

"I'm sorry, Tioni. I could say a lot of things, but I'm sure you don't give a shit. I wouldn't either. I can't change it, but I can apologize."

Tioni stood. Morgan thought he would get punched and was ready to accept it. Instead Tioni reached behind his back and pulled from his waistband an army automatic pistol and pointed the barrel at a place between Morgan's eyes.

"Jesus, Tioni!" Morgan said, instinctively taking a step back. It was Morgan's pistol from the boat, the one used to shoot sharks attacking their catch.

Fishermen behind Morgan got out of the way. No one spoke until Momo, the Sumo wrestler bartender, said, "Tioni! Take this outside, brah."

Morgan focused on Tioni's shaking hand and worried that he'd get his head blown off by accident. He could not believe Tioni would actually shoot him on purpose, he must be trying to make a point, to express his grief, to protect his manhood. But Morgan really didn't know, he just hoped.

"If you do this," Morgan said at last, "it won't change anything in the past, but it will destroy the rest of your life."

"I will feel mo' bettah."

"I don't believe that's true. Regardless, it would be too late for both of us."

Morgan stared at the barrel so close to his forehead that he couldn't see the hole the bullet would come from. It was absurd.

"I done told you, take it the fuck outside!" Momo declared, lifting the bar gate to walk under. "I ain't having dis kine pilikia in my place." The audience parted to let him pass.

"Maybe if you had just told me something first, maybe if you didn't just goddamn go on and fuck her behind my back."

"It's the worst thing I've ever done and I did it to my best friend."

Momo appeared beside Tioni. He reached up and put his hand around the barrel of the pistol. "If you go shoot this buggah in my bar, brah, it's me got to clean it up. You be on your way to jail, and me, I be all over the place with da kine mop and bucket. You know what I'm saying?"

Momo steadily and confidently pulled the pistol away from Morgan's head, then took it from Tioni's hand.

"Now you crazyass motherfuckers take you beef outside and finish this fucking pilikia like gentlemen." Momo stuck the pistol into the waistband of his apron and went back to the bar. "You can come back and get this fucking thing when you cool down." He put the pistol behind the cash register.

"I can't do anything to change what happened, Tioni. I'm not going to lie about it. Even if I could change what happened, I wouldn't do it. I fell in love with her and there's nothing I can do about that."

Morgan knew it was coming. Tioni telegraphed the punch. But he didn't try to avoid it. He actually wanted Tioni to hit him. The punch was stunning, knocking Morgan backwards and onto his ass, where he plopped in an unceremonious sprawl as his head fogged over. He could hear voices urging Tioni to kick his ass. Morgan didn't mind, he thought it would be all right. He would survive it and Tioni could have some sense of revenge. He fully deserved to have his ass thoroughly kicked.

He heard Tioni say, "Now we even, I don't owe you nothing. Ever." By the time Morgan shook off the punch and got up, he saw that Tioni had walked out.

Tioni went to work for Ross Thomas on the Kona Pearl. Sometimes, trolling the ledges, the Kona Pearl and the Dolphin passed within hailing distance. Ross offered a wave from his flying bridge helm and Morgan waved back. Tioni did not find it necessary to pretend distraction in the cockpit or to hide in the cabin, but neither would he acknowledge Morgan's presence on the island, on the planet. That piece of the world constituted a black hole in the field of Tioni's vision. Not only Tioni. Few of the Hawaiian fishermen would have anything to do with Morgan. He was an outcast.

After taking a week of charters solo, Morgan hired a haole deckhand, an Aussie named Josh Archer. No local deckhand would work for him now and Morgan knew it was a waste of time to ask. What he'd done was unforgivable. Morgan Cary was a haole who stole the girlfriend of a local. Maybe worse, a captain who took something of incalculable value from the deckhand who worked for him.

It was never clear how much of this Morgan understood at the time, if he understood the way his life had altered completely. Victoria had replaced everything of value in his world. She was all his eyes could see, the only voice he heard.

Morgan no longer took his evening meal at the Red Pants or ate breakfast at the Seaview. After helping Josh clean the Dolphin and putting her on the mooring, he went straight back up the hill to his mauka house in the jungle, where he ate dinner with Victoria. She quit her job at Huggo's bar and moved in with him. She looked for a day job, maybe secretary at one of the real estate companies, or a day waitress. Morgan went to bed early in order to get up early; he spent all day at sea. If Victoria continued working nights at Huggo's, they would hardly see one another.

They were past-less, future-less. Their lives before that time merely a prologue to a single story, a story fully revealed in each moment, the common but always original story of lovers.

"I want to know everything that pleases you," Victoria said.

"Everything you do pleases me."

"That can't be true."

"But it is."

"What about when I shit."

"I love it when you shit."

They created tunes from the squawking sound of the bed springs when they made love, Morgan softly humming something as Victoria heated up, driving her crazy in a mix of focus and distraction. It was quiet on the mountainside, dominated by fallow coffee fields. The nearest house was half a mile away. The mauka highway two hundred yards down a rutted trail, was seldom traveled. There was a better road along the coast. It was so quiet that a dew drop rolling down a broad leaf and hitting the tin roof clinked like a metal pellet, so quiet some magic nights that the moon might be heard rising like a soft, low groan at the horizon. The squeaking bed springs roused birds, screeching as Victoria moaned with orgasm. Later, after sleeping again, they were awakened by the fluttering coos of a dozen mourning doves feeding and preening in the open yard behind the house.

"If we have a baby," Victoria proposed, "do you prefer a boy or a girl?"

"A boy."

"What if it's a girl?"

"I will throw her into the sea, like the ancient Hawaiians did."

"They didn't!"

She tickled him and they wrestled across the bed, falling to the floor.

Later Morgan told her that he would love equally any child they made together. Victoria did not really believe that Morgan wanted children, regardless of gender. But they were reckless.

Victoria, heavy with the weight of sex, often slept in. Morgan arose refreshed, light in spirit, as if he had sent his burdens into her with his sperm. He ate some fruit and bread, drank juice and coffee, then headed down the mountain to the pier, where Josh would have brought the Dolphin in from her mooring to prepare for the charter.

They had been living together two months that Saturday. There was no charter, so they took the Jeep to drive along the coast road toward Ka Lae. Victoria had never been there and Morgan wanted her to be able to say that she had stood on the southernmost piece of land in the United States. That highway, the only one to circumnavigate the island, wound through coffee fields and kiawe scrub brush and across lava flows as black as coal. Tourists in rented, uniformly red, Mustang convertibles flew by the creaking, slow, war surplus Jeep. Victoria in a laughing, playful mood, put her hand inside Morgan's shorts and made him hard.

He turned off the highway and down a twisting, narrow asphalt road toward the sea. A plain sign read: Miloli'i. It was a village he only knew from the sea, a visible point on the shore marking a turning point in the five hundred fathom ledge.

"Is this South Point?" Victoria wondered.

He told her that it was not, that it was an ancient fishing village.

"Are we going parking?" She laughed, poking his ribs.

He looked down at his swollen dick.

"I can take care of that while you drive, you know?"

"Don't! I'll wreck the Jeep."

"Let's be brave, let me do it anyway," she whined.

"You are crazy!" Morgan pulled up her head.

"What I am is very, very happy."

It seemed as though Miloli'i would never appear, that they would run into the sea first. It was a slow five-mile descent from the highway, with no places to turn out from the rough, narrow road, lined close with green bushes and old lava rock walls. There were no houses along the way, no reason to believe the road would lead anywhere but into the sea.

They stopped at a dirt cul-de-sac just a few dozen yards before the ragged lava shoreline. The village appeared through the trees and dense undergrowth.

There were only fishermen's houses with tin roofs and weathered wooden walls stained by rust like brown sweat. Houses nearer the water's edge rose on stilts. On the steps of one, a poi dog slept in a haze of no-see-ums and sand crabs patrolled nearby. The beach was strewn with odorless bougainvillea blossoms, brown palm fronds, and coconut husks.

There was a small church with bright yellow walls, a red tin roof and a blue door, a steeple, but no cross. An outrigger canoe lay abandoned in the small burial yard, its bow resting on the rock wall surrounding the church on three sides.

Along the shore were open sheds with palm frond roofs, tables for cleaning fish. A dog sniffed around one table. There was a pickup truck and a motor bike parked under a grove of trees, a rusted bicycle missing its front wheel leaned against the scooter.

Behind kiawe trees sat a corrugated tin building with a sign: Miloli'i Grocery Store. A louvered air vent in the upper wall had a cracking peace symbol painted on it. An old man sitting on the steps read a newspaper. Beyond that, as the road narrowed to become a sandy trail, a few more houses. Two girls played along the beach there, a boy watching.

Morgan parked the Jeep beside the sea wall and they walked along the shore path.

"Look at that thing!" Victoria pointed to a remarkable phallic rock on the shore where some outrigger canoes were tied up. "You sure you've never been here before?" She posed coyly beside it, hugged it, then danced away in a tease.

He wanted to show her something he'd found and called her to a flat-topped rock. "Petroglyphs," he told her. "It's amazing to me that we can find such things just about anywhere."

"It looks like this was carved with a fingertip when the rock was still molten," Victoria said. "Like drawing with your finger in a tub of butter."

There were stick men, stick fish, a crescent moon, a bone fishhook.

"In Hawaiian these drawings are called *pohaku ki'i*. Such a rock makes this place sacred, you know? The Hawaiians put these in places they believed to be the focal point of tranquillity and goodness in the universe."

Victoria smiled. "But I thought the ancient Hawaiians were horribly vicious and cruel."

At first Morgan didn't realize she was teasing and felt offended.

"I'm just teasing," Victoria said quickly. "But you know something?"

"Tell me."

"I love the way you are so much in love with this island."

"It's nothing against how much I'm in love with you."

"Well, I love that even more."

"This is a contest we can't lose."

Jungle surrounded the village, thick and fast growing. If one of those houses were taken away, its place would disappear beneath the vegetation in a matter of weeks. They followed the winding path near the shore, entwining their fingers, their steps light like children. Occasionally a wave breaking over the rocks sprayed them with a salty mist. Victoria's long hair made its own waves in the damp air. Her nipples responded and pressed against the white T-shirt, her legs, wet from a dousing, looked oiled: a tropical Botticelli's dream, a tanned, voluptuous Venus arisen from the sea.

Soon all signs of the village were left behind and they walked alone along the lava rock ledge between the jungle and the sea. Victoria let go of his hand and pulled the T-shirt over her head, dropping it behind as they continued. Then she stopped and supported herself against his arm to pull off her shorts and sandals, leaving each item where it dropped. Now nude, she stood with her hands impatiently on her hips and watched him gather her clothes. She took his hand when they continued along the shore.

Morgan thought, this is how a god lives.

He knew she hoped they would be seen. He knew how much she liked her body, how comfortable with it she was, how much she enjoyed approving looks, the validation. Victoria had such a perfect body that only the gods ought to see it. Not a body for mortals. Not a common body. Morgan told her that all the time, although there was no doubt she already knew. It was like falling in love with a work of art, a statue, a painting, or maybe something less accessible: a mountain, a country, an idea.

The lava was hard and hot in the sun. It must have burned her feet.

Victoria said, "Let's swim, darling. Just right here off the shore. No farther out than the reef. Okay?"

"There are currents." Her face pleaded. "Okay, but if we stay in close."

Morgan began removing his clothes while Victoria, crying out, "Last one in has to give the other a one-hour massage," ran a few feet across the lava and dived head first into the lagoon. She swam quickly out beyond the shallow in-shore breakers to the calm, deep water forming the lagoon in front of the village, only a few hundred feet behind them.

She was a porpoise.

He messed around inside the reef, poking his head under from time to time to look for something interesting, maybe a cowry shell for her, happy to lose the bet, an hour massage wouldn't take more than a few minutes anyway, before their attention moved to other things. Because he was long acclimated to the omnipresent tropical warmth, the water felt cold. "Let's get out," he suggested. She waved him off, gesturing toward the shore, and called back that she would swim along the inside reef and meet him at the beach in front of the little store. "Don't forget my clothes!" she added.

Morgan left the water, gathered her abandoned clothes and walked back to the store. He got a package of Twinkies and a Hilo Soda and sat on the tilting lanai of the tiny grocery store.

"Where is everybody?" he asked Mr. Kainoa, who owned the store.

"Fish," he answered, gazing toward the sea. "Shop up Captain Cook way. Nothing for stay here."

He seemed bitter, Mr. Kainoa. Morgan wanted him to love this life, the life of Miloli'i that he could only imagine. He wanted Mr. Kainoa to fulfill Morgan's own hope of having this fantasy of a fine life. He did not want to find out that Mr. Kainoa might rather live in Los Angeles and own a 7-Eleven store.

He looked toward the lagoon but couldn't see Victoria. He dropped the empty soda can into a barrel filled to the top with other rusting empties and walked back toward the beach.

Maybe she had already come out? Maybe she was over there in the palm grove. Waiting for her clothes? Teasing him? Morgan shaded his eyes and scanned the lagoon. The water was flat and there were no white caps, just swirling foam marking current paths. He would be able to see some signs of movement if she were still swimming.

Then he saw her far out to the left, almost around the point. How the hell did she get over there, so far out? He could see her waving toward him. He waved back, but angry because she went out so far.

A sound carried on the breeze. His name. Faintly but clearly she called his name.

"Mor-gan."

Was she waving or signaling?

What was that sound? His name again? No. What was it?

"I . . . love . . . you." He heard it clearly that time.

She was caught in a rip. But why hadn't she called for help? If she needed help, why didn't she call out? Maybe it was a joke. It was like her to think something scary was a joke. This was definitely not very funny.

He didn't pause to undress. He ran across the shell-covered beach toward the lagoon. Two short surfboards leaned against a palm tree and he took one. He was going to kill her if this was a joke.

Paddling the board, it didn't take very long to reach Victoria. She wasn't actually so far out. A couple of hundred yards. A little more. He paddled next to her and told her to get on the board.

"What the hell were you thinking!" he said, pushing her onto the board. "If you saw you were getting into trouble, why didn't you scream for help?"

Victoria lay curled up on her side. He could see now, even though her face was wet, that she was crying.

"I did scream for help," she said weakly. "You didn't hear me. I kept screaming for help. Over and over. You didn't hear me, Morgan!"

"I'm sorry. I really didn't hear you until I went down to the water to look for you. What happened? Are you all right?"

"You didn't hear me," she moaned.

Morgan could feel the rip current tugging them seaward, so he began pushing her on the board toward shore.

"What is it?"

"I don't know. I'm sick. My stomach . . ."

"A cramp?"

"No . . . oh God, Morgan, this really hurts."

He could see a boy coming toward them on another surfboard. It stupidly occurred to him that Victoria was naked and the kid would see her. Then he noticed the blood. It seemed to come from between her legs, a diluted string of it flowed back over the board into the water around him. A second later he felt the oddly dull thud as the shark took his right leg into its mouth and jerked him away from the board.

He went under. Through the turgid water, he could see the blood flowing from his leg, still in the whitetip shark's mouth. His first thought was, it's a small shark and can't eat me. He was surprised that it still didn't hurt as badly as it looked. It was only an intense pressure, an insistent tugging. Mostly he felt angry that such a little shark had pulled him away from Victoria, who needed him. He reached down and rammed his index finger into one of the shark's eyes and it let go.

The boy, pushing his board with Victoria on it, was already approaching the beach. Morgan pulled himself onto the other board and paddled hard to catch up. A woman in a flower-patterned muumuu and carrying a white bed sheet, waded waist deep into the water.

When Morgan got to the beach, the sheet had been draped over Victoria. With the surfer's help, the woman turned Victoria over and carried her toward the store. It surprised Morgan when he came out of the water that now his leg hurt horribly and he couldn't put weight on it. There was a ring of teeth marks and a red swatch of ragged meat marred his calf.

Morgan limped for a few feet before Mr. Kainoa took his arm and helped him along.

"She bad sick, brah," the surfer said. "She all bus' up inside."

Morgan followed the surfer's eyes down the sheet to the red spot the size of a coin and rapidly expanding.

"Victoria!"

"It fucking all to hell hurts!" she moaned.

The woman in the muumuu knelt over Victoria and whispered something to her. Victoria moaned again. Like an animal. A feline warning.

"My God, call an ambulance!" Morgan cried.

"No ambulance," Mr. Kainoa said. "Malia, bring that one mattress from you lanai. We go up Kealakekua in my truck."

"We need an ambulance!" Morgan insisted.

Mr. Kainoa had already run off. The surfer looked at Morgan and said, "No time for send ambulance. It go all the way here, then all the way back. Mr. Kainoa's truck only go one time."

"It really, really hurts!" Victoria cried out. "Morgan, I can't stand this!"

Morgan dropped to his knees next to Victoria and put his hand on her face. Her skin was clammy, trembling. Her eyes closed tightly when she grimaced. Her lips trembled and he could see convulsive ripples across her stomach.

"Were you bitten?"

"No shark," the surfer answered for her. "No fish. Shark follow her but find you, man."

Morgan looked up, searching for someone to answer. A woman he had not noticed before squatted opposite Victoria and put a hand on her shoulder with an air of authority, then looked beneath the sheet. She whispered to Morgan, as if trying to keep Victoria from hearing, "Mister, I think maybe you losing the baby."

"The baby?"

"I don't know. I just think. Bleeding from da kine place."

"Baby?"

"Baby?" Victoria repeated.

Two women lay a cot mattress next to Victoria and rolled her onto it. With everyone pitching in, they got the mattress lifted and into the back of Mr. Kainoa's little primer gray Datsun truck.

Mr. Kainoa drove. Morgan sat in the open back with Victoria. He hardly noticed who wrapped the towel around his leg and was surprised to look down and see blood oozing through it, reminding him that it really did hurt now.

It was five hard, rough miles back up to the highway, then another twenty-something miles to the only hospital on the Kona Coast, in Kealakekua.

The bumps were bad. Victoria bounced on the thin mattress, even though Morgan tried to hold her down. It surprised him to notice the beauty of the jungle along the road, to think how odd a scene like this seemed in such a place.

Victoria kept crying and moaning.

Halfway along the road, through gritted teeth, but trying to smile a little, Victoria looked up at him and said, "I'm not very stoic, huh?" She had already started dying from internal bleeding, he would be told later.

The Kona Hospital was long and narrow, like a shoe box with a pitched tin roof, jalousie slat windows, and dark green plank walls. It backed up into a steep pali that rose to become a ridge line on Hualalai mountain. A lush garden in back had long benches. Two men sat there, smoking; lawn in long shadows by then. In the view from the window in Morgan's small room, he could see that Tioni was one of the men smoking.

Behind the emergency wing, the top of the mountain bathed in the last sunlight. He watched the sky turn red, then purple; ridge lines going up the mountain looked like finger smudges across the sky. When he looked for Tioni again, the smokers were gone.

Mr. Kainoa and the woman from Miloli'i had left before Morgan could thank them. He never saw them again. Pain medications left him feeling smoothed out. A tendon had to be reconnected, nerves were severed, the calf muscle ripped. Because of the shortened tendon, he would limp slightly for the rest of his life.

It was dark an hour later when a doctor with a surgical mask hanging on his chest came to Morgan's room to say that Victoria had suffered a ruptured ectopic pregnancy. They were going to perform a hysterectomy. She would have died in another hour had they not gotten her to the hospital. He wondered if Morgan was her husband. Then who would take responsibility for signing the consent forms? Victoria had told a nurse she had no family.

"I think maybe she must have parents on the mainland," Morgan said. "I can try to find them."

"We're going in anyway," the doctor answered. "At this point there just isn't a choice."

There are things by which we are completely undone.

FOURTEEN

Morgan didn't want any more pills. He wanted a drink. The nurse figured he was joking and pretended to believe that the sweats and the tremors were the product of the concussion. He knew exactly what caused them. He'd had them before without the stimulus of a concussion.

The nurse left a paper sack filled with brownies and a "get well" card, signed Ben Iki and Ana Napela. She told him that he might be able to have a brownie for breakfast, then put them on the shelf out of his reach.

"What happened to the man they took out earlier?" he asked the nurse.

"Mr. Aguinaldo pass on, I'm sorry to say. Better for you get some sleep, Mr. Cary, and not be talking about wanting some alcohol."

The nurse smiled, but in a serious sort of way, then left. Morgan was alone with the tinkling rain and the quiet machines beside the old Filipino's empty bed. Dying seemed hardly more than a disappearance, he thought. Here, then not here. Being, then nonbeing.

He slept a few minutes. The haole nurse's knock awakened him. She brought his clothes. A damp scarf covered her hair. She removed it with a flourish.

"I'll put these in here," she said, opening the cupboard door. "I hope you won't mind, but I kind of cleaned up your room a little. And did a load of laundry. It's nothing, so you don't have to say anything."

"I'm sorry?"

"It's too late to protest, so just forget it."

"Thank you," he said, hoping that didn't sound like any kind of encouragement.

"How's your headache?" She touched a fingertip to the front of his bandage.

"All right."

"I can give you a ride home when you're released."

"That's nice, but you don't have to."

"Well, I know that."

When she left, he turned toward Mr. Aguinaldo's empty bed. His eyes burned, his head ached, his heart thudded against his chest.

He got up slowly and swung his legs over the side of the bed. From the open door of the room across the hall, a little boy, maybe five or six years old, watched. Morgan pushed closed the door and got dressed.

There was no way out but past the nurse's station. He tried to walk by like he was supposed to be leaving, but the old Filipina nurse stopped him immediately.

"Mr. Cary! What you doing? Where you going, you think?"

She came quickly around the desk and took his arm.

"I feel okay. I'd be more comfortable out of here, is what I think."

"You not the best one for making that decision, Mr. Cary. Why don't you just turn around and let's get you back in that bed."

Her grip stiffened his resolve and he pulled free.

"Let's don't make a big deal out of this, okay? I'm going out. Bring whatever papers you want me to sign. I'll pay the bill right now."

"I think you at least better wait here until I go find Dr. Takiyama. We can't release you without we have his signature anyway. Why don't you wait for the doctor in the room? Maybe he will go have to come from his house. But you got to have the doctor's name on the release before we can let you go home, Mr. Cary."

"I know that you can't keep me here against my will, if I take the responsibility. And I do take the responsibility. So just give me what needs to be signed." He obviously wasn't going to stand in the hall arguing about it.

"You stay right here, Mr. Cary, please, and I will get one of the doctors. You will stay right here?"

"Okay. But don't take forever, please."

As soon as the elevator doors closed behind the nurse, he went down the exit stairs.

Outside, it occurred to him that he would have to walk back in the rain to his room off Kamehameha Street. He caught his reflection in a dark, wet window by the Emergency Room entrance. He did look like a swami.

Morgan walked directly to the first liquor store he could find. He was addicted to this stuff, to the whiskey in the bottle now in his hand. There it is. But he knew that feeling better was only an illusion that had to be sustained by drinking even more. He also knew why he had to eat, why he had to shit, sleep, breathe. Most of a life must be lived in spite of what one knows, rather than because of what one knows.

He knew where this would lead. He understood the course he had taken. Regardless, he knew what it looked like walking out of a package liquor store with a pint of whiskey in a paper sack, which he took into an alley. He stood beside a trash bin and took a long drink.

"Well," he said to the raised paper bag in toast, "at least you're not Ripple yet." He laughed, but of course it wasn't funny.

He became a part of that dismal surrounding, immersed in the perspective of his perceptions. That phenomenological notion occupied him for a minute or two as he stared blankly at the wooden wall opposite. He brought the bottle to his lips again, the whiskey burning less in his stomach that time. The sordid atmosphere surrounded him like a cocoon. Sounds: a truck on the street, electrical humming in the wires overhead, a reefer motor, distant percussive notes, the sea, wind stirring the palm fronds, all inside the cocoon with him, not aspects of the objective, external world.

A voice from some other world entered the cocoon while his eyes were closed: "Say, brah! You like go share with one friend?"

He wasn't an old man, maybe only a few years older than Morgan, but he was surely a lost cause. He smelled like an outhouse; he must have pissed on himself. He seemed to be a mix of Hawaiian and Chinese, smiling expectantly with many missing teeth. It was dark in the alley and although Morgan tried not to stare, he could see that the man wore a greasy tank top, baggy plaid shorts, and a red billed cap; there were sores amid the hairs on his shoulders and arms, a vicious boil or in-grown pimple on his forehead, and his beard looked like a dog's fur matted with mange.

"I got one cup," the man said, holding it out on display, a tin cup, or maybe the top of a thermos jug.

"Help yourself," Morgan replied, handing over the bottle in the sack.

The bum poured slowly, careful not to spill as his fingers trembled. He handed the bottle back to Morgan, hoisted the cup for a polite toast, and said, "May the Lord of Hosts bless you, my brother," before drinking it straight down.

"What does that mean, 'Lord of Hosts'?"

"Beats the pee-waddy outta me."

Morgan had another drink himself.

"Woo! Shee-it! Have mercy! What *is* this stuff?"

"Whiskey."

"My ass!"

Morgan pulled the bottle from the sack, turned the label around so the man could see it.

The bum leaned forward, squinting.

"Chivas Regal." Morgan pronounced the words for him.

"Shoo. I thought you meaning Jack Daniels kind whiskey, or like that. It's scotch, ain't it?"

Morgan nodded and let the bottle slip back into the sack.

"I can't say I never had no scotch-kind whiskey before. Ain't sweet like that Jack. I had that Jack plenty. It's American-kind, you know? Chivas Regal, huh?" He held out his cup and raised his eyelids solicitously. "It's Japanese kind, am I correct in what I'm saying?"

"It's made in Scotland; why they call it scotch. Help yourself," Morgan handed over the sack.

"You're a scholar and a gentleman," the man acknowledged, then quickly poured his cup brim full, not returning the bottle.

"My name's Joe."

"Morgan."

"Yeah. Like the pirate, huh?"

Morgan eyed the bottle, wondering if he should make a grab before the bum killed it. "Like the pirate, right."

"They call me Joe," he went on, filling his cup again before handing the bottle back, "cause my name's Joseph. Got one sistah, name Mary. Joseph and Mary. We was always from one religious Lord of Hosts family. Lord of Hosts, see?" Joe reached for the bottle again after Morgan had a drink. "Where you live at, Morgan the pirate?"

"In town."

"I used to live in town myself. Nowadays I live here and there. Know what I mean?"

"Help yourself, Joe."

Joe turned the bottle over and watched the last drops fall slowly into his cup. He looked at Morgan, shrugged, then drained his cup. "Well, shoo! You saving da kine?" He offered the bottle, presumably in case Morgan might want the deposit.

"Nah."

Joe slipped the empty into his pocket.

"Nice meeting you, Joe." Morgan started to leave.

"Whoa! Hey there. What you say, Morgan my brother, we get us another one of them bottles? I'll go halves with you." Joe fished deep into the pocket of his shorts and pulled out two carefully folded dollar bills. "I got two bucks. How much for one of them?"

Morgan didn't want to do this. He didn't want to stand around in an alley drinking scotch with a pitiful piece of human residue, who forecasted his own future.

"This is kind a 'uptown' drinking. Whoo, brah, scotch whiskey, Chivas Regal. From the Scotch-land it is. Shee-it. Let's go halves on it."

Morgan took Joe's two dollars and they went back to the package store. From the counter, he could see Joe peering through the window keeping an eye on his money. That notion brought a smile to his face. He bought a fifth, for twenty-something dollars.

Outside, Joe started to put his arm around Morgan, then seemed to think better of it. Morgan turned toward the alley, but Joe suggested they go the other way.

"Gentlemens shouldn't not be drinking no Scotch-land Chivas Regal in no damn alley, don't you think, Morgan? Come on. I know a place. T'ain't far. Always room for another."

Morgan hesitated, but it had all become so foggy.

"Come on, Mister Pirate. It's a nice place. Ain't nobody gonna bother us. It's maybe about two blocks."

They walked to a small park beside a Japanese bank. There were benches on both sides, a strip of flowers down the center, loulu palms between the benches.

"Hey? Huh?" Joe spread his arm wide, as if laying claim to the park.

"It's nice." Morgan tried to orient himself. He had no idea what street they came down.

"Come on, brah." Joe planted himself on the first bench and patted a spot for Morgan, who sat and opened the bottle.

"You haoles know how to drink. Shoo."

Maybe, Morgan wondered, if he stopped answering, Joe would quit talking. He wondered what time it was? It had to be close to midnight. Stars were visible through gaps in passing clouds, a sliver of moon soon to set. Morgan leaned back and craned his neck to look toward the sky. He heard the clink of the bottle neck against Joe's cup, then a long gurgle.

"Ahh. Say anyhow, what the hell you go and do to you head?"

Morgan had forgotten. In spite of the nagging headache, he had already forgotten that his head was wrapped in bandage. That was what he desired, to forget, and thanks to the whiskey it was working again.

"You been in some fight, Morgan the pirate? Made you walk the plank, did they?"

"I just fell down."

"Shoo. I'll say!"

Morgan wondered about that sound Joe made, that long, hard, expelled S that found its way into so many of Joe's sentences. Was it short for shoot, for shit? Wasn't shoot a substitute for shit?

"Drinking such as this, brah, I can sure see how you'd be falling down. Kind of like some dessert, a liquid kind a cake."

Morgan's opinion of the whiskey was that it was affordable and available, but not that it was liquid cake.

The bottle clinked against Joe's cup again.

"Hey, you better get some before it's all gone."

Joe handed the bottle to Morgan and it felt half gone. He resisted the temptation to pull it from the sack to see how much remained. He took a long drink, then another before handing it back to Joe.

"Man, shoo, you haoles sure got all the money," Joe observed. "How come you haoles ended up with all the money?"

Morgan started to say they worked for it, but he knew that to be true only trivially. Not in any way that would make sense or be meaningful to a man like Joe. Did he work for his money? He didn't have an answer. Morgan was so involved with considering how he earned money that he didn't realize Joe had stood. He noticed when Joe kicked his foot.

"Hey! I asked how much you carry around with you right now?"

"Shit!" Morgan wondered how he could have missed something so obvious? "Not much, I'm afraid."

"How much not much, my man?"

"I don't know."

"Why don't you look? Then you know." Joe leered.

Morgan shifted his weight, but Joe shoved him forcefully back to the bench.

"Nah. Now you don't want to get more hurt. Just look while you sitting there."

"You don't have to get excited. There's nothing about money that makes it worth getting somebody hurt over."

"That's what you say. Just take a look-see."

Morgan removed his wallet, opened it, took out all the bills, which Joe immediately grabbed.

"You're welcome to it. It's obviously a lot more valuable to you than it is to me."

"Shoo. Yeah. You can say that because you can get some more easy enough. Am I right, brah? Me? I never know if I'll ever see any one day to the next." Joe counted the cash. His eyebrows rose and fell. There must have been a lot in there, Morgan figured.

"You are a scholar and a gentleman, Morgan the pirate." Joe bowed. "You ain't that bad, for a motherfucking haole."

Joe backed up a step or two, then turned and walked quickly to the street, glancing back to make sure Morgan wasn't coming after him.

Joe had left the whiskey, what little was left. Now Joe could buy another easily enough. Morgan pulled the bottle from the bag and held it out toward the distant street lamp. About half remained. He put the bottle back into the bag, might as well look like one if you're going to act like one, he thought, and took a deep, long drink that plunged into his stomach like lava.

He finished the whiskey in half an hour. His knees wouldn't support his weight when he tried to stand, so he lay back on the bench to watch the stars come and go, to wait for his legs to work again.

"How did it come to this?"

Soon he was asleep.

Morgan awakened to a policeman's boot kicking at his feet.

"Move on, man," the cop repeated. "Get up, now. Move on out of here. You can't be sleeping on this bench."

Morgan jerked upright and swallowed the eruption of acid surging into his throat.

"Unless you wanting to go to jail, man, you get on out of here right now."

There were two cops. The other stood back with nothing to say. They were big Hawaiians with wide faces, hats perched on their round heads like party decorations.

Mourning doves fluttered around on the dew-damp grass, still in dark shadows behind the buildings, traffic noises not far away. He tried getting oriented to the world, but the nearest cop jerked him off the bench and made him stand up straight.

"I ain't gonna fuck with you, man."

"I'm leaving already," Morgan stuttered, deeply embarrassed. Men in business suits walked by, pretending to ignore the not unusual scene of cops rousting a bum.

"Don't forget you garbage," the other cop spoke finally, referring to the sack on the ground.

He almost passed out bending over to pick up the bottle. He had to support himself on the bench.

"Put it over there," the first cop ordered, pointing to a trash barrel just outside the park.

The cops followed him to the street, where he dropped the bottle into the can and wobbled off toward the city center. He could feel them watching, but didn't turn around. He wanted to turn and scream at them: I went to college, I published a book, I have been loved, don't judge me!

He wasn't sure how to get to his room from there. Turn right at the next corner? How far had he walked last night after leaving the hospital? Must have gone straight down Waianuenue. But which way? Mauka, toward the mountain, or makai, toward the sea? He could hear water not far away. At the end of the street he could see the river. One way there were more houses, the other seemed to be a park. Carvalho? I must have gone makai, he decided.

The Wailuku river flowed like a cool, dark invitation to oblivion.

When he found his wife dead on the floor of their Claremont house, she had written only one word on a scrap of paper on the table: *Why?*

Two dogs harassed him half a block until he crossed the street and turned away from the water's edge. The street paralleled the river. A sign: Kaiulani Street. He figured out that he was behind Hilo High School, a mile or so from his room downtown. From there he knew the way.

The room smelled like lemon cleanser. His clothes were put away, the bed made, the bottles and trash taken out, the books stacked. The candy-striper nurse had left this bomb for him and it exploded in his stomach, reminding him of how far down in the chain of humanity he had fallen. He opened the window then went to the toilet. He looked into the mirror and unwrapped the tape and gauze from his head. He couldn't see the back, where the black stitches stood out on the shaved scalp, but could feel their strange ridges. The face he saw was barely a razor's edge from the face of the man who stole his money in the park last night. He studied himself, both fascinated and repulsed, the face of hopelessness. The fascination came from a desperate kind of knowing. But so did the repulsion. He knew what he was and what he had done, he knew what he deserved. The sanctuary of ignorance and forgetting was tentative and brief.

"God, I am so lonely," he informed the bum in the mirror.

He could still hear alcohol's siren song calling to him from the edge of the storm. He saw the allure of that black tranquillity at the eye of the whirlpool. He could imagine death, but he could not believe there would be sanctuary, even there.

FIFTEEN

Sculpted clouds draped over Hilo. Like a blanket lowered over a bed, they settled over everything on the green and red-brown wet earth, over the dark, glistening ribbons of asphalt; heavy, water-burdened air adding to Hilo's moody, tropical, neglected atmosphere. A calico cat, its tail high, came around a jade hedge and cut across a yard of freshly cut green grass. Dainty steps left spots the size of coins in the dew-damp lawn. Pausing, one paw raised, the cat turned to inspect a boy walking near, then pranced off through a gap in the hedge.

A girl on a motor scooter buzzed past. The wind raised her skirt and showed the soft flesh of her thighs and molded the thin white blouse around her breasts, enticingly visible in the back light. Desire to touch the soft, brown thighs of the girl on the motor scooter made him shudder.

He usually walked to the dock along this residential street. After the scooter passed, it was again quiet enough to hear his rubber thongs slapping the sidewalk with each step.

He took only a few books, along with clothes and toiletries, in the duffel bag over his shoulder. He was moving onto the boat until . . . until whatever came next. The candy striper had ruined the room for him. He couldn't say why. It was just ruined.

He wore a hot wool watch cap to cover the stitches in the back of his head. He thought he was feeling sort of okay, although he had drunk breakfast from a quart bottle of beer. He stopped in Poppy's Hot Snacks and picked up a couple of heavily sugared malasadas, eating one while he walked, and it left swatches of powdered sugar on his beard.

It was after nine by the time he reached the waterfront, the commercial boats were already at sea. The Noho Kai, orphaned by his missing days, strained in the current against her lines. The pickup truck sat where he parked it four days ago, keys still dangling from the ignition. There were grains of salt, like fine grit, left behind on the windshield after the rain evaporated.

The boat was very clean, clean enough that it must have been hosed off earlier that morning, the glass polished with ammonia and newspaper. Ben Iki, of course. Before school.

Morgan had no memory of falling but could see where it happened. Part of the cockpit sole near the aft bulkhead, although it was obviously scrubbed, showed the residual darkness of a blood stain. Following a line up from there, he could see where his head hit the engine box and left a crack in the fiberglass.

It made him smile: Ben Iki had organized the lure drawers. It must have taken some time. There was an obvious system: the straight runners, short and squat, were lined up along the front, with the longer Konaheads in back. All the rubber lures were in the small drawer where normally eating utensils would be kept if any were ever needed. The feather lures were laid out in two cigar boxes. All the wire leaders were neatly coiled, hooks grouped by size and held together with rubber bands.

The tools smelled from the rich lubricant, WD-40. The charts were folded with titles visible in the upper right corner of each, then stacked in the rack above the navigation table. The fish flags, two blue ones for marlin, a yellow for mahimahi, a red for ahi, and a white for aku, were laid out on one of the forward vee-berths. The rods were stored in their racks on the overhead, descending in size from port to starboard.

It seemed to Morgan a shame to touch anything. Maybe he should take a picture? He tried to imagine what Ben Iki's room would look like.

He ran the bilge blower for a minute before starting the engine. A thin stream of bilge water trickled from the thru-hull fitting into the harbor. The boat's vibrations were like a friend's casual touch on the shoulder.

He released the spring lines, the bow, then cast off the stern line as the bow drifted through a slow turn in the current's urging. In a minute the Noho Kai made her way from the dock into Hilo Bay and out toward the channel opening.

His head ached. He couldn't stop touching the rough ridge of stitches at the back of his head. That ragged texture, the bumps of stitching, was how Victoria's had felt, the line arcing across her abdomen, when she pulled up her green hospital gown and asked Morgan to touch her scar.

"I think I would rather have died," Victoria said in a flat tone.

"No you don't."

She stood by the bed still in a hospital gown. He had come to take her home. But she refused to get dressed. She said she was going to live in the hospital from now on, she had friends there.

"Victoria, come on. Get dressed. You know we have to leave."

"It's safe here."

"Where it's safe is with me. Come on, stop doing this."

"Safe with you?" She lifted the hospital gown. Above the fine triangle of pubic hair she kept so carefully trimmed ran the latitudinal fresh scar, stitches like a train track. "Touch it," she demanded.

He did.

"What about this?"

"I don't know what you're saying. That I am the father of our baby? Is that what you're saying? Because you got pregnant, this happened?"

Morgan also assumed he was the father, but knew that there was just as reasonable a chance that the baby was Tioni's. The timing was ambiguous.

"Don't lie and tell me that you can still love this body."

"Please, Victoria. Don't keep doing this. It's not about your body. It never was. I love you. That's all there is to it."

"I'm mutilated. Look at this damn hole," she pointed to the entry point for a medication tube.

"Big fucking deal. So am I." He glanced down at his leg, still wrapped from ankle to knee in glistening white bandages. "So now you don't love me?"

"I love you desperately, Morgan. Madly. Insanely. Stupidly." She began crying so hard her body shook.

Morgan held her tightly, rocked her gently in his arms.

"You blame me for that, don't you," she blurted out.

"For what? I don't blame you for anything."

"I know you think it's my fault, because I didn't want to come in when you did and that's why everything happened."

"You didn't do it. A shark found me the most appetizing thing around. I'm glad he didn't find you first."

He had her lie on the bed and put his hand gently on the slope of her hip. Her muscles trembled slightly.

"He came and got you because of my blood. Or was it my baby's blood?"

"The baby was ours. I made it."

"You didn't want it. I wanted it this time, I really wanted it this time. So it's my baby. Was . . . my baby."

Morgan had not heard her say this time, or it had not registered in a meaningful way. "Please, let's not do this anymore. Can we stop doing this now?" He stroked her hip and leg.

"What did I do, Morgan? All I wanted for just a little bit of happiness. Why is God punishing me?"

"Damn it! Victoria. Just . . . damn it!"

"I'm going to lose you, aren't I?" She turned over and reached her arms out toward him. Morgan held her.

"You're never going to lose me, Victoria. I promise."

"I'll never have children. They gutted me, you know? Gutted me just like one of your fucking fish! Look at what they did to me!" She tried to pull up her gown again, but it was caught between them.

"I promise you won't even be able to see it after the stitches come out, after a little time."

"You're a liar. They said I can't have children. Ever."

"Victoria, please! You can't have it both ways. You can't say I didn't want the baby and then say I want children."

"You will leave."

"Never."

He packed her things while they talked. "We're going home," he told her. He helped her dress and she didn't argue anymore. It was as if a switch had been turned inside her brain. She said he looked interesting with the cane he had bought at the hospital pharmacy. She tried it while he leaned against the bed frame.

"Would you die for me, Morgan?" Victoria asked as he walked her out to the Jeep.

"Yes. And live for you."

"Am I lost?'

"No. I found you."

"Men are such liars, aren't they?"

"Some, certainly, but not this one, not to you, ever."

Morgan and Victoria lived together in his rented mauka house until it became untenable. It went irretrievably bad because Morgan had done a rotten thing and rotten things of certain kinds were not suffered well in the islands. He was a haole; it was not relevant and never would be that he was born in Hawaii and lived there much of his life. He was born white, to transient military parents. Nothing Morgan could have done would have given him the status of a local, a kamaaina. The rotten thing was taking the girlfriend of a local man. Bad enough. But worse, that the man worked for Morgan, that Morgan was the captain and Tioni the deckhand. Morgan took something valuable from Tioni's life, when from the locals' point of view, as a white man he already had life's critical advantage—white skin. It did not matter that what Morgan took Tioni never had, never could have had, because Victoria was the only person who really knew that.

Back home in Kona after his first year of college at the University of Hawaii's Ala Moana campus, while drinking beer with friends at the Red Pants bar, a local man Morgan knew as Sammy the Shaking Samoan, crewman on a long-line trawler, walked in, strode directly to the rear of the bar and straight up to a haole, and pulled a monstrous old military-issue .45 automatic from the back waistband of his ragged shorts. Sammy shoved the barrel a few inches from the haole's forehead and splattered chunks of his brain, a lot of his hair, and pieces of his skull all over the back wall. The hapless haole had been fucking his secretary, the wife of Sammy's brother. That image rushed into Morgan's mind the evening Tioni held the barrel of the shark pistol to his forehead in the very same bar. Some nights he woke in a sweat from the nightmare of seeing his brains exploding across the Red Pants' beer-soaked floor planks.

Not that Morgan felt threatened by Tioni, his friends, his family. He was granted a bit of sanctuary because he was *sort of* a local, because he was a fisherman, which in Kona was the most prestigious of occupations. Maybe also because Tioni was the better man, he supposed. He did not really expect to have Tioni or one of his many cousins blow his brains out some night at the Red Pants. But he did not know what might have happened because they did not stay.

Tioni Brown was not just Morgan's deckhand. They were pals and had been since high school. They worked together for three years, every day, drinking away their evenings, going out fishing together even when there was no charter. Morgan knew from the start that he could not stay on the island and face Tioni again and again, not with Victoria sleeping in his bed every night. The decision had not been to leave, but where to go and what to do.

After Morgan finished at the pier and walked up the hill to the house where Victoria waited, they discussed how they would live if Morgan left Hawaii, with his useless degree in English literature and knowing only the trade of sport fishing. It was Victoria who suggested he go back to university and get the doctoral union card that would allow him to teach.

She slept in one of his T-shirts, also wearing it when they had sex, only letting him have her breasts if he put his hands under the shirt. She was hiding the scar, he understood, and her obsessing about it was ridiculous, the same way she would focus on an idea and right or wrong cling to it all the way until hell froze over. But then she could just as easily change her mind and the previous notion would cease to exist. Hell froze and unfroze rather often in Victoria's world. He never called her scar phobia ridiculous, although it is what he believed, and he never urged her to be naked with him, knowing she would get over it eventually. It wasn't even much of a scar, just a thin, long, raised, reddish dark stripe that basically followed the panty line across her lower abdomen. The hole where the medication and drain tube had been looked like a bullet wound. He

missed her standing naked before him, smiling with unselfconscious pleasure at how much he enjoyed just looking at her. She was oblivious to the
much more ragged and ugly scar on his leg. When she stroked his body,
crawled over him like a snake twisting around and over a limb, she never
touched that part of his leg. Absolution existed as an aspect of blindness.

"So we will go to California?" Morgan said, both question
and statement.

"You could do that. But I don't want to always have to live with
something in your mind where you blame me for taking you away from
here," she answered.

"That's not the case." He noted that he said we and she said you.

"If you've decided to go, then there's no reason to talk about it
anymore. I just want to be with you. I don't much care where. I like it
here. A lot. I do understand how you feel about Tioni, though. It would
be difficult."

"It is difficult."

The evening breeze slid around the palms and found its way into
the room. Morgan inhaled it and relaxed. I just want to be with you, she
had said.

"I would rather we decided together."

"We, me, you, it's the same thing, isn't it?" Victoria lay her hand
tenderly and possessively on the side of his face.

"Like being married, the two shall be as one."

"Like that."

"Do you want to get married?"

"Sure."

"Okay, then."

Sudden rain borne on the fresh breeze rattled the tin roof and he didn't
hear what she said next. He wasn't joking about getting married, although
actually asking did surprise him. Why had he spoken in that offhand way.
He didn't know if she was joking when she said sure. He flipped her over

and onto her back, then moved on top of her. Maybe he asked in that way so he could deal with a negative answer. Maybe she just said sure because she figured he was only joking anyway. He put his hands under the T-shirt and held her breasts as if they were the rounded, slippery edge of a precipice. She turned her head and her hair fell over her face. He nuzzled her hair and put his lips to her ear, a surprising salt taste there.

She wasn't muttering or moaning, she was crying.

"Victoria? You're crying?"

"Don't stop."

"Am I hurting you?" He pulled away and let go of her breasts.

"Don't you stop! Don't you stop, goddamn it!"

"I can't make love to you when you're crying for Chrissakes!"

"I'm not crying now." She reached down and tried to put him back inside, but he was already soft. "Don't stop. I'll make it hard again," she pleaded. Morgan rolled over and propped on his bent arm. He moved the tear-sticky hair from her face like sliding away wet leaves.

"Well, if you aren't going to properly fuck me, would you at least roll a joint?" she stated frankly.

Morgan walked to the other side of the room and into the small kitchen area. "You have a really nice ass," Victoria said. Morgan turned and smiled at her. She scooted up and leaned against the wall, her golden legs outstanding against the disheveled white sheet.

"You know?" he said, attentive to shaking marijuana into a Zig-Zag paper, "I guess I'm wondering if maybe we should make some kind of plans, I mean, if we're going to get married?" He thought it was a sly way to broach the subject again.

"Maybe I shouldn't marry a man whose pecker wilts at the slightest provocation."

"Crying is not a slight provocation. I was serious, you know?"

"I do know. Why do you think I was crying, dummy?"

"I'm sure you've been asked before."

"Well . . . yeah," she said sarcastically.

"And?"

"And no, I've never said yes to anyone. Until now."

So yes, she had agreed to marry him? For a moment he considered the amazing irony that he was living with this girl, that he would marry her if she was willing, he loved her madly, yet he was almost afraid to ever question her about anything. Sometimes questions made her crazy, so he didn't ask often. Was there some knowledge that would matter? He loved her and he lived within that lovely, impenetrable bubble; he would do anything to avoid popping it.

He came back to bed, handed her the joint and set a match to it, then scooted up and sat next to her. She inhaled noisily and handed it back to him. His wilted, sticky penis looked pitiable. He threw a corner of the sheet over his crotch and lay his hand on her thigh.

He waited. They smoked. He enjoyed the herbal smell drifting over the bed and around their bodies. He handed her a clip to finish the roach.

He waited. The rain stopped. The breeze passed on. It was so quiet he could hear the quick, steady drip, drip, drip from the rust-stained roof falling into muddy puddles around the front steps. One bird, then others, called to announce that the clouds were parting and the moon appearing. The window across the room brightened slightly and Morgan could see the wet, dark fronds of the fat loulu palm out there.

He waited and thought she really did not believe he was serious.

He was right. After a few minutes, she asked: "You weren't kidding about getting married? Because it's all right if you just said it in the moment and even if you meant it before, you don't have to mean it now. I understand, you know?"

"As a matter of fact . . . ," he did not like the sound of matter of fact. "I have never been more serious about anything." He leaned over and kissed her cheek as if that were her guaranty. "I think it came into my mind the first time I saw you, just like I fell in love with you instantly. I was serious even before I knew I was serious. Now I can't imagine my life without you."

"I should marry you," she stated, "but I don't think you should marry me."

"That's not how it works," he joked. "We can't do this in one direction and not the other."

"We'll be bi-directional. I need you, you would be good for me."

"Cool! Are you trying to tell me something of sexual interest?" he teased.

"Bi-*directional*. Just dream on, sucker."

She laughed, then he did. "Bi-directional," he repeated her phrase in a skeptical tone. "I heard bi-*sexual*."

"That is so stupid," Victoria cried out, laughing harder.

"Yes, it is," he said. They crushed themselves together and laughed like crazy.

Later, when they had calmed themselves and it felt safe to speak again, Victoria said, "I will marry you, Morgan. I want to live with you. I don't want to live without you."

"Ditto."

"Ditto, you said? Fucking ditto!"

They again collapsed laughing and Morgan forced himself to get up and walk to the porch because laughing was hurting his stomach. "Stop it!" he called out.

In a minute, she came out and stood next to him, her arm around his waist. He was naked and she wore only his T-shirt. They were surrounded by fallow coffee fields and the upland jungle. He kissed her hair and she stroked his side.

"I need you," Victoria whispered, as if the natural world would be disturbed by human noises. "You are stable, you have no wild edges, you are completely dependable. Tioni told me that you were the only trustworthy, loyal, and responsible haole he ever met."

"Did he say that before we . . . ?"

"Before, of course."

"Well, ask him again. Besides, I'm not sure I like that description. Who wants to be thought of as fucking *stable*?"

"But that's exactly what I need, you see. It's one of the things I love so much about you."

"If you think so and if it pleases you, then I'm happy to go along. If you want 'stable,' I'll give you super-stable. I am now the rock of stability. Gibraltar is a pimple in the water compared with my rock of stability."

She smiled and kissed his cheek, let her hand drop lower to stroke his ass.

"Then you won't leave me one of these days?" Her tone unmistakably serious.

"I don't know why you think you have to ask me that all the time. It is more likely I who should be worried about you! Have I ever given you one shred of evidence that I would leave you?" Had he said the wrong thing, the reminder of how she had so quickly left Tioni for him?

"Please say it again, really mean it."

"I will never leave you, Victoria. I mean it. Is that why you were crying before? You worried I would leave you?"

"I was crying because I love you so much and I just don't understand it, or maybe I mean I'm not sure I ought to trust it. Because you just asked me to marry you. If I love you, then you own me, you know? Morgan, I've not been in love before. Do you believe me?"

"I always believe you. But maybe I'm having a hard time with that one."

"I have been in lust, I have been in desire, I have been in . . . what? I have been in heat." She smiled and slapped his ass. "But I have never loved anyone the way I love you."

"Well, since you waited, I'm glad it's me you waited for. I won't push my luck by asking why. Just tell me what you want from me."

"What I want is for you to take up where you so rudely left off."
She moved her hand from his back to his front.

He would always claim that she was the moodiest human being he
had ever known, but also easy, because his love for her could cut through
any mood she offered. Every time she began to wander, it was nothing at
all to bring her back, to refocus her. It was more difficult to calm her down
before she blasted off than to bring her back after the explosion. She could
be brilliantly exhausting, endlessly exciting.

Stable? He thought. Am I? He really didn't think he liked that char-
acterization very much. Maybe that's why I'm such a failure, he supposed.

A frigate bird dive bombed into a swell far ahead and Morgan changed
the Noho Kai's heading to see what the hunter bird found. Hilo Bay receded, the open ocean beckoned.

He relished the feel of the wooden wheel spokes in his hands. Oh,
Victoria, he thought, continuing to remember. A liar? Had he lied to her?
No, he hadn't lied to her, not about how much he loved her. He had never
loved anyone so much. But she was right about the baby. He hadn't wanted
then to be a father. He could never be sure if he was the father. He was
sorry for her pain, crushed by what happened to her, but not for the loss
of the baby. He did lie about that. But it was not the worst of the lies to
come.

Possum mori ergo sum. He lashed the helm and went to the cockpit
to set out two rods, connecting their lines to the outriggers. He watched
the lures begin to work. Because I can die . . . I am.

In the hot sun, he sat waiting for the fish, remembering.

How they left Hawaii in the evening tropical rain on the red-eye flight
to Los Angeles, married that noon by a Honolulu justice of the peace,

witnessed by his receptionist and a secretary from the real estate office next door who cried, although for their evident happiness or in sadness for the spare and lonely wedding, he did not know.

Victoria slept on the plane. Snuggled against Morgan with his numbed arm around her. She breathed softly against his neck and he was happy. He had not thought very much about being married. His parents had not provided the best model, divorcing when he was twelve, his mother disappearing, save the occasional postcard (always from somewhere different) and an envelope containing a warm greeting card and a small amount of cash on birthdays and Christmas; then they stopped altogether because, as her latest husband informed her first husband on a postcard, she died of breast cancer. Now Morgan was married. He looked out at the star-punctuated darkness high over the Pacific Ocean and noticed his smiling face reflected in the window.

It was exile. He thought it was. It occurred to him that they had known each other less than six months. Which did not in any case mean he wasn't in love with her. He was madly in love with her. Blind and stupid and hungry in love with her. Loving Victoria was a condition he would never question, like having blood in his veins.

The plane bumped from turbulence, Victoria squeezed his leg without really awakening. In the dark cabin he put one of his hands beneath her blouse and held her breast as if it were a soft, warm, miraculous lucky charm. The fat woman behind kneed the back of his seat and stank of copious ginger perfume; her seatmate slept with his mouth wide open. The fat lady smelled awful, but that's not why he felt sorry for her, and for everyone else inescapably encapsulated with them. Only he had this woman sleeping on his arm. A cabin attendant passed in the aisle and made a point of not noticing where his hand was and they flew on toward sunrise.

Morgan stared at Victoria sleeping. They would make their discoveries about one another as required through the passing of days. But now they were in an expanding moment, without past and without future, just the two of them enveloped in a romantic fog. She told him she was an orphan and grew up in the Midwest. She said she went to college but quit because she was bored. She said she had dropped acid a couple of times and wouldn't do it again because she didn't like feeling being so radically out of control. She said quite unnecessarily that she really liked sex and he said, incongruously, thank you. She enjoyed art, liked to draw (and proved it by drawing his portrait with a pencil); they never walked past a gallery that she didn't want to go inside. He wanted to surprise her with something she liked, but she never liked anything he could afford. There were certainly things she hid, this didn't matter to him. He liked having no competition for her attention, he liked the sense that she belonged entirely to him, that they were both orphaned, an independent, autonomous unit with no one able to penetrate their private world from the chaotic morass outside. She was volatile and unpredictable, but wildly exciting and maddeningly beautiful. Both men and women stared openly at her. The world threatened endless temptations and potential invasions from outside and he prepared himself for this.

The sun had just appeared as their flight arrived in California, stunning the land in a golden light, exactly as advertised. They had two large bags each to retrieve, all the rest left behind or sold. They took a taxi and were surprised how far they had to go. Claremont, the Claremont Graduate School that had accepted his application, was in Los Angeles County, but far from the airport and not as close to the city as he had guessed from the map. Compared with Kona, Los Angeles was as busy as a kicked ant hill, dry and desperately ugly, in spite of the golden light.

They were in love, they were married, and they were going to make a life together.

SIXTEEN

Ben Iki was at the dock when the Noho Kai returned. He sat on a bollard, a can of soda pop in his hand, a chubby boy. Wind pushed his hair into a V over his forehead. Wind ripples carved the stream. Palm fronds waved like a hula dancer's arms.

Morgan brought the Noho Kai's bow around and let the current neutralize the wind's effect. As the boat slid side to the dock, Ben Iki was there to take the line.

"How's it?" Ben Iki asked.

"Not bad. No fish, though."

"Not even one strike?"

"One strike, but I lost him. He never took the hook. He just wanted to tease me a little bit."

"That's too bad. How's your head?"

Morgan touched the bald patch on his scalp, below the hat. "Healing up pretty well, I guess."

He locked the wheelhouse.

"Want for me to hit her with the hose one time?"

"Sure, if you want to."

Ben Iki quickly uncoiled the dock's water hose. Morgan stepped up to the dock and walked over to the truck, waiting, watching the boy work.

The sun rolled away, moving behind the mountains. Long late shadows stretched out toward the water. Sea birds afoot patrolled trash bins next to the harbor office. A patch of bilge oil shimmered like a soap bubble as it moved downstream. Ben Iki hosed the salt spray off the Noho Kai. Morgan could hear Christmas music coming from the supply store. He did not think they would be dashing through any snow anytime soon.

"Want a ride home?"

"Okay, sure."

How strange this must be for him, Morgan thought. Riding in his grandfather's truck with a stranger. Is this how the boy remains connected with his grandfather? The boat. The truck. All the things Ben left behind.

"Where do you live?"

"Not so far. You know where the university is?"

"Yep."

"Go by there on Kumukoa Street and I show you where to turn. Okay?"

"Okay, compadre."

"What is compadre?"

"My buddy, in Spanish."

"You speak Spanish?"

"Not really." He lit a cigarette, aware of Ben Iki watching. "Filthy, rotten habit. It's an addiction. Do you know what addiction means?"

"Like dope. We study it in school."

"Good. You pay attention. Do you like school?"

"Not so much."

"Why not?"

"Because. I just don't like going to it."

"I went to school for a long time," Morgan remarked, apropos of nothing.

Ben Iki had no answer for that.

"You go by Kalili, then turn right on Noe."

"Okay."

The sun was behind the mountains then. He turned on the headlights. They followed a Japanese man going twenty miles an hour in an old Jeep. Once Morgan and Victoria had an old Jeep that would not go very fast. He didn't want to remember that, but he did in spite of himself.

"I hope your mother knows where you are."

"She knows I go down to help take care of the boat after school."

"I should give you a job."

"Better than school," Ben Iki said hopefully.

Probably, Morgan thought, but didn't say it.

The small house, a bungalow, sat at the end of a cul-de-sac. The Wailoa canal ran not far behind it. A blue Nissan Sentra sat in the driveway. He could see Ana Napela's head and shoulders through an open jalousie slat window as they pulled up. An hibiscus bush with pale orange flowers encircled the windows. From her position, she could be doing dishes. She wiped her hands on a towel and waved.

He said to Ben Iki, "Thanks for helping out with the boat while I was laid up."

"You're not laid up so long."

"You think it should have been longer?" Morgan teased.

"No. Better nothing happen at all."

Ben Iki got out. His mother opened the front door and gesturing for Morgan to wait, started across the yard. He turned off the truck engine and got out to greet her. The door was encircled by a strand of blinking multicolored lights. The wreath had written on it: *Mele Kalikimaka*.

"How are you, Mr. Cary?"

"No more swami."

Which made Ben Iki laugh.

"You must have a very fast metabolism. Mine has gone and turned off itself." She looked down over her body.

They shook hands politely. Her hand felt warm, large, firm, but soft from hot water and dish soap. Morgan didn't think there was anything wrong with her body.

"Ben Iki is a fine boy, Mrs. Napela."

"Sometimes yes, sometimes no," she ran her hand through Ben Iki's hair before he leaned out of range.

"I hope he hasn't missed his dinner."

"Oh no. But it is ready. Won't you join us, Mr. Cary? It's nothing special, but there is plenty and we would be happy to have you join us."

"Sure," Ben Iki added insistently.

"I wasn't fishing for an invitation."

"Of course not. Still, we would like it if you would. It really is nothing special, I'm afraid. A fruit salad, fish sticks, French fries. Do you like mayonnaise? There's a lot in the fruit salad."

"Would you like to see my room?"

"Sure. And I do happen to love mayonnaise."

"Good," Ana Napela said. "Show Mr. Cary your room, then we eat."

"Thank you for asking me. Is my truck okay there, Mrs. Napela?"

"Yes. And my name is Ana, please."

"Mine is Morgan."

Ben Iki grabbed his hand and pulled Morgan toward the house.

"Two minutes," Ana warned.

Morgan slowed to look at a photo montage in a frame in the hallway, but Ben Iki pulled him along. The only men in any of the photos were Ben and Joseph Kamakani. Ben Iki's father? All Morgan knew, Ben told him one day when they were fishing, was that Ben Iki's father "took off" some years ago.

It was an Hawaiian-style tract house, not very large, with a nice backyard stretching all the way to the canal, filled with tropical vegetation and a small vegetable patch. From the window in Ben Iki's room, he could see an overloaded guava tree, part of a set of swings, and staked-up tomato plants in a garden.

Ben Iki stood on his bed and pointed to a brilliantly mounted mahi-mahi on the wall.

"This is the first fish I ever catched with a rod and reel. On Papa Ben's boat. I was only eight."

"That's a really nice fish," he told Ben, leaning over to look more closely. "What did it go?"

"Thirty-eight pounds!"

"That's a big fish for an eight-year-old."

"Big fish for anybody."

"For anybody. What test?"

"Fifty."

"Really? Ben Iki, that's a good fish."

Ben Iki leapt to the floor with a thud and went to his desk. From the drawer he removed a yellow and white feather lure and handed it to Morgan.

"With this feather. Papa Ben let me keep it."

"Next time we go fishing, maybe we should bring this. It seems to be lucky."

"Yeah. Okay. That's great." Ben Iki smiled widely, returning the lure to the drawer. Then, thinking about it, said, "Maybe not. Might get lost."

"Yeah, you're right. It's better staying right here."

One wall was covered with posters: Aloha Stadium with a rainbow stretched over it, a row of female dancers from the Merrie Monarch Festival, a rock group named after electrical currents, an advertising poster for Bertram sport fishing cruisers, the Brothers Cazimero with their guitars. As expected, the room was neat. Four small trophies from a Little League baseball team were lined up on the window ledge. Half a dozen books lay stacked on a corner of the desk and a few more in a case by the bed. Pencils in a Kona coffee can. Stereo earphones hung over the bedpost. A pair of casting rods and reels stood in a corner, a tackle box next to the desk. There wasn't much kid stuff. He noticed a photo of Ben Kamakani, a photo of the Noho Kai, a photo in a beautiful koa wood frame of his mother when she was young enough for it to have been well before Ben Iki's life began.

What about Ben Iki's missing father? What kind of man would a woman like Ana marry? What kind of man would leave her, could leave a boy like Ben Iki?

Ben Iki had opened his tackle box when Ana appeared in the doorway, calling them to supper.

They ate in the kitchen, next to a bay window facing the street. It was dark by then. In the tropics the shift between evening and night came suddenly, especially in the rain.

Ben Iki talked about school, about baseball, and about fishing with his grandfather. Morgan could see them, Ana, Ben Iki, himself, reflected in the window glass; could see Ben Iki eyeing him, watching him eat; Ana's eyes sometimes looking up at the same reflection Morgan saw.

Ben Iki was banished to work on school lessons. It rained hard, a sound like pebbles sprayed over the roof. Trees shook vigorously in the wind. In the living room a television set flickered like a fireplace, its sound covered by the wind and rain. Ben Iki had left it on. Lights on the Norfolk pine Christmas tree in the corner blinked randomly. Ana and Morgan remained in the kitchen. They had cleaned up and were seated at the table, drinking rum and Coke. His cap sat on the window ledge and in the reflection he noticed that his hair had flipped up like little wings over his ears and the back of his neck. Ana looked at his hands, bright and clean from hot dishwater. Not a fisherman's hands.

They were made to gesture, to indicate, to describe and explain, not to haul line, fix engines, bait hooks, and turn to leather in the sun.

With Ana's coaxing, Morgan told stories from his life. It surprised him to want to tell her, surprised him she wanted to hear, but most of all he was surprised by the sudden desire to create a presence of himself in her life, in anybody's life. He had become used to being the familiar stranger.

Ana wanted to know why Morgan left Hawaii if he loved it so much?

"Who can say?" he answered. "Not just one thing."

Ana raised her eyebrows, silently questioning him.

"You don't want to hear all this," he said, taking a drink.

"You know it's exactly what I want to hear."

Rain streamed over the windows in sheets, but it had slowed. Now they could hear the television.

"Ben Iki!" Ana called out. "You left the TV on. Turn it off, please."

Ana rolled her eyes and shrugged. Morgan smiled sympathetically.

"I am a cruel mother," Ana remarked.

"I doubt it a lot."

Ana stood, picked up her drink. Morgan also stood, expecting to depart.

"We don't have to sit in the kitchen. Would you like another drink?"

Ana took his glass. Morgan went into the living room and sat down on the long sofa, at the end of which rose the Christmas tree sparkling with tiny multicolored lights. There were no packages beneath it yet. A wreath identical to the one outside hung above the door to the hallway and also spelled out *Mele Kalikimaka*. He didn't want to go. When Ben Iki came in to turn off the television set, Morgan smiled and gave him a little wave of comradeship.

"I hate school, *compadre*," he proclaimed.

Morgan shrugged helplessly. Ben Iki sloughed off to his room.

"Compadre?" Ana wondered.

"Spanish for friend. He got it from me today. But why are we talking about me?"

Ana handed him one of the two sweating drink glasses she carried and took the chair opposite.

"Because you are more interesting than I am," she said.

"Hardly."

"I am thirty-one years old, married and pregnant when I am eighteen, I have never been outside these islands. I can count on this hand how many times I have even been off this island. I work as a circulation clerk at the Hilo Public Library for almost ten years. That's it."

He shakes his head.

"Yes, that is it."

"Okay. Then I am thirty-six years old, married once and never had children, I have been in maybe a third of the states and a couple of foreign countries, if Mexico and Canada count. Once I was a fisherman, then I was a writer, then I was a teacher. Now I'm a fisherman again."

Ana paused, staring intently at him, then said, "*That* Morgan Cary. Can't believe I didn't see it all this time."

"What does *that* Morgan Cary mean?"

"You know? The writer Morgan Cary."

"There was only one book."

"Some book! I read it, by the way. Everybody in the library read it, Mr. Cary . . ." His expression caught her eye. "Morgan. We all loved it. Loved isn't a good word, is it? Fascinated, compelled . . ."

"You're really flattering."

"I have to say, this is something of a shock for me. Now I have a million new questions. I never made the obvious connection with Hawaii."

Morgan sat his drink glass on the coffee table and shifted uncomfortably.

Around his silence, rain sounded like an approaching war. He shrugged his shoulders and stood to say good-bye.

"I'm sorry," Ana said urgently. "People always tell me I can be very pushy."

"No, please. It's not that. It's late. I still get these headaches a little."

"Rum and Coke, just what you needed." She slapped the palm of her hand against her forehead.

"Will you say goodnight to Ben Iki for me. I don't want to disturb him."

"Of course."

They came to the door. The Christmas lights made multicolored flashes against the skin of her face and reflected back from her eyes.

"I hope we see you again, Morgan."

"Sure. I'm sure."

"Ben Iki for sure."

"Yes," he smiled. "Ben Iki for sure."

PART TWO

VICTORIA

[*Iowa 1956–1970*]

SEVENTEEN

"You are my darling little waif," her mother said, leaning across the seat to push open the car door.

Victoria got out reluctantly and stopped beside the open door.

"Go get 'em, tiger girl. Go on. Go on now."

Victoria moved aside just far enough to allow her mother to pull closed the car door. She shooed Victoria toward the school with a fluttering hand gesture, mouthing silently: go, go, go. After clipping the bumper of the car in front, her mother lurched back into the street.

Victoria would not see her mother again for four years, in the fall of 1960, when she was ten years old.

She approached the school entrance in a swarm of children, the lone penitent among a parade of celebrants. The Minnetonka Elementary School, where she was enrolled only two weeks ago, her first school, resembled the monastery it had once been. Victoria was already six and could just barely read and write, although she drew colorful and imaginative pictures with crayons. She had a box with forty-eight colors.

Children funneled through the wide doors like packets of small explosive charges, leaving Victoria lost in their smoke. She had no significant experience with children, who were as mysterious and frightening to her as if she had been abandoned on the wrong side of the wall in a zoo. Children were wild animals, out of control, loud, threatening, and compelling at the same time.

Because Victoria had spent most of her little life in adult company, she was more comfortable with the teachers. She tried from the first day to find sanctuary near her teacher's desk and during the trauma of recess to stay within touching distance of one of the adult playground monitors. When urged to play with the others, Victoria responded by cautiously and then desperately clinging to a monitor's leg. No one had the heart to peel her off and force her into the fray.

"Go play with the other children, Vicki," they would tell her.

"No," she asserted, and wouldn't.

"All right then, dear, but you have to let go of my leg." This required peeling off her pleading grip. The monitors did not laugh at her, they worried about her.

Victoria trailed any playground monitor, curious but alert for signs of danger. Her circle of exploration was limited to the area of sanctuary around any adult.

She could write her name and a few other words now. She liked to write her name in the dirt with a stick and she always wrote it all, Victoria, never just Vicki. Her mother always used her full name. Her father had a million names for her, but it was a simple *Vic* most of the time. Victoria never wrote just Vic in the dirt. While some of the monitors stood around talking together, Victoria squatted by them and wrote her name. When the monitors separated or moved somewhere else, Victoria tagged along, so that after a twenty-minute recess there would be three or four places in the yard where *Victoria* would be neatly scratched into the packed dirt. But by the time recess ended and all the other kids rampaged across the playground, her name would be scuffed away.

Victoria was happy to have been given a seat in the front row nearest the teacher. Mrs. Carmichael's battered metal desk, cluttered with intrigue, was Victoria's refuge. From the first day, Mrs. Carmichael lavished praise on Victoria's artistic talents, but was dismayed to learn that she had entered first grade having virtually no ability to read and write. She asked Victoria to have her parents call and arrange a meeting; she gave her a note for them. There came no call, no meeting.

Victoria did seem to be bright. In two weeks she had learned the alphabet and how to form each letter very nearly like the examples on cards across the top of the chalkboard. She liked drawing the letters, but not having to arrange them in specified ways. She was still confused by how meaning changed entirely just from arranging the shapely letter forms to more pleasing designs. It was the look of words and the design of them that most attracted her. She more enjoyed the pictures that appeared by grouping letters according to size and shape. She preferred these "picture words," where letters created shapes: mountains by putting a tall letter in the middle of shorter letters, also ascending and descending slopes. It did not concern her when these patterns produced nonsensical words, since meaning wasn't the point.

Most adults were pleasant and patient. Two girls seemed to want to be friends. Everyone was nice. But Victoria missed her mother and hoped that going to school would be a brief experiment. She had never been away from her mother for so long and she did not trust anyone else.

Her mother was late for everything; sometimes she lost entire days. She was pretty and every man looked at her as if she were a public event. Victoria's mother also forgot things, like feeding her, so sometimes she found something in a trash bin when she got too hungry; she had developed a bit of a taste for mushy fruit with the super-sweet tang of rot.

Victoria could see and believed that her mother, whose name was Pat, or sometimes Patty, loved her father, whose name was Paul, or sometimes Paulie, more than anything. Her father was concerned with sleeping, needles, and beer. Victoria's first life-lesson was to never bother her father when he was sleeping and not to stand there staring at him. Her second life-lesson was to never touch Daddy's needles. Her mother said they were worse than snakes and would bite her.

Even though his name was Paul, her father often said his name should be Murphy, because "Murphy's Law is my middle name." This was a reference to his deficiency of luck: "If I didn't have bad luck, I wouldn't have no kind of luck." Her father made lists, not written lists, just things he talked about with everybody, about what he didn't have but deserved. She respected her father and wanted him to see her and love her, but he had other things to worry about. He patted her on the head sometimes, but he had never once hugged her, much less held her. That was her mother's job.

Victoria was especially afraid that maybe something else would happen and her parents would no longer have room in their lives for her. They obviously needed each other more than they needed her. They were always forced to leave things behind as they went from place to place. What would happen then? What if they left her behind one of these days?

What she feared most is exactly what happened: They lost her.

At two-thirty Victoria sat on the steps below the entrance to the Minnetonka Elementary School while all the other children flowed around her. It was cloudy and sometimes a reluctant mist grazed her cheeks. It was warm and humid. She removed her once pink denim jacket and lay it across her lap. She kept the plastic Pic 'n Pay bag safe between her feet. Anything could be stolen, Mother warned. Inside the bag were all her new books with the school's label pasted on the spines, books from which she could still manage to read only the most basic words; a thin box of new pencils—one red, one green, one black, one yellow, and one blue; a new coin purse, which still possessed a quarter and a nickel from her lunch money of one dollar; a lined notebook with Bugs Bunny on the cover; her rabbit's-foot key chain with no keys.

After a while the deluge of children down the steps slowed to a trickle until there were no more. Victoria watched them disappear through the gate in the wall. Teachers began leaving, two patted her head and smiled like her father did sometimes. Mrs. Carmichael appeared and squatted next to her. "Still waiting for your folks?" Victoria smiled and nodded hopefully. Mrs. Carmichael must know her mother would come. Mrs. Carmichael looked at her watch. "Shall I wait with you?" "Mommy is always late," Victoria answered, but desperate to have her wait. "Well, then, see you tomorrow." Victoria's teacher hesitated an instant at the gate, gave Victoria a big wave, then disappeared behind the wall like all the others.

The dark red brick building with chipped gargoyles lurking at each corner loomed over her like a ship trapped in a pond. The pea-sized gravel bits in the yard were smoothed by shadows stretching toward the narrow quiet street.

Victoria did not know how to tell time and didn't have a watch anyway. She had been sitting on the steps forever. She needed to pee, her bony rear end ached, and she had to wiggle her legs to keep them from going numb. No matter what, she couldn't get up or move away. This was precisely the spot where she waited for her mother at the end of each school day for two weeks. If she moved, maybe her mother couldn't find her.

The building's shadow crawled across the wall and the yard darkened. The school building, now an alive-like thing, swallowed her in its shade. A shiver shot up her back and she began to cry.

"Hey there, young lady." An apparition of the shadows appeared and sat beside her. He put his hand on her shoulder. "Don't be telling me somebody could forget a pretty thing like you?"

He, the security guard, had seen her through the glass doors when he came to lock up. Victoria thought he was a policeman because of his uniform. Would he take her away like they had done once to her father? Her mother would never find her then. She cried harder, but he kept his big hand on her shoulder, patting her like a puppy.

"Don't cry now, little lady. You know they're coming any minute now." He put his arm around her shoulders, which Victoria thought was a friendly thing to do, not what cops were like. Cops were bad and bad things happened when they were around. "What's your name?" he asked.

"My name is Victoria Novak," she answered emphatically.

"Well, that's a fine name. Do you know that Victoria's the same name as the queen of England?"

Victoria did not know this or what it meant. Her mother told her she was named for her grandmother, who was likely not the queen of anywhere. Her granny was dead and disappeared. She decided to stop crying. If she kept crying, he might leave her alone. That's what her father did when she cried. He always said, "If you're going to do that shit, then go where I don't have to hear it." He sent her away to some other room; sometimes she had her own bedroom, but usually she was sent to the bathroom because it was the only other room with a door. Every place they lived, at least the ones she remembered, had a bathroom.

"Well, Victoria Novak, it's kind of late. Did your mommy tell you to wait here, not maybe someplace else?"

"No, no. Here! Here, right here! Every day," she insisted.

"What are your parents' names, sugar?"

"Pat Novak and Paul Novak."

"Can you tell me where you live at?"

"That place with the Indian house."

"Indian house?"

"And the Indian on his black and white pony."

"You mean the motel?"

"The big red building with the Indian house in the front yard."

"Well, then now, Queen Victoria, I'm just going to call up some-body who can help us to figure out where you live at. But what you want to bet your mommy and daddy will get here first?"

"My daddy won't be coming, just Mommy."

The security guard took the radio from his belt and made a call. By then the school's shadow had spilled over the top of the wall and into the street. When the police cruiser pulled up by the gate, Victoria stiffened, folded her arms tightly across her chest and began to cry. Her worst fear had come to pass: Her parents had lost her. The police would take her away. But she did not fight when the security guard helped put her into the backseat.

When the patrol car struck a pothole hard, Victoria wet her pants and abandoned her desire to speak.

There was only one red brick motel in Minneapolis with a teepee in front and an Indian astride a pinto on its sign: The Chippewa Hut. The room rented by Paul Novak, for which one week's rent had just come due, was abandoned, although Victoria's clothes and coloring books and a few toys remained, along with a note written sloppily on an empty envelope:

I am so sorry but I had no choice really. Please take my darling baby to her aunt's house in Iowa. Tell my baby that mommy didn't forget her and I'll come back for her really really soon. I am so so sorry. Tell her not to worry and be a good girl.

It was not signed and she had forgotten to add the aunt's name and address.

Victoria was placed with a foster mother, Mrs. Swenson, in Minne-apolis. She had another foster child, a boy named Baron, two years older than Victoria, and a Jack Russell terrier that petrified Victoria with its uncontrollable exuberance. Her voice had not returned. Baron teased her muteness when Mrs. Swenson wasn't paying attention. He would stick

out his tongue and pinch it between his fingers, taunting her: "Cat got
your tongue?" He sneaked up behind her and grabbed her, hoping for a
scream. But Victoria, though terrified, uttered only a spontaneous sound,
a loud hiccup, and did not cry out. She liked the peace of her own silence,
preferring it now. Silence felt natural. It was noise that seemed not to
belong in this new world.

There was no Mr. Swenson. He had died. Mrs. Swenson earned her
living as a professional foster mother. She was good at it, patient and almost loving. It didn't worry her that Victoria wouldn't speak. She had
spoken before, in school and with the security guard; certainly she would
again in her own time. She told Baron to stop teasing her about it, and he
did desist whenever Mrs. Swenson was paying attention. After all, Victoria
never complained. Who would know?

Indeed, who would know?

Baron had recently discovered the pleasure attendant to his penis.
Not so much how it affected him, which it certainly did, but how much
more intense the pleasure when someone else shared his discovery. This
revelation occurred one evening after he'd been playing all day in the
woods at the end of the street and Mrs. Swenson had him strip for his bath,
then checked him for ticks. He stood by the tub, she sat on the rim edge.
Mrs. Swenson turned him around and around, then cupped and ever so
gently lifted the sack holding his suddenly eager testicles. "The little critters go for dark crevices," she said, exploring his.

One tick found and flushed, Baron got into his bath. Mrs. Swenson
washed her hands and left him to bathe in privacy. "Wash your hair!" she
ordered, closing the door behind her.

The next day, Baron introduced Victoria to the "find a tick" game.
First he explained what a tick was and that if she missed one he might
die. Then he explained what *to die* meant: "You disappear," he said,
snapping his fingers. "Pop." Then added, "that's what happens if a tick
gets you."

Victoria pondered this notion of dying as disappearance. Did this mean her parents died? She didn't notice Baron was taking his clothes off. Did a tick get her parents?

Baron put his hands on her shoulders and guided her to sit on the toilet seat. He stood quite close in front of her, his belly button at the level of her eyes. "You have to look everywhere. The critters go for dark places."

The first of what would be many male sex organs in her field of vision appeared like an errant thumb, lacking only its nail. What could be the purpose of such a thing in the first place? Were it necessary, wouldn't she have one?

"You have to look under here," Baron explained, placing her small hand beneath his balls and lifting.

Victoria looked but saw nothing like the nasty little black crawly thing Baron described.

"Look again," Baron said.

She did. His thumb grew, nearly doubling in size before her curious gaze. This surprised even Baron, who marveled at this bodily event erupting beyond his control. It felt sort of like when he needed to pee. Then he did, a stream right into Victoria's lap. She ran from the room, leaving Baron laughing and peeing all over the place.

A month later, after Victoria was already long gone, Baron learned to masturbate with an image in his mind of Victoria's hand under his balls.

What Victoria liked best about her brief stay with Mrs. Swenson was that she was allowed to cry. Rather than banish her out of sight, Mrs. Swenson either ignored her (when she thought the tears unjustified) or comforted her with a pat on the back and a few sweet words of consolation. Victoria sometimes cried just to hear herself make a noise; it was easy to do, she was profoundly unhappy. Just thinking of her mother saying goodbye to her forever was more than enough: *Go get 'em, tiger girl*.

Mrs. Swenson said Victoria couldn't go back to school if she wouldn't talk. This Victoria didn't understand, because she went to school already for two weeks and did little more than listen. If someone asked her a question, she tried to answer, but few questions were directed to her. She had no particular reason for not speaking. She hadn't thought about it. Although she had no reason, she could not speak. She could make sounds, crying, or a gasp when the dog or Baron frightened her, a moan when she felt pain. It was not sound she needed to avoid, it was communication. Anything she might say could only make everything worse. Talking to the security guard was why the police came and took her away. What if, maybe just one minute later, her mother had come for her? She was late all the time. What if her parents had not died from the tick, but were looking for her?

That evening her aunt arrived from a little town near Des Moines.

EIGHTEEN

Victoria would not learn some things that could have been important to her until the essential shape of her life was already chiseled. Irene Henry, Victoria's aunt, the only blood relative she would ever know, did not think this history was any of Victoria's business. How could, Irene made clear often enough, her obscenely lost little sister have named her bastard offspring after their mother, who deserved sainthood for what she lived through, abandoned by a useless, atheistic husband, forced to clean other people's houses to feed her daughters, and the event that finally crushed her, the untimely death of a child.

Among other things Victoria would not know for a long time was that there were three sisters, not two, and the other had been Irene's twin, Paulette. What a slap in the face it was when Patty took up with a drug addict, which of course she did on purpose. She always was one to spit in your face. Of course his name would be Paul, the name itself a flagrant insult to the follower of Jesus from whom it originated, not to mention their departed sister.

When the twins were eight years old, Paulette fell from a tall oak tree in their front yard and broke her back on the very last limb before reaching the ground. Irene, who was higher and was kicking at her sister to keep her from catching up, saw Paulette strike the branch at the small of her back and fold like a closing pocket knife.

The next year was born Paulette's replacement, Patricia.

Irene could have blamed God for what happened to her sister or she could have believed God absolved her. She already had blame hovering over her like a tumultuous cloud; she would have to struggle all her mournful days on earth to achieve and maintain absolution, hoping to avoid the bolts of God's vengeful lightning flashing all around her. To this end, Irene fell in love with the son of God to the exclusion of all others, real or hoped for. Irene's prayers to Jesus revealed that, although she was doubtlessly to blame for her sister's death, she would only have to suffer through the days of her mortality, since she repented for her sins and accepted Jesus Christ as lord of all, offering unquestioning obedience to the divine will. At death her suffering would end.

The unfortunately named Victoria, whom Irene would only call Vicki, regardless of Victoria's pleading to be Victoria, not Vicki, was spawn of the devil, issuing from the unholy carnality of Patricia's godless life. Irene would bring the child to Christ, or . . . what? There are only two choices in this world: to take the righteous path shone by the light of the savior of man, the path to eternal heaven, or descend the heathen road to the nuclear fires of infinite, everlasting hell. Vicki was born into the hands of the devil, but with conversion being the absolute duty of every true believer, the love of Jesus would set the child free for salvation.

It was a small square house Victoria moved into with her aunt, a bungalow of sorts, without exactly being one. A garage sat detached to one side, with a fenced dog-run reaching out from the back. There was no dog, to Victoria's relief. She had never had an altogether pleasant experience with any dog. The street, itself named for an elm tree, was lined its whole length with abundant, full-leafed old trees, like a deep green cavern in the full blooming of late spring. Although the trees along the street weren't elms, which had all died a long time ago. There were oaks and some maples scattered throughout the ten blocks. So in fall the cavernous street turned red and gold, official colors of the local college.

The administration building for Warren College was halfway along Elm Street. The rest of the compact pastoral campus spread out over a few blocks in two directions behind the pseudo-colonial main building, along the only reasonable version of a hill for miles in any direction. In a dozen years Victoria would briefly attend college there.

Warren was a small-town midwestern American mix of corn farmers, shopkeepers, housebound women, fortunate children, lazy academicians. Almost one thousand of its nine thousand residents were students at the college. A small courthouse (Warren was the county seat) sat alone at the center of a small, tree-bedecked square, surrounded on flanking spoke-like streets by shops, beauty parlors, a couple of banks, a pizza restaurant, and a bar. It was not the students' bar, because farmers and workers who listened to country music went there. One had to be like an Okie from Muskogee to feel comfortable in Pete's Bar and Grill.

Irene Henry was a library clerk at the college. Most of her days were spent cataloging books, which she did sequestered in a closet-like basement office with a small dirty window, where she could exercise her habit of talking loudly to and with herself without being so distracting to everyone else. Although even had she noticed the effect her babbling had on others, she wouldn't have cared. The library director moved the cataloging site from the glass-enclosed staff work area upstairs down to the basement cubicle fourteen years ago, to stop the flow of staff complaints about Irene's exterior monologues.

Using her own special set of moral imperatives, Irene cataloged many more books destined for the "closed stacks" than actually ended up staying there. Closed stacks held books with dirty pictures, pornographic content, and criminal or medical mutilations. Even after the director gave Irene a specific list of what sorts of books could be cataloged to the closed stacks, Irene continued to use her own religious discretion.

When Victoria was not in school, Irene had her stay in the library until she got off work. Victoria was allowed some latitude in roaming within the building, so long as she never disturbed anyone. Far from being a disturbance, she was the library mascot. She never had so much attention in her life, all of it positive, an unintentional attack against the monastic-like life at home with Aunt Irene's phantom biblical friends and Bible readings. Victoria wished they could live in the library and never have to take that four-block walk along Elm Street to the house with the dog-less dog run.

The Warren College library had glass walls stretching up both floors and lined with study tables and comfortable chairs. In summer, leaf-laden trees so thick that only a muted greenish light came through the shade, dotted the lawn outside; in winter, especially after a new snow, the bright white unfiltered light was warm and tempted sleep. Students flowed past the lower windows all day. The stunningly cute little girl curled up in a big green chair and often sound asleep was as much a fixture to students from those years as the library itself. In the Warren College yearbook of 1957, there is a picture of Victoria with a red knit cap pulled low over her soft blond hair, curled in a ball asleep in her favorite green chair. The shot taken from outside the window looking in, was framed in a crystal ring of frosted glass. The caption reads: "Warren's most beautiful bookworm." Victoria never saw it. Aunt Irene intended to make sure Vicki's all-too-evident beauty was not allowed to compound her congenital sins.

Victoria had dozens of mothers and sisters, fathers and brothers, among the student body, particularly among the library regulars. But where was her mother, her father? Aunt Irene didn't know and didn't care and especially didn't want to keep talking about it with Victoria. "Your mother is in the fiery hands of Satan himself. You are better off without her as long as she chooses to live in a state of damnation." Victoria didn't understand much of Aunt Irene's religious rants. Just enough to see that the world was in fact a horrible and terrifying place. She did not understand why only she and Aunt Irene seemed to understand the gravity of the horror of the world. So many people simply seemed to be going about living without being afraid of it or unhappy about it. Aunt Irene's vision was probably right, though, since Victoria couldn't find all that much to be happy about when she let herself think about it.

Victoria was not so particularly unhappy, not without pleasant and playful times; it was powerlessness that haunted her. She fantasized about running away, but to where? She saw herself running down the wide sidewalk along Elm Street toward the big square with cars all around it. Her mother and father would be in one of those cars and she would leap full-tilt-boogie into it, into the wide, friendly backseat, and they as a family again would drive away into a glowing pink cloud, which is how Victoria imagined heaven.

Victoria was happiest in the college library, where she had all those college students playing with her. Maybe the world wasn't such a horror, maybe it was only a horror for Aunt Irene. Victoria called her college friends by their first names and after explaining so carefully that she was Victoria, not Vicki, all of them remembered. Soon reading came easily to her as a result of occupying herself for hours each afternoon in the library, where pictures in magazines were so compelling that she was desperate to read about them.

Halfway through first grade, the principal called Irene Henry to say that her niece was testing well beyond her age and they might consider skipping over the next grade. It took Victoria a while to figure out exactly what was being proposed and what the implications would be. She

146 · DONIGAN MERRITT

didn't want to skip a grade, she already felt isolated and excluded. When she figured out that she was selected because her work was so good, she stopped being so good, in spite of discovering that being a poor student was harder work than being a good one. No one except Irene Henry could understand this change in Victoria's schoolwork. Irene knew the devil had a hand in it. After all, she was the daughter of a drug-addicted, devil-besotted, atheistic slut, congenitally doomed to failure.

The only friend Victoria had, the one she most feared leaving behind and losing if she skipped a grade, was Alice next door. They were the same age to the month and likened themselves to sisters. Alice was adopted and Victoria and Alice figured out that more or less they were in the same predicament. Alice limped slightly. She had developed severe rickets just as she was trying to walk, and braces had not completely corrected the bow in her legs caused by weakness in the bones. Her hair was jet black, Victoria's summer wheat blond. Victoria was taller and proportional, Alice short and dumpy. Kids teased Alice because of her last name: Higgenbottom. Victoria told the other kids at school that her last name was Nebuchadnezzar, which she thought was a lot worse than Higgenbottom, but they didn't believe her. Nobody liked Alice, so Victoria loved her beyond measure.

Aunt Irene allowed Victoria to play with Alice because Alice's parents were prominent Christians. Alice's father was a deacon in the Methodist church and her mother had published a children's book illustrating the parables of Jesus. That respect was not returned.

"My mom and dad think your aunt isn't playing with a full box of colors," Alice told Victoria. They were sprawled across the floor of the den in Alice's two-story, Victorian-style house, big sheets of paper before them, a shoe box filled with crayons, erasers, old watercolor brushes, some pencils, a pink barrette, and the like.

Victoria guessed this wasn't a good thing. Nobody ever said much of anything good about Aunt Irene. "What's 'a full box of colors' mean?"

"That's what my dad says when he thinks somebody's kooky," Alice explained. "They aren't making pictures with a full box of colors."

"Aunt Irene calls it missing some marbles." Victoria was careful not to display the sin of pride and since she was a thousand times a better artist than Alice, she did not point out the obvious contrast between what she had drawn using only dark green and beige crayons and the multicolored stick figures marching around a purple globe under a plain yellow sun with needle-like rays shooting out in all directions.

"How would you like to live over here, maybe?" Alice proposed.

"Every day?"

"Every day and every night, like sisters."

"I can't do it. I live with Aunt Irene until Mommy and Daddy come back to get me. If I wasn't at Aunt Irene's house, how would they know where to find me?"

"It's only next door," Alice pointed out. "I heard my parents whispering about it. I don't think we're supposed to know."

"They were talking about me living in your house?"

"Uh-huh. They adopted me, they can adopt you, too."

"Why?"

"Because your aunt is kooky," Alice said, exasperated.

"I don't think she's kooky, specially."

"She talks to herself, for one thing. She talks to people who aren't even there."

"That's what kooky means?"

"Of course."

"You're kooky, too."

Alice looked slapped, but quickly decided that Victoria was only teasing her. So she said, "You live with her and you're my best friend, so that makes you kooky, too."

"You talk to Mr. Peabody."

"Mr. Peabody," Alice cried, "is my bear!"

"Mr. Peabody is not a real person and you talk to him all the time. I've heard you doing it even when you think there's nobody around. I heard you even in the bathroom talking to Mr. Peabody."

Alice didn't know what to make of this. It smacked of disloyalty, an attack against her by her best and only true friend.

So they had nothing more to say. Alice colored the borders blue-green with a sketchy overlay of lime green and colored the sun with sparkling gold over the base yellow of the sun to "see it shining" and then drew flying birds by making a lot of M's in black. Victoria drew something that existed only in her imagination: bands and swirls of dark green and beige, then added tiny faces, like apparitions in black shadows.

Mrs. Higgenbottom brought juice and one crumbly ginger cookie each. She gushed over the art work, admiring Victoria's brilliant sense of color and her daughter's beautiful visual sensibility. Alice momentarily pondered whether brilliant or beautiful was the more important adjective before deciding that they carried equal value. The girls put those pictures aside and took new paper. They lay in a V, feet touching, toes playing. Victoria brushed cookie crumbs aside and a bit landed on Alice's new paper. Alice pinched it up and popped it into her mouth. "Umm," she teased. They pretended to fight over yellow ochre.

"Do you think your mom and dad will come back for you?"

"That's a dumb question."

"I'm just saying I'd hate to see you be unhappy for always. That's what my mom and dad were whispering about when I heard them telling that your aunt Irene is kooky. My dad thinks your parents won't ever come back . . ."

"They will!" Victoria yelled.

"No yelling, girls," Mrs. Higgenbottom said from the kitchen.

"They will," Victoria insisted in a hissing whisper.

"You know I believe it, too, Victoria. You know I do. I always believe you. I know you wouldn't tell me a story. I am your best friend in the world. If you believe it, I believe it. All I was saying was what my mommy and daddy believe and what it might be like, I mean, what you have to think about if you really might be stuck with Aunt Kooky."

Victoria cried softly in spite of herself and a tear dripped onto her fresh paper, leaving a little stain in the middle.

"Oh, Victoria, please don't cry, please, please. I believe your parents are coming back to get you." She scooted closer and put her arm around Victoria, laying her head on her shoulder, stroking her forearm. "I was only saying how great it would be if you didn't have to live with your aunt, if you could live here and we could be really and truly sisters. That's all. Don't cry, please." Alice curled up to Victoria.

Victoria actually also thought it would great if she could live with Alice and they could be sisters. But the fear that when her parents came back for her they might not be able to find her, which might have already happened when the police took her away from school, overwhelmed everything else in her world.

It was a year before Aunt Irene got tired enough of Victoria and just before her eighth birthday that she gave Victoria to Mr. and Mrs. Higgenbottom.

NINETEEN

Neither girl thought that being sisters lived up to the advertising. Now there was no escape when they tired of constant contact, when jealousy appeared, or when privacy mattered. For a long time the Higgenbottoms treated Victoria more like a guest than a member of the family. Alice used her proprietary position to treat Victoria like a kid sister, in spite of the fact Victoria was eight days older and at least eight years more mature.

There was nothing official about the transfer of Victoria from Irene Henry's house at 422 Elm Street to the Higgenbottom house at 424. Victoria didn't have much to move, she didn't even own a suitcase. The two girls took Victoria's underwear and socks in plastic shopping bags, her shoes in two paper sacks, and carried her clothes on their hangers. They made four trips, giggling and teasing all the way.

In September, Mrs. Higgenbottom registered Alice and Victoria together at Warren Elementary. As an afterthought, Mrs. Higgenbottom asked Victoria, as if it were just so simple, if she'd like to be registered as

Victoria Higgenbottom, Victoria Henry, or . . . ? Victoria said she wanted to keep Novak. Changing her name would make it impossible for her parents to find her. Mrs. Higgenbottom patted Victoria's head and said, "Of course, honey."

The Higgenbottoms discussed formally adopting Victoria and consulted their lawyer. It would simplify issues with insurance and clarify responsibilities in an emergency. For the time being, legal responsibility remained with Victoria's aunt, the only blood relative who could be accounted for. But Irene Henry, barring the deaths or formal abdication of Victoria's parents, did not have authority to place Victoria for official adoption. Irene Henry washed her hands of Victoria and signed a document prepared by the Higgenbottoms' attorney assigning to them power of attorney to make any and all decisions regarding her niece. Aunt Irene signed the paper, shook Thomas Higgenbottom's hand, and left the office muttering to herself about the wages of sin and power of salvation.

Victoria preferred living at Alice's house. Mrs. Higgenbottom, who suggested that Victoria call her Aunt Isabel, stayed home all day and she liked to cook. They had a maid who cleaned the room Alice and Victoria shared, who also washed and ironed their clothes. Victoria acquired many new clothes and shoes for school. She got her first pair of Keds trainers. Aunt Isabel enjoyed taking the girls shopping.

They said a prayer before meals, always the same one: First Mr. Higgenbottom thanked the Lord for creating His world in a manner conducive to abundant agriculture, then for creating farmers who prospered from their hard labors in the fields of the Lord to produce the tasty items Mrs. Higgenbottom could purchase from the HyVee supermarket and then so beautifully prepare to offer her family, and finally, of course, to thank the Lord for giving them life to enjoy the bounty He bestows so lavishly on the blessed. They all said Amen and ate. They also prayed before sleep, the girls kneeling beside their twin beds. They were allowed to pray about anything; Isabel and also sometimes Thomas watched from the doorway. Otherwise there was no religious ranting and raving in the house of Thomas and Isabel Higgenbottom, although they all attended church twice on Sundays and for Wednesday evening prayer meetings.

Thomas Higgenbottom, who said Victoria could call him Thomas, allowed Victoria to come into the manly sanctuary of his garage, where he smoked his pipe and built his airplane. This had never interested Alice, not until it interested Victoria. Under strict orders to never touch any part of the piecemeal little yellow Piper Cub airplane, Victoria could play with the tools, if she returned them correctly and specifically. Victoria didn't want to do anything in particular with the tools, she just liked the variety and abundance, the feel of different metallic shapes, the clank they made when tapped together. She also liked the syrupy sweet smell of pipe tobacco, the warmth of the pipe bowl against her fingers when she dared to touch it in the ashtray, the fact that Thomas was building a real airplane in the garage and he had promised to take her flying in it. She liked Thomas's attention. It only took a couple of days before Alice began to feel jealous of the time Victoria spent in the garage with her father. But both girls liked to play there, examining the tools, making geometric shapes by placing them on the worktable in interesting configurations, clanking them until Thomas said to stop the racket.

The girls didn't argue much, but when they did, making up came quickly. Isabel often told their friends that the girls were as close as twins, even though the physical differences between them were stark. Victoria became more compellingly beautiful by the day, while Alice appeared to be shrinking into a gnome; Victoria was smart, Alice plodding; Alice tried to always be kind, Victoria had a volatile temper and held grudges.

Many of their classmates teased Alice brutally, but she employed Christian tolerance to shut out most of it. Although Victoria also believed herself to be one of Christ's little crusaders, she had none of Alice's tolerance or patience. Many times Alice had to take Victoria's arm and pull her away from launching herself into a group of taunting third graders. When Alice wasn't looking, Victoria would present her opinion as illustrated by the middle finger of her right hand from behind her back. She couldn't let Alice see this because she knew it was not a Christian way to express one's opinions.

What Victoria valued was loyalty, steadfast dependability. Once offered, it could not be withdrawn except under conditions of severe provocation. In spite of invitations from favored clumps of girls to join their group, to be included in the activities of their special lives, Victoria would not accept without Alice. Occasionally some of these girls pretended to accept Alice, but it always became evident that Alice wasn't even a mascot to them, much less a member of the group. Then Victoria and Alice again went their own way. These groups of girls began to hate Victoria for her rejection of their exceptional company; Victoria hated them for their manifest rejection of Alice. Alice sailed more or less unfettered through these events. Victoria seethed.

Life in the Higgenbottom house was as tranquil and unexceptional as anyone might expect life to be in a nice house in a nice town in Iowa. Victoria thought of it as a pretty way to live. Everything she had now was pretty: her pretty bed covers with teddy bear prints, her pretty house slippers looking like furry white bunnies on her feet, her pretty woof-woof pink socks, her pretty blue flowered barrettes holding her pretty blond hair back from her pretty blue eyes and pretty white skin, her pretty clothes and pretty hair brush and pretty pink book bag; she even had pretty dreams sometimes. What wasn't pretty was the rage she felt, the powerless rage. She was too smart to bite the hands feeding and clothing her, but sometimes she hated all three of them and wanted to drown them in the pretty claw foot bathtub by the window, from where when the window wasn't steamed she could see part of Aunt Irene's house beyond the corner of the garage. The window in the bedroom she shared with Alice was in back and from there she could see the side of the garage and a piece of the cream gabled house of the old man and woman who tended their large garden connected to Aunt Irene's backyard.

She almost never saw Aunt Irene, who only went outside her house for three purposes: church, work, and marketing. It was a rare event when Victoria might catch a glimpse of Aunt Irene coming or going. When that happened, Victoria wanted to open the window and call out, "Have you heard from my mommy and daddy?" But more often than not Aunt Irene was arguing with herself about something and waving her arms at the phantoms, not likely to have heard Victoria's small voice calling out from the bathroom window next door.

Isabel and Thomas wanted Victoria to believe that she belonged with them, in their pretty home on Elm Street. Victoria pretended to try, but how could she split her familial allegiance? It could be any day her parents returned for her. It didn't matter all that much that day after day after day, hundreds and hundreds of days, had crawled past while she waited for the sound of their car, her mother's voice. She almost loved Isabel and Thomas. She did love Alice and knew they would be sisters forever, even after her parents returned. She dreamed that then Alice could live with them sometimes. Why not?

When Victoria told Alice about this dream, Alice didn't seem as excited as Victoria thought she should be. "We'll see," Alice said. Nothing more.

Days passed. Weeks, months. A year, two.

The pretty world stopped being pretty in the fourth grade.

One morning as Alice and Victoria walked the four blocks to school, neither one noticed the slow car trailing them. When it pulled close, Victoria's heart raced. She thought it was her mother and father coming for her. But it was a police car. The policeman behind the wheel leaned over and asked Victoria to approach. But Victoria, who had no reason to trust the police, backed up and walked faster toward the school. "Come on," she told Alice.

Then Alice, who had been taught to always trust the police, approached the passenger side window, pleased she could be helpful and wondering maybe if she was about to become part of something exciting and important.

"Alice!" Victoria called out urgently. "Don't go there." Victoria didn't want Alice to have anything to do with the police, who might be trying to take her away again.

Suddenly the policeman reached through the passenger window, grabbed Alice by her hair and jerked her screaming into the car, which screeched in a lurch to the left and U-turned in the street. Victoria dropped her pretty pink book bag and raced after the car. Before it disappeared over a rise, she caught just one glimpse of Alice's feet kicking in the air.

Victoria screamed repeatedly as other children ran toward her to see what happened. "The policeman took Alice!" she screamed over and over.

TWENTY

Two police officers tried to coax Victoria into their patrol car in an attempt to calm her down and get a coherent statement, but their efforts only made her more hysterical. She kept crying and repeating, "The policeman took Alice." She wouldn't get into their car and she wouldn't talk to anyone until finally Isabel Higgenbottom arrived.

Isabel first hugged Victoria, then guided her to a nearby bus stop bench and sat beside her. Keeping her arm tightly around Victoria's trembling shoulders, she prodded Victoria to speak: "Victoria, please, what happened to Alice? A policeman took her? What do you mean?"

"The policeman stopped his car right there," she pointed, "and he asked me to come over by the car. But I wouldn't. I was afraid he would take me away." She began to hiccup.

Now there were police everywhere. Probably every single law enforcement officer in Warren. A pair of opposing sheriff cars blocked the street at each end of the block, while more police cars came through the blockade and stopped scattered across the street. The chief of police, who had just dropped off his son at the junior high school, arrived in his private car. The two initial responding officers stood like bookends by the bench where Isabel sat with Victoria, both taking notes. It was about to rain. Dick Hardy, principal of Warren Elementary, with two teachers gathered the remaining student voyeurs and shooed them off toward school. Mr. Hardy stayed in case he could help and, of course, from curiosity. Two housewives stood across the street and watched, coffee mugs in hand. A mother with her baby in a stroller stopped behind the bench and listened in horror, bending over beside the stroller as if she needed to confirm that her baby was still in it. People got out of their blocked cars to see what was going on, speculating with each other in whispers. Thomas Higgenbottom and his minister drove up in the minister's black Buick and were let through the barricade.

"Ask what she means by 'police car,'" one of the officers asked Mrs. Higgenbottom.

"It was a police car?" Isabel asked, her voice rising, but oddly controlled.

"Yes," Victoria insisted again. "I was afraid the policeman would take me away again. I told Alice not to go over there. I screamed at her! I told her not to go."

"It's not your fault, sweetheart," Isabel said.

"It is my fault," Victoria stated flatly.

"Why does she say it was a police car?" the officer continued.

"Victoria, darling, how do you know it was a police car?" Isabel asked.

"It had a light on top. It had a blue stripe on the side like that car over there," she pointed to the police cruiser parked at the curb.

Thomas Higgenbottom knelt beside the bench and put his arms around his wife. Dr. Honeycutt, minister of the Third Avenue Methodist

Church, sat on the other side of Victoria and patted her leg, telling her that everything would be all right.

"For the love of God! What happened to Alice?" Thomas cried, looking toward the nearest police officer.

"That's what we're trying to find out, Mr. Higgenbottom."

"Victoria," Thomas shouted, "what happened to Alice?"

"She said a policeman took her in his car," Isabel answered, her voice becoming shaky now that her husband was near, as if his arrival made it all a reality.

Victoria, sinking in fear and frustration, began sobbing and hiccupping.

"What does she mean a policeman *took* her?"

"Listen, honey," the officer said to Victoria, "the more you can help us, the faster we can find your friend and she can come home. The car had a light on top and a stripe on the side like that one?"

Victoria nodded and sobbed.

"What color was the car, sweetie?"

"Kind of light brown, just like that one." She pointed to the police cruiser at the curb.

"How could a policeman take Alice? What are you talking about, Victoria?" Mr. Higgenbottom raved.

Victoria nestled against Isabel's side. "I told Alice not to go over there, but she did. Then the policeman just reached out the window, grabbed Alice's hair and pulled her right through the window. He did it so fast all I really saw was her feet hanging out. I ran as fast as I could but he turned the car in the middle of the street and . . . the car went too fast, I couldn't catch up. I couldn't catch it."

"Why were you afraid of the man you think is a policeman?" Chief Ruble asked.

"How could a policeman take Alice?" Thomas interrupted, his tone pleading for any sensible answer.

"I am quite sure, Tom," Chief Ruble said, "that the man who took Alice was not an officer." He leaned toward Victoria and asked, "Did you see the word *Police* written anywhere on the car, little lady?"

"No. I don't think so."

"Were there any words on the car? Any writing?"

Victoria shook her head vigorously.

"So you thought it was a police car because of the color?"

"It looked just like that car," she explained in frustration. "Light brown, a light blue stripe on the side, and a light on top."

"Was the driver wearing a uniform?" Chief Ruble continued.

"Yes, yes, yes. I told you! A policeman's uniform. And cap. Just like his," she pointed to the nearest officer, the one taking notes. "A policeman in a police car took Alice, I told you!"

"All right, honey."

"What in Christ's name is going on here?" Thomas Higgenbottom turned on Chief Ruble.

Ignoring Thomas, Chief Ruble said, "Victoria . . . it is Victoria, yes? It's a pretty name, very sophisticated and grown up." He knelt in front of the bench so his face and Victoria's were level. "Did the light on top look just like the light on that car there?"

"No. That car has two lights and the one that took Alice had one. On top. On the side where the policeman was."

"Not in the middle? It was on the left side?"

"Yes, on the driving side."

"A big light or a small light?"

"About this big," Victoria said, cupping her hands to form a shape about the size of half a football. "It didn't have light mirrors like that, either."

"Just a plain, dark glass ball?"

"Uh-huh."

The officer behind the chief had already begun transmitting that information into his two-way radio.

Chief Ruble took Thomas's arm and led him away from the bench where Isabel and Victoria held onto each other. "Why did she say she's afraid the police will take her away?" he asked.

"I have no idea," Thomas answered. "I've never heard her say any-thing like that before. Maybe her being afraid of the police is why she's sitting there on the bench and my Alice is . . ."

"We'll find her, Tom. Now, you know we damn well will."

Were they angry with her? Victoria wondered. Was she not help-ful? She was trying as hard as she could, but it was a struggle against the stronger impulse to stop speaking and sink into the sanctuary of silence.

Victoria sensed that the unspeakable had entered her world. She knew, without knowing exactly what she knew, that everything in the world had changed and it was not good and because of it something hor-rible would happen to her. She had not kept Alice away from the police-man and now Alice had been taken away and it was her fault. They would all blame her. Thomas and Aunt Isabel would hate her, they would give her back to Aunt Irene. Or the police would take her away. Everything she had worth living for had disappeared in a screeching of tires and the sight of Alice's small Keds-clad feet kicking the air like a rag doll.

Victoria was not asleep. Maybe she had slept before for a little while, like a nap, but she was awake now and she could hear voices rolling down the hallway from the living room, a mishmash of mumbling she couldn't understand. Alice's bed next to hers was still made up, Mr. Peabody still sitting on the pillow. Alice's school bag, which she had dropped on the street, now sat in the chair at the small white desk where Alice did her homework, beside the identical white desk where Victoria did hers. Alice's desk was cluttered, Victoria's spare. Alice had photographs, sticky notes,

a teddy bear key chain, and a broken state of Iowa charm from her bracelet tacked to the corkboard on the wall behind her desk. Victoria had some
water colors, which she changed every week or so. Sometimes they mixed
up their school bags because they were identical: pink with flying brown
teddy bears—bears in biplanes, bears straddling a DC-3 airliner chug-
ging by white clouds in the pink sky, bears with wings, angel bears, bouncing bears, parachuting bears.

When Isabel put Victoria to bed, it was a quarter to nine. Isabel had
forced Victoria to eat a turkey, lettuce, and tomato sandwich that Julia,
the housekeeper, made for her, although Victoria could not imagine that
she would ever feel like eating again. So Aunt Isabel might not become
angry with her, Victoria forced herself to eat the sandwich, except the
crust, but as soon as she went to the toilet, she made herself vomit, dis-
guising the sound by running water in the sink, surprised by how good it
felt to empty the feeling of poison from her stomach. She didn't hear
Thomas wondering out loud how Victoria could have an appetite after
what happened. She also didn't hear Aunt Isabel saying they should not
be blaming Victoria. Even were she not in the bathroom then, Victoria
was no longer listening to the adults. She had moved inside her mind; what
was going on in there was confusing enough.

Dr. Honeycutt was still with them, joined by his wife Marilyn, who
was choir director at their church. Chief Ruble was there until around
eight. Late in the afternoon a pair of agents from the FBI field office in
Des Moines had arrived. Now one remained and sat at the dining table
with a third cup of decaf while waiting for a ransom call. Had Victoria
looked out the bathroom window she might have seen Aunt Irene, but
probably not, because Irene was sitting in the dark. The old couple who
lived in back, Mr. and Mrs. Gruber, came over at six bringing a pot of
vegetable soup and expressing their sympathy, as other neighbors began
to do. The soup pot sat on the kitchen counter, growing cold, although
the remaining FBI man did eat a cup of it earlier. Marilyn Honeycutt

brought with her an inspirational book from her own library. The Higgenbottoms wished good-hearted, well-intentioned friends would please stop calling. Each time the phone rang, and it rang often during the first hours, Isabel thought her heart would explode.

When the phone rang at one-thirty in the morning, Agent Higgins answered. Thomas's head jerked up from his cradled arms resting on the dining table, where he had fallen asleep only minutes before, and Isabel dropped and broke her mug of tea. Dr. and Mrs. Honeycutt had left at eleven-thirty. Victoria heard the ring, for she was still awake, but could not make out the voices. But she did hear Aunt Isabel's scream.

Victoria knew that it was the worst of all possible moments in her life. It was such an unspeakable moment that she couldn't express it with words. Her imagination failed. Whatever could have happened to Alice, Victoria had no ability to understand it. She knew only that it was the worst of all possible things, without knowing exactly what the worst of all possible things could be. Maybe it's hopeless disappearance; she had experience with that. Victoria pulled the covers tightly over her head and sobbed madly.

She didn't hear the door open and didn't know Aunt Isabel had come into the room until she felt the settling weight on the side of her bed and a hand on her back.

"Victoria? Darling?"

Aunt Isabel gently pulled away the bed covers from Victoria's head. The only light came from the hallway through the open door and in this shaft of light Victoria could see Aunt Isabel's tear-marked cheeks. Then something else, a smile.

"My dearest, we have the best of all possible news! The police found our Alice. She is all right, thank the Lord. They are bringing her home right now."

"Oh, oh, oh," Victoria cried out, little puffs of air, as if she were being punched again and again in the stomach. "Oh, oh, oh!"

Aunt Isabel pulled Victoria up and hugged her tightly enough to squeeze air from her lungs. Crying hard, Victoria repeated, "Thank you, Jesus, thank you, Jesus, thank you, Jesus."

"Yes, our prayers have been answered." Isabel cast her eyes toward the ceiling.

It would be some years later before Victoria confronted the inherently irrational contradiction of thanking Jesus for fixing something that Jesus, given his access to God, must have been responsible for causing in the first place. She would realize that it was like thanking someone who smacks you in the face and breaks your nose, for resetting and bandaging it and giving you an aspirin.

Alice was a star. Everyone wanted to hear her story. Everyone wanted to be in her company, as if her brush with infamy might also illuminate and excite their lives. It was a story of amazing adventure, a story that made her new friends shiver and squeal in the telling. She displayed again and again the spot on her scalp where a clump of her hair was ripped out. Girls got to see the big bruise on her stomach where she was jerked across the window frame; not boys, of course. Boys gawked at the yellowish and too quickly fading bruises on her wrists where she was bound. She almost, but not really, kind of wished that maybe just a little more had happened to her, something terrible at the time, but something easy to overcome. Alice, at the age of nearly nine, was not aware of all the sexual horrors she had been spared by a simple occurrence of fate. When she sort of wished something more had been done to her, she meant another few bruises, more visible bruises, in places where everyone could see. Maybe a little cut with the knife he waved around at her, just a little cut like a scraped knee. She neither knew nor would have understood that her kidnapper intended to rape her, sodomize her, torture her, strangle her until she was dead, cut her into pieces, then bury her dead, cold, little, white body parts in the rock quarry with her two Iowa predecessors, as he had done to a girl in Nebraska, two girls in Missouri, and a girl in Idaho. Her parents knew but did not tell Alice. They told Alice she was saved because she was a good Christian girl, saved by the mercy of her loving God, which meant that God must have a special plan for her. They did not tell her what the police had told them, that her abductor was a paroled pedophile who had now confessed to murdering eight young girls. They did not tell Alice that it was Victoria he wanted, not her. Alice was only the consolation prize.

Victoria knew this without having to be told. She knew the policeman who was not a policeman had called to her, beckoned to her specifically, projected his old stinky voice directly to her, summoned her with his evil hand. She knew he had only taken Alice in her place, because she ran away and Alice didn't. Victoria, almost nine years old, had a better idea than Alice of the sexual possibilities. She already suspected why boys chased her, teased her, called out silly pretend insults to her, stared at her. She was going to be like her mother, men would stop dead in their tracks and marvel at the blessing of her presence in the world, would want to thank her just for passing on the sidewalk at the same time they did.

Fate intervened in the lives of Alice and Victoria. Fate that jerked Alice headfirst into a murderer's car instead of Victoria and again fate that saved her by the coincidence of a highway patrolman noticing the fake police car, now without its magnetic light on top, parked around the side of a rest stop on the Interstate north to Minnesota. The old man, he was sixty-six, with his shiny bald head and paunch of a belly like a little pregnancy covered by a mat of crinkly hair, was arrested while squatting on a rank toilet with his blue police pants crumpled at his ankles, in the midst of an episode of astonishing diarrhea. The patrolman found Alice in the trunk.

TWENTY-ONE

A year passed. Victoria grew prettier. Alice had unrelenting nightmares and counseling sessions with Dr. Honeycutt. Victoria came over to Alice's bed and held her when she cried. Victoria knew that Alice's tears should have been hers. Alice had by now figured that out, too, and was not above using it.

Now Alice had friends. Victoria did not. Victoria had enemies and was proud of it. She didn't want friends, at least, not friends like the girls in school. The girls of Warren Elementary hated Victoria because the boys of Warren Elementary were mad about her. Worse, Victoria let them admire and lust for her, even though none of them were quite yet able to imagine just how lust was to be directed.

Alice was voted Miss Personality in the fifth grade. She was in the glee club and was learning to play the flute. She played softball—captain of the team—although because of her bowed legs she always had a designated runner. Alice had experiences, Alice knew things no one else knew or could even imagine. Victoria was only beautiful; besides, her aunt was absolutely spooky, her parents had totally abandoned her, she got angry over nothing, and she was not a member of anything, except maybe the only member of a club with the sole membership requirement of being the primary object of brand-new desires in not so little boys.

Victoria missed her mother and father, missed them more as her memories of them cracked into small, disconnected pieces. She did not believe for one moment that they were dead, nor did she believe that they had left her on purpose. She knew it was an accident, that something had caused her mom to be late coming back for her and if the police hadn't taken her away, none of this would have happened, their lives would have gone on perfectly well, just like it was before. She knew they were searching for her and as soon as she was old enough she would search for them, too. She believed that Aunt Irene must have lied to her mom if she looked for her in Iowa. She hated her aunt for this. She did not believe for an instant what Aunt Irene said about her mom and dad: They were evil, possessed by the devil, that they were drug addicts, that they left her on purpose and didn't care what happened to her. What Victoria knew was that Aunt Irene was crazy as a loon, so besotted with God that she was drowning in one huge religious sea. So she did not talk about her mom and dad anymore, partly because it seemed to upset Thomas and Aunt Isabel, but mostly because she didn't know what to say. She drew secret pictures of them, which she kept hidden, rolled up in the box her Keds came in. These drawings were realistic. Anyone could easily have recognized Pat and Paul Novak from Victoria's pictures of them. She drew them to save her fading memories, like ghost images on a photo negative. She drew their car and motel rooms where they'd stayed. She drew her mother's face framed in the window of the car the last time she saw her on the street in front of the Minnetonka Elementary School. If Alice came in or awakened when Victoria was drawing, she covered the paper with her arm and shoved it under other papers. Therefore, Alice teased her about having a secret boyfriend, speculating endlessly and obnoxiously on which boy it could be.

While Victoria didn't have a boyfriend, Alice did and they held hands. His name was Michael Potter. He was in the same grade but thought to be socially advanced. Which meant that he knew what being a boyfriend was all about. He gave Alice a bracelet charm, a jagged half of a silver heart, and he wore the matching half on a chain around his neck. His father coached Alice's softball team; in fact, he coached all sports at Warren Elementary School.

Sometimes when Alice was being obnoxious, Victoria almost told her that Mike Potter flirted with her and said she was prettier than Alice. But Alice was her only true friend and Victoria could under no circumstances hurt her feelings. As for all the rest, she thought they could all go to hell and the world would be a better place.

Victoria helped Alice look less plain, she helped her try better hairstyles. Although cosmetics were not allowed on Higgenbottom females, Victoria seemed to have an instinct for how different kinds of clothes produced various effects. Sometimes the two girls spent an entire Saturday pretending to be models and movie stars, trying on all their clothes, then switching with each other. The girls were, as Isabel Higgenbottom often proclaimed, just like twins.

The year passed and they were ten years old. Victoria still liked to hang out in the garage where Thomas worked on his airplane, which was nearly finished. But Alice now had other ways she liked to spend her time; not in her father's garage, smelling of kerosene, where anything you touched or brushed against made you dirty. Victoria could hardly believe there was an airplane in the garage and one day it would fly and she would be in it, like Thomas had promised. He showed her how the yoke moved the rudder and ailerons, showing her how an airplane flew. During these times she almost forgot that her parents were certainly going to find her and they would go away together. The garage was her refuge, Thomas Higgenbottom her protector, the place where she almost belonged.

Victoria remained a mediocre student. She liked handwriting and all her teachers proclaimed she had the most elegant penmanship in Warren Elementary. She also liked reading because she liked living in the stories, having new and otherwise unavailable worlds to explore. She especially disliked physical education. She was not picked for teams until last. She knew that sometimes when they played softball, the pitcher tried to hit her on purpose. The first time she did get hit, it was Victoria who got into trouble for rushing the mound and tackling the pitcher. She was flagrantly tripped when they played basketball. The other girls teased her emerging breasts in the shower. They hid her clothes in the trash bin and Victoria had no qualms about striding across the gym wrapped in a towel to recover them.

But none of that mattered because Victoria hated them all and had no interest anymore in their games, their clubs, their cliques. The only thing that truly bothered her was that Alice almost never stuck up for her, and this made Victoria sick to her stomach. Alice did not participate in her harassment, but neither did she interfere or object. Victoria did not ask Alice why she would not defend her. She thought it ought not be necessary to ask.

To get out of physical education, Victoria learned how to get sick. She knew which variety of illness would work best at which times and how not to push her luck by repeating the same sickness more than once every few months. Stomachaches came first and were easiest to pull off, not requiring a fever, and she could easily vomit at will. Headaches were good, but not as effective, since more often than not she was given two aspirin and sent to the gym anyway. Through diligent concentration she made the accidental discovery that by focusing on certain thoughts she could produce a fever. That was a source of joy for her because it was so effective and made her feel that she had power over her body.

Too effective. Aunt Isabel sent her to the family doctor, who tested her in various ways without finding a legitimate source for Victoria's fevers, nor could he account for her frequent stomachaches and vomiting. He pronounced them to be psychosomatic. "What we need to find out," Dr. Wiley told Isabel, "is why she thinks she needs all these excuses to avoid going to gym."

Thomas and Isabel arranged for counseling sessions with the reverend Dr. Honeycutt. Alice went at ten o'clock Saturday mornings, Victoria at eleven. Alice and her mother had an ice cream at the Dairy Queen while waiting for Victoria to finish.

Dr. Honeycutt was not a religious loon like Aunt Irene and he did not presume with regards to Victoria that her difficulties were religious in nature or would necessarily need a religious cure. He was a comfortable man to be around. He was short and had white hair cut around his head in the pattern of a soup bowl. He liked stark white shirts and shiny black slacks, loafers with tassels, which Victoria often stared at. Victoria enjoyed talking with him. She didn't mind when they prayed together, she liked asking God about things. Although it occurred to her that it hardly seemed different from just thinking to herself or talking to herself; nothing really came of her conversations with God and she had yet to actually see a prayer answered, a request fulfilled, unless she went to the trouble of making it happen all by herself. Isabel explained that such was God's intention, the appearance of making it happen all by yourself, while of course it was God behind everything all along. Victoria had a hard time simply ignoring things that didn't make sense, no matter how hard she tried to find anything sensible in the religious world. She didn't think that Aunt Isabel's double talk was of much help. She asked Dr. Honeycutt about this problem with God and liked his answer. He told her something that she couldn't get out of her head for weeks. He told her that there were two ways a person could think about knowledge, which he likened to our having a body and a mind. The mind is the spiritual:

We can't see it, we can't watch it work, we can't test it; it's so private that only by reference can any other person be aware of it. But we never doubt having one; we even *know* that other people have one, too, he said, adding that one must be pretty careful about using *know* in this way. The body is the physical proof of our existence: we can see it, we can watch it work, we can test physical theories with it, we can lose pieces of our body and the mind will continue on unperturbed. Faith exists in the realm of the mind, that spiritual place, and we cannot use what we know and trust about the physical to understand it, although we do use the mind to understand how we conceive the body. Dr. Honeycutt told Victoria that what she thought of as a physical problem, a problem of her body, was really a problem with how she thought about things. "We can think ourselves into trouble," he said, "and we can think our way out of trouble, too."

Victoria liked the power of knowing that if she thought herself into trouble that she could think herself right out of it again.

Except it didn't work, in spite of Dr. Honeycutt's explanations.

TWENTY-TWO

Victoria only by chance caught a glimpse of her mother from the bathroom window. She couldn't be sure, it was only a glimpse of a woman in profile walking past Aunt Irene's living room window in the direction of the kitchen. She could have wanted it to be her mother so badly that desire created the image. But no one ever visited Aunt Irene. No one. Ever. There was a pretty little red car parked in front of Aunt Irene's house. Victoria put aside how badly she needed to pee and ran as fast as she could out the back door and across the yard, through a gap in the hedge and up the back steps to the kitchen door of Aunt Irene's house. From there she could hear her mother's voice screaming at Aunt Irene: "Fuck that shit, Irene! You think this is easy for me?" Irene's response was quieter and Victoria struggled to understand. It sounded like, "I pray for you every day."

"Pray, don't pray. I don't give a pink poop. I'm not here so you can have more to babble prayers about."

"You're not here for your child, either."

It was certainly her mother, but then different. She was not so skinny; in fact, she was plump all over. Her hair was so blond it looked metallic, like slivers of aluminum, Christmas tree tinsel. Victoria pushed on the door and it opened to the kitchen where her mother and Aunt Irene stood on opposite sides of the small Formica table with their hands propped on it like wrestlers preparing to go at each other. Aunt Irene faced the door and saw Victoria first. Her mother looked back then spun around and held her arms out: "Oh my God! Look at you!"

"Mommy!" Victoria sailed into her mother's arms.

"I will not countenance this evil deed in my own house," Aunt Irene said and left the room muttering, "I will not watch you keep destroying this child." Pat gave her the finger with her arm stretched above her head. "You didn't see that," she told Victoria and laughed.

"Mommy!"

Pat knelt and let Victoria hug her.

"How you doing, tiger? Jesus X., you're big!"

"I love you, Mommy. I told everybody you would find me."

"I love you, too, sweetheart."

"I knew you would find me."

"And here I am. But you weren't the one lost, you know?"

"Mommy, mommy, mommy." Victoria squeezed as hard as she could.

Pat tried to get up, but Victoria's weight was too much. "Wow! You are really big! I mean, you're almost a young woman. Could you really be only ten? Is that a bra?"

"Aunt Irene says I am just like you were when you were ten."

"Your aunt Irene . . . never mind. How about we get out of here? Want to get some ice cream?"

"Aren't we going home?" Victoria realized she had no image for that word, *home*. All she could envision was a common motel room.

"Let's get us some ice cream, what do you say? You don't think it's too cold for ice cream, do you? Never too cold, I say."

"It's never too cold, I say too. Where's Daddy?"

Pat took Victoria's hand and led her through the house to the front door, then out to the porch. "Ice cream first, talk second."

Victoria held her mother's hand as they walked to the car and didn't want to let go, even after her mother guided her to the passenger seat.

"How can I drive if you don't let go," Pat laughed.

Victoria suddenly remembered how badly she needed to pee.

So, Victoria thought. There is a God and there are miracles. She knew her mother had been looking everywhere in the world for her every day for the last four years. Now she was found. She couldn't take her eyes off her mother: her beautiful mother who had cut her hair short and swept it back and made it silver. She had never seen her mother with short hair. It used to fall to her waist. She wore nice makeup, perfect eye shadow, and just a flattering dab of lip gloss, none of which she ever wore before, beautiful cosmetic touches Victoria was not allowed to use in the Higgenbottom house. She had a tan while everybody else was pasty and smudgy. Her clothes were casual but smart, the kind of clothes Victoria only saw in magazines. Her earrings sparkled like diamonds. Hers was the most beautiful mother in the world. Even big now, she was still pretty. She scooted as far toward her mother as the seat would allow and put her hand on her mother's shoulder, as if she always did that. Her mother drove fast and stirred up piles of fallen leaves on the street that swirled like a mini-tornado in their wake.

"What do you think of this car, tiger?"

Victoria didn't know much about cars, some were big and some were small, some were ugly and some were not. Her mother's car was red, the seats were gray leather, there was no usable backseat and there were a lot of dials and gadgets on the instrument panel. "It's the prettiest car I've ever been in," she said.

"It's a Thunderbird."

"I really like the color."

"Candy-apple red. You were the best with colors. I remember that. You could draw anything, like a whiz."

"I love you, Mommy."

"Mommy loves you, too, tiger."

Pat drove in next to the ice cream parlor and the car slid noisily in the gravel. Victoria feared for an instant that they might slide all the way into the wall ahead and ruin the beautiful candy-apple car, but it stopped more quickly than she thought it would.

"What would you like?" Pat asked, opening her door. Victoria opened the door on her side.

"No, baby, why don't you just wait here? I'll get it and come right back."

Victoria hoped to go in and use the toilet, but wanted to do what her mother wanted her to do. "I don't mind going with you. I can help."

"Oh come on, really! It's faster. I can carry two ice cream cones. What do you like?"

"But I can go."

"Hey, baby, the keys are right there." She gave Victoria a big smile. "If I don't come back, you keep my car."

"I don't know how to drive."

"You are so funny! Come on, what do you like?"

"Vanilla."

"Vanilla and what?"

"Usually just vanilla."

"Oh, come on. Never mind. I'll get you something special."

The door closed and she was gone. The interior cooled quickly from the opened door. Victoria had run to Aunt Irene's house without her coat. The engine ticked and popped and Victoria didn't know why it made those sounds. Mommy's little red car was almost a toy. It smelled like perfume mixed with the odor of oiled leather. A car stopped beside Mommy's candy-apple car, a big car, the kind Thomas called a gas hog; a huge family piled out making more noise than necessary. Pat then knocked on the roof with her elbow for Victoria to open door.

"Try this," Pat said, handing a waffle cone to Victoria.

The top ball was green with black spots, the bottom orange.

"Pistachio," Pat said. "with tangerine."

"I never heard of it."

"Go on, give it a try. This is popular in Florida, you know?"

Victoria took a bite. It was different. Not bad, not good, just different. "I like it," she proclaimed, looking at her mother for verification.

"You've got to take chances, try new things," her mother said. "Adventure; that's all life is."

"I do that," Victoria said, wanting to make sure that her found mother would want to stay found. Victoria licked her confusing ice cream; her mother took big bites from hers.

"How's school?"

"I like it okay."

"That's good. Keep liking it."

"Where's Daddy?"

Why wasn't her mom looking at her? Why did she pay more attention to the ice cream than to her daughter? A leaf let go and slid across the front of the car and her mother seemed more interested in watching that than her.

"Tiger girl, I hope you can understand this. It's not a happy thought." Pat waited, but Victoria didn't respond. "Sweetie, your father is gone. I mean he's dead."

"Dead?" Victoria repeated, as if she didn't know the meaning of the word.

"You know, don't you, that even things that seem the most terrible might have a hidden meaning that isn't so terrible, that might even turn out to be good? In the great scheme of things, of course."

Victoria was still processing the concept of dead combined with the memory of her father. She knew now that dead was something more than just a disappearance; it wasn't a tick bite. Now she knew that death was a transfer from earth to heaven or hell. Processing this stunning information, she tried to form a clear picture of her father. In her mind he had already diminished to concepts: beard and hair, long legs and skinny arms, his leather vest with its dangling fringe, his cowboy hat that looked like a dog had played with it. How did she feel realizing she would never see him again on earth? It occurred to her that she had not really missed him, not like she had longed for her mother. "Is Daddy in heaven?"

Pat laughed. "I should never have left you with Irene."

Victoria understood then that she hadn't been lost, she'd been left.

Pat finished her ice cream cone, wiped her fingers with a napkin, and lowered the window enough to toss the napkin out. She started the engine and moved the heater setting warmer. Victoria didn't want to finish her pistachio and tangerine; she didn't like it all that much and now she felt truly sick in her stomach. Aunt Isabel would have a hissy fit if she ever threw anything out the car window. She had no choice but to eat the whole thing and put the sticky napkin in her pocket so she wouldn't make the beautiful car dirty.

"Let's go for a drive. Do you know your mommy hasn't been back to her home town since five years before you were born? That makes it fifteen years ago. Let's have us a little look around."

"Okay, Mommy." If Victoria told her mother she needed to go to the toilet, what would happen? Would she wait? Would she disappear?

Pat backed quickly out of the parking lot and into the street, then had trouble getting the car into a forward gear. A man in a pickup truck honked at her and made an extravagant point of driving around. Pat honked back and give him the finger, calling out, "Go fuck yourself, asshole!" Then turned quickly to Victoria and said with a smile, "You didn't hear that."

Victoria was more worried that she would wet her pants. "Mommy, I need to go to the bathroom."

"Why didn't you tell me while we were at the soda shop?"

"It wasn't so bad then."

"All right, all right. You can go at the gas station."

Pat swerved the red T-bird hard right into a gas station and parked next to the toilet door. "Hurry up," she said, looking at her shiny wristwatch.

"Okay." Victoria fumbled with the door handle and Pat reached across to open it for her. "You'll wait here?" Victoria asked.

"Where else would I wait? Go, go!"

Victoria felt her mother's exasperated impatience and was afraid that her need to pee had made her angry. What would happen now? She peed as quickly as she could but her bladder was so full and the hole so small that she felt like it would take an hour to empty. Why didn't God design an easier, faster, and less nasty way to do this?

Her mother was still there, smoking a cigarette in her small red car, the radio on the country music station. Victoria ran to the other side and got in without needing to get her mother's help with the door. Now she could think better. They drove to the courthouse square and around it twice. People stared at them and Victoria liked to think it was because her mother had found her and now everyone could see that she was right all along when she told them that her parents would find her. But actually they were staring at the peroxide blond in the cherry red little Thunderbird with Florida license plates, as odd a sight in Warren as a tractor on Broadway in New York.

"How's school going, tiger?"

"It's all right."

"You're doing good, though?"

"I'm passing everything."

"Wow! Well, you sure put your mom to shame."

"It's not hard. I mean it's easy what teachers want us to do."

"Speak for yourself, tiger," Pat laughed.

Is this what they were going to do? Drive around Warren? Were they going home? Home? Where is home? "Where are we going now, Mommy?"

"Oh, I'm just showing off a little bit for the local yokels, then we'll take you home. How do you like living with—?"

"Home?"

"Who are those people next door to Irene? Do you like living with them? You have a, a kind of a sister now, yes?"

"Thomas and Isabel Higgenbottom. Alice is their daughter."

"What a ridiculous name. But they are good to you, right?"

"Yes. But I am only living there because Aunt Irene didn't have, didn't want—. I was not always so nice with Aunt Irene. I'm sorry. I'm grown up more now."

"Don't be sorry. She's *my* frigging sister and I can't stand to be around her for five minutes. I'm sorry you had to put up with her as long as you did, honey. I had absolutely no idea in the least that we would . . . I would be away for *years*! I thought it might just be a couple of days or maybe like a week, but your daddy . . . Let me park someplace."

Pat charged the T-bird into the parking lot in front of the administration building of Warren College and turned off the engine. She looked at Victoria and put her arm across the back of Victoria's seat. Victoria carefully lay her cheek against her mother's forearm. In a nonstop but staccato voice Pat began explaining to her daughter what had happened during the past four years:

The day Pat dropped Victoria off at school and disappeared, she had gone back to the motel and found Paul gone. She looked everywhere for him and kept hearing different stories from people they knew, mostly drug dealers, junkies, and denizens of the bars where they conducted what social life they had. Eventually she found out that he was seen getting on an Omaha-bound bus. Then she knew where he was going. Paul's first wife, from whom he was not exactly divorced, lived there. Pat, to whom he was not exactly married, knew what was up. It was what he always threatened to do when they fought and they had fought uproariously the night before, not a rare event. "It just made me crazy!" Pat told her daughter. "As you can imagine." So Pat drove to Omaha to get her man back. But he had already been there and left again, after a confrontation with his sort of ex-wife's new kind of husband. "I looked all over frigging Omaha for him," Pat continued.

The parking lot filled as they sat there and the car cooled off inside. Students buzzed around them. Boys looked at the car, but mostly at the platinum-haired driver. Victoria didn't understand why they had to sit in the car in a parking lot and why they couldn't just go home, wherever it might be. She didn't need to know all this. She just wanted to go home with her mother. It was not so important to her what happened, where her mother and father had gone or why. If her father was dead she couldn't change anything and bring him back. She understood that the past was fixed and what mattered now was that she was with her mother and they would never be lost from each other again.

"I didn't find your father until the next morning. He was . . . well, it doesn't matter where he was. I tried to get us out of there as fast as I could, you see? Guess it was too fast. We got busted by radar before we were hardly out of Council Bluffs. I was only doing eighty." Pat winked and giggled. "Your father was wasted, of course, and this blob of a cop didn't have any trouble figuring that out. He found Paul's junk in the glove box and that was pretty much it for old Mom and Dad. You see? I completely expected to be back in a few days to pick you up from Irene. But when we got busted . . . I think you can understand why I figured it was better for you to be safe here in Warren, even if you had to put up with

Irene's freakiness a little bit. If you weren't with Irene, who knows what the frigging state might have done with you!"

"You and Daddy went to jail?"

"I'm not proud of it, you know? But that's water under the bridge."

Victoria tried to process this information. Her parents had talked about their fear of "getting busted" and going to prison all the time. There was nothing that could have been done and clearly her mother had protected her by sending her to live with Aunt Irene.

"Some freak-o black dude killed your daddy there. We were in different prisons, naturally. But all this doesn't matter now, does it? Water flows on, the river of life."

Victoria couldn't respond to this. She was sinking into the leather seat with the ponderous weight of all this information.

"I think you can understand that leaving you here was better than any of the alternatives, yes? I was afraid some social services do-gooder would take you away from me permanently. That's why it had to go this way. You can see that."

Victoria gave her mother the forgiving affirmation she kept tacitly asking for. "I understand, Mommy. But I'm sorry about Daddy." There were tears in spite of her fear that crying would upset her mother.

"I know you are, baby. Me, too."

"Can't we just go home now? I don't have to get my things. I have hardly anything we need to get. We can just go."

"Are you crying, tiger?"

"No."

"What's that there?" Pat touched a fingertip to her daughter's damp cheek.

"It's sad about Daddy."

"Yes, it is. It's a tragedy. But, darling, your daddy's life was not a good one. He was sick and the sickness made him . . . his life was . . . he was just a poor, lost little lamb, pretty girl."

"I am thinking how I won't ever see him again until heaven."

"I should never have left you with her . . . if that's where he is now."

"Can't we just go home?"

"Well, we have to talk about that."

Victoria sensed impending disaster. What could there be to talk about? Hadn't her mother come for her, to take her home at last?

"What, Mommy?"

"I have good news and bad news," Pat began, then laughed gracelessly. "Not bad really. Only temporarily bad, just for a little while bad, and after that bad part is over everything will be perfectly wonderful for always. Here's the good news. When I got out of prison I went to Florida because . . . well, because I was sick of being cold, for one thing. This girl I worked with in the kitchen talked about Florida all the time, so I decided to check it out. For us. A place we could have a good life together, you know what I mean? I figured if I could get something started down there, then I'd come get you out of Irene's clutches and we could just go right down to Florida and have ourselves a fine life in the sunshine."

Victoria didn't understand why her mother didn't just come get her when she was on her way to Florida, why she made her wait. Pat picked up on her daughter's unasked question.

"I figured it would be better for you if I made sure I could get work first before bringing you all the way down there maybe for nothing and have to go somewhere else. You needed to be in school, not wandering around the country like some ragamuffin vagabond while your mommy tried to get things, you know, settled."

"Like a what?"

Pat laughed. "Like some lost street kid."

"Mommy, why are we sitting in the car in this parking lot? Why don't we go home now?"

"Let me get to that part of the story, tiger. That's going to bring me around to the good part."

Pat stroked Victoria's cheek with the back of her hand and pushed aside a strand of Victoria's hair. "Oh, I really do love you, tiger." Pat looked everywhere but into her daughter's eyes. The parking lot was busy, cars coming and going, students passing, stylish professors. Victoria felt chilled. A car stopped behind the T-bird, wanting the parking place if it was leaving. Pat waved it away.

"This is a long story and not all that interesting in the details," Pat continued. "There's more to it than this, of course, but you could put the whole thing on a few note cards: *Mommy went to Florida. Mommy got a job—*"

"What kind of job?"

"Doesn't matter. Waitress. But in a really nice place, steaks and seafood. Great tips! *Mommy met a man, a good man. Man falls in love with Mommy and Mommy falls in love with him. Mommy gets married.*"

Pat shrugged her shoulders and smiled benignly, as if the note-card version of her recent life was as common as all those leaves falling from the trees around them.

"You got married in Florida?" Victoria blurted out. Maybe raising her voice wasn't a nice thing to do. Wasn't she supposed to be happy and give her mother a big congratulatory hug?

"I sure did, baby, and that's my good news."

Victoria didn't want her mother to think she wasn't happy for her, so she leaned over and kissed her on the cheek. "That is good news," she said. "That's wonderful."

"You are so precious," Pat said, kissing her daughter back. "It's getting a bit chilly in here, don't you think?" Victoria nodded and Pat started the engine to run the heater. Another anticipatory driver stopped behind them until Pat also waved him away.

"I went to school here," Pat announced. "Did I ever tell you that?"

Victoria shook her head and looked out the window at the Warren administration building as if trying to picture her mother walking up the steps with books under her arm, like these students.

"Just one semester. Well, and half of the second. Almost a whole year, really. This is where I met your father."

"Daddy went to college?"

"No," Pat smiled, pausing as if to remember something. "Your daddy never went to college. He was friends with this guy I dated for a little while. They were going to have a band. You didn't know your daddy was a musician, did you? All water under the bridge now; flowed on down to the sea to nothing."

"What's his name, Mommy?"

"My husband?"

"Uh-huh."

"Melvin R. Cohen. Everybody calls him Mel, of course. That makes me Mrs. Melvin R. Cohen now. Mrs. Patricia Cohen."

"It's a nice name," although Victoria didn't believe it was, really.

"Tiger, Mel treats me like a total frigging princess. I might as well be wearing a tiara." She laughed and preened in the rearview mirror as if adjusting a tiara in her aluminum hair.

"I think you look like a princess," Victoria said.

"You are the real princess, my sweetie."

"We can be princesses in Florida now," Victoria said.

Pat's expression turned grim and she waved away another hopeful driver.

"Oh, to hell with it! Let's just go."

Pat reversed and headed around the circuit back out to the street.

"What's the bad news, Mommy?'

"Yes, bad news, too. But not permanent bad news, just temporary, for a little while bad news. Then everything will be good for us again.

Not just good, better than ever before, better than we dreamed. Let's say it will be flat frigging perfect!"

They turned onto Elm Street toward Irene's house.

"Here's the deal," Pat began as she pulled into Irene's driveway. Victoria noticed Irene's face appear in the front window and then just as quickly disappear. "Mel wasn't expecting to get a built-in family right away. He's got plans. That was pretty clear right from the get-go. Fact is, tiger, I haven't actually told Mel about you just yet."

"You married somebody and didn't tell him about me?"

"Not yet, is what I said. I will, of course, and I am sure he will love you like crazy then. It just made sense to provide that information after he was hooked on me and would see you as the better part of me. You get it, don't you?"

"I don't understand, Mommy."

"It's not so hard. I'm going home to Florida after I pick up Mel in Chicago, where he's visiting his mother. Then, just the very second that the time is right, I'll tell him all about you and then we'll be family like we never was before but should have been."

"When?" Victoria could hardly breathe.

"The very instant I know he's ready to have his family."

"Do you know how long that might be?"

"Not long at all, tiger."

Victoria's look was a plea.

"When do you get Christmas holiday?"

"I don't know exactly. A few days before, I think."

"That's when it will be, then. Perfect time, you see? Christmas is the perfect time for family love and togetherness. That's what we'll have. Plus, you'll be on school holiday and won't have to miss any until we get you into a Miami school."

"Is that where we're going to live, Miami?"

"One block from the beach, in a building so tall you can see damn near all the way to Bermuda. That's an island where Mel wants to take me, us."

"Christmas?"

"Christmas. It's the perfect time. Now give me a hug and a kiss that will last till Christmas."

Victoria threw her arms around her mother's neck and kissed her first on the cheek and then on the lips when Pat turned her face that way.

"Just two measly nothing little months, tiger. Not even that long, really."

"I can't wait!" Finally Victoria let herself feel some excitement. She knew a lot about Florida, she know that they would have palm trees at Christmas; she was going to draw pictures with palm trees.

"It'll fly by so fast you'll think it was two days. But now you have to get out and let me get on the highway. I need to be in Chicago before midnight and damn it, just look, I think it's going to rain."

Victoria leaned over again and kissed her mother's cheek. Pat tousled Victoria's hair and then opened the door for her. Victoria got out and Pat closed the door. She blew her daughter a long kiss and mouthed the words, two months, and held up two fingers. She clashed the gears into reverse and backed quickly out. Victoria waved wildly and blew a kiss to her mother as she disappeared down Elm Street. Then she ran to the Higgenbottom house to tell Alice the fantastic news.

Victoria never saw her mother again.

TWENTY-THREE

According to Isabel Higgenbottom, who would ask her unofficially adopted daughter to leave her home in 1966, poor Victoria's sad descent into hell began the year she became a teenager, 1963. Victoria wouldn't have to move far, just back to Aunt Irene's house next door, where she would live uncomfortably the remaining few years of her ailing and senile aunt's life.

Isabel Higgenbottom enjoyed gossiping that Victoria was cursed by her extraordinary beauty and by the kind of body and soft, compelling visage that cursed all gorgeous women. Just like that new song the girls played on the radio all the time: "*If you wanna be happy for the rest of your life, never make a pretty woman your wife.*" It was simply much worse if they were also smart; just think about Marilyn Monroe, who was smart enough to play dumb, or that poor sad poet, the Plath woman, who had recently stuck her head in an oven, obviously due to excessive mental acumen, Isabel pointed out, wondering if anyone ever knew a happy smart person? Or a happy rich person, for that matter. The golden mean in all things, she told everyone who would listen to her.

Alice Higgenbottom had rather dramatically moved on from being Victoria's *sister* and was none too subtle about dropping hints that she wished Victoria would "go home." She despised Victoria's expanding beauty and believed that Victoria spent so much time naked in front of her because she was showing off, and probably to taunt Alice over that thing that almost happened to her, which Alice was now old enough to understand and to have even more desperate nightmares about. Alice had grown into a different world from the one she had shared with Victoria when they were children. Alice made the cheerleading squad that year, was asked to join four clubs, and had a boyfriend who played tennis on the school team. Alice hated a show-off and that's all Victoria was, and a guileless one to boot. Besides, none of Alice's friends would have anything to do with Victoria, who was the worst possible sort of snob, the sort who ignores the fact that you are ignoring her.

The discord in the Higgenbottom house was made all the worse because Victoria had stopped going to church. She had actually stopped even before making a flagrant announcement, only pretending to go. She would get dressed, ride to church with the family, she and Alice pointedly ignoring one another in the backseat, enter the vestibule, then engage anyone in an irrelevant conversation that gave her an opportunity to make her break outside while the congregation settled into pews. Then she would sneak back in an hour later and wait in the vestibule to join some exiting group. She told Aunt Isabel that she had talked too long and sat in the back so she wouldn't disturb everyone by walking all the way down to the front where the Higgenbottom trio always sat. They believed her two or three times because Isabel was pleased that Victoria had finally made friends at church. Then Alice went to the rear one Sunday to check. After being caught in the lie, Victoria stopped the pretense and refused to get out of bed and get dressed the next Sunday morning. No amount of cajoling, persuasion, or threatening could change her mind. She wouldn't even explain. "I'm not comfortable with it anymore," was all she said. This caused an uproar in the Higgenbottom house of proportions rarely experienced. Still, Victoria would not be goaded or threatened into changing her mind. The Higgenbottoms wondered if she was secretly drinking alcohol.

Victoria had started drinking, beginning soon after the assassination of her idol, John Kennedy. She was in love with the president. She stared transfixed at the television whenever he appeared, and sought out articles and photos about him in magazines and newspapers. She had romantic and sometimes distinctly erotic dreams about him. The most powerful man in the world was going to find her and save her and bring her into womanhood. No matter what people kept saying, she did not believe he had been killed. Surely it was a political ploy of some kind. Then she watched his funeral on the Higgenbottoms' DuMont TV. She still didn't really believe until John-John saluted. No one would ever trick a child like that into believing his father was dead if he wasn't. The weight of this crushed her. This was the worst thing that had ever happened in the world.

They were all crying during the funeral. Alice bawling like a lost calf. Victoria sick to her stomach but unable to peel herself from the floor in front of the TV, vomited into her lap.

"Oh my goodness!" Isabel cried. "You have to do that now, here?"

"Ugh," Alice said, holding her nose.

"Don't just sit there," Thomas ordered. "Go clean yourself, young lady."

Victoria shook her head and didn't move.

"Why do you do things like this?" Isabel demanded, as she got up from the sofa and went to bring a wet bath towel. She plopped the towel into Victoria's lap, then went back to the sofa, wrapping her arms around Thomas's arm.

Then Thomas Higgenbottom said, "The Lord has taken our president to join Him in His eternal heaven."

"God did this!?" Victoria cried out, turning to look at Thomas.

"God didn't 'do this,' Victoria. You know what I mean."

Victoria shook her head.

"He means that the Lord called President Kennedy to His side," Alice explained with some exasperation.

"Why?"

"God's will is not ours to know," Thomas said, dabbing at his cheeks with a cotton monogrammed handkerchief.

Victoria covered the vomit in her lap with the towel. The damp soaked through her skirt. She watched her hero and future lover, the man God murdered, be taken into the black-and-white world of history; her misery melted into hatred. She looked over her shoulder to where Thomas sat on the sofa and blurted out, "You're never going to finish that airplane, are you! You're never going to take me flying, are you!" She bolted from the room, leaving the Higgenbottoms staring at one another in disbelief.

Victoria first experienced friendship when she began skipping Sunday services. There were others also skipping, a regular clique of four or five teenagers, outcasts like Victoria, although in their own distinct fashions, who used some ruse that allowed their parents to believe they had attended church when in fact they had sneaked out a side door. Victoria got the idea when she saw the same group disappearing Sunday after Sunday. She was the only girl, as usual. She didn't really know any girls, except Alice, and if Alice was the model, Victoria wasn't interested.

They spent the church hour in a café two blocks away, drinking Dr. Peppers and eating ketchup-drenched French fries. It was at this time Victoria begin wondering with whom she could dismiss her annoying technical virginity. She chose the maddest, wildest one of the church escapees, even though he was a year younger. His name was Toby and he was a beatnik. Toby had read two Kerouac books and had seen a beatnik movie set in North Beach, San Francisco, where they all talked about going to live one day; they would drive together cross-country, they would be on the road. He owned a set of bongo drums and a guitar. He had seen every episode of *The Many Loves of Dobie Gillis*. Maynard G. Krebs was his hero. He wore a wispy goatee and could exclaim, "Work?!" exactly the way Maynard did. He had threatened to kill himself when the show was canceled a couple of years earlier and sent a letter to the local TV station so stating. He was the only one of them to have, thanks to an older brother in college, smoked marijuana. Beatnik marijuana words like *pot*, *grass*, and *weed* salted his conversations.

Even after Victoria stopped the pretense of attending church with the Higgenbottoms, she continued to meet her group of delinquents at the Magnolia Café on Sunday mornings. There was Toby and his best friend Gus; Tommy, who was very fat; Bob, who was tall and fence-post skinny, a basketball player, and at seventeen the oldest. Gus was youngest, thirteen. Victoria was fifteen. She picked Toby because she liked his name best and he wore a black turtleneck pullover and was easily the most beat of their tiny group of church evaders. Toby, who had read the beatnik books, refused to show any bourgeois social skills. He wasn't all that nice-looking, but his attitude served the purpose of distracting from his appearance; his hair was cut too short, pushed up like a hedgerow in front and glistened with grease; his eyes darted all over the place; he didn't have much of a chin, and the goatee he tried to grow made him look like Confucius with a flattop. Gus had a pretty good name, but he was only thirteen and had too many pimples, which she feared might erupt on her if she made him too excited. Tommy was just way too fat, she imagined herself crushed like a grape under his gigantic belly, but he was far and away the funniest of them; his belly laugh made them grab the table edges to protect their drinks. Finally, she didn't like Bob and made it plain, so he didn't like her much either. She didn't like him because he acted like he could have her anytime he was in the mood, which meant she would never allow him to touch her under any circumstances. But he smoked Lucky Strikes and she thought that looked cool. He said the letters LSMFT on the package stood for Loose Strap Means Floppy Titties. Everyone laughed so loudly that the waitress gave them a dirty look. Bob could strike and ignite his Zippo by snapping his fingers over the flint wheel in a cool way. Cool was the word for Bob, but she didn't like him in spite of that.

One Sunday they talked themselves into making an ill-considered suicide pact. It was Toby's idea and he was the only one who wanted it to be successful. Toby talked about death like it was a trip to Chicago. The others at least subconsciously considered that just enough success might direct some important attention their way. Toby read about suicide and professed the idea of living fast and dying young and having a good-looking corpse, like James Dean. He said they should just check out of this stupid and crazy world. At first there wasn't much serious interest in this idea, but Toby kept at it and after a few minutes Victoria supported him and put her hand on his thigh under the table. If she was going to die a virgin, at least she wanted to do *something*. Toby gulped and lost track of the message when she slid her hand up his leg. After Toby and Victoria said they were going to do it, the other two were challenged to prove their manhood as well as their novice beatnik credentials. After proposing various methods and rejecting anything that could hurt, they settled on an aspirin overdose. Aspirin were the only pills easily available to them. Tommy joked, "Who wants to die with a fucking headache?" But the laughs were just not as riotous as usual. Bob collected some money from around the table then went to the cash register and bought four tins of St. Joseph aspirin from the rack by the register displaying, along with aspirin, small boxes of Alka-Seltzer, rolls of Tums and Life Savers, and packs of Wrigley's gum. Each tin contained twenty aspirin. They only had ten minutes before the boys had to get back to church so they could mingle innocently with the emerging congregation. It did not occur to Victoria until later, when she was left alone in the café, what difference would it make now to get caught skipping church, which their parents probably as much as knew anyway? Maybe none of them really thought this would actually work? Victoria was ambivalent. Her list of things to live for was critically short. At first they swallowed each aspirin one at a time with a swallow of cola, but then Toby emptied the entire tin into his glass of Cherry Coke and stirred it around with the straw. Then he drained the glass and licked his lips—ahh! Gus, Tommy, Bob, and Victoria did the same.

Singing in his best James Darren imitation, Bob stood to leave: "Goodbye cruel world, I'm off to join the circus . . ."

Victoria impulsively decided to kiss each one, a goodbye kiss, she said. Bob, Tommy, and Gus got a nice kiss on the lips, Toby got a full exploration from her tongue. Then she was alone at the table, looking at the four empty aspirin tins, which she gathered up and dropped into the trash bin outside when she left.

Victoria had a premonition when the phone rang during lunch, because they almost never got phone calls during the day on Sunday, a day when the family first worshiped together, then ate together, then did family things outside in good weather and inside otherwise. She had a strong appetite and did not feel untoward. She had no idea how long it took to die from an aspirin overdose, or even if they had taken enough. She wondered if it would hurt and then what being dead would be like, even though she was still rather dubious. Would her soul really endure eternally somewhere; up or down, who could say? Would she see her mother again in heaven, or elsewhere? Would she be able to meet President Kennedy? Maybe she would only get sick and that would be stupid. What would death be like if the religious stories were not true? Sleep? If you go to sleep expecting to wake up, but don't, then how would you know you were dead? It would just be a longer sleep; instead of some hours, it would be infinite . . . maybe. What does that mean? If the religious beliefs were correct, would God be so angry with her that she would be condemned forever to the fires of hell? What would that be like? Would her father be there? At least in hell she wouldn't have to be around the Alice Higgenbottoms of the world.

Aunt Isabel returned to the table from answering the phone and said, "Victoria, did you take a bunch of aspirin with those juvenile delinquents at the Magnolia Café?"

"I don't even know what you're talking about?"

"That was Sarah Palmer who just called to say that her son Gus told her that you and those boys ate an entire box of aspirin, each. Did you, young lady?"

"What?" Thomas Higgenbottom sputtered, spitting a wad of mashed potato onto the table.

"How retard is that!" Alice exclaimed.

"Thomas, go call Dr. Gould and find out how many aspirin can kill a person," Isabel ordered. "Alice, go to your room."

"Mom!"

"Alice! And don't say that word."

"What word?"

"You know what word: *Retard*. Now go!"

"What did I do?" Alice muttered as she left the table. "I'm not the re— idiot around here."

"You, young lady, come with me." Isabel took Victoria by the arm and pulled her into the kitchen. She bent her over the sink and ordered her to stick her finger down her throat. "If you don't do it, I surely will, young lady."

"How many aspirin did she take?" Thomas called out from the phone in the hall.

"Victoria? How many?"

"One of those little tins. Twenty, I suppose."

"Twenty," Isabel yelled back. "One of those little tins." Then to Victoria, "your finger in your throat *now*!"

Victoria made herself vomit into the sink. Thomas came into the kitchen and said, "Dr. Gould says it's not enough to kill her but it could damage her stomach. He wants to see her at the hospital. I hope they pump her stomach."

"Why, oh why, did you do such a stupid thing, Victoria?" Isabel pleaded.

"We were just goofing around," she said, the taste of bile burning her throat.

"You call this goofing around!?" Thomas cried. "Was this your crazy idea?"

"Sarah said the Blanchard boy started it," Isabel said, handing Victoria a dish towel to wipe her mouth. Victoria splashed water into her mouth from the tap.

"Toby Blanchard?"

"Nobody thought it was any big deal. We just wanted to see what would happen."

"You take twenty damned aspirin and you think it's no big deal?" Thomas said. "You'll see a big deal now; you're going to have to eat a bunch of charcoal and get your stomach pumped."

"I find it just amazing to believe a boy like Toby Blanchard would come up with something this childish and dangerous without some help," Isabel said, casting her suspicious glance at Victoria, trapped at the sink. "We've known the Palmers forever. This is not the kind of thing Gus would think up."

"It wasn't anybody's idea, exactly. We just sort of did it, like a joke."

"This is just damned amazing!" Thomas said.

"There's no reason to curse," Isabel stated. Then to Victoria: "Get your jacket, young lady."

They saw the Blanchard family in the hospital parking lot but none of them spoke. Victoria shrugged when she saw Toby looking at her. Toby made a slashing motion across his throat, but Victoria didn't know if he meant to indicate what was going to happen to him when he got home or what he was going to do to Gus Palmer.

Two weeks after happily failing to kill themselves, Victoria and Toby abandoned their virginities to one another after smoking so much marijuana that Victoria couldn't remember how it worked or much of how it felt. What she remembered was learning to appreciate Bob Dylan, who until that night she thought was such a bad singer that his records had to be a joke.

They were in a ratty apartment overlooking the Warren town square where Toby's older brother, Peter, a student at Warren College, lived with two roommates. Toby had a key and knew that his brother and roommates were gone that Saturday afternoon to an away football game at some Podunk college in Illinois.

This is how Victoria would live when she went to college, she decided. She would have her own apartment and it would be right in the center of town, like this one, but she wouldn't have roommates. Her bookcase would be made from planks and cinder blocks, like Peter's, and she would have plenty of books—art books and Russian novels she knew she should read some day. She would have her own art on the walls and casual flowers in fruit-jar vases with paint splatters on them. She would have a hi-fi record player and a special rack to store the albums. In place of curtains she would have bamboo-slat blinds, like Peter did. She would set up her easel, when she got one, by the window overlooking the square; people looking up could see her there, a bottle of wine on the window ledge, and hate her for having a perfect life.

Victoria splayed across the blanket-covered sofa and watched Toby, who looked so much like this was the world to which he belonged, take a bag of marijuana from behind one of the cinder-block bookcase supports. They smoked it in a pipe. Victoria adjusted herself on the sofa to make it easier for him to lie beside her. They had done plenty already, but still hadn't gone all the way. She wanted it to happen now. But Toby got up and brought back a guitar. He played and sang for her "Don't Think Twice, It's All Right" and "The Times They Are A Changin'." She asked him to sing the first one again. She remembered this more clearly than when later he finally removed all her clothes and put his penis where before only his finger had ventured. When Toby saw Victoria naked, he could hardly breathe, managing to whisper only the plea, "Oh my God!," before closing his eyes and taking the plunge. "Don't Think Twice, It's All Right" became their song, and Victoria thought she had fallen in love with the boy who could sing Bob Dylan songs a lot better than Bob Dylan could. It was an appropriate choice for their song because less than a year later Victoria would decide that indeed it wasn't her he was looking for, babe; not if he could also be looking to get into Annie Bacon's panties, which he did, and it didn't sway Victoria when he pleaded that it didn't mean any more than jacking off. Toby could have done anything with her and to her that he liked, and pretty much did, except be unfaithful to her. It was the only thing she asked and it was the only thing she would not forgive. Ever.

TWENTY-FOUR

Getting pregnant was the last straw. Thomas and Isabel Higgenbottom told Victoria that she could no longer live in their house. She was sixteen and had little more to carry back across the adjoining lawns to Aunt Irene's house than she and Alice had carried over six years before.

She passed her seventeenth birthday, actually the day after, with an abortion, the money for it a birthday present from Donald Estes, who was, as close as she could estimate, probably the father. There were four possibilities. Donny didn't go with her, he just paid from his college savings. She had known him longest, although they had broken up last month, a couple of weeks after she was probably impregnated. Bill Murphy offered to both accompany her and pay, but Victoria did not want to share this with someone she hardly knew. In fact, she didn't want to share at all. She just wanted someone to pay so she wouldn't have to go through any hassles with Aunt Irene, who was as oblivious to Victoria's life as she was to some peasant in China. Victoria got a D and C, which was not what it sounded like, just bad grades on a couple of tests. Instead, she got her uterus scraped out.

Victoria didn't particularly desire any of the boys she had sex with that year. She just wanted to take them away from their girlfriends, which turned out to be so easy that there wasn't nearly the satisfaction in it she hoped for. Donny moved her along the drug line from pot to pills. Bill tried to move her back to pot, but it was too late by then, the rush had become necessary to getting through the stupid days. The yellow jackets wound her up so tight that she passed through school in a series of barely controlled explosions. Bill was too good for her, so she dumped him the week after her abortion, thinking of it as her good deed for the senior year; his girlfriend took him back, but he never stopped staring at her like a puppy urgent for praise. After the abortion and since she had no access to birth control pills, and absolutely hating the feel and tainted odor of condoms, she required her sex partners to pull out before dousing her insides with all those slimy tiny squiggly worms that erupt from their dicks. They didn't seem to mind spilling that snot-like goop on her stomach or breasts. This policy continued all the way through Tioni Brown, only stopping with Morgan Cary after she fell in love with him and decided they would be together forever.

There probably wasn't a single female student at Warren High School who didn't at least dislike Victoria and at worst hate her guts. Quite a long string of emotional debris trailed behind her. More than a few of the girls either knew or believed or at least feared that their boyfriends had betrayed them with the Slut of Warren, or would if given any chance. They were pretty much right about this. Victoria had also seduced Mr. Greene, the young history teacher, and Mr. Sizemore, the old math teacher, who was over fifty and had a daughter in Victoria's class. None of Victoria's lovers—they were really just sex partners—talked about her among themselves, although most knew who had been with her. None of them said anything about how violent she could become, how easily her anger was triggered. Most thought the result was worth the threat; in orgasm more often than not Victoria would pummel her partner with her fists, often biting them somewhere, taunting them to hit her. One or two did hit back, but that just made her wilder and even more violent and they had to run away with their clothes clutched to their chests. Had they compared, these boys might have discovered that most of them shared the stigmata of having fucked Victoria Novak—the scar somewhere on their bodies of her teeth marks. It was worth it. Even the ones who in spite of themselves tumbled into love with her believed, even as they stifled cries of secret pain, that it was worth it. Not just because of the sex. She was the most exciting and adventurous girl in Warren. Maybe, some thought, the most beautiful girl on the planet.

She managed to just graduate from high school through good luck and grade inflation from teachers who wanted her or had her. She skipped Commencement and spent most of graduation day in a stoned frenzy in a motel room in Des Moines having sex with the Drake University student who got pills for her.

Irene and Victoria had spent her last two years of high school living like incompatible, suspicious strangers cast up on a deserted island. In all their years together, Aunt Irene had taken Victoria into her arms and held her and called her Victoria instead of Vicki only once, almost eight years before, after the phone call from the Illinois State Police informing Irene that her sister, Patricia, was killed in a five-car pileup during an ice storm on Interstate 80, just east of Moline. Victoria was so shocked to be hugged by a tearful Aunt Irene that minutes passed before she realized that her mother was dead. Her mother's new husband claimed the body and shipped it to Florida for burial. Pat's pretty little red Thunderbird had exploded and burned down to an unrecognizable blob of charred bits of metal and shapeless plastic. Her casket was closed. Melvin Cohen sent a telegram to Irene regarding the particulars of her sister's funeral. He never responded to the telegram Irene sent back informing him that his dead wife had a ten-year-old daughter. At the hour scheduled for Pat's burial, Irene was in her bedroom praying. Victoria walked back to the Higgenbottom house and sat alone in her bedroom crying. She was utterly alone now.

As a generous by-product of Aunt Irene's employment at Warren College, Victoria, as her ward, was admitted to the college in spite of her academic record and received the standard tuition waiver. Otherwise she would not have been able to afford to study beyond high school; she had no money of her own whatsoever. When Aunt Irene died at the end of Victoria's sophomore year, the tuition waiver was not revoked. But by then she was flunking out anyway. Victoria had gone into the library to study during her lunch break and one of the clerks asked if she'd seen her aunt that morning. As soon as Victoria realized that Aunt Irene had not come in for work and had not called, she knew her aunt was dead. Heading home to check, she imagined that Aunt Irene had taken a fall and hit her head, or something like that. She had become wobbly during the past year and had dizzy spells. Victoria expected to find her crashed out of the tub, or perched stone cold in bed with a Bible on her lap. She did find Irene in bed, lying on her side looking peacefully asleep. Victoria, stunned by the hopeful possibility that Aunt Irene had overslept for the first time in her life, felt an odd sense of relief because she had not found her on the bathroom floor. But she didn't stir when Victoria called her name and she didn't respond when Victoria nudged her shoulder. Victoria pushed back Aunt Irene's hair and recoiled as if she was jerked back with a rope. Irene's eyes were wide open, popped out like in cartoons. She had suffered a brain aneurysm and, Victoria was told, died instantly. But Victoria knew that Aunt Irene had known she was dying, she saw it in her eyes—not the eyes of someone happy to be going to heaven.

After the funeral, which was well attended by many members of Irene's church and a few of her coworkers, Victoria received notification that she was Aunt Irene's sole heir. Irene left her the house, which had only a small mortgage payment with only a couple of years remaining to term, and, although Irene had no private life insurance, there was a five thousand dollar insurance policy provided by the college and a savings account with thirty-six hundred dollars in it. It did not take Victoria long to spend most of it.

TWENTY-FIVE

Victoria's lifestyle as a single college coed with an off-campus house confirmed in the public mind every horrible thing the Higgenbottoms had ever said about her. Victoria's grades were so low after sophomore year that she was placed on academic probation. She began junior year, but attended classes randomly and then often stoned, and was likely to be expelled when grades were issued. Alice, who was in Rhode Island studying divinity at Brown, sent a postcard showing the Brown library and all it said was, "Why don't you just grow up! Your ex-friend, Alice." The Higgenbottoms felt it necessary to call the police about goings-on next door about once a month. "Irene must be flip-flopping in her poor grave," Isabel told everyone.

Victoria had learned a long time ago not to care what anyone thought, which only served to increase the ill-will directed against her. There were always people around, but she never thought of them as, or referred to them as, friends. Not even the ones she had sex with. Her lack of interest in the world outside the opaque bubble she maintained around her space made it easier for her to be used by people who only wanted her house for parties, her dope supply for highs, her astonishing body for sex. After Woodstock, but especially after Arlo Guthrie, Victoria's house became commonly known among students as "Alice's Restaurant," because you could get anything you want there, *including* "Alice." Some new students thought Victoria's name was Alice, because that's how most of the coolest students referred to her house. "Let's go to Alice's."

During the fall semester of 1970, Kevin and Bob entered Victoria's space and began the process that would take her to Hawaii. Bob was Barbette, a tagalong groupie; Kevin was a folk singer making the rounds of small colleges in the Midwest, booking himself using a mimeographed flyer featuring fake testimonials. ("Don't hold being white against him. Kevin Clark is all black inside."—Big Bill Broonzy.) It did not occur to Kevin that someone might notice that Big Bill died in 1958, when Kevin was twelve years old.

After Toby, who hated her and would always love her beyond any other woman in his life, Victoria was a mark for boys who sang and played guitars. Kevin did both, and in spite of needing to hype himself with bogus testimonials and lies about who he knew, had a good voice for folk music, reminiscent of Phil Ochs, whose songs made up a large part of Kevin's repertoire. In faded black denims and scuffed tan rough-out cowboy boots, the Indian beaded necklace and woven horsehair wrist band, Martin guitar, and a perpetually dangling cigarette, he believed that with the right break he'd be the next rough-hewn John Denver. He had been wandering around the Midwest for a year, in a limping-along canary yellow and turquoise VW bus with a Day-Glo purple peace symbol where the VW logo used to be, playing college student center one-night stands for fifty bucks, seventy-five when he got lucky. Most of Kevin's luck also came in the form of one-night stands, at least until Bob latched on a few weeks ago and kept him off limits.

Bob attached herself to Kevin at Carlton College in Minnesota, where she was hiding as a runaway with a boy she met in a bar. She was small, one of those self-assured but childlike girls that the word *gamine* best describes. Her body went straight up and down, without the spread of hips or the distraction of breasts. She cut her hair short and could have, at some distance, been taken for a teenage boy. She was fifteen years old and wasn't likely to do things like run off with folk singers when she stayed on her Thorazine, but she was off. She told Kevin she was eighteen, which he did not believe but did not question. Kevin was attracted to madness in women and Bob was mad enough to need a variety of psychotropic aids to keep her secured to the planet. Bob supposed that Kevin had a thing for girls who looked like boys and made the most of it.

Victoria went to Kevin's coffee house concert at the Warren Student Center and afterwards invited him back to her house to smoke some dope. This happened to Kevin more often than not, so he seldom had to pay for a room or sleep in the bus. He stayed at some colleges for three or four days before moving on to the next gig, especially if his free room came with free dope and free love. Victoria was a little surprised when Bob came up while she was talking with Kevin and put her arm tightly around his waist. She had thought Bob was a boy.

Instead of accepting Victoria's offer, Kevin invited her to go with them to a farm outside town where Kevin knew somebody from the last time he toured through central Iowa. "It's a hippie commune," he said. "Probably a dozen good folks live there. Can you dig it?"

It was midnight, just beginning to rain. Victoria played roadie and helped Kevin and Bob load the bus with speakers, amps, and guitar cases. Bob looked like a wet puppy, Victoria thought, watching how she hovered around Kevin as if waiting for him to toss her a stick. "Woof, woof," Victoria muttered under her breath. She had decided that Bob was more likely a girl than a boy; she had breasts and large dark nipples distinctly visible under her white T-shirt, though small for a girl, too large for a boy. The only word Bob had said to Victoria was: "Hi." She didn't need to speak to let Victoria know what she was thinking.

Kevin and Bob got into the front, Victoria sat on an amplifier behind and between the front seats. A pair of black and white fuzzy dice dangled from the mirror, with a decorative little hash pipe on a string and a large metal peace symbol on a chain. Some paperback books lay about on the floor; *Thus Spake Zarathustra* was under her foot. In back, the guitar cases rested on an army duffel bag and a red suitcase. The interior walls of the bus were plastered with posters—*War Is Not Healthy for Children and Other Living Things*; *Make Love Not War*; Jimi Hendrix with an American flag exploding from his guitar; Che Guevara puffing a stogie; a marijuana plant; a Day-Glo pink peace symbol. The bus engine wouldn't start. Kevin hit the steering wheel and got out into the rain to check under the hood.

Just making conversation, Victoria asked Bob, "Are you a musician, too?"

Bob took a quick look over her shoulder, then opened her door to get out. "Kevin might need some help."

Victoria shrugged. She was used to having girls take an immediate dislike to her. She wondered how Bob got her name. The van reeked of marijuana and dirty laundry; behind her there was a plastic laundry basket heaped with clothes. She could make out their voices, but not what they were saying. In a minute, Bob came around into the driver's side. "Okay, try it," Kevin called out. Bob turned the key and the engine started. Bob crawled over to her seat, Kevin banged closed the hood, and got back into the bus.

"She's a quirky little bitch," he said, "but I love her." Victoria assumed he meant the bus. "Bob, my sweet little slut," he said, "how about we have us a little something for the road?"

Bob bent down and pulled a multicolored woven string bag from beneath her seat and fished around before retrieving a pack of Zig-Zag papers and a dime bag. She rolled a fat one while Kevin found his way out of the student parking lot.

"You don't know Jesse's farm?" Kevin asked over his shoulder. Marijuana smoke filled the bus. Bob coughed hard and handed the joint back to Kevin, instead of to Victoria. Kevin passed it back and gave Bob a cut-it-out look.

Victoria inhaled, shook her head, then said, "No. I don't think so."

"How could you live around here and not?"

"Don't know."

"Maybe she doesn't get out much," Bob said to Kevin.

"Actually," Victoria said, "I don't. What for?" The dope began slowing her down, smoothing the more ragged of her edges, intensifying the 'lude she dropped before the concert.

Kevin produced a tape from a box on the floorboard and put it into the player in the dashboard. Victoria was surprised to hear a sappy Elton John song, to which Kevin began to sing along. Bob plopped her hand possessively on Kevin's shoulder and kept squeezing it. Victoria felt her ass banging uncomfortably against the amp as Kevin turned onto a dirt road about halfway along the highway between Warren and Des Moines. It occurred to her that maybe Jesse's farm was some Charlie Manson cult. It rained harder and the windshield wipers finally made some headway cutting through the dead bug debris. They passed a farmhouse, then another, and kept going. Bob rolled another joint.

"How you doing back there?" Kevin asked, looking over his shoulder.

"Mellow," Victoria purred.

Kevin turned the bus up a muddy track off the gravel road and followed a fence line into deeper darkness.

"How do you know this farm?" Victoria asked.

"I was here once last year."

"Once? And you can find it?"

"Maybe. We'll see." Kevin laughed, causing Bob to giggle.

Victoria bounced on the amp as Kevin turned again, fish-tailing a little on the mud track. They entered an open gate. The bus's single working headlight darted across an old pickup truck, a motorcycle, a bicycle on its side, a wheelbarrow on its side, a barking dog, and a white shingle old farmhouse with a tin roof and a broken, wraparound porch. A barn of indeterminate color leaned dark in the shadows. A gray dog bounded just in front of the bus, barking hysterically. Victoria noticed a huge piece of rusting iron sculpture in the shape of an X before Kevin turned off the headlight.

"That's Comfy," Kevin said. "He won't bite. He just wants you to rub his butt."

A shadow moved across a lighted, curtained window, then the door opened, spilling a strange, flickering reddish light onto the porch. A man covered like a monk, his head beneath a peaked hood, stepped out. Victoria could see another figure behind the monk.

"There's Jesse," Kevin said, opening his door and jumping out into the slackening rain.

The men embraced perfunctorily, Victoria could not hear what they said to each other. Kevin then gestured for Bob and Victoria to get out and come in.

By the time Bob and Victoria came inside, the robed Jesse and Kevin were gone. The only light in the big front room came from a few candles, which were placed behind pink theatrical gels. Panicked with Kevin out of her sight, Bob continued through the only open doorway. As Victoria's eyes adjusted to the dim glow, she noticed a big mattress on the floor, with an indeterminate number of people sleeping (or something) under big Indian blankets. There was a single overstuffed arm chair with a plate of pasta debris in it. Tottering, overflowing bookcases. A table covered with cans of paint, splattered jars holding brushes, rags, ashtrays, a hookah. Loud music from somewhere else clashed with the tinkling rain on the tin roof. As her eyes adjusted more thoroughly, she noticed that the walls were covered with graffiti, or maybe an amateurish attempt at art, a terrible blend of colors. The dog nuzzled her leg, so she patted his butt and wondered if she should close the open front door.

She was rubbing Comfy when someone touched her shoulder so lightly that she at first thought it was a spider dropped from the dank ceiling. When she raised up and turned, she thought it must be Jesse; she could only see the whites of his eyes from the dark hole of the hood over his head. Then his teeth when he smiled.

"Your name is Vivian, Kevin tells me."

"Well, not really. It's Victoria. I just met him tonight," she explained.

"Ah, yes. Vivian is, of course, totally wrong. Victoria. Yes. Victoria. You would never accept Vicki, am I correct in this?"

"You are."

"There is nothing Vicki about you."

The voice from under the hood was a bass rumble like thunder a dozen miles away. Or a god from a burning bush. She wondered what he looked like.

"Take my hand, Victoria."

She took his hand and felt hers disappear within his warm grip. "Do you want to leave that door open?"

Apparently so.

They went in darkness toward the music. "Is that Iron Butterfly?" she asked, as they passed through a chaotic kitchen, where a single candle burned atop an old oven. "*Heavy*," Jesse said.

"Yes."

"Name of the album," he continued. "*Heavy*."

"Yes, I know. I've heard some of it."

"What else have you heard, dear Victoria?"

What answer could there be to that?

All she could see of Jesse as he led her deeper into the caverns of the farmhouse was the robe, the hood peaked like an old-time sleeping cap.

His feet made not a sound, except causing the floorboards to creak from his weight. They entered a hall. The first opposing doors were closed. She could barely see anything. At the end of the hall, they passed into a large room that could have been the end of the house. Blankets hung from what were probably windows. She felt hot, smothered. There was smoke everywhere, marijuana, cigarettes . . . PCP? The music was here, the tangible smells of human sweat and sexuality, the sticky sweet odor of incense. A fat candle melted over the wooden floor in the center of a circle of seated, lying, squatting people—eight, she counted, including Kevin with Bob's head in his lap. She felt bumps beneath her feet, the clumps of melted candle wax all over.

Jesse turned Victoria to face him and leaned close. "Just a moment to tend to the needs of my little flock of acidheads." Victoria shrugged her answer and watched Jesse handing out what he told them was Owsley on sugar cubes, passing each to his acid celebrants like a priest offering the Eucharist. "Soon you will touch the hand of God," Jesse said three times. Why, Victoria wondered, was she being left out? She wouldn't mind touching the hand of God; she had more than a few things to tell Him.

Victoria had dropped acid twice before, only three months ago and a week apart, thanks to her Drake University friend who gave her speed for sex. She had not touched the hand of God either time. She had spent hours the first time folded into a beanbag chair that contained her like cuddling arms, while colors she knew and colors yet to be known flashed by her, around her, and through her body, which she could sometimes see from a position above and outside the room, an X-ray through the ceiling; her body as smooth and alabaster as a Greek statue; sparks of neon passing in and out of her body, seeing herself naked although she was not. She had sex with Willie, her Drake supplier, the next time. From the same vantage point outside and above the ceiling, she watched herself absorb Willie into her body until she was able to see Willie inside her, through her transparent skin, humping her from the inside, his penis emerging from her vagina backwards, so she thought his penis had become part of her, that she had both sexual organs and could fuck herself.

But that was not touching the hand of God.

The hand she touched was Jesse's. He led her from the room and back into the hallway. He opened a door and she followed him inside. More candles. Fat candles on the floor, tall thin candles in bottles. Windows, again behind Indian blankets. In the center of the room, dominating the large space, an orange and white parachute canopy draped over a king-size mattress on the floor, with a slit in the chute to crawl inside. There were a dozen or more big pillows in gaudy patterns. Sprawled among the pillows, an emaciated naked girl.

Jesse let go of Victoria's hand and knelt at the foot of the bed. He touched the girl's foot, then ran his hand up the inside of her leg. "Cat," he said in his low, rumbling voice, "go."

She turned over and stretched and took Jesse's hand to pull it further up her leg. She was not exactly a girl; she looked like she was at least forty and had had babies or lost a lot of weight. Victoria noticed that her pubic hair was shaved clean, her pudenda bulged oddly, like a small, misshapen pear fallen between her legs.

"Go," Jesse repeated, withdrawing his hand.

Cat raised up on her elbows and saw Victoria standing at the end of the bed. "This is for you, dear Cat," Jesse said, helping her get up. He had taken another sugar cube from somewhere in his robe and put it into her hand. Cat stood awkwardly, glared at Victoria for a vicious second, popped the cube into her mouth and said, "Fuck you, Jesse," as she careened out of the room.

"Nice parachute," Victoria said.

Jesse crawled through the parachute slot and beckoned her by waving his fingers, all she could see of his hand emerging from the robe sleeve. Victoria kicked off her shoes and followed, sitting cross-legged in the middle of the mattress. Jesse lotused himself in front of her and withdrew an envelope from the mysteries of the robe. Somewhat ritualistically, he fished out a tablet and silently offered it. Victoria stared at his hand but didn't reach out. "It's just a 'lude," Jesse explained. "Not just any. Home-made." He inclined his head in the direction of the barn. "Shit you can put your faith in."

"I indulged earlier," Victoria said.

"Ah. In that case."

He replaced the tab and the envelope returned to his robed myster-ies. He lay back and crossed his arms over his chest like dead monk's wake. He began speaking to her but it had the character of a monologue. It seemed he was going to tell her his life story: growing up black in Geor-gia, the Army and Vietnam, where he was a medic, and now this commu-nal farm. Victoria was falling asleep.

Apropos of nothing he'd been saying, Jessie lay his hand on her thigh and said, "Shall we make love not war, darling?"

"Actually, I'm ninety-nine percent out of it. It's not you. It's the 'lude and a few joints on the way here."

"No harm done. But if I say 'pretty please'?"

The little boy tone he used made her laugh.

"Is that a yes laugh or a no laugh?"

"It's just a laugh. Maybe I should take a nap. After that?"

"Let's have a nap."

"Do you ever take that off?" she asked, lying on her side next to him.

"Never," Jesse said.

"You take a bath in it?"

"I do everything in it. I think, Miss Victoria, that you would like to live among our little band of happy campers."

She smiled and nodded, beginning to fall asleep.

Then someone screamed. Victoria didn't know if she had been asleep or how much time had passed.

Jesse rose and jumped through the parachute slot. There was another scream and another, then voices yelling. Victoria scooted off the bed and ran toward the noise.

Leaning around Jesse's bulk, Victoria watched people scampering away from each other like cockroaches caught in quick light. Psychedelic music blared from a big reel-to-reel tape player. Kevin on his hands and knees bent over a girl lying on the floor, blood oozing from a slice across her cheek, her eyes wide with surprise. An animal scream erupted from Bob, plastered against the far wall, naked, covered in swirls, dabs, circles, psychedelic finger paints. Red target circles went around her negligible breasts. Wiggly arrows pointed to her vagina. Bob sliced madly at the air with a long knife.

"What's this motherfucking bullshit!" Jesse cried. "What the fuck!" Two people scrambled out of the room.

"She just freaked out, dude! I mean, totally fucking freaked out!" Kevin cried. "She cut this girl. I mean, like, for fucking nothing. She just . . . I don't know, got this knife from someplace and started hacking away at her face. Some fucking shit, man."

Bob still screamed and sliced at the air.

A guy behind Kevin said, "Far fucking out, dude!" A girl in a granny dress and combat boots cowered behind him in a fetal position, the fat toes of her boots pointing in nearly opposite directions.

"Somebody get that goddamn knife away from her!" Jesse ordered. "How'd she get all painted and naked, anyhow?"

Like let go from a spring, Bob bolted toward Jesse and Victoria, the knife carving a path through the space in front of her. Jesse jerked Victoria around in front of him as a shield and pushed her into Bob as he ducked and fell back.

When Victoria felt the sudden, powerful shove from behind, she lurched and stumbled toward Bob and the knife, feeling herself speeding up and rising into the air, compelled to the knife blade sparkling in candle light and slicing toward her face, the dazzling knife appearing disconnected from the hand wielding it, flying alone through the darkened room toward the inevitable target.

But Victoria was not the knife's target; Bob was after the hulking robed figure of Jesse scooting backwards on the floor behind Victoria. Victoria's momentum moved her forward and when she ducked to avoid the knife, she collided head first into Bob's stomach. As she raised up, Bob had staggered back a step, clutching her abdomen with one arm, her mouth wide open and sucking air. Now she focused on Victoria, lunging toward her with the knife thrust out like a spear, jabbing, jabbing, jabbing. Victoria could not get out of the way. She knocked the knife aside and grabbed Bob around the neck, the momentum taking them both to the floor. "Stop this shit!" Victoria screamed as she tried to get away from Bob. But Bob was no longer struggling. Victoria quickly rolled out of the way and got to her knees. She looked over at Bob and saw first the bubbling pool of blood coming from the side of her neck. This is not right, Victoria thought. There's this child she doesn't even know, naked and painted like a psychedelic poster, with a knife sticking out of her neck and blood pouring out. This could not be real.

Suddenly Kevin was beside her, grabbing her arm and pulling her down the hall. They could hear Jesse yelling and a girl screaming as they ran through the living room, shoving their way through half a dozen people trying to look down the hall.

"My shoes," Victoria said as Kevin dragged her down the steps and across the muddy yard toward the bus.

"Fuck your shoes! You better hope the fucking engine starts this time."

Kevin got lost trying to find the highway and it took them almost two hours to get back to Victoria's house in Warren. He wasn't able to explain what happened. "I was wasted as hell," he said. "Somebody got this idea of body painting Bob, and this girl, the one who got cut, started teasing Bob about her body . . . 'You a girl or a boy? There an itty-bitty prick hiding in there?' She tried to open Bob's pussy to see what's inside. Shit like that. I haven't a goddamned idea where she got that knife from. It was just there. I mean, she was fucking naked! Maybe it was lying on the floor somewhere."

Victoria put her shoeless feet against the heater vent and considered that she had somehow stuck a knife into that girl's neck. In the dark, the blood spots on her arm and the side of her face looked like splattered mud. She was responsible for killing that girl. She killed herself, Kevin told her, but it didn't seem to be the kind of inept consolation she needed to hear.

"We've got to get out of here," Kevin went on.

"You didn't do anything."

"Bob's fucking fifteen!"

"Guess you did do something then." Shit, she thought, I left a fifteen-year-old girl with a knife in her neck.

"Do you think she's dead?"

"What do you think?"

Victoria nodded. "But it wasn't my fault." She felt herself avoiding hysteria because the whole event was so unreal. She flashed on a brutal future of courts and prison for the rest of her life.

"Think about where you were, what was going on there. Just think about it. How far do you think 'it was an accident' will travel? Even if they buy it, we're both in plenty of trouble. You want to hang around and find out how much? All we've got going for us right now is that nobody at the farm knows who we are . . . you didn't tell anyone your name?"

"Apparently you did that for me, since Jesse knew my name."

"Well, all he knows is our first names."

"And your bus and that you're a musician. This is major fucked, man." Now she did feel hysteria rising in her throat, starting to choke her.

Kevin parked the bus behind Victoria's house so it would not be easily visible from the street. "I'm going to Hawaii," Kevin blurted out when they went inside, "and you can go with me. You can't stay here whatever you decide to do, with me or not. I am not trying to shit you, Vicki."

"It's Victoria," she corrected him. "I can see you're serious." She sat on the end of the bed, crossed her legs and swung her foot back and forth. She took in the smoke from a joint and made a face holding it in. "Why Hawaii?" she asked as the smoke billowed back out, helping her to slow down.

"My brother lives there. He works for the Honolulu newspaper. It's a long way from here and a free place to crash."

"Um," Victoria muttered as she inhaled again and considered how the word Honolulu sounded. She said it out loud, pronouncing each syllable distinctively.

"I want you to take me seriously," Kevin said insistently. "Don't get stoned."

"I like it." She repeated the word. "Ho-no-lu-lu." Getting stoned was the only way she could dampen the fear and think about what she should do.

Kevin closed the duffel and latched it with a padlock. He sat next to Victoria on the end of the bed and put his arm around her. She lay her head on his shoulder and he let her put the joint to his lips.

"All right," Victoria said.

"All right?"

"Sure. All right."

"You'll go? It's not like we have a whole shit pot full of choices."

"I like the sound of Honolulu and I've never seen a real palm tree."

What she wanted was to disappear and to make the night so far into the bleak past that maybe it just never really happened at all. In a place so far away, she could begin her life again, become someone new, have a life that didn't make her feel crazy all the time.

"What about your bus?"

"It's not mine anyway. It belongs to this guy who loaned it to his friend who loaned it to me. Long as we clean out all of Bob's shit, we can just leave it abandoned at the airport. We can find someplace to dump that stuff on the way."

"To where?"

"Chicago. O'Hare. We can't leave it anywhere around here, for damn sure."

"It's a nice bus," Victoria said.

"Do you have any money? I mean, like on you?"

Victoria rose, pulled Kevin up, then lifted the corner of the mattress and removed a flat zippered notebook case. She put the case on the bed and unzipped it. "I have this," she announced.

"Shit! How much is that?"

"A couple of grand, a bit more, I guess."

"What are you doing keeping two thousand bucks under your mattress?"

"For when I need to make sudden, special purchases." She waved the joint around. She kept her money in cash because she was afraid that for some reason the bank might not let her have it when she wanted it.

"Far out. Looks like we'll be traveling in style."

She plopped Aunt Irene's one brown leather suitcase on the bed beside Kevin's duffel bag and threw in a bag of marijuana, summer clothes, a magazine for the airplane, and left the house without even locking the door.

TWENTY-SIX

Kevin's brother Keith lived in a single-wall-construction bungalow in a planned suburb of similar bungalows distinguished mostly by the different color paint on their ubiquitous window shutters, along winding fresh asphalt streets named for battles in the Pacific War: Tarawa, Iwo Jima, Guadalcanal, Wake. It wasn't far inland from Pearl Harbor. On relatively flat ground, the neighborhood bumped up against the steeply rising leeward slopes of the Koolau range, which took on a deep, rich purple hue at sunset. Keith lived with his wife Renee and three-month-old daughter Leilani on Tarawa Street. Because Leilani still slept in a crib in her parents' bedroom, Kevin and Victoria got an air mattress on the floor of what would eventually be Leilani's room, already painted tropical pink; Renee called the color lilikoi, Hawaiian for passion fruit juice. The wall separating the two bedrooms was just the thickness of two thin layers of sheetrock tacked to the framing and Leilani did not sleep well or long.

Keith wouldn't allow dope-smoking (or any other kind) in the house so they had to smoke in the backyard.

Kevin called the house a little box made of ticky-tacky, just a bourgeois tract house with a tract yard in a sad little tract suburb that could be anywhere, except for the view, the thick tropical odors, the air clinging to and stroking the skin. The yard was a nice place to sit and get stoned. There were two young palm trees and a new guava tree, a lemon tree, two huge banana plants; the yard glowed in the rich light sliding down sunset slopes. They sat at a white plastic patio table, making the embers from their cigarettes dance like fireflies in the dark. Sometimes they noticed Keith watching them through the kitchen jalousie windows, like an ersatz father. Kevin wanted to leave the day after they arrived, but they had no money for rent and he had no prospects for a gig. He told Victoria she should have sold her house, money like that could have staked him to get a demo tape made. Sure, Victoria told him, why didn't I put the house on the market and hang around until a buyer showed up? Kevin complained that Keith had lost the cool he had when they were kids and had become just another bourgeois lapdog of the system. He wondered if Victoria might be able to get a job, maybe wait tables, secretary somewhere, anything to get them out on their own. Victoria pointed out a full page of construction jobs in the Sunday *Honolulu Advertiser*. Kevin held up his hands and wiggled his fingers, saying that these were too valuable to get crushed digging ditches in the lava. We need to figure out some way you can safely sell that house, he insisted.

Victoria had not thought much about the house she left unlocked and dark in Warren, Iowa, more than a week ago. She had not considered that it had some value. It had not occurred to her that she could sell it. But what now? Kevin made it clear that they couldn't go back there and they couldn't let anyone know where they were. He was convinced he would go to prison for statutory rape; Victoria for worse, of course. "Don't you have some friend you trust enough to act for you selling the place?" Kevin proposed. "No," Victoria answered, and the fact of it made her feel sad.

"If the cops are really looking for you," Victoria explained, "don't you think they'll find out you have a brother and he lives in Honolulu? It's not, you know, like a foreign fucking country."

This possibility made Kevin crazy for most of a day, because now he expected every car coming down Tarawa Street was the police. He didn't like Hawaii as much as he thought he would anyway: hot, sweaty, people treating each other like they were in some private club, not much of it white, Japs everywhere. They should consider going somewhere else. Keith called his brother's complaining "rock fever." Kevin felt trapped and broke, having used all he had plus some of Victoria's on the plane tickets. He had to borrow from her for cigarettes, even.

Whatever happened in Iowa, it had not made the papers in Hawaii. Kevin looked every day for a week. He could hardly ask his brother to check at the newspaper office. He began to relax and started writing songs again.

Victoria slid easily into a new life in a new world. She loved everything about Hawaii that Kevin hated. It was the only foreign place she had ever seen and it only mattered that it was one of the United States because she didn't have to learn a new language or figure out the money. All the rest was foreign to her. Spending her life until then in Minnesota and Iowa, she had seen few people who weren't as white and slick as she was, as Kevin was, and within a day she wished her skin was the color of fine milk chocolate or polished Hawaiian wood rather than a colorless, creamy insignificance. She relished every smell, every sound, every sight; the enveloping humidity stroked her skin and made her feel postcoital between her legs. She adopted the deficiency of clothing style, most of the time barefoot or in flip-flops, wearing shorts, more or less covering her breasts with something like a wraparound bandana.

Kevin drastically disappointed her. He took it for granted that because she had sex with him that they were in some kind of relationship and he became proprietary. She would just as soon abandon the sex than have to feel like some guy's property. When she wanted to feel a sense of belonging with a man, she knew it would not be simply because they happened to screw. Besides, his continual crapping on Hawaii got on her nerves. Why couldn't Kevin be more like his brother Keith? Victoria liked Keith and Renee, envying their soft, comfortable, normal life together. That's what belonging looked like. She enjoyed playing with the baby and didn't mind helping out by babysitting so that Renee could go shopping or meet her friends when Keith was at work. Kevin had no interest in the baby; having babies is a bourgeois affectation in a population explosion, he said. He spent a lot of time in their bedroom, strumming his guitar and claiming he was writing new songs and he would borrow some money from his brother to get a demo tape made.

It lasted only two weeks. Until the night Keith asked Victoria if she'd like to go along with him to drop a story off at the newspaper office, suggesting she might enjoy seeing the sparkle of downtown Honolulu lights at night.

"Kevin, you want to go into the city?" she asked.

"Not especially."

"I do."

"Fine."

Kevin took his guitar and headed for the backyard with a joint in his hand.

"What about Renee?" Victoria asked Keith.

"Oh yeah," he laughed, "and leave Leilani with the doper?"

"Right."

They got into Keith's Ford Pinto and headed down the slope, past the ticky-tacky houses and into the noisy, blinking city. Victoria kept her face toward the window, watching the chaotic tropical nightlife. Without a car, she had been stuck in the suburban neighborhood except for the one time she and Kevin went on a picnic with Keith and Renee to a beach up north, where they watched surfers on waves as high as houses. After they turned away from the tourist area, the city seemed out of place, a kind of Des Moines with incongruous palm trees here and there. Keith's office was in a steel and glass high rise. Inside it was just another office. She waited by his desk while he stacked a pile of papers and put them into a plastic bag. The papers were brown, like a paper shopping bag. He introduced her to a coworker as "my brother's friend, staying with us a while." Victoria thought it looked like a boring place to spend much time, not what she expected from a newspaper office.

Keith offered to show her the view of Diamond Head at night from Ala Moana Park on the opposite end of Waikiki. He stopped the car on the point, where the smattering of hotels at the foot of Diamond Head twinkled against the darkness and Waikiki flashed like a multicolored neon python slithering along the shore. Victoria thought it was the most beautiful play of lights she had ever seen. It made her want to paint it. They talked a few minutes about how Keith ended up applying for and getting the newspaper job in Honolulu and he told her that he was a poet, but a poet with a family has to have some way to pay the bills. When she asked, he said he would show her some of his poetry, warning her that "I write rather epically, in the T. S. Eliot style." He put his arm across the top of the seat and touched her shoulder. They were already close in the small Pinto. She smiled politely, not surprised. It always happened eventually. He told her that it was not easy being able to hear them through the wall and to imagine what she looks like making love. "We hear Leilani," she said, thinking she ought to distract him with a dose of reality. Letting him do what he obviously wanted to do would only complicate an already complicated and uncomfortable situation. "That's because there's nothing else to hear lately," he complained, leaning closer to her and putting his hand now on the back of her neck. "I don't know about this, Keith," she said. "Are you worried about my idiot brother?" he supposed. "Don't." "And Renee?" Victoria wondered. Keith shook his head and stroked her neck and shoulder. Victoria stared at the brilliant lights of Waikiki, not yet sure how she wanted to deal with this. Keith slid closer to her and using his arm urged her closer. He reached across with his other hand and turned her face toward his. She let him have the kiss. Maybe a bit of this would be enough. He kissed her and opened her mouth with his tongue, his other hand slid over her shoulder and cupped her breast. She let him have that too for a moment. Then in the sudden, magical quickness that men knew, his hand had gone down the waistband of her shorts and already he had a finger inside her.

"Okay," she said, pulling his hand from her shorts and pushing him back a little. "I think that's enough, don't you?"

"You're kidding." He put his hand on her leg next to her crotch.

"I'm not kidding, Keith. Really."

He stiffened and looked shocked when she pushed his hand off her leg and leaned toward the door, away from him. "What kind of deal is this?" he whined.

"Oh, come on. You know this is dumb."

"I didn't take you for a cock tease."

"You can go fuck yourself!"

He reached out and cupped her breast while pulling her head closer with his other hand.

"I mean it!" Victoria cried.

When he tried to kiss her again, she said, "I'll slap you, I mean it. I'm a whole lot stronger than you probably think I am."

He jerked away from her and started the engine. They drove back to Tarawa Street in silence. In the driveway, Keith said, "You aren't going to say anything?"

"No. I just wish you wanted the life you have more than you seem to."

Keith shook his head as if her remark struck him as stupid, then followed her into the house.

An hour later, Kevin and Victoria had just started making love when they heard voices through the wall. "Sounds like a bit of a marital tiff," Kevin said, then went back to sucking the nipple on one of her breasts. The voices grew louder and the baby began to cry. They could hear everything quite clearly, Renee accusing Keith of being with someone, Renee crying that she could smell her on his hand. Fucking Christ, Victoria thought, the idiot didn't even wash his fucking hands. Kevin raised up on his elbows and looked at Victoria. "What is this?" he asked in an accusing tone.

"You fucked your brother's girlfriend," Renee screamed.

"I did not fuck anybody," Keith screamed back with the righteous authority of a technical fact.

"She leaves her smell all over the house, you think I don't know it? You think I'm that stupid?"

"If you think I fucked that little bitch, then yes, I think you're acting stupid."

"What the fuck!" Kevin said, raising up on his hands and knees.

"I want them out of here!" they heard Renee cry through the wall. "Her anyway."

"Did you fuck my fucking brother?" Kevin asked.

"No, I didn't fuck your fucking brother, which does not mean he wouldn't have welcomed the opportunity."

Kevin slapped her. Victoria jerked her knee up into his genitals and Kevin rolled onto the side of the bed clutching his crotch and moaning. The door burst open and Renee exploded into the room. "I want you to get out," Renee cried. "Now! Tonight! Right this minute!"

"I'll pack, if you don't mind. And you're wrong about what you think happened."

"I'm not a fool."

"Maybe. Believe what you want."

Keith appeared behind his wife and brushed past her. "Tell her I didn't fuck you," he said.

"He didn't fuck me," Victoria answered, already up from the bed and shoving her clothes back into the suitcase. "But he sure as shit wanted to."

"Goddamn liar!" Keith screamed.

"Just get out," Renee ordered, screaming but sobbing at the same time.

Kevin sat on the edge of the bed, still doubled over moaning. "That fucking hurt," he whined.

"So did this," Victoria said, touching her reddened cheek.

Victoria did not notice or consider that she was still naked. When her things were in the bag, she only then, as she started toward the door, realized she didn't have anything on. She took shorts, a top and flip flops from the bag and pulled them on, then shut the bag again. "Will one of you call a taxi?"

Renee shoved her way past her husband and went to the phone. Victoria could hear her making the call. "What are you doing?" Kevin said, getting up, also still naked.

"I never touched her," Keith said to Kevin. "I've never seen Renee fly off like this. It's nothing. Nothing happened." He shook his head somberly. "What kind of girl did you bring here?"

"Your taxi's coming," Renee said to Victoria as she went out the front door.

"Thank you," Victoria answered, and went into the street. She could still hear the raised voices from the house.

Just as the taxi pulled up, Kevin and Keith tumbled through the door, fighting. "Go, go," Victoria ordered, and the taxi pulled away. She glanced back and saw Renee tugging at her husband, who was sitting on his brother's chest.

"Go where?" the driver asked.

"I guess, the airport."

"International or domestic?"

The taxi turned onto the highway and after thinking about it for a minute, during which the driver repeated the question, she answered, "What's your favorite place in Hawaii?"

"Um, me, maybe I say Kona. Got the best fishing."

"Domestic terminal," she said, from where she would fly to Kona and into Morgan Cary's life.

TWENTY-SEVEN

She had thought Honolulu was Hawaii, but now realized it was not. Honolulu was Des Moines with palm trees. This, she exclaimed to herself, is Hawaii! The Kona airport terminal was like some East Indies Quonset hut in a Conrad book and even while still on the tarmac, across which she found her meandering way with the other Aloha passengers, moist warm scents from the tropical sea and jungle flora floated through the night. She asked a taxi driver if he knew an affordable hotel. It doesn't have to be nice, she added. He suggested that she could stay at his place; she declined politely and smiled. He was quite plump and told funny jokes and wore a brilliant shirt stretched over his basketball belly. Maybe in her past life the old Victoria would have simply gone with him, but this was the new Victoria in this new and amazing place. She got into the front seat of the taxi and leaned her head out of the open window. Wind tangled and tied knots in her hair. Tall bamboo pole torches glittered along the Kailua sea wall from the pier to the old royal summer palace, fishing boats moored in the bay were noted by swaying anchor lights. She commented on the odd name of a bamboo-walled bar with a tin roof across from the shadowed pier—Red Pants. Don't go there, the driver told her. "Rough place for one pretty wahine." He didn't know why it was called red pants when she asked.

He took her to the Sunset Lanai and told her to be sure to have the papaya pancakes for breakfast. "You say to da reception, Kimo he brung you. Okay dat?" On the drive to town she had not always understood what he said, as if the English he used was his own personal version. It made her feel more deliciously foreign. The Sunset Lanai resembled a small-town motel in Iowa, except no Iowa motel would paint its cinder-block walls a crispy black and no Iowa motel would be fifty yards from the Pacific Ocean and have palm trees lining the driveway. The next day she would figure out, after hopping along the lava rocks in the tiny bay across the road, that the black cinder blocks were meant to resemble lava. Lava! From a volcano! Far fucking out, she thought. It was all outrageous and wonderful. She stood on a big rock with the Pacific Ocean swirling around and touched her bare heels together in a clicking motion, you're not in Iowa anymore, she announced to the preposterously blue sea.

She had a job before the end of the following day, waitress at an expensive restaurant called Huggo's, which happened to be barely a hundred yards from the Sunset Lanai. Maybe she could have found something else, something better than being a waitress, but she didn't worry about this. She had been there only two days and already had an income. She had a uniform, a scoop-neck Hawaiian print peasant blouse and bright white linen slacks. Huggo's was a nice place and even though the pay was hardly minimum wage, the manager said she could count on her share of the tip pool to at the very least triple her salary and what she declared to the tax man was her business. She thought it precariously amazing and beautiful how the restaurant extended far out over the swirling white water; at night, illuminated by spotlights, an astonishing array of wildly colored fish and spiny red urchins surged with the swell of the sea over the black rocks.

She needed to find a place to live and Huggo's manager gave her two leads; she took the first. It was a just a short walk from the restaurant and since it was essentially just one big, cinder-block, rectangular room, it was cheap enough to afford from her salary alone, not counting any tips. Anyhow, she still had most of the cash from Iowa. The apartment came basically furnished. The long room was divided by a sliding shoji door to create a bedroom, where there was a double bed, a pair of wicker night tables with reading lamps, a tan woven jute rug at the foot of the bed, and a framed print from an old Hawaiian calendar on the wall. A wicker three-cushion sofa, matching wicker chair, floor lamp, round glass coffee table in a wicker frame, and another framed Hawaiian calendar print filled the space in front. A galley kitchen ran along the opposite wall; squeezed against the front corner, by a small window, was a Formica table with two plastic chairs. The bathroom was as narrow as a hall closet and had a sink, toilet, and shower stall in a row. No window, but there was a shiny aluminum palm tree on the long wall reflecting light from the sliding glass shower door in the morning. She bought a cheap, colorful rug for the living room, three squat potted palms, and a young bamboo plant. Out front there was only a narrow, long driveway, but the bedroom window overlooked a garden and an impenetrable wall of tropical plants and trees beyond that, just marred by a single strand electrical wire drooping between creosote poles.

Her neighbors were a gardener and his wife, a sushi chef, and the night desk clerk at the Kona Inn, who was gay. They all found themselves in love with Victoria and took great pleasure in teaching her the things dearest to them: Mr. Nakamura gave her bonsai lessons and Mrs. Nakamura taught her flower arranging; Mr. Sato helped her learn to choose fish for sashimi and showed her how to prepare sticky rice for sushi; Dale Messner, who called her Sweet Victoria, offered tai chi lessons in the backyard and fell in love with her, spiritually, and taught her the degrees of gayness.

Victoria was young, healthy, inquiring, and dangerously beautiful. She liked men, she liked their touches, their smells and tastes. She couldn't live without their praises, without their explicit attention, even if sometimes she hated them for giving her so easily what she wished she didn't need so much. Then she would suddenly feel disgusted with herself and disappear; she made her way to the pali above Keahou Bay where she would sit for hours with her arms locked around her knees, watching the fishing boats passing along the five-hundred-fathom ledge, or sometimes lie undisturbed on the black lava rock ledge at the City of Refuge, where waves broke soft and white at her feet and the salt-laden trade wind cooled her tanned skin. After a day alone, she could return to her life at Huggo's and with her neighbors.

She thought it odd how little Iowa now meant to her now, how little time she spent thinking or wondering about it: about college, her house, people she had known, the bad things. Maybe it was stupid to walk away from whatever value there was in the house, but what could she do? Kevin's skinny girl might be dead and Victoria did not want to be caught up in such a thing. She decided to be reborn here. Not that silly religious kind of notion, but something more important, something about this life, her life, as lived, starting fresh and new from right here and right now without memories.

She saw Tioni Brown her first night waiting tables at Huggo's. He was by himself at the bar, drinking a Primo beer, so she did not serve him. The manager had assigned her to serve the best tables in section A along the low open wall overlooking the bay and down to the lighted fish show below. He gave her this section even after she turned down his offer to walk her home after work; maybe he found hope in the way she smiled and looked into his eyes even while saying no. Tioni's skin was the exact color of a Hershey's milk chocolate bar and she wondered what it might

be like to lick him. But she did not go out with him until he had assumed
a regular place at the bar and watched her politely and without approach
for two weeks. Nearly every man in Huggo's tried to pick her up, but none
were polite enough and she only flirted with them for tips. The owner of
Kona's largest construction company tipped her fifty percent, but another
waitress warned her that he was married and had a bad temper. This was
how it would be in her new life. She wouldn't go out with just anyone
because she was bored or lonely. She was learning how not to be lonely
when alone with herself, she was learning the interesting difference between solitude and loneliness and had begun to rather enjoy solitude. She
had her neighbors, who were friendly and inclusive, but gave her solitary space, as well. The Japanese couple who lived at the other end of her
building took her under their wing and began educating her in the life of
islanders. Victoria spent the late quiet evenings after work lying on her
sofa with the radio on, dreaming about the possibilities of this hoped-for
new life into which she didn't allow her past.

After his two politely patient weeks, Tioni waited for her until closing. She liked his name and his skin and his bright brown eyes, especially
his patient, almost embarrassed way of glancing at her when he thought she
didn't notice. She said he could walk her home and along the way she happened to wonder if maybe he knew where she might be able to buy some of
that famous Hawaiian marijuana? He said, ain't no beeg thing, smiling like
he had won the lottery. The next night she had off and agreed to an afternoon date with Tioni. He wanted to take her snorkeling at Keahou Bay.
He brought mask, snorkel, and fins for her, along with a dime bag for which
he adamantly refused payment. She let him kiss her and he was pretty good
at it, tasting like a sweet lemon. He told her that he ate half a lemon every
morning for what he called his fish breath. He brought up a red spiny sea
urchin and showed her how ancient Hawaiian women used the spines for
cosmetic decoration; the red from the spines did not show up well against
his darker skin, but it was as bright as pink lipstick on hers. They lay on the

rocks by the water and let the sun dry them. Impulsively she licked his cheek and he tasted more like sea salt than milk chocolate.

She believed, because of the way Tioni acted from then on, that he probably fell in love with her when she licked him, if not before. She sort of loved him a little because he was so polite and respectful and treated her like a treasure. He was cute and so not full of himself. The pidgin-flavored English he spoke made her feel like she was in an exotic land, as foreign from her past as anything could be. She expected him to ask her to marry him and could not decide how she would respond if he indeed did. She thought about it during her quiet nights on the sofa, with the radio and the dreams, but wondered what they would talk about over time? This was a problem. It was also a problem that she thought love ought to feel more overpowering, more . . . desperate?

Tioni worked the charter boats. There were a lot of sport fishing boats in Kona, since it had a significant reputation among big game sport fishermen around the world. He liked to talk about big fish and boats. That seemed to exhaust the list of things that interested him, besides Victoria, who interested him very much. Because he worked days, his nights were always free to meet her after work. After they started sleeping together, they went directly from Huggo's to her apartment and sometimes, although not every time, Tioni stayed over, slipping carefully from her bed before the sun rose so he could get to the harbor and bring the boat in before his captain arrived with their charter group. Victoria slept soundly and did not awaken much before noon. Tioni was trying to survive on just three or four hours' sleep the nights he spent with her.

Victoria spent the afternoons exploring Kailua and the Kona side of the island. She didn't have a car and there was no bus service, but she had no trouble hitching rides when she wanted to see what was higher on the mountainside or further down the coast. Not much, she decided: mainly a few widely scattered villages even smaller than tiny Kailua, which the taxi driver had told her had a population of about six hundred, not counting a thousand or so tourists on any particular day. There were Haight-Ashbury—reject hippies living in some sort of colony in the jungle near the village of Captain Cook and on the beach at Keahou, and many of the rides she got were from hippies in VW buses, Army surplus Jeeps, and on motor scooters. They freely shared their joints with her and sometimes offered to share their freethinking sexual adventures. Victoria always took the joint but not the other stuff; she wanted to see what it was like to be faithful to the man she was with. She was rather proud of herself because of this, because she had never managed to do this with any success before. Other interesting items were on offer, frequently an invitation to share a few tabs of acid inside one of the surplus parachutes used for shelter at Keahou, but Victoria had sworn off acidheads forever. She was not tempted by the free-spirit lifestyle of Kona's hippie community; many did not often bathe and the women did not always shave under their arms or their legs and Victoria didn't like that, she thought it was ugly. Not to mention she was sick of hearing "like wow, man," used in every sentence.

One day in the rain Tioni took Victoria to meet his boss and his friend, the captain of the sport fishing boat Dolphin.

There was no explanation for what happened to Victoria that day. She had seen in his eyes the moment Morgan fell in love with her; she had seen it before, she had already seen it in Tioni's eyes. What was different this time? Victoria was ready for Morgan, or someone like him. It just happened to be him standing there falling in love with her when she was ready, although Victoria did not know it was Morgan she was ready for until she realized that she was thinking about him even when Tioni was making love to her, and then for sure, when Tioni said, Morgan is the most honest, stable, and dependable man I ever known; you can trust that man with your life. And that is exactly what Victoria needed: a man to trust with her life. Falling in love with him was easy after she opened that long-locked door.

PART THREE

MORGAN *and* VICTORIA

[*California 1971–1980*]

TWENTY-EIGHT

Before they left Hawaii on the day they married, Morgan was accepted into the English doctoral program at the only one of the six universities he applied to that responded favorably. They rented a one-bedroom duplex bungalow a few blocks from campus. Victoria took a part-time job as a checkout cashier in a grocery store. Morgan found an evening job cleaning a community college's gymnasium and field house. They set up housekeeping and worked on being perfectly married, perfectly like everyone else, moving toward a tandem vision of a perfect future, or, as Morgan said only to tease her, sailing safe and stable in the unstable currents of connubial life.

Morgan enjoyed cleaning at the community college because it was solitary, quiet work requiring little mental activity, leaving him free to study. It didn't bother him to clean toilets and mop floors and empty trash. Most of the time he rode in diminishing loops around the basketball court on a small tractor outfitted with scrubbing brushes. He was able to read and drive at the same time. The reading lists were overwhelming, and reading while working was the only way he could hope to keep up. He liked riding around on the tractor more than he liked going to classes.

Just a month passed before Morgan began to regret moving to California, especially the decision to work on a PhD in English. He believed that his classmates were snobs and felt as if the coursework was designed for snobs. How could graduate school be so different from college? As an undergraduate, he read literature because it was good in itself, because it expanded experience, because . . . well, because life was just emptier without those truer than real worlds. Now he felt that they were being asked to think about literature another way: something that needed to begin with a capital L, a subject, an entity unto itself; even worse, a product resulting from a process of production that could be deconstructed, reconstructed, valued, devalued, revalued, and made lifeless after the academic process of analysis had its way. He did not enjoy this; he barely understood it.

This was not a popular attitude among his teachers, who conjectured among themselves that Morgan Cary was the snob, a not appropriately educated Hawaiian beach boy whom they had admitted under the weight of his excellent academic record and the brilliant essay he submitted. Between the paper version of Morgan Cary and the real thing in their classrooms, they bemoaned a major disconnect.

The rented bungalow was spare. Their living-room furniture consisted of a sofa and a chair and a pair of floor lamps from a Goodwill shop. They ate at a card table with a pair of folding chairs, below a small kitchen window from which they could see a wildly purple and desperately messy jacaranda tree. The bed was a mattress on the floor and the reading lamp sat on a stack of books. Their art consisted solely of a pictorial calendar of Hawaiian waterfalls and a thumbtacked poster of the previous year's annual Hawaiian International Billfish Tournament. His work space was a table made from a closet door across a pair of construction sawhorses appropriated from a building site two blocks away, and angled in a corner of the living room so there was a window at each end. He had a typewriter, a Royal manual bought used at the university book store, but he didn't like it, and he couldn't type as fast with two fingers as he could think with a pencil in his hand. He had always written everything in spiral-bound notebooks, including the stack of journals he'd kept for years. Victoria without complaint typed his class assignments. She typed as fast as a secretary and told him that touch typing was her favorite high school class. "The functionality just made a lot of sense to me," she said. Besides the little red typewriter, he lined up along the back of the worktable his textbooks, a glass of pencils, and a framed picture of Victoria in a bikini on the Kailua pier. Every day Victoria put a fresh flower (picked from the garden of the tenant sharing the bungalow) in a Coke bottle on the window ledge in the corner. She kissed the flower before putting it into the bottle, he had seen her do it. From that window he could see the quiet street in front, Cambridge Street, which Victoria thought prophetic; she told him she had married the finest English-literature scholar in America and of course he would be offered a job at Harvard and they would live in Cambridge. He wasn't sure she was exactly joking. Indian Hills Boulevard, a four-lane highway, part of Route 66, made its roaring way along the other side. At night they lay in bed forced to listen to the unrelenting rumble of passing cars and trucks instead of the soft moan of the moon sliding through the clouds and the dripping of rare winter rain from the roof into transient puddles.

Morgan had been isolated from the cultural and social shifts occurring on the mainland during the previous half-dozen years. He had lived most of his life on an island in the middle of the ocean, leaving him both incredulous and naive about their new life in California; psychedelic flower power music, protest banners strung everywhere on campus, the prevalence of drugs and their signifiers in the burned-out faces of his often-stoned classmates, wildly patterned mismatched clothes, scruffy wild hair and Jesus beards, girls wearing granny dresses with combat boots and their breasts roaming free, even the new, private language of the young, all made him feel like he was an outsider. Twenty or thirty derelict hippies camping out around Keahou Bay had not prepared him for Southern California in 1971, although Victoria hardly seemed to notice what he found astonishing and perplexing.

They bought a car, a rusting Ford Maverick found for sale on a notice board at the university library. It was some version of yellow and Morgan said it looked like a baby puked over it. Victoria asked how he might know what a baby's puke looked like, but Morgan let it slide. Morgan didn't much like cars and this was the first one he had owned. He only got a driver's license so he could pick up charter fishing customers from their hotels using the company's truck. He had never even driven on a highway.

The L.A. basin smog was usually so thick that they had lived there for almost three months, it was Thanksgiving weekend, before seeing Mt. Baldy, barely a dozen miles to the north. Their first sighting showed a dusting of snow on the summit and Morgan wanted to drive up to see it. Before they had gone five miles, the Maverick lurched to a stop on the highway and they had to get it towed to a garage. It was the fuel pump. The tow truck driver drove them home. Victoria had to sit squashed between them and Morgan was annoyed by the way the driver kept his leg tight against Victoria's, especially how Victoria seemed to just accept it. The Hispanic driver could have been, as far as Victoria was concerned, a sack lunch or a seat cushion. But when his hand dropped to her thigh, Victoria lifted it like a dirty rag and dropped it into his own lap, whispering almost sensuously, "Do that again and my husband will feed you your balls like a pair of Hershey's kisses." Both Morgan and the driver laughed and everything was okay. *My husband*, Morgan repeated to himself and smiled, impossibly happy with the world and everything and everyone in it.

Morgan trusted Victoria. He had not considered otherwise. Trust was subsumed within the marrow of his love for her. He was not anyway inclined to be jealous. Not because he was confident, necessarily. It was because he had learned to suppress feelings that frightened him. Not once had he thought that if Victoria left Tioni for him, she could leave him for someone else.

Their first Christmas together they were invited to a party in a student apartment. One of the roommates was in the English doctoral program with Morgan, the other studied ancient languages. Some thirty students were crammed into the two-room apartment, where they displayed the usual pretensions of graduate students, producing an atmosphere like a savannah over which roamed and grazed a large pride of scholastic lions, anxiously prowling for something to drink, something to debate, something to fuck. Dixieland jazz was an odd accompaniment to a Christmas party, but Morgan liked it. Perfume from a dozen scented candles and the stale odor of beer cloyed the room. A fat plastic Santa stuck perched atop a beer keg, a candy cane jar containing instead ready-rolled marijuana joints, and a tall student wearing a red and white elf cap topped with a tinkling bell, were the only signifiers of the season. From time to time the elf could be heard over the jazz from the stereo singing: ho, ho, ho. Smoke lay across the middle of the room like a swamp fog and the elf cap floated along and above the haze like a cruising shark's fin.

Morgan found himself with the ancient languages roommate, mainly because she had focused her attention on him, although he kept forgetting her name and at various times called her Cindy, Sarah, or Susie. Each time she reminded him it was Annie, like Annie Greensprings wine, she always added. She had coaxed him into the kitchen where they stood by the sink, occasionally having to move aside so something could be rinsed or recovered or dumped out. People jostled them with automatic empty apologies. A large red flag with a white peace symbol in the center, mimicking a red cross flag, covered the kitchen window behind them. A white peace dove flew along on a sky blue flag draped across one of the living-room windows. A photo poster on the kitchen wall depicted a war protest march with hecklers lining the route and one redneck in a Bud cap offering his middle finger salute to the nearest hippie, a balloon caption above his head stating: "Peace on you too, brother." Morgan's favorite was the poster of an all-girl, all-nude, bike race.

"What might one do with a degree in dead languages?" Morgan asked.

"My parents are stinking, filthy, obscenely, righteously rich," she answered with a bored sort of smile, "so I can do whatever pleases me. It's *ancient* languages, by the way."

"Fortunate birth," Morgan said.

"No fucking shit, Sherlock."

"Do you actually like *ancient* Greek and Latin?"

"I like puzzles. Languages are like puzzles that finally become clear when you get the pieces all where they're supposed to fit."

"What can you say for me?"

"In which tongue?" She seemed to wink without moving her eyelids.

"How many do you have?"

"So far, only Greek and Latin, but I'm adding Sanskrit next semester."

"Greek, then."

She said something that might or might not have been Greek, since he wouldn't have been able to know either way.

"Meaning?"

"Do you like sex?"

"Interesting choice of phrase."

"Just testing you."

"Did I pass?"

"Don't know yet. It's early." That bored smile again, and Morgan wondered if he bored her, why did she stay?

Morgan deliberately reminded himself that he was married, because for a moment he felt like Victoria had receded too far to protect him from this obvious seduction. "My wife also has a talented tongue," he announced, intending to bring his wife back into this competition.

"Linguistically or sexually?"

"She can tie a knot in a cherry stem using only her tongue."

"Far fucking out. I am impressed. Is that why you married her?"

"Well, she didn't show me that trick until after we were married."

"Guess she wanted to know if you wanted her for more than her talented tongue. Your wife is the gorgeous one you came in with, right?"

He nodded and said, "She is gorgeous and we did come in together."

"I hate her! Your wife intimidates me. Let's not talk about her."

"What does that mean?"

"As long as there are women in the world who look like your wife, all the men like you are never going to be interested in someone like me. I'm just smart. That's not enough if your boobs look like eggs sunny side up. Not like those delicious melons on your wife's chest."

Morgan laughed; he had noticed she was flat-chested. "So is she," he said.

"You mean that astonishing cleavage is fake? There is a god."

"No, I don't mean that; she's very real. I meant that she's also smart."

"I hate this conversation. Please change the subject. You two are like something from a fucking magazine, man."

"Want another beer?"

"Of course. It's Christmas. Santa's going to pass by my chimney this year anyway."

"Not a good girl, huh?"

"I'm only good when I'm being bad."

"Guess that means you go everywhere," Morgan joked and she laughed.

He excused himself and went off to get the beers, but really to look for Victoria. He felt guilty over the erotic intimacy of his conversation with the ancient-languages student. He scanned the room on his way to the keg and didn't see her. He put the empty cups on the table by the keg and made his way into the other room, the bedroom, and didn't see her there, either. Nor was she on the balcony or the stairwell landing. He couldn't believe that she had just gone home by herself without saying anything to him. He was a little angry. He didn't want to leave the party yet, although it would be childish to stay just to punish her. He went back to the keg and refilled their cups, then went back to the kitchen and the waiting whatever-her-name-is. He supposed he could have sex with her and some part of his instinctual male core wondered what it might be like. He looked at his watch, timing just how long it might take to properly punish Victoria for leaving without telling him.

But what if something happened to her? What if she didn't just leave? What if she had been kidnapped? What if she got hit by a car? What if she were a Jane Doe in the morgue?

"Are you fucking stoned?" Annie asked.

"I'm sorry?"

"Hello, hello!" She waved her hand in front of his eyes. "Ground control to Major Tom."

"I need to go," Morgan said.

"Chasing your too-fucking-gorgeous wife?"

"Did you see her leave?"

Annie nodded. She took her time draining the cup of beer and handed the empty to him. Morgan stared at it as if she had put a piece of trash in his hand.

"She left alone, if that's what's bothering you, dude. Although who can say what happened when she got outside, if you know what I mean."

"I better go anyway," Morgan said, handing back Annie's empty cup along with his still full one.

"I have to admit," Annie said, "that were I of the Sapphic persuasion, I'd probably get a candy ass over a woman like that, too."

"Thanks for the Greek lesson," Morgan said and turned away.

She shook her head and shrugged as if it was nothing. He glanced back at her when he got to the door and she was already lost in the crowd.

It took only fifteen minutes to walk back to the bungalow. Seeing lights through the windows diminished some of his anxiety. When he reached the yard, he saw piles of clothing outside the door, shoes scattered across their small yard. His shoes. His clothes.

Both the front and side doors were locked with both the key and the slide bolt, so his keys were useless. He could feel anger rising because he knew he hadn't done anything to deserve this. It was almost midnight and he wasn't going to stay in the yard and make a fool of himself by shouting or banging on the door, like a bit-part player in a soap opera cliché. She had pulled the curtains so he couldn't see inside. So maybe he should just go back to the party, maybe he should do something so he wasn't being treated like this for nothing. Maybe he should just fuck Sarah or Susie or whatever the hell her name was. Of course not, but he also wasn't going to give Victoria the satisfaction of banging on the door and pleading to be let into his own damn house.

He stood in the yard looking up at the clear sky and the few stars not blotted out by the nuclear glow of Los Angeles. There was a Turkish moon. It was chilly and he was glad he'd worn a jacket.

He retrieved his shoes and lined them up in matched pairs near the front door, then began picking up his clothes. What else could he do? He folded the shirts and stacked them by the shoes, then his slacks and jeans. He scavenged around the yard, using the glow from the street lamp on the corner to gather socks and underwear. He found his only belt and his only tie. She had pitched it all. He guessed this would eventually end in some sort of fight, some stupid shouting, probably, then they'd just laugh it off and make love. She had never done anything like this before. He had no model for it. He realized that he should not have left her alone in that mob of people with whom she had nothing in common. It was rude. Of course he should never have been stupid enough to flirt so flagrantly with what's her name. He could see that all this was his fault and he should just apologize and love her a little extra to put an end to his silly episode.

What now? Standing in the yard with his clothes and shoes stacked up by the front door, some cars slowed to look at him, maybe someone called the police, for Chrissakes! But he was no longer angry because it was his own dickhead fault.

Then he remembered that the little window in the bathroom had a broken lock. He had meant to fix it because the bushes below that window could easily disguise a burglar. It was small, but he thought he could squeeze through. If somebody had called the police, he hoped they wouldn't show up while he was climbing through the window and shoot him on top of everything else.

He made some noise with his feet pushing against the wall as he climbed through the window and then fell head-first into the tub, with his arms out to catch himself. He could hear loud music from the bedroom, from the clock radio, a Joni Mitchell song. He got up and stepped out of the tub. The medicine cabinet door was open and he noticed his Gillette razor, the top open, laying incongruously on the side of the tub. She had never before used his razor to shave her legs. Quietly, he went into the short hall and leaned forward to see into the bedroom; Victoria on the floor, leaning back against the mattress, her legs bent at the knees with a notebook stuck between her legs and chest, her arms wrapped around her knees as if protecting something, the reading lamp on the floor, books scattered around. The beer case where he kept his private journal and the three fat spiral notebooks that held the novel he had finished more than a year ago was on its side and empty. The notebook Victoria clutched was one of those.

Coming into the room, he called her name. She clenched her arms more tightly around the notebook and looked at him.

"What is this?" she asked, indicating the notebook.

"Stuff I kind of . . . where I wrote down some of my thoughts. Why are my clothes outside?"

Had she been crying? Her face so flushed and puffy.

"This one is not like the others. This one is a story. I want to read all of it."

Not like the others? Had she been secretly reading his journals?

"I guess there's no reason you couldn't. There's nothing in it I would hide from you. I just didn't . . . well, I just didn't think anyone would . . . frankly, I guess I was embarrassed."

"I'm sorry about your clothes. And I hope you will forgive me for violating your privacy." Victoria got up and placed the notebook proprietarily on her pillow. "Let me get your clothes. I am so sorry."

"No, that's okay. I'll get them."

"We'll get them together. Oh, Morgan, please let's do everything in the world we ever do together. Always together, only together."

"Deal."

She kissed him quickly on the cheek and then hugged him tightly. She took his hand and they went to bring his clothes back inside.

"I'll do it," she insisted, beginning to hang his clothes back in the closet.

Morgan picked up the scattered books. "I don't suppose I need to ask why," he said, "but I need you to know, to completely believe, that is, that nothing at all happened there, nothing at all like that will ever happen. I want you to believe me, Victoria."

He could see that she was crying as she put one of his shirts back on its hanger. He walked over and placed his hands firmly on her shoulders, but she refused to turn. "I was so scared," she said. Her shoulders quivered under the palms of his hands. "But it was for nothing," he answered. "I love you, Victoria. Only you, always only you." "Really?" "Of course, really. Really and always." She turned and let him hold her. He felt her trembling.

She spoke softly with her lips close to his ear. "I love you more than you love me." He started to speak but she shushed him. "No." She put her hands on the back of his head. "When we started, you loved me more and more truly . . . yes, I'm right and you know it. I loved you then, I did, of course. You know that. But not like now. Now I love you more. I think I always will, you could not, no one could, love anybody more than this."

"It's not a contest."

"I know. It's a fact. I wanted you to know this fact. You have more power over me than any god ever could."

"Whether or not I do, power is not something I think about when I think about us, it's not something I would ever abuse. Believe me."

He could feel her tears against his neck and shoulder. "Don't cry," he kissed her hair. "I hate to cry," she said. "It's just so stupid." Morgan stroked her face with his fingertips. "Please promise that you will never leave me," Victoria pleaded.

"That's the easiest promise in the world to make and to keep," he told her.

When later he went into the bathroom to wash himself, he saw his razor again. He picked it up and screwed closed the top, the blade still inside. He did not allow himself to think about it any further and put it back into the medicine cabinet. In spite of that, he subconsciously let his eyes scan the pill vials, checking to see none were empty. Later he checked the speed and downers hidden in a tin in the kitchen cabinet.

TWENTY-NINE

Morgan had written a short novel without any idea what he might do with it, except put it away with all the other notebooks, his journals, where he had written about and wondered about the content of his days since his sixteenth year. He had kept all of them, eleven in all, not counting the three that held the novel. The novel, if that's what it was, he wasn't sure, came out of a dream so intense that he had awakened from it sweat-soaked and gasping. He drowned, watched himself inhale sea water when the demand to breathe conquered the will to live. At the moment of his death, encapsulated in an eternally blue sea, he sensed that he had accomplished an awareness of the entirety of his life and to have seen everything that both was and, especially, would never be. The novel he wrote over the course of a single year took place entirely during the last seventy seconds in the life of a drowning man. Morgan knew this character's life story as well as he knew his own; he had seen it revealed in the dream. He didn't know why he thought to write a novel nor what he could possibly do with it, except to assuage the compulsion to tell this man's story. The three spiral-bound notebooks went into the box with all the journals and he never looked at it again until Victoria had pulled it out of his stash.

Victoria said it must be published. She was going to type it. But she wanted to know, "Is the main character dead? I mean, was he always dead, the whole time?"

He had not given the narrator a name. "Did you think he was dead from the start?"

"I didn't know for sure. He could have been. Isn't it possible that he was always dead?"

"That's a bit too much magical realism for me."

"So then, the whole story takes place in his mind during those few seconds when he's drowning?"

"Well, that's what I intended. It is more than a few seconds, though. I think it's about a minute and a half."

She laughed. "It's not a criticism. I think it could work either way; it's all in his mind, or it's not. I don't think you should tell the reader what to believe about it. Ironic, though, that the massive guilt he carried was not his true burden, really. Imagine the arguments your readers are going to have. He's dead and the story is about him, an omniscient narrator, kind of, or no, it's what went through his mind during the last seconds of his life. It could even be a dream. He could still be alive, or he could have been dead all along."

"I don't know if it was his true guilt to carry, or not, but I suppose it is ironic if it isn't. What would it mean to suffer as much as he does from a guilt that does not belong to you? But I didn't mean it to be a dream. For me, it's what went through his mind during the last minute of his life. Maybe I should fix that, make it more clear."

Cradling the notebooks against her chest as if protecting a baby from attack, she screamed: "Don't you fucking touch this! Not one fucking word!"

"All right, all right." Morgan smiled and put his arms around her, the notebooks compressed between them. He loved her more for this affirmation, even though there wasn't a chance a strange and obtuse piece of writing like this would be published.

Victoria typed the manuscript with two carbon copies on the Royal manual she had moved to the card table where they usually ate their meals, forcing them for the duration of the month it took to type what turned out to be three-hundred-twenty pages to eat on the floor, their backs against the sofa. It's just an extended picnic, she proclaimed. She typed after coming home from her cashier's job and while Morgan was at his night job cleaning the gym. She corrected misspelled words but nothing else, including what she thought were punctuation mistakes, but maybe he did that on purpose, maybe that was part of the creativity of the way he wrote.

It was during this period that Morgan realized he would not survive the doctoral program in English. He thought getting his union card and finding a teaching job at some university was the life Victoria imagined for them and he put off telling her that he probably wasn't going to make it. He figured out that with a year of course work and a thesis he could take a master's, so the move, the money, the time wouldn't have all been wasted. He talked about this option with his department chairman and without telling Victoria made the decision to take the master's and then opt out after that. The manuscript Victoria was now typing would be offered as his thesis. She provided the title that would stick: *Decompression*.

During that year, Victoria made a list of the names and addresses of likely publishers from a book in the university library. The preface of that book warned the novice author to cultivate superhuman patience and to be aware that rejections should be seen as common and not necessarily reflective of the quality of any particular manuscript; rather, to understand that timing and luck were the real criteria involved in getting published.

But when the first rejection letter came, in spite of two long paragraphs of compliments about both the writer's talent and the "profoundly artistic vision" of the story, Victoria said she was going to New York and "beat the holy shit out of that stupid bitch." That was only the first. That year would come a second, a third, a fourth, a fifth, sixth, seventh, and eighth rejection; mostly complimentary, some apologetic that they were forced to turn down such a beautiful and artistic piece of work simply because they did not know its market or because it was not the kind of novel published by their house. One sent only a form-printed postcard and Victoria was sure they hadn't even bothered to read it. She said she was going to go to New York and dynamite their building.

One evening in the library, while she went through the *Writers' Market* making a new list of publishers she had not yet tried, she noticed a student reading a newspaper page on a screen. It was the front page of the *New York Times* dated three years earlier.

"Excuse me," she said.

The boy turned and looked at her standing above him with a there-is-a-god look on his face.

"How does this work? If you don't mind my asking. You can read old newspapers from anywhere on that machine?"

"It's a microfilm reader. You can read all sorts of things with it, including the *New York Times* archives."

"How far back does it go?"

"Pretty far, I guess. It depends. Do you want to give it a try?"

"Can you show me how?"

"Not a problemo." He reached over and dragged the next chair close to his and Victoria sat down. He focused on her cleavage, but that was all right. She was used to it. "So?" she got his attention back to the reader. "What do you want to find?"

"Is the *Des Moines Register* in here?"

"Hey, that's interesting. I knew this girl once from Des Moines. Never mind. It's not very interesting anyway." It was evident where his current interest resided. "This roll is just the *Times*. We'll have to check the microfilm index to see if they have your newspaper here."

"Can we do that?"

She followed him to the librarian's desk and he asked if they had the *Des Moines Register* on microfilm. They did. The librarian brusquely pointed out that they had the major newspaper from the capital city of every state in the union. He took the film roll and they returned to the reader. He fiddled with the machine, scrolling quickly through pages, so fast she couldn't read any of it, just a black and white blur. Then he slowed down. "What date are you looking for?"

"Could you try the last week of October 1970? The twenty-fifth or twenty-sixth."

There it was. She didn't want to call attention to the article in front of this guy for what she feared finding in it, even if he didn't know her name. She had watched how he brought up the page and she could do this herself later. Maybe she should think about whether or not she wanted to do this at all. She thanked him and stood. Rewarding his helpfulness, when picking up her book, she bent over the table in such a way to enable him to see more of the part of her that so distracted him. "Are you a writer?" he asked, noticing the book title. "Oh no," she answered, now covering her cleavage with the book, "my husband is."

"Of course," he muttered, shrugging with profound disappointment.

She thanked him again and returned the writers' market reference book to the shelf.

It took her a long time to fall asleep that night. Morgan fidgeted in his sleep beside her. She liked the feeling of him moving in bed because it made his presence beside her real. He had kicked off the sheet and she lay on her side looking at the curves of his body, white in the dim glow sliding through the blinds from the street lamp. He looked so vulnerable asleep. His penis lay in the configuration of its more utilitarian purpose. His belly moving slightly with each slow, shallow breath. She wanted to protect him. The brutal scar on his leg, less raised and red now, someday to be almost lost in the rest of the skin, a slight discolored tarnish, not a morbid focus, still frightened her. She only looked at the scar when Morgan was asleep, and that was the only time she allowed herself to think about it: he had come out to save her when she went too far and was stupid, he had taken a shark for her, she knew he would die for her. She wanted to cry, she loved him so furiously, so desperately.

Would she return to the library and search for that story? She had glimpsed the headline before looking away: "Knife Attack at Local Farm Leads to Drug Arrests." It was on the front page. It did not say anyone died. She could hardly go on pretending that it happened in another life, nothing that applied to her life now, not with a real story about it in the Des Moines newspaper. She had seen just the headline but she knew it was about what she had done. Sometimes she dreamed about people with knives and lots of blood on walls and awoke crying. Morgan did not know this. He slept like a dead man. He lay beside her now, on his back, his mouth open because his nose always clogged up during sleep, and he did look, maybe a little, dead. She looked away, as if her gaze could make it become fact. She stared at the wall and watched car lights split through the blinds and race across the far wall.

She waited three days before going back to the library.

Victoria sat staring at the blank screen on the microfilm reader for some minutes before finally turning it on and rolling the film spool to the date she wanted in the *Des Moines Register*. Then, even when the story was blown up on the screen, she looked for a while at her fingers tapping on the table and avoided the microfilm reader. Could she stand it if she read that she is a murderer and the police are looking for her? What would she do then? She had a different last name now: Cary. She had never been fingerprinted. Could they find her if she didn't want to be found? Wouldn't it be better to just leave well enough alone? She would not let her eyes move beyond the headline. There was still a chance to not know. She looked over each shoulder to make sure no one was watching.

So she read.

Slowly, word by word, trembling inside with worry over what the next word might be, and the next. Then faster as she began to realize that she was not a murderer. In fact, the story implied that she was a kind of hero, that she had saved people from a knife attack by a psychotic teenage girl under the influence of a *bad trip*. So Bob—her real name was Barbette Johansen—did not die. Jesse, Jesse Fuller, had been a medic in Vietnam and he stopped the bleeding in Barbette's neck. No one at the farm admitted calling the sheriff's office. Barbette was only fifteen years old, a runaway from St. Paul, Minnesota, reported missing by her parents three weeks ago. She was a psychiatric outpatient who did not come home after a visit with her doctor. There was no mention of Kevin by name or any other way. Nor did they know Victoria's name. She was described as the "young mystery woman who, at great risk to her own safety, put herself between the knife-wielding girl and her targets, comprised mostly of students from Drake University . . ."

"The mystery woman," she said under her breath. "I am the mystery woman." She sang the Mighty Mouse tune *sotto voce*: "Here I come to save the day . . ."

The remainder of the article related how sheriff's deputies discovered a variety of illegal substances in the farmhouse, including LSD, peyote, a variety of amphetamines, and ten pounds of harvested marijuana divided into a box full of one-ounce ten-dollar bags; an acre of marijuana was discovered planted in back of the cornfield. There was a lab in the barn turning out Ecstasy. For the first time since Hawaii, Victoria felt a wisp of nostalgia for her hazy drug days. An acre of pot, she thought. Now that's farming! They were not able to determine the exact number of people living at the farm, which the article referred to as a *hippie commune*. Two of the residents had to be hospitalized as a result of bad acid trips. One Drake student was picked up by a sheriff's car as he ran naked down the farm road half a mile from the house. He told the officers he was being chased by an iron butterfly. They arrested Jesse Fuller. Poor fucking Jesse, she thought. Barbette's parents had arrived that morning and were hoping to take their daughter back to St. Paul as soon as she could be released from the hospital.

Victoria scanned the papers for three consecutive days before finding a follow-up article, a note about Jesse's arraignment with a mention that Barbette was in good condition but it was too early to determine when she might be released to her parents. Barbette told the police she had hitch-hiked out of St. Paul and had no idea how she ended up in Des Moines and she couldn't remember how she got to the hippie commune. She said she thought she might have hitched a ride with a golden fairy or a hairy faun. She said she couldn't remember where the knife came from or what she was doing with it. And no, she didn't know who the mystery woman was who took the knife away from her. "Just some girl there," she supposed. Is that true? Victoria wondered. Did she really forget? But what reason would she have to protect either Kevin or me? It was that simple? She forgot.

She rolled her way through another week of the *Des Moines Register* without finding any other references to the story. Had she also been able to look at the *Warren Weekly Record*, she would have found an article with her high school yearbook picture saying that Victoria Novak was missing, had not attended classes for two weeks, and her house had been left open, as if she expected to return. She had no known family and no missing persons report had been filed with police. She would not know any of this until she went back intending to sell Aunt Irene's house. She turned off the microfilm reader and sat for a moment to think about the conversion from murderer to hero. Then she went home and waited for her husband to return from class. She met him at the door, nude behind a bath towel.

THIRTY

Two months passed. Victoria did not tell Morgan that she owned a house in Iowa and Morgan did not tell Victoria that he had essentially dropped out of the PhD program. Another rejection arrived in their usually empty mailbox. At least the rejections were getting longer and nicer, Morgan noted, attempting to assuage Victoria's typical angry outburst, her threats to go to New York and cut the throat of whomever was so stupid and so blind and so idiotic and so . . . so . . . such a fucking literary dunce! She cried about his orphaned masterpiece and he made love to her on the sofa and the floor and beside the table.

Later that evening he asked what she thought about him dropping out of the doctoral program and taking a master's degree, not informing her that it was a fait accompli. She stood naked in the kitchen, making a mess of an omelet. He leaned across the pass-through opening above the card table into the kitchen. She turned toward him, a glance, then looked back at the pan and tried to flip the crumbling omelet. "Do what makes you happy," she said, and it sounded to him as if she meant it.

"I don't know if happy is the point."

"Can you eat this screwed-up thing?"

"I'm sure what it looks like doesn't affect the taste."

"Don't be too sure."

She cut the omelet into halves for two plates and handed them to Morgan, who put them on the table. She tore a baguette in half, picked up the last two hash brownies, and came to the table. Morgan poured two juice glasses full of grocery store red wine. They ate naked. A bit of mushroom dropped into the cleavage between Victoria's breasts and Morgan reached across the table, plucked it between his fingers and tossed it into his mouth. "That was my mushroom," she teased. "Want it back?" he asked, opening his mouth wide. "You swallowed it already, you pig." "No, I didn't," he answered, reaching in and taking it out. She leaned over and grabbed his arm by the wrist, guiding the bit of mushroom into her own mouth, giving his fingertips a bite as well. He faked a loud "ouch," and she blew him a kiss with a smile, then chewed with dramatic exaggeration.

"Why do you want to quit?" she asked, finally.

"A lot of reasons."

"I didn't think you were happy with this school. You're a writer, anyway."

"But isn't that what you wanted?" he continued. "Me a university professor somewhere?"

"Maybe such a fantasy passed through my mind. But that was before I *discovered* your writing. That's what I want you to do. If it makes you happy, I mean."

"Your faith in me is wonderful."

"Do I hear a 'but' in there?"

"The 'but' is money. Needing some way to earn it."

"I have a job. So do you."

"That's our future? You a checkout girl at Safeway, me a janitor?"

"Of course not. You will sell this novel, and then lots more. We will live in Paris."

He laughed. "Lots more? I don't know about that. But let's be serious about this, baby. Even if the novel sells . . ."

"When!"

"*When* the novel sells. You've read those writers' market books. How much money do you think I would get? A couple of thousand dollars? Five at the very upper limit?"

"Don't be so fucking negative."

He laughed. "I'm just being realistic. I'd probably get less for a book than I earn as a part-time janitor in four or five paychecks."

Victoria stood and cleared the table. "Well, I don't happen to think it's just about money. You are too good, your book is too good to sit in that damn beer box. Let me think about it," she said. "But I have to take a shower and go to work, speaking of making the big bucks."

Morgan refilled his wine glass, slipped on a pair of shorts and a T-shirt and went to the sofa. He picked up the paperback copy of Yeats poetry he had left there before Victoria brought in the mail, containing the next rejection in what he fully expected to be an endless chain of them. Victoria sang in the shower. He loved the sound of her voice, even though her pitch was pretty far off.

She came out in her Safeway clothes. He got up to kiss her goodbye. He did not have to leave for work until ten o'clock.

"Maybe there's a way we can solve this money problem," she said. "Let's talk tomorrow."

"Selling your body is out of the question," he teased. "Even if it would make us richer than God."

"Would you watch?"

"Get out of here!"

"I love you," she said, embracing the words.

He blew a kiss to her at the door.

She told him about the house in Iowa. She told him more than that. She told him her story, everything to the point where they first met on the Kailua pier. She left out the long string of sex partners and even when he pressured her about it, she just said that she was never in love before him, and that was true. She told him about the drugs, well, some of the drugs, leaving out the fact that she still swallowed a bit of speed to get through work and some downers to get to sleep; she described the incident at Jesse's Farm. She told him about her father, her mother, Aunt Irene giving her to the family next door, who kicked her out when she was sixteen. She did not tell him about the abortion. She wanted to go to Iowa and sell the house. She would never live in it again, they wouldn't live in Iowa. She had no idea what it might be worth, but must be enough for them to live on for a few years, certainly long enough for the novel to sell and Morgan to write another one. He told her he planned to apply for teaching jobs at community colleges after he finished the master's. She said it probably wouldn't be necessary, and if worse came to worst, there was always her body, but only if he watched, she teased.

What Morgan heard that evening while he sat on the sofa and she lay with her head in his lap talking about her life was her history of betrayal and loss. He began to understand why she became so explosive and irrational when she just suspected, on the slimmest of evidence, that he might be interested in some other woman, why she clung to him regardless of how reassuring he thought he was being. He understood why she had chosen him: stable, dependable, true, unlikely to betray her or leave her. He had no trouble fulfilling these needs of hers. He was mad about her and he would be whatever brought her security and happiness.

In January, Victoria flew to Iowa alone. Even if Morgan didn't have classes and his job, they could only scrape up enough extra money for one airfare.

She drove back into Warren in a rented Oldsmobile that made her look, she thought, like a kid who had borrowed Grandpa's car. She seldom drove and it was snowing. The recently plowed highway south out of Des Moines to Warren made her nervous and she drove at half the speed limit, causing some cars to pass her with a blast from their horns, their drivers doing a double take when the old Grandpa they expected to see behind the wheel turned out to be a gorgeous young woman.

She had been gone just over two years. The college closed during January and without students the campus and buildings looked as static as a Currier and Ives postcard in the pristine snow and stark old trees. Elm Street had been plowed and parked cars along both sides were half buried. Victoria turned carefully into the driveway and stopped behind a big-as-a-boat wood-paneled station wagon. What is this car doing here? she wondered. The house, at first, appeared just as she had left it, until she looked closer. There was a child's wagon on the swept porch, the window curtains were different, and on the front window to what had been Victoria's bedroom was a round sticker alerting the fire department that it was a child's bedroom. She had not formed any expectations, naively assuming the house would be exactly as she had walked out of it that November day more than two years ago.

It was dumb, she thought, to have just assumed nothing would change over two years. But how did other people come to be living in her house? They couldn't have bought it, or even rented it. Squatters? She sat in the car with the engine running for a minute or two, just looking at the house and trying to decide what to do next. Should she go to the door, knock? She didn't even have a key. She had walked out with Kevin and as far as she could remember, maybe didn't even close the door. This was Warren, Iowa. People didn't lock their doors or take their keys out of their cars. Nothing happened here. The front door opened and a woman appearing to be only a little older than Victoria came onto the porch, pulling on a down vest over an oversized flannel shirt. Victoria opened the door and got out, but stayed next to the car. It was so cold. Snow pellets tapped her nose and cheeks.

"May I help you?" the woman asked, staying on the porch with her arms crossed over her chest.

"This is going to sound strange," Victoria said, staying by the still open car door. "But this is my house."

"I'm sorry?" The door opened and the head of child peeked out. The woman turned and said, "Go back inside, honey. Close the door." The child looked at Victoria then did what her mother asked.

Victoria closed the car door but stayed beside it. "My name is Victoria Cary . . . Novak. This is my house."

"I think you should contact the bank, the Farmer's National. We, my husband and I, bought this house almost a year ago at a repossession auction."

"That's not possible."

"I'm sorry, but I'm afraid it is. We bought it from the bank, we have the full title. My husband isn't here at the moment, he knows where the title is, but I might be able to find it. I think you should talk to the bank first though. I'm sorry. What a terrible way to find out something like this. I am really sorry."

What could she say now? There had to be some explanation, some way to resolve this unexpected dilemma, but not by standing there freezing to death. "I will go to the bank," Victoria said, getting back into the car. She had not even turned off the engine.

The woman went back inside and closed the door. Victoria saw her glance through the curtains, then she backed carefully into Elm Street, the street where she had lived most of her life, from the house left to her in Aunt Irene's will, the street her mother drove down that cold November day. Victoria thought about her mother and that day, the last day she saw her and the last chance they had to be together. She thought about how her mother died on the icy road and left her forever and wondered if she had gone with her mother that day maybe she wouldn't have gotten into the wreck or maybe Victoria would have died that day, too. She was crying over the mother she had seen only once after the age of four, driving slowly up the street until out of sight of the house, the house where her mother had once lived and where her mother abandoned her, then pulling into the Warren College administration building's empty parking lot and stopping in almost the same place she had sat with her mother in the red Thunderbird. Victoria couldn't drive and cry at the same time.

She remembered there had been a small mortgage left on the house, but there was only a year, or maybe it was fifteen or sixteen months, left on it. She had made at least three payments, she thought. They could take her house and sell it when there was just a few months remaining on a mortgage of thirty years? Without even telling her? How could this be possible? Isn't this tantamount to stealing her house? What was she going to tell Morgan if she couldn't fix this? He would think she was stupid, a real space cadet. She cried, more from what Morgan would think of her than having maybe lost the house and the money she had expected to get from selling it. Snow fell thicker and layered over the recently plowed street and the lot where she parked. This is really fucked up, she thought. She didn't even know where she could stay; she had expected to stay in her house. Where is my stuff? She had left most of her clothes, her books, all her art supplies, her drawings and watercolors. What happened to all her things? You don't suppose they found the pot stash in that hole behind the oven?

The clock on the Oldsmobile's dashboard said it was two-fifteen. When did the bank close? But wait, it's Sunday, isn't it? Shit, she muttered. Where was she going to stay? Maybe the Higgenbottoms would put her up, she laughed to herself. She wondered if they had seen her standing in the driveway? Isabel was always spying.

Before the snow trapped her in the Warren College parking lot, she drove back to the Des Moines highway and checked into a motel. Next door was a hotdog joint called Dog and Suds where she had often eaten as a high school student. She took the car, even though it was only a hundred feet away, so she could eat in the car and avoid going inside.

She had a shower later and wanted desperately to call Morgan, just to hear his voice, but then she would have to tell him that his wife was stupid beyond belief. Besides, maybe tomorrow she would have better news. She watched a TV movie and fell asleep with it on.

Victoria was taken directly to the branch manager's office after announcing herself and her purpose to the receptionist. He rose when she entered and came around his desk to shake her hand. His professionally friendly greeting did not disguise a more distinctive look of astonishment. He pulled close a chair for her.

"I must say what a surprise this is. Could have knocked me down with a feather, Miss Novak. May I call you Vicki?"

"I prefer Victoria."

"Well, Victoria, do you have any idea the uproar it caused around here when you just disappeared?"

"I didn't think of it as disappearing. I just went on holiday and found this good job and well, one thing seemed to lead to another."

"Where have you been all this time?"

After a moment's hesitation, "Mexico."

"Mexico. Well, I'll be. Have you told the police you're back. I would imagine they are still looking for you."

"Oh, yes," she lied. "They weren't very happy with me."

"I imagine not."

"Mr. Fowler, please. There's a problem with my house."

He pursed his lips, clasped his hands together and rested his chin on them. "Problem is putting it mildly, Victoria. Fact is, your aunt's house . . ."

"My house."

"Well, yes, your house." He flipped open a file folder on his desk and glanced at it. "Fact is, Victoria, you didn't make a single mortgage payment on your house since . . ." he ran his finger down the page, "since October 16, 1970."

"Okay. I understand that. The truth is, I forgot the house still had a mortgage; it was such a short time left that I just assumed . . ."

"We sent out reminders for four months. Our only obligation is for three, you know? Ninety days."

"As you said, I was missing. Is that what you do when someone goes missing? You take away their property?"

"Not exactly. But we waited . . ." running his finger further down the page, "let's see, we waited a year, Victoria, before issuing the repossession order. A year. Some students from the college were living in it, you know? The sheriff had to evict them. What a mess they left. You couldn't imagine people, even kids, would live like that."

"Someone was living in it?"

"More than someone. They had turned the place into a . . . what do you call it? Crash pad? Whatever. The sheriff would move one group out, then another showed up. Imagine how this upset your neighbors. Freaked out," he added, pleased with the phrase.

Victoria shook her head. This was too much information all at once. She needed time to understand what had happened.

"Can you do that? I mean, can you just take someone's property, a missing person, and sell it? Just like that?"

Mr. Fowler looked up and closed the file. "It's not exactly just like that. There are strict procedures and I assure you we followed them even beyond the call of duty, as it were. This is terrible, I know. It's just terrible. But it's a done-Nelly, I'm afraid. We had the legal right to repossess the property for nonpayment on the mortgage, a full year, I remind you, and then to resell it. Which is what has happened. It is all completely legal, and I'm afraid, you have, at this point, no recourse. But you should check with a lawyer, of course."

"Oh, you can be sure I will see a lawyer."

"You have that right, Victoria. Just let me say how sorry I am things worked out this way. But please try to see the situation from our side, from the bank's perspective. We can repossess a property after ninety days in arrears. My dear, frankly, a lot of people thought you had been murdered by drug dealers or run off with types like that. A bag of marijuana and some sort of illegal pills were found in the house—*before* those hippie students started crashing there. Anyway, in your case, we waited a full year before feeling that we just must take the property for the unpaid mortgage. Just imagine if we waited a full year before repossessing a property that far in arrears. The bank would go out of business pretty damn quick.

"The Lieber family who bought the property are wonderful people. He's a new English teacher at the college, they have a baby. They love the house. I would hate to see them have to suffer just because . . . well, you know what I mean."

This is ridiculous and out of control, Victoria thought. She felt like a snowball rolling down a hill, the problem getting bigger, the path down inexorable. She shook her head then stood. Mr. Fowler stood with her.

For a moment she couldn't move, still trying to process this information and decide what to do next.

"Your bank account is still fine," he said. "It's inactive, but we can activate it with a signature."

"Oh." She had forgotten the bank account. "How much is in it?"

"Let's just go to the teller window and find out, shall we? You know, this is a very pleasant surprise. How great that you are all right, after all. I'm sure the police were relieved."

"Oh yes, they were quite relieved. Me, too."

He laughed. They went to a teller window and Victoria closed her bank account and withdrew the balance of $886.32. At least, she thought, she wouldn't go home with nothing at all.

What could she do? She wasn't about to go to the police or get a lawyer. There was too much to explain and too much she couldn't predict and she had no doubt that the bank manager had picked up the phone and called the police the moment she walked out. She didn't spend another night in Warren, driving directly back to the Des Moines airport that afternoon. She would never again be in Iowa.

THIRTY-ONE

On a night some years later, alone in their bungalow, stoned and scared to death she might have lost Morgan, Victoria briefly remembered that trip back to Warren. That was, she believed, when she opened the lid to Pandora's Box. Before that trip, she and Morgan were happy beyond description, beyond belief, and in spite of her cautious worries, she saw the rest of their lives together continuing exactly in that way. Then, after just one small misstep, one little thing, she started losing everything.

Morgan did not know this was how Victoria felt. Not because he was unobservant, although sometimes he was, but because Victoria hid from him her feelings of inadequacy, and like a threatened animal, she believed that showing fear exposed her true vulnerability. The strong, aggressive, self-confident, even egotistical façade disguised a girl cowering in a corner with her face buried in her knees.

On the return flight to Los Angeles, Victoria planned the best way to explain all this to Morgan. How could she make being that stupid look

less so? She had essentially thrown away a house worth . . . whatever.
Instead of coming home with thousands, dozens of thousands of dollars,
she had about eight hundred. So she created an elaborate lie. The house
was never hers in the first place. It was a terrible misunderstanding. Aunt
Irene had in fact left the house to her church with the stipulation that
Victoria could remain living for free in it as long as she was a student. So
when she left school and went to Hawaii, that triggered the clause allowing the church to take the house. The probate lawyer had not made this
clear to her, so she thought that living in the house for free somehow meant
she owned it. That's how she would explain this to Morgan. A misunderstanding, really the lawyer's fault, combined with her naïveté about such
matters. Being naive and taken advantage of was much better than being
stupid; experience takes care of naïveté, but stupid sticks like tar.

Morgan was disappointed, but believed he had not let it show. He
chastised himself for having counted his chickens even before the hen got
pregnant. But it didn't really matter to him all that much. It was not in his
nature to worry about what never was in the first place. That's what he
told Victoria. She chose not to believe him. They had almost no money,
her artistic novelist husband was working as a janitor, and she was stuck
behind a Safeway cash register where half the assholes in Pomona slob-
bered over her. This was their future? She thought it would be better if
she found a secretarial job. She was a fantastic typist and a good speller.

By the time Morgan took his master's degree, using *Decompression* as his
thesis, the novel had been rejected by three more publishers. He began
sending applications for teaching jobs to the many community colleges
in the Los Angeles area and often daydreamed wistfully about returning
to Hawaii and becoming a fisherman again. Victoria never told him that
she had the same daydreams, that she also missed Hawaii. She couldn't
tell him; she was the reason they felt compelled to leave.

Morgan rather liked driving the floor-scrubbing tractor around the gym floor and didn't mind emptying trash bins and cleaning mirrors, sinks, and toilets. He still worked part-time nights, but had received a decent pay raise each year, now beginning his third year in the maintenance department of Western Hills Community College. When he put in an application for a teaching job, the academic dean joked that it would be the first time they had someone move from being a janitor to the faculty at their school, but said anyway, if a position in the English department did arise, Morgan would definitely be a contender.

And then it sold. April Fool's Day, 1974.

After all those rejection letters, the acceptance came in a phone call. Victoria took it while Morgan was at work. Alert to April Fool's jokes because Morgan liked to pull one on her every year, Victoria nearly peed her pants when she finally believed that the woman who had introduced herself as Sophie Greene, fiction editor for Metropolis Literary Press, where Victoria had dutifully and with shivering hope mailed the well-worn copy of *Decompression* only two weeks earlier, was not joking. Sophie Greene asked, "Am I speaking with Mrs. Cary, then?" Victoria happily claimed to be one and the same. "Well, Mrs. Cary, would you please ask your extraordinarily talented husband to call me collect in New York at this number? Believe me, this is not April Fool's." Unable to find a piece of paper handy, Victoria wrote the number along her forearm. After hanging up, she exploded around the living room like Chinese firecrackers.

That night, just half a dozen years later, alone in their bungalow, wanting to disappear, Victoria would remember that day, that phone call, as another demon she had let out of the box.

THIRTY-TWO

The success of *Decompression* surprised everyone, even the publisher. Everyone except Victoria. The earliest reviews glowed and Victoria put each clipping into a plastic folder and filed them by date in a marbled stationery box she appropriated from the manager's office in her Safeway store. The typical first printing of one thousand books sold steadily and well enough for an unknown author from a small literary press. Then it made the front page of the *New York Times Book Review* in a review calling it "arguably the finest debut in literary fiction in a decade." Translation rights sold in German, French, and Spanish. The second printing was five thousand, the third another five thousand. Metropolis Literary Press brought Morgan to New York and took him to lunch at the Four Seasons, where a tie had to be provided for him, and sent him around to book signings. Western Hills Community College offered him a job the fall semester after the book came out and he took it. In addition to the standard introductory English courses, the first course in creative writing ever offered by the two-year college was designed just for him. It was the most popular course in the Western Hills English department, particularly with young women of an artsy-craftsy inclination.

He got a royalty check. The foreign editions sold well enough. They couldn't have lived for many years on the income from *Decompression*, but they could live well on it with his teacher's salary. They finally had health insurance, the book money bought furniture for their Claremont bungalow, which they purchased with a substantial down payment; they got a water bed in a massive oak frame with a bookcase built into the headboard, they traded in the Ford Maverick for a newer, bigger car, a Ford Fairlane with four doors, and Victoria was able to quit her job at Safeway. She had taken the dust jacket photo of Morgan and there was her name in all those books: photo by Victoria Cary. She wished she could have had some input about the cover design; she thought it plain and unappealing. The title was at the top in wavy navy blue letters, as if seen through water, with bubbles rising from the bottom of the pale blue cover, where Morgan's name was. Morgan had only insisted there be no people on the cover.

Metropolis held the option for his next book, which he began working on the same month the teaching job began, writing the first page fifty or sixty times before giving it a rest. The demands of his teaching job were unexpectedly difficult and time-consuming. He was used to more mindless occupations. Victoria was used to having not only more of his time, but more of his undivided attention, although she liked watching him grade student papers and she liked how it made her feel to be the wife of a professor and, most importantly, a renowned novelist, renowned at least in her private world, and that was enough.

Morgan taught four courses: Introduction to World Literature, two sections of Rhetoric and Composition, and Creative Writing 101. They represented thirteen hours a week of in-class time, but Morgan realized that making sure he didn't sound like an idiot in class and trying to give each student a fair evaluation required three hours in homework for every hour spent in class. He was surprised by how much he enjoyed every hour of it, in class and out. Victoria bought him a tweed sport jacket for his birthday and she thought he was handsome in the extreme with it on. Too handsome?

Housewifery was not especially interesting and not useful as a way to occupy the hours, and Victoria thought of finding another job, something more interesting than clerking in a grocery store, but couldn't decide what that might be. Secretarial work, because it would require sitting in an office all day, had no appeal. Maybe a gallery, Morgan suggested, but Victoria complained that she didn't know anything about art; doing it is not the same as knowing it, she told him. He had a similar feeling about trying to teach writing, so he understood why she would be hesitant. He suggested she consider going back to college, but she had flunked out the first time and would probably not have the basic GPA necessary to get in somewhere else now. He said she could try, but she said she had no idea what she could study, even if she got in. Art, he said. She just shook her head. Months passed with Victoria in this limbo.

In the park where she walked for daily exercise, dumbfounded that she was getting a belly roll and that she could put a pencil under her breasts and it wouldn't fall out, there were mothers, younger than Victoria, pushing strollers in a lazy circle around a small pond, toddlers toddling into things and crying loudly when they inevitably fell. There were children old enough to form miniature societies as they began to learn inclusivity and exclusivity. Dogs yelped and played. Pigeons bobbed and fluttered. On Sundays during summer, families and lovers picnicked on blankets around a bandstand gazebo where musical groups performed all afternoon.

Victoria did not enjoy being around so many mothers and children. She would rather watch the dogs playing than children playing and appreciated the good luck that she could not have children, as if her own body had known best what she was mentally capable of. She told herself that she was not patient enough for the demands of a child and could not stand the idea of being trapped with all those babbling and cooing mothers. She reminded herself of these feelings every day during her walk in the park.

Sometimes she smelled marijuana on the breeze. After a while she realized that the pot smell didn't come from the clumps of mothers on benches, but from behind them, down the slope to the concrete drainage ditch, where a little tribe of hippie kids gathered to play guitars, tap bongos, and plot revolutions and sex.

She bought a sketch pad, a box of charcoal sticks and some pencils, and began drawing scenes in the park. No human figures at first, just trees, a study of benches and their shadows making stretched-out smudged designs across the dry grass, a water fountain, a robin bathing in a bird bath, the gazebo from up close and from far away. After a while she brought a blanket and a picnic basket and ate lunch on the wooded slope that angled down to the concrete ditch, where after eating she would smoke a joint and lie back to find shapes in the cotton-ball cumulus clouds. When summer came she planned that they would come here for the Sunday afternoon picnics; she would proudly kiss her husband and make out with him in public.

She started sketching the hippie tribe, particularly a boy with a guitar. She supposed he couldn't be much more than sixteen or seventeen and wondered why he wasn't in school. She liked that they cleaned up after themselves, gathering up their Ripple and Annie Greensprings empties, the bread wrappers, even the cigarette butts. They were always in the same place, a flat spot near the canal, blocked by a hedge row from the bourgeoisie up there in mother-and-baby-ville, and separated by the ditch from a busy street. There were plenty of shade trees, and sometimes after dipping in the canal they dried their clothes on the limbs, and sheltered behind the hedge, dried their bodies in the nude. She drew the guitar boy more often than the others. He looked like a teenage Jesus wannabe in multicolored striped bell-bottom pants, a paisley shirt, Indian beads, a filthy, tangled mat of blond hair draped over his skinny shoulders, and a hoped-for wispy beard, Ho Chi Minh style. If things had gone differently in her life, she thought that she could be one of them, a hippie chick in some Jesse's Farm tribe just like this, smoking dope and making music, riding the roads in a psychedelic bus, making love and not war. That would have been all right if she had known nothing else. But she liked being the wife of Morgan Cary, the novelist, even if she could not envision their future. It would be all right, she thought, if the next day was just as fine as the one before.

The hippies figured out she was drawing them and began affected posing. The guitar boy began singing in her direction, to her. He could make himself sound like Donovan in ballads, Phil Ochs in protest songs. This went on for about a week before he moseyed up and asked to see what she was drawing. He squatted by her, lay his Hummingbird Gibson on the grass, and looked through her sketchbook. You draw damn good, he told her, relishing the view of her breasts beneath the elastic band of her peasant blouse. He said his name was Pooh Bear and she stopped herself from saying that he looked more like Wiley Coyote. He named the others she had drawn: Mister Wizard, who goes to college; Lady Sunshine, who had actually been to Woodstock; Blue, who's pregnant; Sam, who might be the father of Blue's baby; Billy; Tess; and finally Jay Bird, who scores the pot. He offered her a joint and made himself comfortable lying sprawled on the grass beside her.

"You're an artist, I guess," Pooh Bear said to the passing clouds.

She said she was a doodler and put her sketchbook away.

"You not gonna split already?" he asked, turning and propping himself on his bent arm.

"That's life," Victoria said, getting to her feet.

"Don't scare her away, Poohby!" the one called Mister Wizard cried out.

Pooh gave Mister Wizard the finger.

"If I can ask," Victoria said, "how old are you?"

"I am eternal," Pooh said, rising to a squat and taking his guitar by the neck.

"And that would be something like fifteen, sixteen in trivial time?"

"Why does it matter, lady doodler?"

"It doesn't. I just think you are a very good singer for someone your age, whatever age that might be."

"I'll take that as a compliment and assuage your doubts. I am seventeen . . . in trivial time."

"Assuage? Shit, dude, you do turn a phrase."

Pooh watched her from below. "When you come back," Pooh said, "I will sing a song I wrote just for you."

"That would be nice."

"So you are coming back?" He got to his feet and held the guitar as if he was about to play something.

"Sure. I'm always here. Tell your friends goodbye for me."

"Bring that art book of yours, too. They won't believe me when I tell them how good you can *doodle*."

"Thanks for the toke," she said, offered a wave to the others, who were watching all the while, and walked away.

The following day, the ditch hippies posed for her and she made a portrait sketch of them, posing them among the trees with the hedge behind.

Mister Wizard, who seemed to be their guru, after all, he was in college, stationed himself in the middle. Pregnant Blue lay with her head in Sam's lap, her belly rising like a lonely hill, her hands clasped over it. Sam sat at Wizard's feet. Lady Sunshine and Tess stood on either side of Mister Wizard with their arms around him. Mister Wizard's beard and hair framed his face so fully that he seemed to have only small eyes and a big nose; except for being white, he reminded her a little of Jesse. Pooh Bear, guitar slung across his back troubadour-style, stood next to Lady Sunshine, while Jay Bird, a little hash pipe clenched in his teeth, stood on the other side. Billy was not there. They had naturally posed themselves like a Victorian outlaw family in a tintype.

"Immortalize us," Mister Wizard said when they were in position. Victoria sat on the grassy slope with her sketchbook opened across her lap and drew them with a pencil and then charcoal.

Morgan wondered about those people when she showed him the group drawing of the park hippies. She told him they inhabited the park on Scripps Street, where she went walking most days. Morgan said she was a better artist than he was a writer, certainly a more prolific one. Victoria lost her temper because that was an absurd statement. "I'm not an artist, I'm just a good drawer. You're the artist." But Morgan had meant it. He had begun to worry that probably he had only one book in him and would likely never be able to write another. *Decompression* had come to him in a fully formed dream and he had not had another interesting idea, or dream, since. A flash in the pan, he thought. A damn lucky dream. But Victoria had filled three or four sketchbooks with beautiful drawings, not a bad one in the bunch. He asked if she would like to paint and suggested that she buy whatever art supplies she would like. Victoria said drawing was enough. It was just to pass the time, a kind of entertainment. It's not a big deal, she told him. Maybe, she supposed, it wouldn't be a bad idea to get more serious about finding a job. She was bored. Morgan proposed that loving him and taking care of him was more work than any person ought to be stuck with and he was making a living for them now, anyway. Victoria thought he was saying that she wasn't doing a very good job of it. When he was asleep, she could never fall asleep within hours of when he did, even with the pills, she got up and took all her sketchbooks outside to the trash Dumpster. She didn't go back to the park that week.

Four days later, she answered a knock on her door to find the hippie guitar boy and his guitar standing on the stoop. "I've come to sing your song," he announced.

"How did you know where I live?" Victoria demanded, her voice mixed with confusion and apprehension.

"Don't be afraid of me, Lady Madonna. The answer is, I happened to be walking over to the grocery store on Indian Hills and saw you getting out of a car here. With a dude."

"The dude is my husband."

"Figured that, I did. You never came back to the park to hear your song. I wrote a song for you, like I said. Want me to play it for you, right here on the stoop?"

"No. You can come in. But you better be a good boy."

"Good Boy is my middle name."

"Names, plural. Pooh Good Boy Bear. I can dig it."

She let him in and asked if he wanted something to drink. He asked if she had something to smoke instead, which she did, of course. "Lot of books," he observed while she rolled a joint. He put his guitar on the new easy chair and inspected book spines. She lit the joint and brought it to him. "You in college?" he asked. "My husband was a graduate student here. He's an author," she added probably too proudly and pointedly. That information did not seem to interest him. "So, you wrote me a song?"

"Special, just for you."

"Well . . . ?"

"Have a seat right here," he indicated the end of the new sofa. He picked up his guitar and Victoria splayed herself across the cushions, her feet dangling over the arm. He sat next to her, and she had to twist around so her back wouldn't be to him. He handed the joint to her and made a motion of fishing a pick out of his psychedelic-swirl T-shirt pocket. Victoria took a toke and gave him an impatient look; his appearance at her door was presumptuous enough, he didn't need to push his luck by sitting on top of her.

He began singing in his Donovan voice. She noticed that he could actually play the guitar well. The song was about a magical lady artist who could only live by drawing pictures; she created the world and brought everything to life in pictures. She draws a picture of and falls in love with a young Pan playing a flute in the forest. But they are doomed, because when they make love she forgets to draw and at the moment of climax the world she had sustained by drawing it disappears and she turns into a spirit. Something like that.

She clapped politely but honestly. He was a fine guitar player and even if the lyrics were kind of hackneyed, it was a pretty tune.

"I'm impressed," she said. "But you had to be pretty fucking stoned when you wrote it. Right?"

"Impressed enough for a little kiss?" he asked.

"Not that impressed."

"Enough for another joint?"

"Definitely that impressed." Victoria said and went to the kitchen to roll another.

The boy put the guitar back on the sofa and followed her to the kitchen. Suddenly it bothered her having him standing behind her, having him in the house. "I'll roll a couple and let's go to the park," she said, spreading the papers on the counter. "Let's roll a couple and smoke 'em in the sack," he answered, putting his hands on her shoulders.

She put the baggie down on the counter and turned around, shrugging off his hands. "What you're thinking is not going to happen. Now you can go back and have a seat, play your guitar, smoke a joint, and then leave, or you can just leave now."

He was no larger than Victoria but she was stunned by how fast he moved and how suddenly overwhelmed she was when he threw his arms around her and shoved her back against the counter, trying to kiss her. At first, she just thought what persistent and stupid animals men could be. She did not feel threatened by Pooh Bear, she felt pissed off. She slapped him hard. Then he punched her, knocking her head hard against the cabinet door. The last thing she felt was an explosive tingling in her face.

She came to with the boy on top of her. During the first seconds she could not process what was happening to her. She felt his weight but did not connect it with a person. The tingling she remembered had become a ferocious stinging ache that filled the back of her head. She registered events in sequential moments, first the weight, then her head, then the wet on her face, then a slobbering tongue around her left ear, then the wiggling body on hers, then the wide spread of her legs, and then finally the dick inside her. The realization that she was actually being raped was so farfetched, so ridiculous and impossible, that for a moment she wondered if it was some crazy dope dream. He was grunting, trying to get his tongue into her mouth, humping harder and faster . . . she knew he was coming.

"Get the fuck off me, you stupid fucking moron!" She tried to buck him off and shoved hard against his shoulders. She tried to close her legs but his knees were between then. She began pounding on the side of his head and jerked her body as hard as she could, forcing his dick out of her just as he shot sperm across her pubic hair and onto the floor between her legs.

"Fuck you, bitch!" he said, spitting into her face. He grabbed her hair in both hands and began slamming her head against the linoleum floor. She kept pounding her fists into the sides of his head until again she felt her face explode in a kind of electrical fury until again there was nothing.

THIRTY-THREE

Pooh Good Boy Bear was gone when Victoria awoke and found herself still lying on the kitchen floor, naked below the waist, his stickiness matted in her pubic hair and stuck to the inside of her upper thighs. Her head throbbed and her hair felt gooey when she put her hand back to touch her head, aching like the worst bruise she had ever felt. She raised her head and looked over to see a patch of blood drying on the floor. The kitchen door stood partially open. She forced herself to get up and close and lock it. Her shorts and panties lay in a silly lump by the wall. She picked them up and walked quickly to the bathroom. That he had hurt her, that he had punched her and slammed her head against the floor made it worse, she thought. She had been raped. She made herself say it out loud: "I was raped." Now it was real.

She knew what she was supposed to do and what not. Women absorbed this information about rape even hoping against hope they would not need to remember any of it. She knew, but when it happens to you, she thought, you just want to first clean his goddamn scum off your body and second kill and castrate the bastard. Could she tell Morgan? Why would I not tell him? What would he do? What could he do? What would he think of her now? How do men react to something like this—how will Morgan react? No matter what they say, no matter how sincere, how soothing and understanding they are, a man will wonder just a little how a woman got herself into a situation like this. "I know him from the park. I've drawn sketches of him, in one he's naked. I invited him into our house to sing a song he wrote for me—how fucking romantic!" Maybe Morgan wouldn't be able to get this out of his mind. Maybe he wouldn't be able to love her the same way. Her head throbbed but the bleeding had stopped, coagulating like honey in her hair. Like honey. One time in the Warren Elementary cafeteria two girls who hated her squirted honey in her hair. It came out in hot water more easily than she thought. The blood would come out like that, she supposed. It's not bleeding now and she decided at that moment not to go to the hospital, not to call the police, not to call Morgan or tell him, and to get in the shower and get clean, then buy a gun and kill Pooh Good Boy Bear.

She devised a great story for Morgan about the cut on the back of her head and the gross, already yellowing bruise beside her left eye: she was trying to climb on the kitchen counter to put away some stuff in the upper cabinet they almost never used. She lost her balance. Luckily she did not fall to the floor, but did hit the back of her head on the open cabinet door and clunked the left side of her face on the countertop.

Morgan wanted to take her to the hospital, but she said it didn't hurt now, it wasn't bleeding, and obviously she didn't have a concussion. He didn't think it was all that obvious. He sat beside her on the sofa and held an iced towel against her bruise. In fact, it didn't hurt much now; after a couple of Seconal and four joints before he got home, now a fifth shared with him. It was the right thing to do, she decided. She could see that his imagining something terrible happening to her made him seem to love her even more. When they went to bed he made love to her quite softly, tenderly, and very, very carefully. She did not have an orgasm because she feared it would make her head explode. He said it was all right, he understood. She thought it was wonderful that not once did she compare making love with her husband to being raped by a dumb shit psycho moron posing as a peace and love hippie. It used to be, she thought, that long hair, a beard, beads, the usual hippie ensemble, guaranteed a certain peaceable, loving, humanitarian attitude about life and the world. But now you couldn't depend on that. Look at Charlie Manson!

It was too difficult and time-consuming to buy a gun in California, she discovered. She didn't want to wait. She decided that a knife would be more personal anyway. She fantasized cutting off his penis and watching him writhe around on the ground bleeding to death with his prick squirting like a beheaded chicken. How his face would look as it went pale and his lights went out. She would stick his severed little wienie into his dead mouth, carve *rapist* onto his chest, and in that way put an end to this sick chapter in her life. She would never think of it again. She just had to make sure she wasn't caught; she spent days plotting out the angles.

Three days after the boy who called himself Pooh Bear raped her, she took the largest of her kitchen knives, wrapped it in a dish towel so it wouldn't cut the inside of her bag, and walked to the park. She would not have described her movements as automatic; she would have used the word *determined*, or maybe *resolute*. She had calculated how to do this. She would watch the hippies until they left, they couldn't sleep in the park, so they had to leave sooner or later, then follow them discreetly until she found out where Pooh Bear lived. He had to be alone eventually.

But when she saw the hippies in their spot by the ditch, everything the same, as if nothing in the world had changed in the last few days, Pooh

Bear was not with them. The others were there as always, but without the kid and his guitar. Maybe he just went to take a leak, or something. She waited out of sight for two hours. What did this mean? Everything was exactly the same, except Pooh Bear wasn't there. Had he supposed she would do this, come looking for him? Or the police? Or her husband? Of course he did. He was hiding.

Finally she approached the hippies and they greeted her like she had been there just yesterday, not two weeks ago. Mister Wizard, who now Victoria decided looked quite a lot like Charlie Manson, asked where she had been. She asked what happened to Pooh. Mister Wizard shrugged. Blue, hands clasped over her basketball belly, said that Pooh hadn't been around for a few days. She joked that maybe he joined a rock-and-roll band. "Am I my brother's keeper?" Mister Wizard stated.

"He was a pretty good guitar player," Victoria said. "He said he was going to write a song for me and I'd like to hear it, if he did." Mister Wizard shrugged again. "Anybody know where maybe I could find him?" Blue and Lady Sunshine shrugged. Mister Wizard shrugged.

"Pooh Bear is all I ever knew about the dude," Tess said, then added, "and he was a bitching guitar picker."

Victoria thought she shouldn't pursue this any further or make a big deal out of it. She believed that he wouldn't stay away from the park forever and all she had to do was continue her exercise walks in the park and one of these days she'd find him, if there was any justice in the world. She couldn't close this door until she castrated Pooh Bear.

She went to the park every day that week. She took her sketch book and pencils so everything would look the same, she even sketched the hippies a couple of more times. Pooh Bear did not appear and she knew better than to keep asking about him. The next week she went twice, then once, and after a month she stopped going to that park. It was easier to divert her mind from this than she thought it would be. By the time her head stopped aching and the bruise disappeared, Pooh Bear was not all she thought about. She destroyed every sketch she had made with him in it. On the back cover of her sketch book, she wrote this poem:

> *I won't always think of this,*
> *I know other thoughts will come*
> *And you won't be all my mind can see,*
> *I know this hatred will dissolve into other things,*
> *Like chewing gum and lovely grass*
> *Damp from spring rain.*

Were that words could form deeds. But she could not force the fury, the hatred, from her mind, and she could not banish the nightmares, which woke her like a nearby gunshot. She would quickly turn to see who was beside her, because she dreamed of awakening to find Pooh Bear in her bed, or sometimes standing beside the bed, looking, leering at her, sometimes with a knife as long and shining as a saber. She did not make any noise and did not awaken Morgan. He did not know that she had left the bed and was sitting on the toilet with the lid closed, bent over, weeping. Most nights she hadn't slept but two or three hours, even with Seconal.

She bought speed from the gangs on an infamous drug corner in Riverside, where she drove while Morgan was in class. She needed to balance the downers, so she could get through the day without the crash and burn she felt without the little pick-me-upper. Morgan noticed that she ate less, always taking small portions, always leaving food on her plate; he wondered if she was just bored. He hoped she wasn't depressed. She needed something to do since he was gone much of the day and had so many papers to go through almost every night. He asked if she wanted to buy some real art supplies—paints, an easel, brushes, whatever she wanted. She repeated that she preferred drawing. He asked to see more of her drawings but she said she hadn't been in the mood lately. He gave up easily. His thoughts were filled with his own work, and the guilt over that other work: the writing that wasn't getting done.

THIRTY-FOUR

During the summer of 1976, Morgan decided not to teach a summer ses-sion and instead get serious about working on the next book. He had trashed every attempt to start something new, the time-consuming dis-tractions of teaching full-time his best excuse. He wrote plenty of sketches and ideas about characters, but he had no plot, no idea of what story he wanted to tell. It occurred to him that probably he had only one story and it was already told. Could he wait for another dream?

Victoria liked having him around but had already determined that she was just another excuse. He wanted to go for walks with her in the cool mornings, and they had two-hour lunches at his favorite café in the village, followed by exhausting episodes of afternoon sex that always astonished Morgan at how voracious and tireless Victoria could be. Some-times he took speed with her and he never supposed that she did it when he wasn't there. They went to movies a couple of times a week. But what was she supposed to do? She was there. Was she supposed to spend time shopping, walking, sightseeing, what? Feeling guilty for distracting him and upset because he used her so flagrantly to avoid work, she knew this couldn't continue all summer. Autumn would come, he'd have classes again, and the summer would have produced just more scrap paper in the box where he pitched his literary residue.

She should get a job. There was no other way to give Morgan enough time alone and remove his new best excuse. Safeway would take her back, she knew, but that job was so ploddingly dull that considering it made her feel sick. Morgan made a polite objection when she began looking in the classifieds for secretarial jobs, although it was obvious that he also knew he was using her to avoid facing the empty page. What would happen if Victoria wasn't around all the time and still he couldn't write anything worth keeping? Maybe he should just face the probability that there would be no second book, that he had one good idea and one burst of creativity allowing him to write that one book. What was wrong with being a college teacher anyway? Thanks to *Decompression*, he might be able to get a position in a university, where the pay would be significantly better. Victoria teasingly threatened to leave him if he kept refusing to accept his providence, his destiny as an author. He knew she was teasing about leaving him, but he also understood that his being an author was important to her. She felt like his muse; for him to abandon that fate would be a rejection of her desire to be, somehow, his inspiration. She pointed out that everything he had written happened before they met, nothing since. He said that was an unimportant coincidence of timing. He was not unaware of how vital it was to impress her, to avoid disappointing her, especially to avoid writing some mediocre junk that would bruise the way she felt about him. If he didn't write anything, then he wouldn't write any shit.

Morgan found her the job. He was in the mall to buy a pair of running shoes and saw a help wanted sign in the window of an art gallery. In spite of her lack of art sales experience, the owner, with the unfortunate name of Marilyn Monroe and sick to death of constantly saying the blatantly obvious—"No, not that one"—and offering the same tired smile, hired Victoria because she was as beautiful as anything hanging on the bright white walls. Mrs. Monroe supposed that customers, men without a doubt, would come into the gallery because of her, and the rest she could teach Victoria in a few days. She even moved the clerk's antique oak table near the window. Victoria thought it was a fine job and although the salary was small, she would get a commission on anything she sold. Mrs. Monroe was a pleasant boss, not only allowing her to read art books at work, but insisting on it as part of her training. Victoria sold two paintings in her first two weeks, a Napa Valley vineyard landscape for $2,500 and a funky point of view oil painting of a bathtub with a yellow rubber ducky bobbing in the bubbles, toes sticking out, and the artist's reflection in the faucet, one of Victoria's favorites in the gallery, for $1,200. Mrs. Monroe glowed about Victoria's future and could not fail to notice the immediate increase in floor traffic, just as she expected. "What a fireball!" she always said.

Now alone all day, Morgan went for walks in the cool mornings, spent two hours or more having lunch at his favorite village café, masturbated sometimes in the long, warm afternoons, and watched TV, especially nostalgia-inducing reruns of *Hawaii Five-o*. He barely suppressed profound feelings of guilt and the only way he knew to hide from Victoria his abject laziness and creative impotence was to ask her not to read his work just yet, until he felt more secure about it. There was no work.

Summer passed. Next week he would start teaching again. What was he going to tell Victoria? He had nothing, not one page. Notes, he had. Sketches, he had. Even an outline of an idea he had essentially lifted from the plot of a *Hawaii Five-o* episode. Every day Victoria came home from the gallery and the first thing she said to him at the open door was, "Did you work well today, honey?" He gave her a welcome home kiss and varied his story, sometimes telling her it had been a good day, sometimes that it had not gone well, and sometimes just shrugging with artistic angst. How long will she buy this? He wondered.

The week after Thanksgiving, one of Victoria's charcoals sold. Stimulated by the environment of the gallery, Victoria had started sketching again, portraits mostly. She did a portrait of Mrs. Monroe and it was the one that sold first: to Mr. Monroe, who owned the State Farm Insurance agency in Pomona. The following day, another sold: a portrait of Morgan looking pensive and artistic, hazy in brilliant smoke from the cigarette casually posed between his fingers. A woman in pink pedal pushers and flip-flops paid $500 for it. "My God, darling Victoria," Mrs. Monroe said, "we're going to have to have a bloody showing of your charcoals! And anything else you've created, my dear."

In the spring, 1977, after she had produced enough drawings, pencil, pastels, and charcoal, Victoria had her first show at Mrs. Monroe's Gala Galleria. It opened on Saturday and Morgan came with her. He wore the professorial gray corduroy jacket she had bought for him, and a black turtleneck. People thought he was the artist. It's the beard, he told Mrs. Monroe, stroking it. Victoria could not fail to notice the continual mistake, supposing that at first people guessed she was the artist's trophy wife. She should not have dressed that way, her scoop-neck blouse scooping too low and her skirt cut too short. Her feelings were hurt and after a couple of hours of this, she began to pout and drink too much sparkling wine, which on top of the amphetamines made her feel a bit frantic. She went into the toilet and dropped a couple of reds to get balanced.

Mrs. Monroe, who shared with her namesake an impressive chest and bottled blonde hair, placed herself between Morgan and Victoria and said, "My God! What a gorgeously spectacular couple you two make." She put her arms around their shoulders and squeezed. "A brilliant artist and a brilliant writer, young, gorgeous, just amazingly happy. I hate you both with all my heart and soul." She gave each a kiss on the cheek, sent the now balanced Victoria off to mingle, and took Morgan to the table where bottles of California sparkling wine stayed cool in ice buckets and trays of cheese, nuts, dips, and crackers were quickly disappearing.

"Victoria is a natural talent," Mrs. Monroe began. "I couldn't believe she hadn't a lick of training in art."

"She surprised me with it, too," Morgan said. He was just making conversation and would have already left if it wouldn't have disappointed Victoria.

"Isn't it just truly amazing?"

"Yes, it is."

"She's got that temperament, too, don't you think? You would know more than anyone."

"Not so much, I think."

"Oh, really?" Mrs. Monroe looked suspiciously at him.

"Why would you say that?"

"I just mean she's such a sensitive creature, don't you think?"

"Yes, I guess she is, in some ways." He wondered where this was going, why Mrs. Monroe brought this up?

"Usually women who are this drop-dead gorgeous are just totally full of themselves, but Victoria acts like it's nothing to her, a handicap. She keeps saying she's just a doodler . . . Oh, see that couple who just came in?" she asked. Morgan nodded. "Money, money, money," she continued. "He's on the board of the Getty. I hope you won't mind if I go do a bit of hustling on behalf of your gorgeous wife?"

"Be my guest," Morgan said, just as happy to be left alone.

What Mrs. Monroe might have gotten around to, or maybe not, because it was a territory she wasn't comfortable with, was that she knew Victoria smoked marijuana in the bathroom, and sometimes from the way she acted, she worried that maybe her new prize artist was involved with real drugs. Sometimes she was off at full speed and sometimes she seemed to be in a daze. If she approached Victoria when she was daydreaming at the desk, sometimes she was so startled that she actually yelped. Once she suddenly jumped up, knocking the Chippendale chair over, and bolted out of the gallery. Not a word. Thankfully, Mrs. Monroe was there at the time. Would Victoria have left the gallery empty? She was gone nearly ten minutes. All she bothered to say when she came back was a quick apology, lamely explaining that she thought she had seen someone she knew. Then one time Mrs. Monroe heard sounds from the small office bathroom that sounded like Victoria crying and muttering to herself.

Three of Victoria's pieces sold during her first showing. Mrs. Monroe took forty percent, but still Victoria made almost six hundred dollars. During the three and a half years Victoria worked and showed at the Gala Galleria, her work sold steadily, and in the first year she made more than Morgan had earned on the advance for *Decompression*.

THIRTY-FIVE

Her name was Emily Slojka and she was in Morgan's autumn semester creative writing course and had taken Freshman Composition from him last spring. She was the most talented student he'd had in four years teaching at Western Hills. She often wore her light brown hair in braids that hung over each shoulder to her breasts. Other times she wore a ponytail, also braided. He had not seen her hair loose and wondered how long it would be. She wore jeans and men's shirts and chukka boots. He tried to imagine her legs. It's quite a normal thing for a man to wonder about, he told himself.

The creative writing seminar was limited to fifteen students and they sat on both sides of a long table, instead of at desks, with Morgan at one end, facing a wall of windows. He let them smoke during the seminar because he did. It was the only class at Western Hills where that was allowed. Rather, ignored. There were a few students who could have gone to any of a number of four-year colleges and universities, but who chose

Western Hills because Morgan Cary taught creative writing there, a co-
terie of his small but persistent fan club. All of those students would transfer to major universities after finishing their two-year program at
Western. Emily was one of them, and at the end of the 1980–81 school
year, after Morgan had abruptly quit and disappeared, she would transfer to Reed in Oregon. Fourteen years later, having only known him a
year and having never seen him again, she would write an autobiographi-
cal novel in which Morgan Cary would figure prominently, a character
named Carl Morgan.

In seminar, he suspected that she was writing to him specifically.
Her stories were romantic and sensually descriptive, the characters too
much like Morgan and like herself. He thought some of the other students
weren't missing the similarities, either. He wasn't bothered by this, as long
as the writing was good. It was rather flattering for other students to pick
up on Emily's flirtations with him. He thought about this a lot, about
Emily, about what she was clearly making available to him. He figured
he could enjoy the flirtation without doing anything about it.

They met in his office and talked about her writing. Then they went
for coffee and talked about her writing. Then they had lunch and talked
about her writing. Then they went to bed and afterwards talked about his
not writing. She said she would be his muse and he was sick to his stomach from an upset conscience. Why was he doing this?

She was attractive naked and her hair loosened fell over her shoulders and she could coyly nest her face in it when he was on top of her. He
would pick away a strand, wavy from the braiding, to expose one eye and
she would blink, he would expose her mouth and kiss it. How odd that
she hid her face while at the same time lying with her legs wide open and
her breasts brazenly offered. He had the impression that she was not experienced with this kind of thing, secret love. He was definitely not. The
flattery that she had chosen him almost balanced the extreme guilt he felt.
Sex helped to moderate his troubled conscience, but just until the heat

dissipated. He felt like he was in love with her when they were squirming around naked, but not at any other time. There was no doubt she was in love with him and she said so and lay her opened hand against his cheek as if to impress there her assurance.

The first time, Morgan walked home from her room feeling stupid and mad, exhilarated and desired, profoundly and criminally guilty. His mind spun and he couldn't focus his attention on what needed to be done now; conscience staggered his walk. Of course he would never have sex with Emily again, but he hoped they could remain good friends. But Victoria would smell Emily on him. He had to figure out what excuse he would use to have a shower before she got close to him. He showered in the morning, not at night. Victoria could never find out about this, it didn't mean anything, it didn't change one iota how much he loved her, it was a mistake that he wouldn't make again, she could never find out, it would kill her. He walked past a large truck in a gas station parking lot and decided to rub dirt from the tires on his hands, forearms, and a smudge on his face for effect. He would tell Victoria that he helped a little old lady change a tire, then he could go directly to the shower. That he came up with this excuse so easily surprised him and increased his guilt; such an easy liar. How could he even consider making up such an excuse, which was a lie? He was going to lie to Victoria for the first time. He remembered all his clothes tossed all over the front yard and he hadn't even done anything that time.

It worked, though. Victoria suspected nothing. He had screwed up just that once and not been caught. The feeling of relief came mixed with the fear that Emily might do something if she became angry with him for breaking it off. How had he let himself get into this? He hoped he would be able to explain everything to Emily in a way that did not make her angry, or guilty, or embarrassed. Not her fault, not anybody's fault. It was just one of those things, not bad, good actually, but just wrong. If he were single . . . et cetera, ad infinitum.

Then she was naked beneath him again, naked and offering every-thing but her nested face. Later, when she was on top of him, her hair flew about as if in a wind storm. She leaned forward and held herself with her palms on his chest and her hair fell over him and tickled his nose. She ecstatically gave him her face and he thought her earlier coyness was just her way to be in love. *Had we but world enough, and time, / This coyness, Lady, were no crime*, he thought.

"You can't write about this for the seminar," he said, smoking a joint while lying beside her.

"I know that, of course," she said, taking the joint from between his fingers.

"I'm married."

"I definitely know that, too."

She pouted and he thought it pretty. He took the joint back and sat up, prelude to dressing.

"I have no illusions," Emily went on. "But I do love you. I was in love with you before . . . we did this. It's not just this."

He leaned back and kissed her shoulder, gave the joint back to her. It was down to the roach and she clipped it.

"It's not necessary that you love me for me to love you," she added, stroking his arm.

"Emily, it's not about that."

"It's about your wife. I've seen her. I don't know why you're with me, like this, when you have a woman like that. But I won't think about it."

"Of course it's about my wife. It's about the fact that I'm married and I want to stay married, in spite of what this . . . how I feel about you. You had to have known that from the beginning. I hope you don't think I . . . But there's . . . it's also . . . you are an astonishing woman and you have a fantastic talent, which is compelling to me."

"You don't have to say any of this. I love you. I can live with it this way. I'm not asking you for anything more than this."

But can I live this way? Morgan thought. He felt like the asshole of the western world.

As if she had heard inside his head, she continued, "But can *you*?"

Had she asked him that while she was on top of him with her hair flying and her mouth open in ecstasy, the answer could have been that yes, he could and would happily live with her as his secret lover. Doesn't she know better than to ask a man a question like that when he is dressing to go home to his wife, a wife he loves very much?

"Just don't stop," she said, suddenly rising and throwing her arms around him from behind. He turned so he could kiss her.

"You are very hard to stop," he said, and that was true.

How many times, he wondered as he walked back to the bungalow on Cambridge Street, could he change tires on old ladies' cars? Every time he approached the bungalow he expected to see all his clothes tossed into the yard.

He did not stop. He could not stop. He thought about it every day, but like the nicotine he was addicted to and hated, he was addicted to the time he spent with Emily, which he did not hate, it was only himself he was starting to hate. He almost loved Emily simply for wanting him so much. During the three months before that last Christmas, he was with her almost every day, except on weekends. He learned it was a good idea to shower at Emily's small student apartment, where they always met, rather than take a chance that Victoria would want to make love when he came home, which happened from time to time. Emily had stopped submitting any of her writing to the workshop sessions. She was a good critic and that contribution was enough, as far as Morgan was concerned. But how was he supposed to grade her now? How could he give her anything less than an A without hurting her chances of getting into a university graduate writing program, which she dreamed about, not to mention hurting her feelings, even if she would claim to understand? She was the only student in the class doing truly A-level work, but what would the others think when she got an A and none of them did, when she didn't turn in a single piece of writing after the first month of the seminar? You are really tangled up here, he told himself. Worse, he was really starting to care about Emily. It was more than the sex. She stimulated him to work, and two months ago he had begun a novel. The story line involved a married professor and his best student. He made the protagonist a history professor.

THIRTY-SIX

The first week of December in that part of Southern California was un-usually cold, especially in the valley east of Los Angeles, as a brisk sea breeze stretched far inland from the coast and left the air chilled and smell-ing of salt. A storm the night before had dropped a spotty, thin layer of ice pellets over lawns around Claremont, resembling snow; Morgan joked that maybe they would have a white Christmas and washed the dishes while singing *Mele Kalikimaka*, an Hawaiian Christmas song offering wishes for a green and bright holiday.

Had Pooh Good Boy Bear not actually walked past the Gala Gal-leria window twice, Victoria might have missed him. He had exchanged his hippie outfit for a biker look, with a scruffy black leather jacket, stovepipe black jeans tucked into scruffier black engineer boots, and a faux navy blue Greek sailor cap. He had a pink and black long scarf rolled a couple of times around his neck with one end down his back

and the other down his chest. Victoria noticed the movement but paid
no attention to the person. Then, just a moment later, he walked by again
in the other direction, faster, as if he was making up time after going
the wrong way. He did not look toward the Galleria window, where
Victoria sat not ten feet away.

She was alone in the gallery, Mrs. Monroe out for her typical two-
hour lunch. She was also speeding on a Benzedrine tab she had taken an
hour ago because the reds she took to sleep seemed to never quite wear
off. She went after Pooh without even pausing to lock the door.

He was easy to follow, even from some distance, because of the Greek
cap bobbing in the hatless crowd. Her heart pounded and she began to sweat
through her blouse, even after she followed him outside into the windy,
misty, air. What if he got into a car? But he didn't. He walked across the
parking lot, turned right on the sidewalk, walked to the stoplight at the in-
tersection, waited impatiently for the light to change, lit a cigarette, then
crossed the street and walked into an alley between a furniture emporium
and a famous valley music club, the Puking Buzzard. She remembered one
of the park hippies saying she thought Pooh had joined a band. Victoria bet
he was playing at the Puking Buzzard. She watched him knock on a rear
door and be let in by fat man in a T-shirt. The door closed. Pooh had not
looked back.

She ran as fast as she could back to the gallery. It was still empty,
Mrs. Monroe had not returned from lunch. Victoria, breathing hoarsely,
looked over the walls, at the paintings stacked in the rear hallway, then
checked the cash drawer. As far as she could tell, no one had come in
when she was gone. Mrs. Monroe returned twenty minutes later and
Victoria told her she had to go home, she had horrible menstrual cramps.

Morgan was with Emily. When he came home and found Victoria already there, at least two hours early, already in bed and buried under

the comforter, he immediately believed that she had found out. His chest tightened and he thought he might have a heart attack, his pulse throbbed erratically against his temples, he was going to throw up. She must have heard him come in, but she had not said anything or moved under the covers. He had the ridiculous but compelling impulse to run away. He could not face this. He would rather die than be thrust unprepared into Victoria's pain. Prepared? What could he have been thinking? How utterly stupid could he be? This was the worst possible thing he could imagine. He would not survive being face to face with Victoria's hurt. But maybe there was some way to explain it, or at least . . . what? Could he lie believably? Would Emily lie for him? Victoria was going to kill him, or worse, leave him. This passed through his mind in seconds, then he put on his everything-is-completely-normal voice.

"Victoria, are you all right?"

"I've got terrible cramps," she said, without exposing herself from the covers.

Oh Jesus Fucking Christ, Morgan thought, the relief so profound that he felt suddenly faint: she came home sick. He sat on the side of the bed and lay his hand on the rise made by her hip. "Oh, honey! What did you eat?"

"Menstrual cramps," she said, her head slowly emerging from the comforter.

"Menstrual cramps," he repeated, feeling the fear flood back into his chest. She had her period only nine or ten days ago, how could she be having menstrual cramps? She knew. She found out about Emily and for some reason she didn't want to confront him. Or maybe she was really sick from something and confused it . . . no, how could she not know when she had her last period?

"Just let me lie here for a while," she said.

"Did you take something? Can I get you anything?"

"I've been popping Midol like Life Savers. I'll be all right. Why don't you go roll a joint. Maybe that would help."

"I'm on my way," he patted her hip and kissed her golden hair.

Maybe she didn't know, after all. He didn't understand the menstrual cramps, but what did he know about things like that? They smoked two joints. He did not instigate sex because of her cramps, even when she said she felt better. Besides, he hadn't yet had a chance to shower. She didn't know, but something was wrong, and he doubted the cramps story. Maybe she had done something. What if she really did know and . . . ? Not a chance, he believed; rather, he hoped.

Her first problem was figuring out how to get out that late, without her husband, so she could go to the club. What excuse could she possibly have? Morgan was seldom out at night without her, or she without him. The Puking Buzzard didn't open until nine and the band's first performance, she noted on the poster by the door, started at ten. Pooh Bear was probably with a band called Mother's Helpers. Once she saw them playing, she would know Pooh's real name. But she guessed he was the name listed for lead guitar and singer, Harry Bottoms, although that didn't seem real, either. It was making her crazy, waiting.

Then Mrs. Monroe told Victoria that she was going to San Francisco the weekend before Christmas for four days to visit galleries and do some buying. That gave Victoria an idea: she told Morgan that evening that Mrs. Monroe had asked her to go along on a buying trip to San Francisco for two nights.

The first thought Morgan had was that he could spend the entire night with Emily, then felt disgusted that it was his first thought. He agreed with pseudo-reluctance and pointed out that it would be the first time they had ever slept apart.

"Guess it had to happen one of these days," Victoria answered. She had no idea where she was going to sleep those two nights. Probably the motel two blocks down the street from the club. She began planning how she was going to kill Pooh Bear or Harry Bottoms without being caught.

Morgan didn't tell Emily that he was staying until after they made love. Instead of his usual quick shower and rush home, he turned toward Emily in the bed, spooned himself against her, nuzzled her hair, and suggested they have a nap. Didn't he have to go home? In the morning would be all right, he told her nonchalantly. In the morning? "She," not comfortable using his wife's name in such a position, "is on a buying trip this weekend to San Francisco."

"There is a god, that's proof," Emily proclaimed and excitedly kissed him all over.

The club was dark and smoky and Victoria sat in back in the darkest corner. She swallowed two bennies with a rum and coke. The band was already on stage, engaged in a fair imitation of the Stones. Pooh Good Boy Bear was Harry Bottoms, playing lead guitar and belting out "Satisfaction" while kissing up to the microphone. He had a fan club of girls at the front tables, who squealed and applauded when he swished his thin hips and marched around the stage with his guitar thrust out like a phallic weapon about to shoot off.

Victoria ordered another rum and coke and swallowed another Benzedrine tablet. She thought of jumping on stage and killing him there, with the butcher knife in her purse, cutting off his pecker, and throwing it to his adoring fans. She had ceased to care about herself. What did she have to lose? All she cared about was Morgan, what he would think about her, how horrified he would be discovering to whom he was really married. No, she had to get away with it. Morgan could never know what she had done. Morgan was what she had to lose.

She waited for the first set to end. She was flying too high and too fast. She swallowed a red to slow herself down and focus her attention. How would she get him alone? Would the band go out together later, or would they separate and go home? She wanted it to be tonight, she couldn't bear waiting. As long as Pooh Harry Bottoms Bear was alive, she wouldn't be able to think of anything else.

They played for an hour. When they left the stage, the second band came on and Victoria went outside and around to the alleyway. She had seen him go in that way and presumed he would come out the same way. She waited in the dark, trembling, checking for the knife in her purse half a dozen times. She had wrapped it in a dish towel, the towel she planned to use to wipe off the blood. If she could get him alone in the alley and kill him there, it would look like a robbery; remember to take his watch and wallet, she reminded herself. This is a rough neighbor-hood, she thought.

She had waited more than fifteen minutes before the side door opened and the light from inside raced across the alley and up the wall of the furniture store. She leaned back against the wall. Smoke sparkled as it floated in the light. The smoke preceded the drummer. He came out, flicked the butt toward a trash can, then went back inside. The door stayed open. Victoria had her hand around the handle of the knife, still in her purse. She had to pee and wondered if she would be able to hold it while killing Pooh, so much liquid, she thought, his blood, my piss. She would piss on him, piss into his wound. Yes. She saw him on his back, squirm-ing and screaming, after she had castrated him, and she squatted over his crotch with her pants down and pissed between his legs.

He came out then. Casually tossing the pink and black scarf around his neck as if he was on the set of an Italian movie. He adjusted the fisherman's cap to a jaunty angle. He lit a cigarette with a plastic butane lighter. Would he go back inside? Could she surreptitiously follow him if he left? Would she piss her pants before he even moved? Why did she always have to pee at the worst times? He exhaled smoke in a stream and began walking toward her, leaving the alley. She noted that the door had closed behind him; maybe no one else was coming now. She crouched in the darkness behind a trash Dumpster. His boot heels clicked as if they were metal. He looked normal sized with his big coat and hat, but on stage he was a stick, emaciated. Probably heroin, she supposed. He passed her and turned right. She could follow him by the sound of his boot heels. He walked to the next corner and turned right again. She could smell his cigarette. There were cars; people passed. It was only a little after midnight and there were bars all over the neighborhood. Maybe that's where he was going. Another bar or club. He turned right again and she wondered if he was only out for a walk during the break, making his way back to the Puking Buzzard? She wanted to get this over with, certainly before he got back to the club and she would have to sit through another set. Then what? If he turned right again at the next corner, it would be obvious he was just out for a walk and on his way back. He turned right. There was an alley between the two streets. Victoria speeded up and as if he sensed her approach, Pooh Bear looked over his shoulder. He didn't seem to recognize her. He stopped and looked at her with a curious smile on his face and tossed the cigarette butt into the street. Victoria continued toward him, her hand inside her purse and holding the knife. Now she thought she should have gone to the trouble and bought a pistol. What would she do if he ran or if he attacked her? He was so skinny, she thought she could take him in a fight, especially holding a knife. Still he did not recognize her. The streetlights were far apart and while he was within the glow of one, she was in the darkness.

"Are you following me, sweetheart?" Pooh Bear asked in a curious but nonchalant voice, acting as if she were another groupie.

Victoria entered the glow of the streetlight, close to him now, the entrance to the alley only ten or fifteen feet ahead. She could see as his expression suddenly changed that he finally recognized her. "Shit," he said, tensing his shoulders but holding his arms stretched out in front of him in a what-the-hell gesture. When she was close, she pulled the knife from her purse and pointed it at his chest. "What the fuck!" he cried, thrusting his hands out as if to ward off the knife. "Go over there," Victoria said, nodding to indicate the opening to the alley. "Look, I understand what's going on here, really. Give me chance to apologize, all right?" "Apologize?" Victoria sneered. "Go in there," she ordered, thrusting closer to his chest with the knife. Pooh backed up carefully, not moving his hands down. "Why don't you just report me to the police? You don't have to do something like this, something you are going to regret, I promise."

He backed up to the alley and Victoria ordered him into it. There was a dim light bulb glowing at the far end, trash Dumpsters, empty beer and liquor cases. They were behind some bar, the air reeking of old beer and soggy cigarette butts.

"Stop," she ordered.

"I never done anything like that before. Please believe me. It was the stupidest thing I ever done, no shit. I hope you'll let me show you how sorry I am. You don't want to do something you'll regret for the rest of your life."

"Is your name really Harry Bottoms?"

He was visibly shaking but her question made him smile. "No, it's just some stupid stage name. Dick, the drummer, gave it to me because I got one, a hairy bottom, I mean." He winced, noting a reminder he didn't want her to remember.

"What is your name? Don't lie to me." She raised the knife tip until it was directed more to his throat.

"Tim."

"Tim? Tim what?"

"Timothy Smith."

"Bullshit," Victoria made a slicing motion with the knife and Pooh leaned back, raising his hand to block any cut to his neck.

"Really, it really is Tim Smith. Want to see my driver's license?" He made to reach back for a wallet.

"Don't move," she poked the knife at him again.

"All right, all right. But it really is. I'm not exactly in a position to lie to you about anything, not after what I done to you. I am so fucking sorry. It was the stupidest goddamn thing I ever done. I hope you believe me. I never done anything like that. You are the most beautiful chick I ever seen, really. Just made me crazy."

"It's my fault? You asshole!"

"No, no. That's not what I mean. Not at all. It was one hundred and ten percent my fault. How could I have been so fucking stupid?"

She wasn't going to kill him. She knew this in an instant and didn't know why. Not because he apologized. His apology was stupid. She just knew she wasn't going to kill him, even if that was exactly what he deserved. Maybe she would just cut him somewhere, leave him a memory scar. No. She couldn't cut him, she couldn't kill him. But she was glad she found him, because now she could make him disappear from her mind. Now he would never forget what he did to her.

"Well, Timmy, I know your name, I know the band you're in, I know how to find you anytime I want to find you. I haven't decided what to do with you, or when. Maybe tomorrow, or maybe next week, or next year. When I'm in the mood, you will see me sitting at the back of some club, or behind you on some street; maybe I'll have a knife like this, or maybe a gun, or maybe I'll just run you over with my car. I don't know. Whatever I decide and whenever I decide it. Any day, any time. You think about that. I want you to worry about that everyday until you see me again, which will be the last time you'll ever see anything."

Then she turned around and walked quickly out of the alley. It sounded to her like he exhaled the words *holy shit* as she disappeared from his view and his life forever.

THIRTY-SEVEN

Victoria took a taxi home. She felt good about herself. She had not killed someone she could have killed and who deserved it anyway. It was a god-like power. She could have taken a life, but didn't. She could choose. She tipped the taxi driver five dollars on a twelve dollar ride. She entered the bungalow through the kitchen. It was after one o'clock and she didn't want to give Morgan a start, assuming he would even wake up. She could picture him sleeping like a baby with the blanket pulled up to his head. He slept like an innocent, she thought, smiling to herself at the thought of the man, her man, in her bed, sleeping and waiting for her, for only her.

As quietly as possible, she undressed in the dark and left her clothes on the sofa. Then she crept into the bedroom on her toes. Her eyes were just adjusting to the dark. Light through the closed blinds streaked the opposite wall. As she approached the bed, she realized that it was still made, the way she had left it, and empty. She turned around as if she would see Morgan standing behind her, ready to jump out and scare the pants off her, which he was known to do. She stood there incongruously remembering once when Morgan had hidden in the closet where she would hang her jacket when she came in from work, but she was distracted outside with a neighbor and by the time she came in, Morgan had gotten bored waiting and was coming out of the closet as she came in. "What are you doing in the closet?" she asked. "Never mind," he said, but later confessed.

She said his name, quietly, then loudly. Then she turned on the light. Morgan was not in the house. There was no evidence he had eaten supper there. She went everywhere looking for a note. Surely he had left a note. She looked at the kitchen wall clock and checked against her wrist watch. It was twenty-two minutes past one in the morning.

He had never done anything like this, go out without her or stay out this late if they weren't together, as far as she knew, anyway. Her heart thudded inside her chest and she was sweating, her stomach burning. She had dropped too much speed at the music club. Was he hurt somewhere? Maybe he got hit by a car or something? She had to calm down. She downed two reds with a glass of vodka and orange juice. Where the hell was the phone book? She never could find anything when she needed it. How many hospitals were there around here? Should she call the police? But what if they came here? There was so much dope in the house. Suddenly she wondered if maybe Timmy, or whatever his name really was, might have called the police? She had threatened to kill him, he knows her name and even her address. No, he couldn't be that stupid. But what if the police were on their way here, what if they were going to arrest her? No, don't call the police, just check hospitals. Where is the fucking phone book? She swallowed another red secobarbital pill and made another vodka and orange juice.

By three-thirty she had phoned the emergency room of every hospital within ten miles of their house in Claremont. No one named Morgan Cary had been admitted.

Even after taking more secobarbital than she ever had before at any one time, even with the countereffect of almost a fifth of vodka, she still felt panicked, afraid. Morgan could be hurt somewhere, needing her, calling for her. Why, oh why, she thought, did she lie about where she was going to be this weekend? Oh shit, Jesus Christ, motherfucker! What if he said something to Mrs. Monroe and found out she had lied? How would she explain what she was really doing? Well, honey babe, I lied because I was going to murder the punk who raped and beat me and I thought you'd be upset. Shit, shit, shit! She had not lied to him before, not consequentially, at least. See what happens when you lie? She told herself. Why couldn't she calm down, at least? How could she even still be awake? Baby, where are you?

At five, still pitch dark outside, she first considered that maybe it was something else, maybe he wasn't hurt or dead, maybe he . . . no, not possible, she thought even as the possibility inevitably appeared. But why is it not possible? Because, she thought, because he loves me. She had no doubt about that. But maybe . . . she felt acid churning in her stomach and surging up into her throat. How many reds had she taken? She emptied the vial onto the table and there were only two remaining. How many were there when she put the vial into her purse and went to the music club? It couldn't have been full. But she felt so dizzy and sick to her stomach. Just the vodka and orange juice, she thought, looking at the almost empty bottle on the table. Jesus, I am sick, she told herself.

In the corner of the living room, on a round table at the end of the sofa she had picked out especially for the room, the little plastic Christmas tree sparkled with all white lights. There were a few token gifts under it, but she had not wrapped everything yet, and she knew that Morgan had hidden something big for her. He said he didn't trust her not to peek. He was right, she thought. She had already unwrapped and perfectly rewrapped the two packages for her already under the tree. In one was a set of calligraphy pens, the other a coffee table book on the history of

Hawaiian Aloha shirts. She had no idea what her big present would be. Morgan's carefully extracted hints were no help. Waiting another week felt like a year.

She tried to get up from the table to go lie down on the sofa. She was so sleepy, so sleepy that her head bobbed up and down like a water duck. This is so stupid, she thought. You know better than to take so many reds and drink vodka. What the hell were you thinking? You weren't thinking. Why? Morgan, Morgan, Morgan, my darling, where are you? Please be all right. Please, please, please.

Her head bobbed so far down that her face hit the table. She tried to raise herself up but her neck wouldn't provide the tension. She turned her face sideways and looked toward the little twinkling plastic Christmas tree. Please come home and let's open our presents, she thought. What did you get me special? Where are you? Please be all right.

Why are you so stupid? Why?

She scrawled the word *why* on her shopping note pad. She had meant to continue with *are you so stupid*, but the first word was all she could manage.

"Please, my baby, don't be dead," she muttered aloud.

She tried once more to stand, but slipped sideways out of the chair and hit hard on the floor, breaking her thumb without knowing it. She was unconscious by then. A minute later she vomited.

"I should have brought some clean clothes," Morgan told Emily. She brought him breakfast in bed. It was warming up after a chilly dawn and he had pushed the blanket down.

"You could leave a few things here if you'd like," she said. She brought him toast and jam, scrambled eggs, two slices of bacon, and half a sliced melon.

"This is a feast," he proclaimed.

"Fit for a king," she said, smiling.

"After a royal fucking," he teased.

"Your servant is at your command, sire."

"Sire needs clean clothes."

"Want me to go with you?"

Morgan thought that was a bad idea. He had separated his life into these two distinct and immutable sections: one, the Morgan Cary gloriously and happily married to the most beautiful and wonderful woman he had ever known; the other, some inexplicable element of . . . what? Lover of this bright, talented, and interesting young woman, who treats him like a king. He could only survive this dichotomy by keeping them entirely unknown to one another, in two distinct and isolated worlds.

"No, that's all right. It won't take long. What do you want to do this afternoon? We have one more day."

"Umm, I'll think of something and let you know later."

"Intriguing."

Morgan ate lavishly, in bed, with Emily naked beside him. She had opened the bedroom window a crack to mute their sleep odors and slid her legs under the blanket up to her thighs. He looked at the hair between her legs, which she trimmed into a small triangle, the tip pointing to the magic trigger of her clitoris. He liked being inside her. She was instantly wet and she had learned this trick with her vaginal muscles that was like . . . what? A suction hose. No, one of those Chinese finger puzzles that get tighter the harder you try to pull out.

This would have to end, he thought. There was no future for her in it, which doubled his guilt. He hoped she understood that inevitability from the start, and still did. Maybe it would be all right until she finished her coursework at Western Hills and went off to finish college somewhere; Reed, she wanted. He would write her a terrific recommendation. Then it would end, or fade away, and maybe from time to time . . . oh, stop it!

He finished eating and she took away the tray, walking to the sink with her rear slinking along in the most enticing way. But he wanted to go. It was subtle, but still he felt uncomfortable having spent the night in her bed. It was different; fucking in her bed was in another category from sleeping in her bed. What if Victoria had called home for him and gotten the answering machine? What would his story be? He just wanted to go home, shower, put on clean underwear, at least, and make sure there were no messages. He had been stupid not to consider that Victoria might call from San Francisco. He began working on a list of possible excuses. He should have unplugged the phone, then he could claim that the power went out. He wasn't yet used to needing such excuses. After more practice . . .

He dressed, gave Emily a wonderful kiss, and said he would be back in a couple of hours.

THIRTY-EIGHT

He began to self-destruct.

Morgan didn't even last a month into the new spring semester. He was drunk most of the time and often skipped classes. Alcohol was not an anesthetic, it was in fact a knife stabbed directly into his heart, again and again and again, the weapon of an unrepentant sufferer.

They were knocking on the door for some time, becoming more insistent about getting in. He had no idea how long he'd been locked in his office. He'd made a real mess of it—the books with their colorful spines on the floor, the desk and all around it littered with student papers like jetsam after a storm, papers he should have dealt with weeks before. He was blind, deadly drunk. They stopped knocking and started banging.

On the corner of the desk lay a shard from the bottom of a broken drinking glass, the paper beneath it stained with condensation circles. Sunlight passing through the glass made of itself a prism that flickered against the opposite wall in a Technicolor sort of Platonic cave show.

Morgan looked at the sharp edge of the glass, touched a fingertip to it, drawing fascinating blood. He lay his wrist over the glass and thought, there's nothing like taking phenomenology by the balls and giving them a little squeeze.

Someone had found the key by then and when Helen, the department secretary, and Dr. Thomas, the English department chairman, came into the room, his blood dripped over the edge of the desk and spotted a pile of final exams.

Two days later he was on a plane to Hawaii.

PART FOUR

THE COMMON BOND

[Hawaii 1981–1982]

THIRTY-NINE

Morgan came for Christmas dinner with Ana and Ben Iki and Mrs. Kamakani. Ana called the midday meal dinner and the evening meal supper. He had fretted for more than a week about what to bring for Ana and ended up with an autographed copy of *Decompression* and a pair of small black coral earrings, hoping the earrings wouldn't seem too personal and the book too egotistical. He remembered her mentioning that she liked black coral, not the pink or white. He brought flowers and a crystal vase for Ben's widow. Ben Iki was easy: a gold-plated Fin-Nor offshore spinning reel. Mrs. Kamakani said it was crazy to spend that kind of money on a boy, but she had given him a ten-speed mountain bike costing quite a bit more. Ana told her son as he sat on the floor amid the debris of Christmas that he had made out like a bandit. Mrs. Kamakani gave Morgan one of her husband's favorite Konahead lures. Ben Iki gave him a framed colored pencil drawing of a marlin tail-walking wave tops that he had drawn himself. Ana gave him a Montblanc rollerball pen and he was horrified she had spent that kind

318 · DONIGAN MERRITT

of money on him. They drank eggnog, a drop of rum in Ben Iki's, while Christmas music played from the radio and twinkling lights from the house across the street speckled the walls through the jalousie window slats. Morgan felt his emotions surging out of control and went to the bathroom and softly cried. Victoria dead one year now. A week ago, the anniversary of her death, he had spent much of the night sitting in the Noho Kai's cockpit, drinking and thinking of taking a swim to Japan.

Ana put on the earrings immediately and even after thumbing through the book and thanking him for the inscription—"*To Ana, for being a friend, Morgan*"—held it in her lap for a long time. After making him help clean up, Ana let Ben Iki take off on his new bike. Mrs. Kamakani drove herself home then. Morgan thought he should leave, but Ana hoped he would stay for a while. They finished the carton of eggnog and Ana put the remaining rum in Cokes, with lime and mint leaves. Morgan felt more at ease after she finally put down the book. She noticed when he glanced at it, where she had put it on the coffee table next to the box her earrings came in, and said, "I can't wait to read it again, my *autographed* copy." He just smiled and nodded. He wanted to be there and he wanted to be alone, anywhere else. He wanted to suffer and Ana was not allowing it. But he also held a deep wish to live at ease with whatever life remained for him and Ana offered that. He wanted her to understand why he couldn't just be all right, but couldn't tell her. What could he say? My wife committed suicide one year ago because I was having an affair with a student. "What are you thinking about?" Ana interrupted. Morgan shook his head, afraid his voice would give away his limitless guilt. Finally, "nothing much," he said. Why did she invite me for Christmas with her family? Morgan thought. I must be the worst guest on the island, he supposed.

"So, what are you going to do for New Year's?"

Oh God, Morgan thought, she's going to invite me to some New Year's party. "Don't know yet," he said.

"We never go out on New Year's Eve. It's too crazy. I actually have a hard time staying awake until midnight. We can see the fireworks from the front yard. They shoot them off from a platform in the bay. You'll have them right over your head on the boat."

"Sounds like what I'll have is a lot of ash to clean off the decks."

Ana laughed. "Probably. Papa always complained about that."

"I'm not much of a fan of party crowds, either," he commented.

"What's it like living on the boat all the time? I mean, living and working in the same place."

"Convenient. I don't have far to walk."

She laughed naturally. It did not seem just polite to him.

Ben Iki rushed in to ask if he could ride the new bike to his school with the three brothers who lived at the end of the block. They were going to race around the running track. "At least try to keep that bike in one piece for an entire day." "Mom!" he cried in exasperation, and ran out the door, probably not hearing the order to be home before dark.

"I should go," Morgan said, standing and putting his glass on the coffee table.

"Really? You don't need to rush, I mean, if you have someplace you need to be . . . sorry, that's none of my business."

"No, that's all right. Ahi is going for Christmas prices at auction right now. I'm hoping I can bring up a couple."

"You're going out today, now?"

"I guess so."

"It'll be dark in a couple of hours."

"That doesn't bother the fish, I suppose."

"By yourself?"

He shrugged. "My best deckhand seems to be otherwise occupied."

"That boy!"

"Ben Iki is a fine boy."

"Oh, I know. I often think how lucky I am with him. Some of my friends have kids and you wouldn't believe the stories. Horrible things. Ben Iki is a treasure. But, you know, sometimes . . . oh well."

"Please say goodbye to him for me. I love the drawing. I'm going to hang it in the cabin. And this pen." He patted his shirt pocket where it was clipped. "Makes me feel compelled to write something important."

"I doubt if it would be easy to write something as important as this," she picked up his book from the coffee table, "but I hope you're going to try. Was that a dumb thing to say?"

"Not at all. Maybe I will. You can't use a pen like this to pay bills or just anything."

Should he shake hands with her, kiss her cheek, hug her? They faced each other awkwardly. He tucked the frame under his arm and put the Konahead into his back pocket. Then he hugged her. She kissed his cheek.

At the door, stupidly, he took her hand and shook it, thanked her for a great Christmas day. She stayed in the open door as he got into the truck, started it, and backed out of her driveway. He waved and drove away.

He wasn't going fishing. He was going to get stumbling, reeking, shit-faced, plastered somewhere he could get sick in peace and drown again in his punishing memories of Victoria.

FORTY

January it rained every afternoon but two. In the middle of the month it rained for forty hours with hardly a break. The price of ahi dropped after Hilo's Japanese population finished buying up all the catches for their seasonal traditional Christmas dishes. Morgan made nearly fifteen hundred dollars in two weeks over the Christmas period and he worried less that he would be broke and living on the street like Chivas Joe in a year. He still went to the Paniola Kai most evenings for a burger and beer. He had companions of a sort there, but he still missed Ben, the evenings talking story with him. The barmaid, Leila, an islander mix of Japanese, Portuguese, Filipino, and haole, flirted with him flagrantly, reminding him of what time she got off and pointing out that he could drink for free at her place. He thought she was fifty or so and had a lifetime of difficulties in her face, but she could have been forty or sixty. Not that she was unattractive, even with that hard-edged sarcastic look some women who work behind bars often get as they carry troubles on their skin and in their posture. She wore thin-strapped tank tops offering a compellingly deep cleavage.

The last night of January, after five boilermakers, he stayed until closing and they went to her apartment in an older condo two blocks from the Paniola Kai. He knew what this was about, but was no less surprised when she had barely closed the door before pulling him against her body and giving him the sort of welcome kiss that said there was no point going through any polite chitchat. Her clothes and his landed here and there across the floor as she kissed him to the sofa, which he figured must have been the bed in her studio apartment, although it was not extended. She lay back on the sofa holding out her arms while he stood in front. She had a long scar on her stomach, like a cesarean. Did she have a child, children? He glanced at the walls for personal photos and there were none, just the standard uninspired decorations, like a motel or a cheap rental. "Come here, baby," she said, wiggling her fingers. "Let mama-san fix that for you." He did not have an erection. No matter how she administered to the problem, he never did; it would not bother him if he never did again. By all rights he should have been castrated anyway; better yet, decapitated. She invited him a couple of more times, but after that they settled back into a bar friendship, which satisfied both of them well enough.

He stopped smoking for two grotesque days. There were more night promises to himself, more commitments to do this and avoid that. One day he managed to drink only two beers. The loss of anesthesia was worse than not smoking for two days had been.

At the beginning of February the sun erupted from the sea into a cloudless sky so big and bright that it was hard to open your eyes looking to the east. Such mornings were rare on the windward side. *Vog* still veiled the mass of Mauna Loa.

Morgan puttered around nervously cleaning up the forward cabin, shoving his clothing into the lockers below the berth, rolling up and stowing the sleeping bag. He put a Jackson Browne tape into the player and opened the forward hatch to let fresh air push out the stale sleeping smells. Maybe he could get a plumeria lei from the stall next to Yamachi's Supply, hang it in the wheelhouse for good luck and a bit of deodorizing.

Morgan was walking back from Yamachi's, the lei around his neck, a bag of ice under one arm and a sack of groceries in the other, when Ben Iki and Ana drove up. Ben Iki took the ice bag from Morgan and stepped aboard.

"Are we too early?" Ana wondered.

"No, not at all."

"Ben Iki would have been here half an hour ago."

Morgan smiled. He needed the smiles Ben Iki caused.

"Help your mother aboard," Morgan said.

After she boarded, Ana reached back and took the grocery bag from Morgan.

"Let me show you where we keep everything, Mama." Ben Iki took the sack from his mother and motioned her into the wheelhouse. Ana shrugged her shoulders and Morgan smiled. Of course Ana had been on her father's boat before, probably often, Morgan thought. Ben Iki reached for his mother's hand. Morgan squeezed by Ben Iki and Ana to drape the lei over the compass binnacle. "We changed some things from what Papa Ben did. We put the cans right up against the ice," Ben Iki explained, "and that way they get cold fast." Ana looked back at Morgan and raised her eyebrows. "Thank you for asking us," she said. Morgan nodded, still smiling at Ben Iki, who was now on his knees loading the reefer. "That's how we do it," Ben Iki proclaimed. "Eh, Cap'n?"

"That's how we do it."

"We save the sacks in there for carryout trash," Ben Iki informed his mother as he handed the plastic bag to her. "Want me to cast off?" he asked Morgan.

"Cast off, mate."

"Let's hele mai and chase us some fishes," Ben Iki chanted.

Morgan steered their way clear of the busy channel before turning the helm over to Ben Iki. Ana stood at the transom facing aft, watching the Hilo shoreline recede. She said more or less to herself that Hilo town was beautiful from the sea. Morgan brought out the trolling rods and remarked that everything is beautiful from the sea. You can't see the dirt, Ana agreed, then asked if she could help.

"No, thanks."

"I'm a pretty good fisherman, you know."

"I would think so, with Ben Kamakani for a father." He secured the rubber band and sent the port side trolling line up the stinger pole. "You could do the starboard outrigger while I set up a flat line," he offered.

Ben Iki had parked himself royally at the helm. His mother said, "Ben, put on your life jacket."

"Mama," he said, exasperated.

"I have to confess," Morgan interrupted, "that I only make him wear one when he is outside the cabin or if he wants to go to the rails. Just like his grandfather did," Morgan added.

"Okay, you win," Ana said. "But follow Morgan's rules."

"He always does," Morgan said.

"It's hard for me to believe that he will be a teenager in a couple of months," Ana told Morgan as they continued rigging for trolling. "Makes me feel pretty old."

Morgan just shook his head. He thought that Ben Iki acted much younger than his twelve years; there seemed to be no potential teenager in him at all, as if he planned to skip over all that.

"His birthday is tax day, right?"

"Right," Ana smiled. "My little tax deduction."

"If it's not a school day, I'd like to take him fishing and maybe someplace for a burger afterward."

"He'd like that very much. But not the Paniola Kai."

Morgan laughed. "Well, I was thinking of McDonald's."

Ana wore a white blouse cut like a man's dress shirt, tails out and knotted at her stomach, over tapa print shorts. A black bikini top showed through the thin white cloth. She was a big woman, stout without fat, except where it was supposed to be, in her breasts and hips. When they stood together at the cockpit stern rail, they were the same height. She wore a ball cap with her hair pulled in a pony tail through the back slot and big black plastic sunglasses. Morgan had said if the fishing was bad, they could just go for a swim, so Ana had worn a swimsuit beneath her blouse and shorts. Ben Iki told her the fishing would be good so she didn't need to bring a swimsuit.

She glanced over her shoulder toward her son sitting at the helm of his grandfather's boat. He looked like a child, but somehow grown up at the same time. He was already so tall. He controlled the wheel like a man. She did not think she wanted him to become a fisherman, although she thought it a noble and worthwhile occupation and had nothing against it, of course. She had a small private dream that he would maybe be a literary or creative person, an artist maybe; he drew so well, just look at the marlin drawing he gave Morgan for Christmas. She would take care of him if he wasn't making any money as an artist, except probably he could not respect himself if he lived off his mother. But no, she watched him peering through the cabin window for working birds, her son was going to be a fisherman. It was in his blood.

It was blazing hot in the sun, but the breeze from their motion through the slight swells mitigated the effect. Ana relaxed in the fighting chair while Morgan sat on the cockpit rail facing her, his back to the wake. He looked just beyond her, to the right and front, and called out to Ben Iki: "Bring her three points starboard, skipper."

"Aye, aye," Ben Iki answered and brought the Noho Kai a little to the right.

326 · DONIGAN MERRITT

"Do you know how much he likes and respects you, Morgan?"

He nodded. "It's mutual."

"I can see it is. I have wanted to thank you for that."

"For nothing. I mean, no thanks required."

A female Ben, he thought. But a lot prettier.

Two boats patrolled for fish in the same direction, others crossed ahead and behind. Not as many as there would be on a normal working day. It was Sunday. Few of the long-liners were out. Some boats carried fishermen's families, a day-off outing. Probably only a handful of boats were working. Long period high swells passed beneath them and the Noho Kai wallowed a little. Morgan went into the cabin, patted Ben Iki's shoulder, and told him he was holding a fine course, then got a couple of beers from the reefer and returned to where Ana leaned back in the fighting chair with her feet on the transom, wiggling her toes. He pulled the tabs on both cans and dropped the loose tabs into the cans so they wouldn't fall into the water and end up in a fish's belly. Ana said cheers and they clanked the cans together. She glanced over her shoulder at her son then back to Morgan. She said, "My father claimed that you needed saving?" Morgan laughed. "No, really. Papa was good with things like that, his impressions of people."

After a long pause, Morgan finally said, "Ben was truly a good man. You were lucky to have such a man for a father."

"I know. I miss him very much."

"Me too."

"That was a pretty obvious changing of the subject. Or maybe your way of telling me to mind my own business again?"

"Just wondering if the entire Kamakani family are missionaries?"

"Well, maybe not my brother," Ana said. She smiled but persisted. "Mama said you told her you were one time a Kona-side charter-boat skipper."

"A previous life. Can I get you another beer?"

Ana shook her can a little and said she was not that fast. Morgan shook his as if he needed to show it was empty and went to the cabin for another. He knew she wasn't going to give up easily and they were sort of trapped on the boat. He couldn't just leave and he did not want to offend her. He liked her. He was crazy about her son. He wanted them to like him. In a way, he thought, pulling out another beer, Ana and Ben Iki are all he has, the only tethers to the shore.

"I'm not going to stop," Ana said when he came back, "unless, of course, you really do want me to. I am curious because I . . . we . . . Ben Iki and me, I mean. We feel like we are becoming part of your life, and you in ours. Am I presuming?"

"It's not a good story, Ana. That's all."

"Okay. I understand."

He held his beer in one hand and adjusted the outrigger settings with the other. "Here, fishy, fishy, fishy," he cajoled.

Ben Iki leaned around and called out, "What say we go north, Waipio way? Big ahi up there sometime."

Morgan gave Ben Iki a thumbs-up. The Noho Kai drifted slowly to port as Ben Iki turned the wheel; she squatted down through quartering swells.

Two minutes later, the starboard stinger bobbed quickly twice. Morgan noticed out of the corner of his eye and spun around to look astern. The tip of the long stinger pole discernibly quivered two more times and the rubber band stretched.

"Marlin!" Morgan called out over his shoulder to Ben Iki. Ana sprung from the chair and went to the starboard outrigger rod. "He's playing with it, slapping it with his bill," Morgan said. "It's yours."

"Thank you," she answered, gripping the rod with her left hand and her right on the reel, ready to make the strike and set the hook.

"Steady," Morgan told Ben Iki. "Be ready."

Two more quick taps and then the stinger pole bent nearly double and the rubber band snapped off with a bang. Line raced off the reel.

"Pedal to the metal!" Morgan shouted to Ben Iki.

Ana pulled the rod from its holder and pointed the tip in the direction of the fleeing line.

"Okay, okay, now!" Morgan yelled.

Simultaneously, Ben Iki shoved the throttle forward to the stop as Ana tightened the drag wheel and jerked the rod back. Feeling the sudden pressure, the marlin erupted from the sea like porpoise in a show, tail walking back across the Noho Kai's spreading white water wake.

"He's got the hook," Morgan said. "Go neutral."

Ben Iki pulled the throttle back and slipped the gear lever into neutral; the sudden slowing drove down the Noho Kai's bow. Ana had already worked her way across the cockpit sole to the fighting chair and backed into it. Morgan grabbed the fighting harness from a peg at the cabin entrance. He stood behind the chair and got Ana into the harness, then came around and clipped the harness to the reel. Ana worked the fish, which had gone down again, like an old pro, pulling the rod back to her chest and then reeling in slack line furiously as she dropped it level.

"God, he looked huge, didn't he?" Ana said, already breathless, but as much from excitement as exertion.

"I think he's over five hundred."

"Shit . . . pardon my French."

"You all right?"

"I'm dandy, skipper."

"Mama," Ben Iki called out. "You got a big guy."

"Boy, I'll say."

"Want for me to back down on the guy?" Ben Iki asked.

"Not yet," Morgan said. "Let's see what this guy's going to do. There's plenty of line left."

About a quarter of the 120-pound test Dacron line had been stripped from the reel on the marlin's first run. The bigger marlin were usually female, and Morgan presumed this one was, although all big fish were guys in the vernacular. Ana pulled back on the rod, then as the rod dropped level again, hurriedly reeled in the recovered slack line.

Ben Iki dropped a holding loop over one of the wheel spokes and headed toward the cockpit.

"Life jacket," Morgan said.

"All right, all right," Ben Iki said and grabbed one from the cabin seat. He had it on by the time he got into the cockpit, but not secured.

"Buckle it," his mother ordered, glancing at him over her shoulder.

"All right, already. Did you see the fish?" Ben Iki asked.

"You bet I did," his mom answered.

"Shit fire," Ben Iki cried.

"Don't curse!" Ana said, giving him a quick look.

"I'm sorry, Mama. You ever fought one fish this big?"

"No way." She was breathless, sweat poured down her face and dripped steadily from her nose.

"You're all right?" Morgan asked.

"I am. I am. Thank you. But I've got this guy. Me and him are going to the dance."

He could see that she most definitely had the fish. She sweated beautifully.

A hundred meters off the stern starboard quarter, the fish exploded from the sea again, then again and again, turning a full flip before disappearing below. Morgan saw that more than two hundred yards of line was off the reel. "There's a bow in the line," he said. "We've got to get that back. Stay with your Mom and guide the chair," he told Ben Iki, then went to the helm and popped the steadying rope off the wheel. "Turn the chair starboard and ahead," he called back to Ben Iki. Then he spun the wheel until the Noho Kai's bow was pointed toward where the fish disappeared. He engaged the gear and eased the throttle forward a little. They were chasing the fish now. Ana had to reel quickly to avoid slack line. Such a large bow in the line put more strain on the Dacron than even the desperate pull of the marlin. When Ana had recovered nearly a hundred yards of line, Morgan went back to neutral and let the boat swing around until the fish was again astern. Ben Iki turned the chair to follow the boat's motion. Ana kept pumping and reeling.

The fish jumped again nearer the boat. The lure was easily visible swinging near the marlin's bill.

"I think he's bill-wrapped," Morgan said. "You okay?"

"Stop asking me that!"

Then immediately she apologized for being curt.

"You're right," Morgan said. "You've got this fish good."

"Go Mama!"

Morgan went back to the helm to keep the stern lined up with the fish, letting Ben Iki stay in the cockpit with his mother. They didn't need him. This was Ben Kamakani's daughter and grandson.

An hour passed and another. Ben Iki kept cool wet towels over his mother's head and shoulders. Morgan drank beer and watched the helm. Jackson Browne sang to the soft swells and the hot sky. Three times the fish came nearly close enough to touch, but seeing the boat had turned and stripped off line again. The gaff was by the stern and ready. When Ana rested, Ben Iki gave her some water. She could only rest when the fish rested. Ben Iki liked reporting the time passing. "Two hours, fourteen minutes, eighteen seconds, Mama," he announced. Ben Iki's digital watch had a countdown timer and he had engaged it when the marlin took the lure.

The big metallic blue fish came close again, then erupted from the surface and tail-walked away, the leader wire glistening in the sun, the lure and hooks flopping around loose.

"I don't think this guy's very tired yet," Ben Iki supposed the obvious.

"Oh boy," Ana said in an exasperated exhale.

Morgan knew better than to ask again if she was okay.

"She knows we are going to kill her," Ana said.

"It's a fish, Mama."

"Still . . ."

Morgan had seen this happen many times, had felt it himself. In a long and exhausting battle, the fisherman begins to empathize with the quarry. It rarely happens when the fight is short or easy, only during the long, exhausting battles, when the fish has fought valiantly for its freedom, its life. He realized that Ana would probably let the fish go and that was all right with him. A good fish deserves to live. Taking it to auction would bring a few bucks, but nothing he needed. If Ana needed the money, she could make that decision. There would be other fish, fish that had not earned another chance. This marlin was not hurt, only tired. If Ana wanted to release her, the only problem would be getting the leader off the bill. He thought it best to cut the fish free and let the ocean's natural oxidation rust away the wire leader. It would be too dangerous for all of them, including the fish, to try to keep it at the stern while struggling to unwrap the taut wire. He took wire cutters from the drawer and slipped them into the pocket of his shorts. He would lose the fine Konahead lure, though.

The Noho Kai wallowed in the troughs between the long swells. Birds came and stayed with hope. The current had taken them closer to the Waipio Valley. Other boats were dots further out toward the horizon. Morgan drank beer and sat at the helm. Ben Iki stood behind the fighting chair and from time to time massaged his mother's shoulders and squirted water into her mouth from a squeeze bottle.

Halfway between the third and fourth hours, the Pacific blue marlin quit. Ana could feel her coming to the boat and announced it: "Here she comes."

Ben Iki rushed to the stern and Morgan joined him. Morgan took up the flying gaff, although he was willing to bet he wouldn't need to use it.

"Can you see her?" Ana asked.

After a few seconds, Ben Iki cried out, "Yes, yes, holy moly, it's a big fish!"

"Well over five hundred, maybe six," Morgan said.

"I want to see her," Ana said, "and then I'm going to let her go."

Morgan knew she would and put back the gaff.

"Mama!"

"She fought me well, Ben Iki. She earned her life."

"Jeez, Mama."

"I think your mother's right, Ben Iki. There's a lot of fish out there. This one earned her life."

Ben Iki shook his head. "Papa Ben would never do something like this."

"Oh yes he would," Ana said. "And did. Besides, remember what you said about bullfighting? You said only a coward would kill the bull after what it had been through."

"You want to see this guy, here she is," Morgan said, coming back to unclip the rod from the harness so Ana could get out of the chair and come to the stern. He handed the rod to Ben Iki to hold and took the wire cutters from his pocket. He put on a glove and grabbed the leader wire to hold the fish, which twisted and bucked, even though weakly, against the pull. Ana leaned against him to look over his shoulder. "She's beautiful," Ana said. "Five-fifty if she's an ounce," Morgan noted, feeling suddenly embarrassed for Ana that her breasts were crushed against his arm. They could see that the fish was indeed bill-wrapped and not hooked. Morgan pulled the fish closer and reached down as close to her bill as he could and cut the wire. The lure's metal insert sparkled once like a flash of lightning before it sank out of sight. The marlin drifted slowly back in the wake. "Is she all right, you think?" "Just pooped," Morgan answered. Ben

Iki joined them and leaned over, Ana instinctively clutched the strap of his life jacket. The marlin turned to the side and stared up at the boat with one big gray eye. Ana waved a salute to her. Then the fish turned slowly, flicked its tail once and went deep.

"That feels pretty good, huh?" Ben Iki said. "But we lost the Konahead."

"We can make another with the mold in your grandfather's shop."

"Oh yeah, we can just make another one."

"It feels great," Ana confirmed. "I sure would like a beer now."

FORTY-ONE

In the late, quiet hours, night people walking along the dock and passing the Noho Kai might be curious about the incongruous music coming from the old wooden fishing vessel. Dim yellowish light leaked through the forward cabin port and a brighter whiter light glowed through the long, rectangular window in the main cabin. Some passersby might have recognized the opening Arioso from the Handel opera *Serse*, but surely most would think, whatever the music, it was an odd sound coming from a Hilo haole sampan fishing boat on a cloudy dark tropical night where palm fronds could be ghosts and dark water a Siren's song. Morgan Cary was not visible from the dock where he sat leaning over the chart table with his Christmas Montblanc pen poised above the infernally blank first sheet of paper in the spiral bound notebook he bought from the Ben Franklin store. He had finished a third of a bottle of whiskey, although not yet necessarily anesthetized. He rolled the burgundy pen between his fingers, nearly desperate to use it. He went through this routine many nights and still the first page remained blank. Rain threatened. The bay swell nudged the Noho Kai against her dock fenders from time to time, a gentle bump and rubbery squeak Morgan no longer noticed.

Ana Napela sat on the parking lot railing across from the Noho Kai with her arms lying in her lap and crossed at the wrists, listening to the beautifully sad arioso, which she neither recognized nor understood. A haole tourist couple wearing matching Aloha shirts with hotel leis around their necks walked along the dock on the pathway between where Ana sat on the creosote log rail and the fishing boat that once belonged to her father. They stopped momentarily, as if the music blocked their path. The man said something to the woman before they walked on, fingers interlocked. Ana watched them for a moment then looked back at the Noho Kai's lighted cabin. Between her legs flaking white letters spelled out the name of the boat. Morgan's pickup truck, her father's old truck, parked in its place behind her. She could lean back against the bumper.

She had gone to the movies with two of her library colleagues and then separated from them after a coffee. She walked by the harbor on her way to where her car was parked. Ben Iki, spending the Friday night with his grandmother so she could take him to an Hawaiian music festival at the high school, left her rather aimless. What was she going to do? Nothing, she thought. Just sit there. Was she hoping Morgan would come up on deck or look out and see her. And what? That music made her feel like crying. Don't fall in love with this man, she told herself. Too late, she already knew. But why? It can't be just the book? Something about him? Her father's strange affection for him? Simple pity? A slap in the face of good sense, she was in love with the man on the boat she could not see, who played this sad music. Why did he need to be sad?

The piece ended, but just as it had twice before already, started again. A homeless drunk stumbled by and turned to say something to Ana, but her glare and her damp cheeks moved him on. He said, "Don't cry, wahine, it's gonna be all right, you'll see." A few steps away, she heard him mutter, "That fucking cat-howling music make a dead man cry."

It began to sprinkle. Palm fronds rattled above her and the Noho Kai bumped and creaked against the tire fenders. The music stopped. She got up and made a dash for her car and drove home in a black downpour.

Ben Iki went out with Morgan on the Noho Kai every Saturday and afterwards Morgan drove him home and stayed for supper. It was not something they decided or planned, it's just that Morgan always drove Ben Iki home and Ana always came out to say hello and then asked him to stay for supper. Morgan never presumed to stay, even after he had supped with them every Saturday night for two months. Ana always had to come out and ask. It didn't seem right to formalize it, to admit that Morgan was going to eat supper at the Napela house every Saturday night for . . . until . . . Neither of them made a point of noticing that after a while Morgan happened to have a bottle of wine with him those Saturdays. He often stayed late and they would watch TV, finishing the wine or having a whiskey, since Ana had started keeping a bottle around. She asked the library director, who drank scotch, for a recommendation; she was pleased that Morgan approved. She didn't much like whiskey but always had one with him. She put a lot of ice with hers and waited for the ice to melt before taking a drink. They hugged goodbye when Morgan went out to his truck to drive back to the docks. After a while she kissed his cheek when they hugged. Then, after a few more Saturdays, she kissed his lips, brushed them really, quickly but portentously.

"Sad day for fishing," Morgan told Ben Iki.

"For us sad, for the fish happy," Ben Iki replied.

They had boated one small ahi and five or six bait-sized aku Ben Iki had fun bringing in using a feather lure and his still shiny new Christmas casting reel.

"I was sort of hoping to get you a world-record marlin for your thirteenth birthday."

"We'll get that big guy one of these days. You can bet on it."

"Do you mind taking her all the way in today? I'm beat from the boredom of not fishing."

Ben Iki in the helm chair looked over his shoulder at Morgan to see if he meant it. Morgan feigned a huge yawn and stretched his arms wide. "I'm just going to get myself a beer and park in the fighting chair, if you don't mind bringing her in by yourself."

"Aye, aye, skipper!" Ben Iki settled himself in the helm seat, turned his baseball cap around bill forward, tapped unnecessarily on the gear lever, and headed the Noho Kai into the inner harbor toward her berth. Even his grandfather had never allowed him to maneuver by himself through the crowded moorings near the docks, much less bring the boat into her slot, side to the pier, requiring a deft manipulation of gears, throttle, and wheel. Of course, he was still just a kid when his grandfather was alive. He thought that thirteen was about as close to being a man as he had ever been.

Morgan propped his feet on the stern rail and leaned back in the chair. He wanted to look but didn't want Ben Iki to think he was being watched, like this was some kind of test. Morgan was confident the boy could do it. After all, he had brought the boat most of the way to the dock after Morgan's accident, until a Coast Guard skiff met the Noho Kai and put an officer and medic aboard. There were only a couple of particularly tight places, and although it required some finesse to slip a thirty-eight-foot, single-screw, haole sampan sideways into a small slot against the pier, Morgan wasn't worried.

It was nice to watch. Ben Iki jockeyed the throttle and played the wheel to get the Noho Kai turned in time, side to the pier, and just out far enough for the residual momentum to drift her gently against the tire fenders. Like he had done it a thousand times. Morgan, stern line in his hands, stepped onto the transom and jumped to the pier to secure the line to a cleat. By the time he got forward, Ben Iki had crossed the deck and tossed the bow line.

"Damn fine boat driving," Morgan told Ben Iki. "Let's hit her once good with the hose and then get a burger, what do you say?"

Ben Iki was already on the dock connecting the water hose.

In the truck heading upland toward the Napela house, Morgan asked Ben Iki about his mother's birthday, which Morgan thought was in April, the same as Ben Iki's.

"It's the fifteenth, all right, but in August!"

"At least I got the date right. Got any advice concerning a present, compadre?"

"She totally huhu about those black coral earrings you get for her Christmas present. I think she wears them every single day. It's her favorite, black coral is."

Morgan thought about this for a moment, about black coral and about Ana wearing his earrings every day. Ben Iki twitched, still high from docking the Noho Kai all by himself. "You know what?" Morgan said. "Wonder what she'd think of a whole stalk of black coral, she could have all kinds of jewelry pieces made from it. What do you think of that?"

"Where you going to get a whole stick of it?"

"Dive for it. I know this place Kona side where there's some black coral, if it hasn't been harvested already."

"Really? Like the whole tree?"

"Well, a stalk anyway. I should leave a little."

"Black coral is only in deep water, you know."

"Usually beyond a hundred feet."

"You'd need scuba."

"Well, yeah. I can't hold my breath quite that long."

"I want to go, too."

"You have to get certified, Ben, before you can get tanks and air."

"I can do that."

"I don't know if there are age restrictions, but we can find out."

"I already asked last year. You only have to be twelve. I can get a PADI card in a week, or even less, at the Y."

"Well, go for it, compadre."

"If my mom says okay. She wouldn't let me when I was twelve."

"Well, now you're thirteen. Don't tell her what it's for. We're going to surprise her."

"What can I tell her?"

"I'll think of something."

Ben Iki approved of that idea. If Captain Morgan interceded on his behalf, it was a done deal.

Morgan offered his hand for a high five and Ben Iki slapped it. They pulled into the driveway and, as always, Ana saw them from the window and came out to ask Morgan to stay for supper. Ben Iki followed them inside and not for the first time wished it was always this way, that Morgan came for supper and stayed and was his father.

Morgan couldn't say why he told Ana that night what happened that last Christmas in California, why then and not sometime earlier or at some point in the future or ever. He was not especially drunk nor even all that depressed. Maybe that was it. Maybe because he felt so comfortable in her house, with her and with Ben Iki. Maybe because of what Ana had come to mean to him, her stabilizing presence in his jumbled leftover life. Maybe because he just felt more or less all right. He had been back in Hawaii just over a year and he thought less about swimming to Japan lately. Maybe what he really wanted was to recover, if he could.

Without specifying the nature of their relationship or even supposing what conditions to it there might be, Morgan and Ana were comfortable with each other. In the beginning and for many months, Ben Iki was the medium through which their lives together passed. Now they were more of an indispensable trio, not a family, but close enough to fool any observer. They were not fooling Mrs. Kamakani, as she had already informed Ana.

Ana sat in the TV chair with its wide soft arms, her feet on the footstool, her housedress casually hiked up, a paper towel on the arm to absorb the ice sweat, leaning back with her hair making a mat on the chair back. It was odd. Ben Iki wasn't there. It was the Saturday every month he regularly stayed with his grandmother, because she is lonesome, he explained to Morgan on the drive over.

Morgan had earlier driven Ben Iki to his grandmother's house but then came back because Ana asked him to. It was the first time they were in the house alone, without the boy. Maybe Morgan had not before talked about these things because subconsciously he worried that Ben Iki might overhear. Or maybe it was something else. He hadn't thought about his reticence with her. But Ana had thought about it. Ana had thought about a lot when it came to Morgan. He sat on the sofa, wearing jeans and a white T-shirt, with his bare feet on the coffee table, holding a highball glass of scotch in one hand, putting out a cigarette with the other, when he began, apropos of nothing, "If I may ask? What happened to Ben Iki's father? Your husband?"

"It's not a secret," Ana said. "We were young and we got married mostly because I got pregnant. He's not a bad guy, we were just young, high school students together. He wanted to live in Australia and I didn't."

"That simple?"

"Basically, yes. Well, I guess I don't think he loved me enough, or else he would have stayed here and made it work, no matter what. I also don't think he wanted to be a father."

"What's he doing in Australia, do you know?"

"We haven't heard from him in a long time, but his parents are here. They live up in Waimea town. He's in Cairns, working on a sport fishing boat. He lives with an Aussie girl now for more than five years."

"Shit, he could have done that here."

"He wanted to live in Australia." Ana shrugged.

"What's missing from this tale?"

Ana took a larger than usual drink of her watered-down whiskey and shrugged again. Morgan lit another cigarette and exhaled with exaggerated impatience, dropped his feet to the floor as if he might leave. Ana took another big drink and made a face this time. "You don't really like scotch, do you?" Morgan said.

"It's an acquired taste, that's for sure."

"You don't have to drink it just because I do."

"I know that."

Morgan put his feet back up on the coffee table.

Ana took a deep breath. "I wish there was a better reason, some exotic story to satisfy the storyteller in you, but I just don't think he loved me enough to make any kind of sacrifices, not for me, not for his son. He asked me if I would get an abortion, but never pushed me about it. I hope I'm still not judgmental; we were both kids."

"I'm sure glad you didn't get an abortion."

Ana took another drink and said, "He's the most important person in my life." Then she smiled and said, "You wouldn't by any chance be thinking of moving to Australia?"

Morgan laughed. "Never considered it."

"Well, that's good news."

"I don't understand any man who could walk away from Ben Iki."

Ana shrugged. What could she say? She wanted him to say that he couldn't understand any man who could walk away from *her*.

Morgan started to take another drink but his glass was empty.

"Let me get you a refill," Ana said, extracting herself from the soft chair.

"Are you trying to get me drunk?"

"Would it help?" She asked plainly.

"Help what?"

Ana didn't bother to answer what ought to be obvious, even to a man who was always so damned oblivious. She went into the kitchen and fixed two drinks, a tall scotch on the rocks in a highball glass for him and a watered down version in a short glass for herself. Returning with the drinks, she sat on the other end of the sofa instead of the chair. They clinked glasses.

"Now you know my sordid tale of woe," she said. "It is common, isn't it?"

"I suppose it is. But being common doesn't help, does it?"

"No, I guess it doesn't."

Morgan gulped half his drink and blurted out: "My wife killed herself because I had a lover . . . it's a dumb word, *lover*. The coroner said she choked on her own vomit from an accidental overdose, but I never believed it. What reason could she have had to take so many pills and drink so much vodka if she didn't know what I was doing? She was not unfamiliar with those drugs; I don't believe she could just make a mistake. So there's my sordid story."

Ana's throat went dry and she felt a clutching sensation in her chest, rising into her throat. She didn't speak again, during all the time it took for Morgan to tell her everything, from the moment he saw Victoria on the Kailua pier.

FORTY-TWO

Mrs. Kamakani would bring Ben Iki home at nine o'clock Sunday morning, pick up his mother, and they would go together to church. Morgan wanted to be gone by then, although Ana said it would be all right for her son to know that her relationship with Morgan had *evolved*, the word she used. Morgan thought otherwise. He was dumb about a lot of things, but what a thirteen-year-old boy would think if he came home and found there a man who had just spent the night in his mother's bed was not one of them. And no, he would not join them for church, although he told Ana he would like to go sometime and listen to the choir singing hymns in the Hawaiian language. The church was famous for that.

Morgan did not think that what happened last night was in any way wrong. Maybe it was the best thing that could have happened to him now. As long as Ana was happy about it. He was also happy, in a way. Lying in her arms and feeling her desire for him, he had felt the hope of a future; for the first time in more than a year, he actually wanted a future.

They made love embarrassed: awkwardly, tentatively, and not until near the end did there appear an abandoned passion. They did not experiment, unsure still of one another, of what would please and what would offend and what would increase their embarrassment. Morgan showered, uncomfortable with Ana's personal toiletries, more so when she came into the bathroom and he thought she was going to join him, but instead she just put a clean towel over the rack for him and went back out. He did not think he was supposed to know at this point what creams she used on her skin or what feminine things she kept in the cabinet or what medications she might need. Ben Iki obviously used the other bathroom because there was nothing of his in this one. He came out with a towel around him and Ana was in the kitchen; he smelled breakfast. He dressed in her bedroom and noticed the alarm clock by the bed. Already a quarter past eight and he really didn't want to still be there when Ben Iki arrived with his grandmother. He sat with Ana on the curved bench seat by the window and ate a piece of buttered toast, blew on the hot coffee so he could drink it more quickly. Ana told him he could stay, even if he didn't want to go to church, although they were informal and he didn't have to worry about what he was wearing. He said he wasn't ready for that and she didn't push him any further. When he got up to leave, she held him tightly for a moment and asked, "It's all right, isn't it?" He said it was the most wonderful change in his life since he left California, he let her know at least indirectly that she had given him a reason to hope. She kissed him, grateful for that. Then she let him leave. Ten minutes after Morgan drove down the hill to the harbor, Mrs. Kamakani and Ben Iki arrived and the family went to church.

Ana was waiting for Morgan at the dock when he came in from fishing Monday afternoon. She in her work clothes: a pretty, long, red and white dress with puffy sleeves and an incongruously sensual scoop neck for a library clerk. He noticed the black coral earrings. He helped her aboard and she offered to help him clean up. There were a pair of long silver gray ono on the cockpit sole and a lot of their blood lay sticky by the scuppers. "Not in that dress," Morgan said. She made as if to pull it over her head and he laughed. "It won't take very long," he said, hopping onto the dock to get the water hose. Ana went into the cabin and sat at the chart table. She saw the Montblanc standing alone in a drinking glass beside the spiral notebook, which she knew better than to peek into, no matter how intriguing it was. Would he write his next book with her Christmas pen? Morgan hosed out the fish blood and rinsed salt spray from the windows. The twin pair of ono lay on the concrete dock in the shade; he would need to take them to the fish auction soon.

"I told Ben Iki," Ana said when Morgan came into the cabin to find his shoes.

"That's up to you, I guess." He felt his stomach twitch.

"I hope you aren't upset that I told him."

"What did you tell him?"

"Not everything, of course. Not even that you stayed the night. I think things have changed for us, which includes him, and I didn't want a secret around us."

"I understand. It's all right. What did he say?"

"I just told him that you and I have recognized that we have important feelings for each other and we might start dating."

"Dating." Morgan laughed. "Something like that."

"I guess the word doesn't exactly fit, but I couldn't think of any other way to put it."

"And what did he say?"

"He said, in effect, that he's all for it. He is very happy."

"Whew," Morgan wiped his brow exaggeratedly.

"You want to come up for supper?"

"I have to take the ono to Suisan."

"After that?"

Why couldn't he just say yes and go, which is what he wanted? What was he afraid of now? Being happy? Was he afraid that he would feel good and the second skin of his guilt would peel off? Was he afraid that he wouldn't suffer enough if he let this happen?

"I guess I could . . ."

"But?"

"Not a but, really."

"I know a but when I see one," Ana smiled, but awkwardly.

What was he going to say? He didn't himself know what caused the hesitation. Maybe he was afraid Ana didn't understand enough about him. Did she understand that he was a drunk? Did she really understand what he had done to Victoria?

Ana never said she excused his having an affair while married. But did his wife die because of it? Couldn't it have been an accident, like the autopsy stated? Morgan could not say for sure that his wife knew where he was that night, not from what he told Ana. His wife had died from choking to death on her own vomit and she used drugs all the time. Why did he have to believe it was suicide? Why couldn't it have been an accident? An unfortunately timed accident, granted. Morgan would not let her pursue that possibility. "I know what I know," he had told her with finality.

Morgan continued. "It just seems that with Ben Iki it might seem really fast. You tell him we're having a relationship and wham, there I am."

"All right." Ana didn't feel comfortable arguing about it. It was too new to know how to argue with him. She felt confused and her feelings more than a little hurt. Had she done something wrong already? Was she not good enough in bed? Was she just too pushy, as usual? "You're right. Shall we wait until Saturday, as usual?"

"Maybe I could stop by tomorrow around suppertime?"

"That would be great."

It was going to be all right, she thought. He was right about not pushing all this into Ben Iki's face so quickly. Certainly her son was crazy about Morgan and on one level was happy to see his mother *dating* him, but he was also a thirteen-year-old boy. Morgan understood that. His first thought being about Ben Iki's feelings made her love him even more. Now, at least, she understood why he drank so much and she was going to take that need away from him, replace it with a loving family.

They exchanged a long kiss. It crossed Ana's mind that she would like to make love with him on the boat, in the forward cabin where he slept, on the boat where she believed he must be writing his next book with her gift pen.

When she left to drive home, Morgan took the ono in the back of the pickup to the Suisan fish auction. The fish hardly brought enough money to pay for the fuel he burned going after them. He went to the Paniola Bar, ate a hamburger and drank a few beers, then walked back to the Noho Kai in a light, warm drizzle. He was not drunk. He had sat on a stool at the bar chatting aimlessly with Leila for a while and then talking fish stories with Kimo from one of the long-liners and then just decided to leave, still early. It confused him to feel good. He wanted to think about what had happened to him and what it meant. He didn't want to manipulate those thoughts by setting up some preconditions embodied in how pickled his brain happened to be, what kind of music he played, or how ponderously the past controlled his mind. Is it okay to be happy? Does he deserve this chance to be happy? Why him? Why does Ana want him? Would he do something compulsive and stupid and hurt her? Would he do to her what he did to Victoria? Ben Iki. There was no Ben Iki with Victoria. He had stopped thinking of swimming to Japan.

But he could not sleep sober. He had lost that technique. He opened a bottle of whiskey and had just enough to take the edge off the night and let him fade away.

Tuesday, Ben Iki was at the pier when Morgan came in. He uncoiled the hose and got ready to wash down the boat as Morgan docked her.

"How's it today, Cap'n?"

"Don't ask, brah."

"You don't have your lucky deckhand, that's wassamatta."

"I think you're on to something. Are you going to hit her with the hose?"

"Sure." Ben Iki started and Morgan stepped onto the dock to get out of the way.

"How was school today?"

"SOS," Ben Iki said.

"Where did you pick that up? You know what the letters stand for?"

"Same old shit."

"It wouldn't be a good idea, I think, to let your mother hear that cute little phrase."

"You're right about that."

"Well, since I don't have any reason to go to Suisan, want a ride home?"

"Sure."

Was everything all right? Morgan wondered. Ben Iki acted completely normal, the way he always had, as if nothing had changed. Is this how he deals with change, to just go on like always?

Ben Iki went about the boat chores quickly and efficiently. He was in fact a damn fine deckhand, Morgan thought. One of these days he would make a great captain, and if he lived long enough, maybe as great as his grandfather. Maybe, Morgan thought, he could help Ben Iki study for his Coast Guard captain's license and when he was eighteen . . . when he was eighteen, five years from now . . . Morgan realized he was projecting a future, a future with Ben Iki in it, a future with Ben Iki's mother in it.

Going up the hill, the sun already behind the mountains and the truck's headlights flashing across yards, huge oleander bushes, houses, street signs, Morgan asked Ben Iki what he thought about his mother and him?

Ben Iki looked straight out the windshield. Morgan thought he was embarrassed by this and asked if he was uncomfortable.

"You mean about you dating my mom?"

"Yeah, that, I guess."

"It's the smartest move you ever made in your whole life, Cap'n."

Morgan laughed hard and decided that he agreed.

After Ben Iki went to his bedroom, while Morgan helped Ana pick up the dishes, he talked Ana into letting Ben Iki take a diver's certification course. He explained that Ben Iki could help clean the Noho Kai's hull and maybe they would set a mooring block and tackle on the far side of the bay, between Carl Smith beach park and Leleiwi. They could anchor out there with some privacy, allowing Ana to imagine her own details.

FORTY-THREE

Ana made it clear that it would be all right for Morgan to stay over, especially since they ate supper together nearly every evening, and the few times they did not eat at home it was because he took them out. Why, she wondered, did he keep driving back down the hill every night? But Morgan said he just wasn't ready to bump into Ben Iki in the morning on his way to the bathroom. This meant they made love furtively, except for the once-a-month Saturday night Ben Iki stayed with his grandmother, then Morgan would spend the night. He always left before Mrs. Kamakani brought the boy home and they all went to church. Ana told him that her mother approved of their developing relationship, although he didn't believe it; Ben Kamakani's daughter with a haole boyfriend? The few times Morgan and Mrs. Kamakani met, they maintained a polite distance, flagrantly respectful on his part. Ana tried to explain that her mother's formality with him was because she did not approve of *that kind* of relationship before marriage, that she actually liked Morgan in spite of him being haole. At least, she added with a smile, her mother was happy Morgan wasn't part of that invasion of wacky spiritual haoles living in tree houses and praying to lava rocks and silly stuff like that. He was a fisherman and that compensated for quite a lot. So the next Saturday he brought nicer clothes, stayed that morning and went to church with them. He was not the only haole at the service, but he was the only haole sitting with Ben Kamakani's family.

Morgan struggled to avoid making comparisons between Ana and Victoria, but some sensations were unavoidable. Ana was a much larger woman than Victoria, who, especially the last year of her life had become quite thin. Not only was Ana much taller, but so broad across her shoulders and back that his arms around her felt like Victoria doubled. There was a different smell to Ana's skin, strongly coconut from the oil she rubbed over it and through her hair. Victoria displayed herself during sex, Ana was as reticent as Victoria was abandoned. Ana, though not shy, was self-conscious about some things that Morgan learned quickly to avoid, like noticing that she did not like it when he looked at her sex and only wanted to spread her legs when he was lying between them. They were learning what lovers have to know. Morgan, although he did not understand why, did not doubt how much she loved him. When he was lying atop her with their faces close, her half-lidded eyes cried with an ecstasy that was more about being in love than having sex. Often she placed the palms of her hands on his cheeks and held his face close enough for their noses to touch, especially when he came, she opened her eyes fully and watched him, as if she had just handed him a gift and wanted to see his expression when he received it. He loved her because she loved him and by loving him made him worth something.

After supper Morgan often stayed late before going back to his boat. If Ben Iki had finished his homework, he was allowed to watch TV. They watched with him and Ana was careful about the programs. They watched reruns of *Hawaii Five-o* when one was on because Morgan told them how nostalgic he had felt watching the show in California. Ben Iki would cry out, "Book 'm, Dano," when the show started. Morgan drank whiskey. Ana had given up the pretense of it and went back to rum and lilikoi juice with a big chunk of fresh lime from the tree in her backyard. Ben Iki sat cross-legged on the floor close to the screen and Ana sat in the big armchair. Morgan had found himself a family and was just beginning to understand how much he wanted one. He watched Ana and Ben Iki more than he watched TV. Sometimes Ben Iki asked Morgan to help with a homework problem and they went off to his room, with Ana calling out behind them, "Make him do it himself, don't do it for him." Morgan would have done anything for him.

The days and the weeks passed like this.

A rainy afternoon in early June, Morgan came in early, having not had a single strike and tired of being wet. As he approached his slot at the dock, he could see Ana under an umbrella waiting for him. She was in her work clothes and it was not yet three o'clock. He knew something was wrong but wouldn't let himself think of any of the worst things. As the Noho Kai slipped side to the dock, Ana approached and reached out for a line. Holding the umbrella with one hand, she took two quick whips around the cleat and secured the stern. Morgan jumped off with the bow line. She walked up and held the umbrella over him, although he was already soaked.

"Hi," he said.

"Hi," she answered.

"Let's get out of the rain."

"All right."

They boarded the boat and went into the main cabin. Ana closed the umbrella and propped it against the engine box. Morgan picked up a dishcloth and wiped his face.

"What's wrong?" Morgan asked.

"Tioni Brown's father died yesterday."

"Shit," Morgan exclaimed and sat down.

"How long were you waiting in the rain?" Morgan asked.

"Not long. I came down to leave you a note to call me, but I saw you coming in, so I just waited."

"What happened?"

"Brain aneurysm. He went to sleep and didn't wake up."

"That's a good way to go."

"Yes. I think it must be better to die and not know you did."

"How did you hear?"

"It was on the radio."

"Oh."

"I thought you'd want to know as soon as possible."

"Yes. Thank you. He was a great fisherman."

"I know. You told me."

"Oh, that's right."

"And Tioni is your best friend."

"Was."

"Maybe is?"

Morgan only nodded slightly. Then he said, "you are my best friend."

"Thank you. I'm not trying to tell you what to do, but shouldn't you think about going over?"

"I suppose so. I don't know."

"I think you should go over. Tioni came to Hilo side when you were in the hospital."

"I'll go over."

"I think that's good."

"Samuel Brown taught me how to fish."

"I know. You told me."

"Oh, yes, that's right."

Was he going to cry? Why did he feel like he couldn't control himself? Ana put her arms around him and held him tightly. She kissed his hair.

He took Mamalahoa Highway out of Hilo in a pounding rain that forced him to creep along at thirty miles an hour halfway to Waimea, so he began to think it would take the rest of the day to get to the Kona side. The rain slacked off to a drizzle by the time the road veered away from the coast and he urged Ben's old truck to tackle the increasing altitude. By Waimea the sun was out and the dark clouds tumbled around behind him. The air chilly at altitude, he turned on the truck's heater. It didn't work, he discovered. But by the time he passed the Saddle Road Junction and began to drop down toward the glistening distant coast, the temperature rose. He took Palani Road into Kailua town, drove onto the pier and parked out of the way beyond the fish hoist. It was a beautiful day Kona side and only one lone fishing boat remained on its mooring in the bay, Sammy Brown's boat. Four in the afternoon and in another hour or so the boats with charters would return to the harbor. Had Tioni gone out? He thought about driving up to the house but decided to wait for a while and see who came in. Morgan sat behind the wheel letting time pass in a reverie of memories from his days as a Kona charter fisherman. Tiny Akaka, in his ancient, fish blood–stained, Chevy pickup rattled around Morgan and parked on the opposite side by the small boat ramp. Tiny Akaka had been picking up the day's catch and taking the fish to auction in that truck since Morgan was a teenager. He would get out of the truck, light a cigarette, and walk back to lean against the wooden railing around the truck bed. Like he always had. He would watch everything and wait for the fish. Morgan got out of the truck and leaned against the door, lighting a cigarette, looking toward the sea wall along Alii Drive. There were plenty of tourists walking along, teenage boys perched on the sea wall like brown bottles, a boy and girl played in the shallow water where the sea wall ended at the pier, trumpet fish shot alongside the pier like a fusillade of arrows, and the world smelled exactly the way it was supposed to smell: salt-tinged, floral, fishy and fresh, with an overlay of beer and the metallic tang of dried blood. A few tourists walked on the grounds of the Royal Summer Palace. Jukebox music roamed outside through the open bamboo shutters of the Red Pants and he could just make out the smell of fry grease from the Oceanview Café's kitchen. Only Justin painting by the seawall was missing. Tiny recognized him and offered a simple wave, as if he saw Morgan there every day, as if Morgan had never been away and was not now living on the other side of the island. Just after five o'clock, the first two boats, not a hundred yards separating them, entered the harbor. Another pair not far behind. Morgan got back into the truck and went to find a place to park off the pier, which would start getting busy now. The fourth boat in was Tioni's. They had two large and one small ahi, with three yellow ahi flags flying from an outrigger. Morgan stayed out of the way while the fish were offloaded, weighed, and photographed with the tourist fisherman who caught them. After the fish were lowered into the back of Tiny's truck and the sportsman paid for the boat and left, Morgan approached the stern where Tioni rinsed fish blood through the scuppers. Morgan was not surprised Tioni had gone fishing two days after his father died. Sammy Brown would himself not have been surprised.

Everything was the way it had always been, except for Sammy Brown's boat, Stryker, empty and alone on her mooring in the bay. Then Morgan noticed the maile-leaves lei draped from the wheel on the flying bridge and then black ribbons tied to both outrigger poles. Sammy Brown was unarguably the most noted and respected sport fishing boat captain in the islands; every famous person who came to Kona for big game fishing went out on the Stryker with Sammy Brown. Of course the boats and their crews went out today. Sammy would have, too.

Tioni looked up and saw Morgan and shielded his eyes against the low sun.

"Aloha," Tioni said.

"Aloha, brah."

"Mahalo nui loa," Tioni thanked Morgan, without needing to say it was for showing up at all.

Morgan nodded and struggled to get a grip on himself, with Tioni standing in the cockpit and his father's empty, lonely boat slipping up and down the slight bay chop. "Can I buy you a beer when you finish? Do you have time for that?"

"Anytime, brah."

"Good, that's good."

Tioni hopped up to the pier and turned off the water and coiled the hose. Captain Ross, for whom Tioni had been crewing since he quit the Dolphin all those years ago, came out of the cabin and waved at Morgan. "Looks like you survived the head thing," Captain Ross said.

Morgan rubbed the back of his head. "The head did, but can't say quite yet about the brain."

Captain Ross laughed.

"I got one offer for free beer," Tioni said.

"Better get it while the getting's good," Captain Ross said. "I'll take her to the mooring."

"Mahalo nui," Tioni said, got his flip-flops from the boat and joined Morgan on the pier. "Red Pants?" he suggested.

"If you think Momo will let the two of us in there at the same time," Morgan teased cautiously.

"Momo's gone already. He's like da kine head man for that Hilton restaurant."

Morgan noticed when Tioni glanced over his shoulder at his father's boat in the bay, where now other boats headed out to their moorings. They walked off the pier toward the Red Pants bar like they had a hundred times in the past. A man driving a red mustang convertible laid long and loud on the horn when they sauntered across Alii Drive in front of his car. "Fucking haole," Tioni cried out and sent an obscene message with his middle finger. Then, slapping Morgan on the shoulder, added, "No offense, brah." Tioni pushed open the swinging saloon doors and Morgan followed him into the expanding late afternoon fishermen's world of the Red Pants. Two men were trying to shoot pool in the center of the room but the little round tables were too close and there were too many people moving between the bar and the tables in back. They got a table in back and Tioni asked Morgan what he wanted. "Beer's fine," Morgan said, "but I'll get it. Primo for you?"

"Nothing here changes, brah," Tioni said, "me the littlest."

Some things change, Morgan noted when he made his way to the bar to order. Momo had been replaced by a woman and at the moment she was the only female in the Red Pants. Morgan ordered an Oly and a Primo. She gave him the beers with a small tray of snack pretzels and salty peanuts.

"Look at this," Morgan said, putting the snack tray on the table with the beers, "free puu-puus." Morgan sat and they clinked glasses before drinking. "Some things do change," he said, making small talk. "Momo replaced by a wahine, free snacks at the Red Pants. Who knows where something like this could lead? The end of civilization as we know it."

It stunned Morgan to feel how much he missed this. It wasn't quite the same, sitting there with the man who had been his best friend and his deckhand for so many years, but neither was it all that different. The cacophony of Hawaiian voices and the same old jukebox with the same old Fifties and Sixties rock and roll, the off-kilter torn-felt pool table with a solid red snooker ball replacing the cue ball, the white one lost twenty years ago when it was thrown at somebody and went out the window and into the bay, bamboo shutters flung open to the sidewalk, Alii Drive, then the sea wall where the little brown boys always perched, then the bay blending finally with the infinite sea, all these things unchanged. Yet some things did change. Sammy Brown was dead and that meant nothing would ever again be as great as it was in the best days, the days that always come before wherever you are. Now Morgan had a beard and a hopeful, healing guilty heart, Tioni's skin had leathered and there were streaks of white in his thick, shining black hair; he had lost a molar, Morgan noticed when Tioni smiled widely. When Morgan asked why Justin wasn't painting by the sea wall, Tioni told him Justin had died of lung cancer six months ago. "Maybe it's the season for dying," he said. Tioni tapped the pack of cigarettes Morgan had put on the table between them, then shrugged fatalistically as he took one and accepted a light from a match Morgan offered. "Here's to Justin, a damn fine painter," Morgan said, taking another cigarette from the pack. For that moment he remembered when Victoria told him Justin had asked her to pose. He should have let her, he would have that painting now. Fading light from the setting sun came through the open windows in streams of white to gold to yellow, then red, and then purple before the dark, without at any level or intensity being able to penetrate the Red Pants beyond the window tables. A man riding in the back of a pickup truck lit the gas fueled torches along the sea wall and the bar lady went outside and set alight the Red Pants' torches with a butane lighter. Trying to talk about anything other than Sammy, Morgan told Tioni about the marlin Ana Kamakani caught and released and about what a fine deckhand Ben Kamakani's grandson was. At one point in this story, suddenly, Tioni punched Morgan on the arm and said, "Brah, are you sweet on Ben Kamakani's daughter?" Morgan confessed that he had indeed gotten sweet on her. "Shit," Tioni said, shaking his head and taking a big swallow of beer. "You always was a sucker for any kine a wahine, brah."

They smoked and drank beer, enjoyed watching a pair of thoroughly dismayed haole girls wonder what they had walked into when they opened the Red Pants' swinging doors. Morgan waited for Tioni to bring it up. When he was ready. It was a long time until he did.

"It's going to be private, for just the family, or I'd like it for you to be there," he said.

"I understand. It's okay. Is there going to be a public service sometime?"

"Sammy would be against it, brah. You know how he was about showing off."

Morgan nodded and smiled.

"Yeah, there's going to be this big thing over at Mokuaikaua church day after tomorrow. The mayor's office is doing it. The sport fishermen's association's paying for some beers and puu-puus on the yard behind the summer palace."

"I'd like to go. But yeah, I know Sammy would just blow me off about it."

"He told Momma 'just set me free and put what's left out for the fish.' If he knows we gonna have some service he wouldn't a even died, you know?"

"That's why your father was the man he was. He was a man who had every reason and every right to take advantage of being a great man. I guess part of what made him a great man was that he refused it, it meant nothing to him."

"It was Momma kept his big feet right down on the earth. She would kick his ass if he started showing off."

"I bet she would. How is she? I guess that's a dumb-shit question."

"It's not so good for her right now. You know, she couldn't go get herself all prepare for this. One day Sammy is all Sammy and the next day . . ."

"No chance for you to prepare, either?"

"No chance, brah."

They let the noise cover them for a couple of minutes. Then Tioni said, "Mahalo for the beers, Cap'n. I got to be getting home."

"Sure. Will you please tell your mother and your brothers and sister how sorry I am?"

"Hey, of course."

"You know how sorry I am, Tioni? About everything?"

"Hey!" Tioni got up and punched Morgan's arm. "I always know'd that."

Morgan got a room at the King Kamehameha next to the pier. He called Ana to let her know that he was staying until the day after tomorrow to attend the public memorial. She assured unnecessarily that Ben Iki would take care of the boat and said she would miss him. Before hanging up, he said, "I love you." He heard her gasp.

He went down to the bar and had a couple of drinks before going back to his room intending to watch TV until he got sleepy. But he went onto the small balcony and sat there for two hours, just looking at the lights along the coast and the dancing anchor lights from the moored fishing boats. Kona would not be as good a place without Sammy Brown in it, he decided. But it still offered the most beautiful tropical nights he had ever seen.

In the morning he walked over to the Oceanview Café and ate exactly the same breakfast he had eaten every morning during the years he was a Kona fisherman. He sat by one of the glassless windows on the bay side. He was eating when Sammy Brown's fish truck pulled onto the pier, followed by a car. Morgan watched Tioni and his two younger brothers get out of the truck and went to the car to escort his mother and older sister. Tioni's brothers boarded the Stryker's skiff and rowed out to Sammy Brown's boat. Tioni stayed with his mother and sister while the younger boys brought the boat to the dock. It was easy to see that Mrs. Brown was weeping and struggling not to let it show. Tioni removed a large urn from the back seat of the car and the family boarded the boat. Tioni climbed up to the flying bridge and headed out to sea. Morgan noticed that everything had come to a stop on the pier and along Alii Drive. A fishing boat on its way out sat bobbing at idle until the Stryker had passed.

After breakfast, Morgan wandered around the Alii Drive shops looking at coral jewelry.

The next night, after the public memorial service attended by every Kona fisherman, as well as quite a few from Hilo side, Morgan met Tioni again at the Red Pants for a drink before driving back to Hilo. He came with his brothers.

When Ike and Kolo went to shoot pool, Morgan, shouting over the Red Pants rumble, asked Tioni, "Is that patch of black coral still there, off Kaiwe Point?"

"Not unless it grew back in the last couple of years."

Morgan shrugged.

"Why?" Tioni asked.

"I want to get a branch and have some rings made."

"Wedding rings kind of rings?"

Morgan smiled. Tioni punched him on the arm and Morgan feigned pain.

"You not saying you're gonna marry Ben Kamakani's daughter?"

"I haven't asked her."

"But you're gonna."

"I'm gonna."

Tioni punched him again and said he'd have to see that for himself, a haole marrying into Ben Kamakani's family, then added, "Ike maybe knows where there might be a couple of trees. He's the diver dude from our family."

"I would really like to get a branch. Just a small one. Enough to polish down into two rings, maybe a necklace. Can you ask Ike?"

"I'll ask."

"Thanks, Tioni."

"Maybe I get me one piece too."

"We can go for it together."

"But you think coral is strong enough for rings?"

"Guess I'll have to ask a jeweler. But probably it has to go into some setting."

They went on talking story almost two more hours.

Maybe he didn't need to do it? Morgan thought, as the quieter, later hours came. Maybe it was a done deal when Tioni sat with him in the Red Pants and talked story with him as if nothing had changed during the past decade. But Morgan realized that in these two days and all the beers, Tioni had not said one thing about Victoria, not even mentioned her name.

Morgan waited for an empty space that felt right.

"I'm sorry, Tioni. I just wanted you to know that."

"Way people making speeches at the memorial, I'm thinking they gonna put up some kine a statue."

"I wasn't talking about Sammy."

"Oh, yeah." Tioni took a long drink, making a face over the beer gone warm. "That was a long time ago."

Morgan sensed that it wasn't just a long time ago. Tioni's tone had changed.

"I loved her, Tioni."

"I know that, brah. I know that well as you."

"You loved her, too."

"Yeah, I did. I guess so. But that wahine was a real piece of work, brah."

"We both loved her and that's why I want to ask you to forgive me."

"Forgive your ass? Come on. You haoles are so full of your own shit."

"I suppose we are."

"Let's don't talk about this kind of shit. We don't have to go around forgiving this or that. Maybe I loved her, that's for sure, but I never had no kine a expectations about it. She loved you and she married you. Maybe I took it personal, for a little while. Then you took off. Look what happened anyhow. Sammy said you saved me from getting married to some way too pretty haole wahine and ruining the rest of my life. Maybe you can look at it like you done me one favor. I don't mean to be talking trash about the dead, you know, but she was a real piece of work."

"You never married."

"Jesus motherfucking shit Christ almighty!"

"I'm sorry," Morgan said.

"You gonna be really sorry if you don't shut the fuck up about being sorry all the time."

Tioni was right. Was he going to spend the rest of his life feeling sorry for himself? He was just desperate to apologize: To Victoria, of course. But how he could he do that? Apologizing to Tioni wasn't going to absolve him of this need. Nothing would. He could live or he could die, but he could never tell her how sorry he was.

He hoped Ana would marry him and let him become Ben Iki's father, but right now he was going to buy Tioni another beer and thankfully let Tioni change the subject.

"Hey, you remember when you almost got into that fight with Lee Marvin right over there?" Tioni said. "He looked like somebody's kapuna kane with that long white hair and white beard."

"He was making *Paint Your Wagon*."

"I laugh my ass off, you making plenty pilikia with Lee Marvin."

"I could have taken him."

"Only thing you wanted to take was his wife."

"Hey, that wasn't his wife! She sued him about it later."

"You didn't know that then."

"Well, I had my suspicions."

Tioni laughed hard enough to shake the table and knock over one of the empties.

They stayed until the Red Pants closed and then, Morgan way too drunk to drive anywhere, stumbled to the parking lot where he left his truck and passed out in the back of it.

FORTY-FOUR

They talked about getting married once. Not talked, exactly. Morgan had only said he supposed they should get married so people would stop talking about them. Ana had only smiled and said she supposed so. They were becoming the fuel for Hilo's gossip machine, the haole who bought Ben Kamakani's boat and got his daughter in the deal. Ana sloughed it off, but it bothered Morgan. He was afraid it would bother Ben Iki, too. Then Ana wondered privately that maybe she didn't want to marry him if all he wanted to do was stop the petty gossiping. He had only said he loved her once, when he called from Kailua the week before. Although she believed that he did . . . love her, the best way he knew how. He had almost stopped smoking for them, cutting back to less than five or six cigarettes a day. He was even drinking much less. She had never seen him drunk. Maybe that was more about Ben Iki than her; she didn't know for sure. She could not help but wonder how much of the love she felt for Morgan was because of how he doted on her son, and of course, how much of the love Morgan felt for her was because of Ben Iki. Ana wondered if she was asking for too much, expecting Morgan to express himself her way rather than his own? Her mother told her that you should never try to change a man: Be careful what you ask for, she said. Why would you think enough about a man that you give him your love and then decide you want to make another man that maybe you won't love so much? You think your bicycle would be more pretty without the wheels so you take them off; then what you've got? You got a bicycle you can't ride. You like it better this way? Mrs. Kamakani told her daughter that Morgan Cary was not nearly as bad a man as he thinks he is. All you got to do, she told Ana, is see him one time with Ben Iki. That is not a bad man. Your father knew he was not a bad man, too. Morgan Cary is only a sad man. Sad you can fix. Bad just stays bad. Well, Ana told her mother, he hasn't exactly officially asked me anyway. Do you want him to? Her mother asked, knowing the answer already.

Morgan wondered if he knew how to be in love, or understood what being in love is. If he was in love with Victoria, then why did he do what he did? He remembered one of Wittgenstein's aphorisms from *Zettel*: "Love is not a feeling. Love is put to the test, pain not. One does not say: 'That was not true pain, or it would not have gone off so quickly.'" He had no trouble thinking to himself that he was in love with Ana. He didn't know why, then, he had so much trouble simply saying it. Was it because he said it easily and often with Victoria? They were so different. He couldn't say it to Ana because it was the same word he said to Victoria? Was it the same feeling? No. But love is not a feeling. Love must be tested. Victoria had once said that she knew how much he loved her not because he said it but because he acted it. Did Ana know he loved her because he acted like it? It was not the same feeling, but maybe it was a better one. Those thoughts mystified him.

He wanted to ask Ana to marry him and he believed she would accept, although he did not believe he deserved to be a part of her life, and

Ben Iki's. He had loved Victoria and look what happened, look at how utterly he had let her down. He couldn't live through that again. He never wanted to hurt someone so much. He held back from Ana because he was afraid. Only love can break a heart, as they say.

They walked to Rainbow Falls after church Sunday. There were only the usual mountain cumulus gathering over Mauna Kea when they left, Morgan carrying the picnic lunch and a bottle of wine and a liter of Coke in a rucksack. Ben Iki wanted to go on his bicycle and went ahead, after deciding where they would meet. Not halfway, the cumulus darkened and thickened and tumbled down the mountain slope toward the coast and they were caught in the rain. "Hilo is said to be the rainiest city in America," Morgan announced. "Duh," Ana responded, holding her arms out wide. They laughed and accepted the futility of staying any drier than allowed by the single umbrella they shared. They would dry when the clouds got out of the way of the sun and Rainbow Falls would offer up its namesake.

Covered shelters were limited and it was fortunate Ben Iki went ahead. He had commandeered one and was sitting on the picnic bench with his bike leaning against the table when Morgan and his mother approached.

The rain blew by and in the sudden sunlight a double rainbow framed the falls. Ben Iki went off to explore on foot with his mother's warning to stay well away from the edge of the stream and the falls. Morgan opened the wine. Ana unwrapped sandwiches and opened Tupperware bowls of fruit salad and chip dip.

Morgan impulsively boarded Ben Iki's bike and rode it in a wobbly circle around the picnic pavilion, raising his arms over his head once and nearly tumbling. Ana laughed and then told him not to break his neck or Ben Iki's bike.

Other families arrived. A pair of lovers lay on a blanket by the stream, privately entwined. A father played catch with his six-year-old son. People laughed and their chatter was almost as loud as the falls. Ice chests opened and expelled brown bottles of Primo beer, soda pop cans, and jugs of lilikoi juice. Tabletops were quickly cluttered with tin foil and wax paper debris. Paper plates were placed. A baby cried until its mother offered her breast, a breast so large it was bigger than the baby's head.

Ben Iki came back with a school chum; they decided to ride their bikes along the trail. Ana said it was okay, but what about his lunch? Ben Iki said they were just going to the end of the trail and back and he'd eat then. He hopped on his bike and said, maybe showing off a little for his friend, "I saw you trying to steal my bike, Cap'n."

"Yeah, well," Morgan said. "I gave it a thought, but it's too nice for a bum like me."

Ben Iki laughed and pedaled away at full speed, chasing his friend down the hill.

The young lovers picked up their blanket and disappeared into the brush behind the falls. A dog started to follow, but the guy shooed him away. A big wahine called her family to eat. Morgan poured wine into plastic cups and they tipped their cups together in toast. "Here's to a sunny day," Morgan said. "And clouds with silver linings," Ana added.

A patron Ana knew from the library approached and greeted Ana, who introduced Morgan: "This is my friend, Morgan Cary." The patron, Mrs. Tanaka, introduced her husband and their teenage daughter. Mrs. Tanaka wanted to know if they would mind sharing the table? It was a long picnic table, well shaded, with a direct view of the falls, and there was plenty of room. The Tanaka family unpacked and took places at the end of the table. Ana unwrapped the Spam and pineapple sandwiches and offered one to Morgan. "Breakfast of champions," Morgan said, holding up the sandwich and the cup of wine. The Tanaka family laughed politely.

Five minutes later, Pali, Ben Iki's friend, came racing up on his bike crying out, "Mrs. Napela, Mrs. Napela, come quick! Ben Iki fall down off his bike!"

"Oh goodness," Mrs. Tanaka said, covering her mouth.

By that time, Morgan and Ana were racing down the trail with Pali, who left his bike at the shelter. Instead of following the dirt bike trail, Pali directed them to the stone steps that led to the parking lot. At the point where the steep steps leveled out beside a moss damp banyan tree, they would see Ben Iki's bike sprawled beside the green guard railing, but no Ben Iki. "He flied right over the rail," Pali said when they reached the bike. He pointed into the brush.

"What the hell were you boys doing riding down the damn steps?" Ana shouted as she climbed over the railing. Morgan threw himself over the top of the railing and nearly tumbled into the gulley. Ben Iki was sitting up in the weeds, holding his left wrist and crying.

"Baby, what did you do?" Ana cried, dropping to her knees beside him.

"Ouch!" Ben Iki screamed when his mother tried to put her arms around him.

Morgan knelt in front of the boy and took his left arm in his hand. "Can you move your wrist?"

"Nooo!" Ben Iki cried.

"Looks like you broke your wrist, compadre."

"Are you hurt anywhere else?" Ana asked, running her hands around him without actually touching his body.

Ben Iki didn't let go of his left wrist and nodded toward his knees, which were scraped pretty badly.

"Your legs okay to stand up?" Morgan asked.

Ben Iki nodded. Morgan put his hands under Ben Iki's armpits and pulled him up.

"You scared the shit out of me, Ben Iki!" his mother cried.

"You said shit," Ben Iki said.

"Oh you shut up, just shut up."

"I think you're on thin ice here, Ben," Morgan warned. "You have any idea how much you scared your mother?"

Morgan picked up Ben Iki and lifted him over the railing.

"Pali, I'm not going to call your mother, but I think you better tell her that you were riding your bike down the steps and you see what happened to Ben Iki."

"Yes, ma'am."

"I want you to take Ben Iki's bike home. All right?"

"Yes, ma'am."

"Put it behind the garage."

"Yes, ma'am."

Standing on the steps, Morgan inspected Ben Iki. He noticed when he lifted the boy over the railing that his wrist wiggled a little. Maybe it wasn't broken. The skin was off his knees but he was standing all right. He'd also lost a bunch of skin from his left elbow. All in all, considering all the stumps and broken bushes along there, it's a good thing he didn't get stabbed by something.

"Morgan, please, we need to take him to the emergency room," Ana cried.

"You and Ben make your way on down the steps. I'll run home and get the car. I can be back pretty soon after you get to the parking lot."

"Oh God, thank you, darling."

Both Ben Iki and Morgan looked up at that word.

As Morgan thought, Ben Iki's wrist was sprained, not broken. He got it wrapped in nothing more than an Ace bandage, although by then, after a pain killer, he was hoping for a big white cast everyone could write on.

He got his scrapes painted with iodine, which he thought hurt more than wrapping his wrist.

They had just gotten into the car to go home when Morgan turned from the front seat and yelled, "What in the hell did you think you were doing!" Ben Iki had never heard Morgan raise his voice, much less scream in his direction. "Do you have any concept of how much you scared your mother? What if you had broken your arm, or your goddamn neck?"

"Morgan," Ana said, putting her hand on his shoulder. "He's all right. That's what matters now."

Ben Iki began to cry. Morgan turned back and faced the windshield stone-faced. Ana started the engine and they drove out of the hospital parking lot. She didn't say anything else about Morgan's outburst. She understood and she loved him even more for it. Later, she would explain to Ben Iki that the reason Morgan yelled at him wasn't because he was really angry and certainly not because he didn't like Ben Iki anymore.

"Because he loves you, baby. Because he loves you and you scared him. That wasn't anger yelling, that was fear yelling. Do you understand?"

Ben Iki sort of understood.

After supper, Ana took Ben Iki to his grandmother's house, then she drove to the bay to find Morgan, who had walked to the harbor after they returned from the hospital. The sun was already down behind Mauna Kea and the lights of town began to glow here and there. The bay was dark already. Ana parked on the street and crossed the parking lot to the dock; she could see the Noho Kai's cabin lights.

"Knock, knock," she called out when she came up beside the boat.

Morgan came out of the cabin into the cockpit and took Ana's hand to help her step aboard. The boat tipped with her weight on the cockpit railing and rocked a little when she stepped down, like a welcome.

"How's Ben Iki doing?"

"Oh, he's fine, really. He wanted a cast, so he's a little disappointed about that."

Morgan smiled. He took her hand again and led her into the cabin. They sat together on the single settee berth across from the chart table. "Like something to drink?" he asked.

"Sure, whatever you're having is fine."

"You don't like whiskey, remember?"

"It's not that I don't like it, I just prefer girlie drinks."

"Afraid I'm fresh out of girlie drinks, but we could go over to the hotel bar, if you want."

"Scotch is fine. Let's just sit here and be together."

Morgan poured two drinks. There was enough ice left in the bag in the reefer for hers.

Ana took a cursory sip then sat the glass down. "Would you hold me, please?"

She leaned against him and he held her tightly, stroking her hair with one hand. "I never thought about losing him before," she whispered. "I was terrified."

"Me, too."

"I know."

"I can't believe I exploded that way. I have to talk to him."

"I did. He understands."

She took his hand from her hair and kissed it. "You were so good when we found him. You were so calm and, I don't know, so authoritative. I don't know what I would have been like if you weren't there."

"You would have been fine."

"I hope so. But you took care of everything. You made the decisions and I didn't have to."

"He scared the crap out of me."

Ana turned her head up and kissed him.

"I just needed to be with you right now. All right? I hope."

"More than all right."

After a while they went to bed in the Noho Kai's forecastle berth, where Morgan slept, where he lived.

Before they made love, when they were lying naked holding one another, Morgan almost asked Ana if she would marry him, but he wanted to ask the right way, in the right place, and he wanted to have a ring to give her.

FORTY-FIVE

It was the Fourth of July. Hot, even by the bay reflecting the shimmering glare of a white sun, the water's surface as silver as tin in the harsh sunlight. Morgan and Ben Iki, with Tioni, dragged scuba gear from the back of the pickup and loaded the tanks and kit bags into the outboard skiff Tioni had borrowed from his cousin, Keoki. Ben Iki, who had only had the Ace bandage off for a few days, tried with one hand to pull out the ice chest his unsuspecting mom had packed in Hilo that morning with Spam sandwiches, a jug of lilikoi juice and a fresh pineapple, but Morgan reached over and took the free end. Ana thought Morgan and Ben Iki were going to the big fisherman's supply warehouse in Kona and then snorkeling in Kealakekua Bay; Morgan made sure Ben Iki understood that he lied to his mother for an exceptionally good reason and it was not something to make a habit of. Morgan put a six-pack of beer into the cooler. There were four tanks, two each for Morgan and Tioni, since at the depth of the patch of black coral, they would not be able to make more than two dives in one day. A second dive from that depth would require long decompression stops on the way up, shrinking the amount of time they would have to search the deeper reef to less than ten minutes on the bottom for the first and only five minutes for the second. After the skiff was loaded, Tioni pulled up and secured the sun awning while Morgan started the big outboard engines. They let Ben Iki take the wheel. "He's a real pro already," Morgan told Tioni. "Well yeah," Tioni punched Ben Iki's arm, "he's got the blood of Ben Kamakani in there."

Far out, imperceptibly mobile dots on the horizon, where the tin sea blended with the sun-bleached sky, they could make out three or four, then five charter boats. A thirty-six-foot Bertram roared past them to starboard, its white wake rocking the skiff like a toy in a tub. Tioni waved to the skipper on the flying bridge. "Cap'n Jack," Tioni said. "After you left," explaining why Morgan wouldn't recognize him. The Bertram, speeding bow high on her way to the *grounds*, the long hundred fathom reef line where deep ocean currents surged small fish toward the surface for the pickings of cruising marlin, turned north as Tioni directed Ben Iki to head south, staying closer in.

They were never all that far off the palm-lined shore, less than a mile at most, following a compass heading Tioni provided. He would locate the destination by shore markers. After an hour, Tioni told Ben Iki that it would be another hour or so and did he want a break. Ben Iki declined. He had brought his spinning rod with the Christmas Fin-Nor reel so he could do some fishing while Tioni and Morgan were below. When Morgan picked it up thinking to make a few casts and troll with it, Ben Iki warned him not to let it fall overboard.

"My old man and your kapuna kane were friends way, way back," Tioni told Ben Iki, having to shout over the roaring engines. "I got plenty good stories from the old days."

"I got plenty good stories, too," Ben Iki shouted back.

"When we get back to Kailua town, we can go to the Red Pants and do some share story."

Ben Iki nodded happily and did not see Morgan behind him shaking his head at Tioni. "No Red Pants," he mouthed silently. Tioni laughed and said something Morgan couldn't hear.

They stayed below the flapping sun awning and even with the wind from their motion it was hot. The only relief came from an occasional spray when the skiff got bounced by a quartering swell. Tioni and Morgan had wet-suit jackets in the kit bags and they would need them in the cool, deep, and dark water. The strong sun would weakly slip into those depths and help them find the bushlike fans of black coral, but it would not make the water any warmer.

Morgan felt fine. He sat facing aft, watching the wake peel away to become absorbed by the on-shore swells. He still wondered if he deserved to feel this fine, so much a part of a normal world. Behind him, Tioni and Ben Iki talked in shouts and Morgan didn't try to overhear. He was going to be Ben Iki's father, Ana Napela's husband, and he felt fine. As soon as he got the rings made, he would ask her to be his wife. He still had not stayed the night with Ana while Ben Iki was there. They didn't make a production of his frequent presence, now almost every night of the week. Last night they watched an *Hawaii Five-o* rerun and Ben Iki went to bed when the late news came on, kissing his mother and offering a half-assed salute to Morgan, who said, "Book 'm, Ben-o." Ana came to the sofa then and lay with her head in Morgan's lap. He stroked her hair and she reached up and lay her hand against his cheek. The news frequently disgusted her and she reached for the remote to turn it off, and in the process picked up Morgan's whiskey from the coffee table and handed it to him. She put his hand on her breast and he took it away. "He won't come back in now," Ana said, and put his hand back. They talked in whispers. She said, "I love you very much." He said he didn't deserve it but wishes he did and wants to deserve it. He did love Ana. There were no doubts now. It was not like Victoria, nothing would ever be like that, but it was good and he was not faking it. He loved Ana and he loved Ben Iki and he wanted to be alive. It may have begun as gratefulness but now it was better than that, more than that.

Morgan got up when the skiff turned toward shore and went to stand by the steering pedestal. Tioni gave Ben Iki directions. They slowed and stopped and rode up and down over the low shore swells like a resting gooney bird. Morgan recognized the small village on the shore a little further ahead: Miloli'i. With a momentary shudder he remembered the shark that mutilated his leg and Victoria bleeding on the sand, the racking ride in the back of the pickup truck to the Kona Hospital, the doctor telling him she lost the baby . . . what if? He would not let himself think about any more what ifs.

"Let her drift in a little bit more," Tioni told Ben Iki. He went forward and flaked out the anchor line.

Morgan busied himself preparing, getting the regulators out of the kit bags and checking the gear.

Tioni stood on the bow with the anchor ready. Ben Iki wondered how deep it was and Tioni said he was waiting until it was less than a hundred feet so the anchor could reach the bottom. "We'll go out a hundred and fifty yards from here, beyond the reef," he told Morgan. "It gets deep fast from here."

Tioni tossed the anchor and fed line through the forward cleat. When the line stopped moving, he let the boat's shoreward drift increase the angle, then set the anchor. The skiff turned on the anchor line until her bow pointed into the wind, parallel to the shore and side to the swells, causing her to rock side to side like a bassinet. Morgan, as he raised a diver down flag from one of the outriggers, teased Ben Iki about getting rocked to sleep while waiting. Morgan teased him, but Ben Iki knew how important it was to watch for them, to see when they came up, especially if there was any trouble. He knew a lot about scuba diving now, he reminded Morgan.

Morgan and Tioni checked their equipment. Tioni asked Morgan, "Does it bother you?"

"What?"

"Diving close to this place."

"No."

"Why would it bother him?" Ben Iki asked.

"See that?" Tioni pointed to the ragged scars on Morgan's leg. "He got that over there," he added, indicating the far side of the bay, a few hundred yards beyond them.

Morgan had explained the scars to Ben Iki a long time ago, although leaving out the part about Victoria.

"Wow," Ben Iki said.

Morgan wondered if it bothered Tioni to remember everything that happened in Miloli'i. He wondered if Tioni had ever tried to calculate the timing of Victoria's pregnancy, if he ever thought he might have been the father of the baby she lost and nearly died because of. But he didn't say anything. They squeezed into their wet-suit tops at the last minute because of the heat. They both double-checked the regulators after attaching them to the tanks. Tioni said, "We go that way," he nodded seaward, "one hundred yards, going down slow following the bottom. Ike says we see a long ridge line going up like beyond a narrow but deep valley. He says maybe there's three or four trees on the top of the ridge. Two close by and another farther out. Easier to see looking up from the bottom with the light water behind."

"How deep?"

"Ike says you gotta go down the slope first then look up the ridge. The bottom is maybe a hundred fifty, the ridge a hundred twenty."

Morgan checked the dive table chart in his kit bag. The deepest number in feet for the start depth was a hundred thirty. He traced the line across and told Tioni they would only have five minutes without decompression, ten with a five-minute stop at fifteen feet on the ascent. He said he was averaging because the tables didn't go to one fifty.

"If Ike know his stuff, we can see the two close trees on the ridge line. It takes only a few seconds to break off one branch and come up. We won't be long at the bottom before starting back up the slope."

Ben Iki was already making inshore casts.

"Don't take off that life jacket or you'll be up shit creek without a paddle," Morgan said.

"You said shit."

"I sure did. Take off that life jacket and you'll know what I mean."

"Aye Aye, Cap'n Bligh."

Tioni laughed and positioned himself backwards on the side rail.

Morgan and Tioni sat side by side on the starboard gunwale then unceremoniously tumbled backwards into the sea. After rinsing their masks with spit and checking the regulator flow again, they both gave Ben Iki a wave.

They began a slow descent from the bright, shimmering surface toward the blue darkness. They had visibility over a hundred feet. Morgan looked back and could see the bottom of the skiff, the anchor line descended in a swooping arc toward the much shallower reef, and the steeply sloping bottom seaward. Rhythmically kicking with their fins, they moved in tandem toward the bottom.

The bottom there was shaped like a bowl, rising more steeply toward shore but steadily as far as they could see ahead. In the distance a pair of rays glided by parallel to them and just below Morgan noticed a school of bright silver barracuda on patrol. There wasn't much here in the valley to patrol for, small fish were back around the supermarket of the reef. Fish ahead of them, seaward toward the great depths, were going to be large, the predators. Tioni got Morgan's attention and pointed toward a single cruising hammerhead shark passing in front of them in the same direction as the rays. Tioni made a questioning okay sign and Morgan responded with a head nod. Tioni checked his pressure gauge. They were approximately halfway between the brilliant surface and the layered, shadowed bottom. The top of the rising slope on the other side of the bowl began to take shape. They approached, now swimming just above the bottom. The sea floor here was like a desert under water: rocks, some the size of boulders but most small and scattered, gave minimal shelter to a few scampering lobsters and one small octopus. There were few small fish. Two more hammerhead, one following the other, passed crossing ahead. The barracuda had disappeared behind them, toward the reef. A moray eel waited mostly in its hole between two rocks, its toothy head exposed, waving back and forth in the surprisingly strong current surge along the bottom. Morgan and Tioni kept having to make small right turns to compensate for the current's push.

They followed the bottom as it sloped upward and now they could see the top of the ridge in silhouetted outline against the brighter water above. There were no black coral trees visible on the top of the ridge, but they could be a little off either right or left. After the darker depths, it was strikingly bright to look up toward the brilliant surface. Tioni checked his pressure gauge again and Morgan looked at his watch to see how much time had passed. He calculated they had another twelve minutes if they took the decompression stop, seven minutes if they wanted to ascend directly. He pointed to his wristwatch and gestured to Tioni, flashing twelve fingers, ten then two, then making a closed fingers O for *or*, and flashing seven fingers. Tioni responded holding up seven fingers. Morgan gave him an okay sign. Decompression stops were boring and they had another set of tanks if they needed a second dive. They kicked harder and swam toward the ridge line. Morgan thought they could cover more of it if they went in opposite directions. With the clarity of the water they could maintain sight of one another up to a hundred feet apart. On top of the ridge, they stopped and each diver hooked a fin beneath a rock to keep from drifting apart in the current. With hand signals, Morgan indicated that he would swim to the left while Tioni went right, three minutes each, then turn and meet back at this spot. Tioni agreed, but with a clear reluctance. Flashing an okay sign to each other, they turned away and swam in opposite directions.

In spite of knowing he was in almost no danger from them, Morgan kept scanning to the sides and looking behind for sharks. They had seen only the three hammerheads. He tried to keep his attention focused on the highest line of the ridge, where any black coral trees would stand out. He thought it was beautiful, the blue dusk, like a few minutes after sunset. He checked his watch and looked back. He could make out Tioni and the stream of bubbles rising above, although he was almost lost now in the deep blue of undersea distance. The rubber mouthpiece still tasted rank but he was getting used to it. The whoosh, whoosh of air from the regulator had an odd calming effect, life-confirming. Whoosh, whoosh.

Then nothing. He sucked hard twice. Nothing. No air, no sound. He looked up to see the last of his air bubbles disappearing like translucent pearls toward the vastly distant sparkling surface. Without taking the mouthpiece out and still sucking for air, he jerked off the scuba tank and twisted it around so he could see where the regulator connected to the tank. He looked at his pressure gauge and there was still enough registered for him to get back to the surface, but no air came through the hose. He looked up again and tried to judge how far it was. At least a hundred and twenty feet. He looked at his watch. He had not yet passed the time barrier where he would need a decompression stop, although maybe he had, since he had only estimated the stop based on the tables for a hundred and thirty feet, but he knew they had gone deeper than that. Maybe he could make it if he dumped the tanks and weight belt and kicked as hard as he could. He was guaranteed a pneumothorax from holding his breath on the ascent. Ten seconds had passed since he drew his last breath. But the way his heart pounded he must have used up a minute. *Is this how I will die?*

Ben Iki was sweltering in the life jacket and he unsnapped the front clasps, but did not dare take it off. He didn't know exactly what Morgan meant by up a shit creek, but what he didn't want to do, ever, was anything that would make Morgan not trust him or not like him anymore. So he would swelter. He had caught a baby barracuda but cut it free to avoid the teeth. He was just fishing to pass the time anyway. He was not often struck by the beauty of his island home, he was more used to the rain-soaked lushness of the windward side of the island than the lava starkness of the leeward. The black lava scars made an odd but also appealing background for the clumps of tall palm trees nearer the shore. With his beautiful gold Fin-Nor reel, Ben Iki could cast a weighted lure halfway to the shore, it seemed. After losing a feather when he cut the barracuda free, he changed to a minnow-like lure, which he could toss thirty or even fifty feet further than the light feather. Every minute or two, he looked over his shoulder seaward. He had to be ready to up anchor and go out to them if there was some emergency. He checked his watch every couple of minutes, knowing exactly the point when they would have to appear on the surface; it was getting close now. He wished his grandfather could see him now. He felt like he had become a man already, doing the things that men do together. He cast the minnow plug and reeled in slowly back, day dreaming a little about what it would be like if Captain Morgan could really become his father.

Tioni checked his watch and turned around. Startled, he couldn't see Morgan at all. The last time he looked, hardly a minute or a minute and a half ago, he could still make out Morgan and see his air bubbles. Now nothing. Had he kept going? He should have turned back now. Tioni flipped around and swam fast in the direction from which he had just come. He kicked harder and breathed faster, glancing quickly at his watch and pressure gauge. If they didn't start up in one minute, they would have to decompress at fifteen feet for five minutes or get the bends. Did Morgan leave the top line of the ridge? Why would he? Ike said the black coral was on the ridge line, not in flat deeper bottom area. Damn it! Tioni looked from side to side, where the ridge sloped toward deeper, darker water, then ahead and up for bubbles. How could there be no bubbles? Then he saw Morgan just as he jettisoned the tank and weight belt. If he kicked hard he could reach him in maybe ten seconds.

Morgan was about to push off the sea floor and shoot for the surface, hoping he still had enough breath to make it. Then he saw Tioni. Morgan swam toward him, closing the distance between them, already knowing he could never have reached the surface without reflexively trying to breathe. Morgan and Tioni came together and Morgan grabbed the harness on Tioni's tank to keep from spinning around and past him in the current. Immediately Tioni removed his mouthpiece and handed it to Morgan, whose eyes widened as he took in a gulp of air. Tioni hooked a fin under a rock and they passed the mouthpiece back and forth again. Morgan pointed down at his abandoned tank and made a slashing motion across his throat. Tioni nodded, then held up his pressure gauge so Morgan could read it. With both of them breathing from Tioni's tank, they would not have enough air left to take the decompression stop they would now need, having passed the time threshold their bodies would need to eliminate the nitrogen from their blood. They both understood that they had to go directly to the top before running out of air, which meant they were more than likely going to get at least a mild case of the bends. Morgan gave Tioni a thumbs-up gesture and Tioni responded with the same. He unhooked his fin and they began rising toward the surface, exchanging the mouthpiece, trying to avoid ascending faster than their bubbles. Tioni held up the pressure gauge so both could see it and shook his head. Morgan nodded. They increased their speed and began passing the bubbles from Tioni's tank, courting popped lungs. Better a pneumothorax than the bends? Either better than drowning.

Tioni looked up to determine how close they were. Sunlight shimmered beyond the distant surface. They were still within the blue. How far? Sixty feet? Eighty? He passed the mouthpiece to Morgan and checked the pressure gauge yet again. Morgan passed the mouthpiece back without exhaling bubbles. Tioni realized that Morgan had not taken any air. Tioni took a short gulp and then shoved the mouthpiece back into Morgan's mouth and pointed his finger straight into Morgan's face, shaking it back and forth. Morgan nodded and took a shallow breath; each time the mouthpiece passed they expected it to be the last of the air. They both knew well enough that there was probably not enough pressure in the tank to get both of them buddy breathing to the surface, certainly not with a now impossible decompression stop of five minutes. But just maybe, if they took their chances with the bends.

Morgan raised his face toward the sunlight filtered through the water until it dissipated only a dozen yards below them. It was beautiful, the gradients of blue, aku tuna darted above them. Ones that size could give Ben Iki quite a fight with his spinning reel. Tioni pushed the mouthpiece back and Morgan accepted air. Morgan looked at Tioni, their eyes magnified behind the face plates, and they smiled as the mouthpiece passed between them again.

Methodically, they kicked in unison and rose toward the light like entwined vines, surrounded by their crystal bubbles.